H03

30130505619192

MAGGIE'S KITCHEN

When the British Ministry of Food urgently calls for the opening of restaurants to feed tired and hungry Londoners during WWII, aspiring cook Maggie Johnson seems close to realising a long-held dream. After overcoming a tangle of red tape, Maggie's Kitchen finally opens to the public, but her restaurant is so popular there isn't enough food to go round. Then Maggie takes twelve-year-old street urchin Robbie under her wing and, through him, is introduced to a dashing Polish refugee, digging for victory on London's allotments. Between them they will have to break the rules in order to put food on the table, and, perhaps, find love into the bargain...

MAGGIE'S KITCHEN

MAGGIE'S KITCHEN

by

Caroline Beecham

Magna Large Print Books
Long Preston, North Yorkshire,
BD23 4ND, England.

British Library Cataloguing in Publication Data.

A catalogue record of this book is
available from the British Library

ISBN   978-0-7505-4633-1

First published in the UK in 2017 by Ebury Press,
an imprint of Ebury Publishing

Published in Large Print 2018 by arrangement with
Ebury Publishing

Magna Large Print is an imprint of Library Magna Books Ltd.

Printed and bound in Great Britain by
T.J. (International) Ltd., Cornwall, PL28 8RW

For John – and for Sam and James,
whose love of reading inspires me every day...

On 5 November 1940 the British Minister of Food wrote to his civic heads addressing the problem of food supply:

I believe that many of these problems and dangers can be met by the establishment of community kitchens and feeding centres in every part of the kingdom. If every man, woman and child could be sure of obtaining at least one hot nourishing meal a day, at a price all could afford, we should be sure of the nation's health and strength during the war...

By the end of 1940 a Director of Communal Feeding had been appointed and by midsummer 1941 there were just over two hundred centres operating under the ministry's scheme and another one hundred and twenty operated by voluntary associations and local authorities.

On 21 March 1941 Mr Churchill wrote to Lord Woolton, Minister of Food, in relation to the establishment of communal feeding centres:

I hope the term 'Communal Feeding Centres' is not going to be adopted. It is an odious expression, suggestive of Communism and the workhouse. I suggest you call them 'British Restaurants'. Everybody associates the word 'restaurant' with a good meal, and they may as well have the name if they cannot get anything else.

Chapter One

I saw three ships a-sailing
But not with food for me
For I am eating home-grown food
To beat the enemy
And ships are filled with guns instead
To bring us victory
Marguerite Patten OBE,
Victors Cookbook: Nostalgic Food
and Facts from 1940–1954

LONDON, 17 APRIL 1941

They had been inside the shelter for hours, the familiar warming of atmosphere despite the coolness of the ground, their collective breath forming a moving fog: the sweet sharp notes of mint humbugs; the faint aroma of Gillian's fragrance, no doubt a gift from John; the sour smell of last night's ale; the bitterness of stale cigarettes, woven into their clothes as tightly as the garments' own fabric.

Maggie was conscious of every movement and each and every sound. There was the rustle of clothing, the fragile stillness of her neighbour's breath waiting to be exhaled, the muffled gasps as another bomber roared overhead. And the growl of anti-aircraft fire that followed. Lord knew how many hours she had sat upright with

13

nothing to lean against, the tiny pitch-dark shelter separating them all as surely as it bound them together.

Then the ground shuddered again, but it was only the weight of vehicles on the roads escalating the ferocity of sound, drowning out Henry's coughing fit and her neighbour's cries. She imagined the next blast and the weight of the debris and soil as it pressed down on them, weighing down their flesh and levelling the backyard as they all disappeared beneath... Mrs Armstrong from number fifty-two, soft belly protruding from the earth ... Henry and Julia from number forty-three, arms still locked around each other ... Gillian and her three girls from along the road ... her own body, arms and legs sticking out at awkward angles like sticks from a game of jacks. Discarded clothes and prized possessions, brought to the shelter for safekeeping, lonely artefacts in their communal tomb.

She shook her head to dispel the image. *I'm not going to die, I'm not going to die,* she repeated to herself. If Peter were here he would have found a way to distract her.

Her breathing intensified and she struggled to think of something else, to grasp hold of a thread of something normal. She willed the thudding of blood and muscle to cease, to force her heart back to its normal size and her breathing to slow enough to stop overtaking her thoughts.

She could smell the fear in her own perspiration and sense it in the unease that had overtaken their shared space. Her legs were numb now, and her back locked rigid, muscles set in permanent contraction. The earth was so cold, and pressed against her so tightly, that the pain began to spread through her like the fire that surely engulfed the shattered homes above.

And then it grew quiet again, and they waited for the shelter doors to open so that they could reluctantly reinhabit the streets outside, though they would not be allowed home until the wardens had checked the damage, until the fire brigade made safe or demolished any precarious buildings and any unexploded bombs were defused. She knew the drill by now: knew that there would be those who went straight back home, counting themselves lucky to be alive, while others, like Mr and Mrs Fox, would not take to their beds until they were sure that the local streets were clear and that their neighbours were all accounted for.

To pass the time between now and then she pictured Peter, handsome and authoritative in his uniform, only his dark brown hair unruly.

'You can't change what happens to you, only how you deal with it,' he was saying to her.

It was what he always said.

So she would deal with it by focusing on what she needed to do for her next shift – if the radio factory was still standing, of course. There were new recipes from the ministry to master, food inventories to be done, the butcher's order, two hundred factory workers to cook for...

As thoughts of store cupboards and frugal dishes replaced the darker images, she started rubbing the sodden dirt between her fingertips, feeling the same cold coarse texture as if she were simply making breadcrumbs for shortbread or the topping for a fresh fruit crumble. But the sensation that was so completely natural and reassuring evaporated as she remembered that, only a few miles away, people were likely being blown to bits.

Nearby, Mrs Brooks exhaled, providing the first movement of air since they had been down here. The poor old woman had been whimpering from the moment they were ushered into the shelter by the shrieking sirens and the brief gathering beam of light. It had taken them five minutes to get Mrs Brooks out of her house and securely stowed in the underground shelter; she was not very mobile at the best of times, hampered by her arthritis and considerable bulk. They had half lifted, half walked her along the cracked concrete path, across the uneven grass and down the seven steep steps to the shelter.

There was a loud explosion and a ringing in her ears as something whistled too slowly through the air a few hundred yards away. Screams shredded the space around her and the ground vibrated, setting her teeth chattering, and for a few moments it seemed as if they were caught at the epicentre of the blast.

Then she smelled the smoke and the acrid burn of rubber and Maggie knew that she was still alive.

From outside came the pandemonium of sirens and explosions. And as it subsided, the three girls began to cry: first Alex, the youngest, then her sisters Molly and Beatrice. There was the sound of boots scraping across the dirt as Gillian pulled them closer to her and began to sing.

Mary had a little lamb, little lamb, little lamb.
Mary had a little lamb, its fleece was white as snow,
and everywhere that Mary went...

But their mother's verse wasn't working and Molly became more and more agitated.

'Come on, love,' Gillian whispered. 'What happened to my brave, brave girl? You've done this before...'

Then she heard a faint whooshing noise and a familiar grassy smell, as the thin warm stream found its way through a groove in the earth.

'I'm sorry, Mummy. I'm sorry,' Molly cried.

'It's alright, pet.'

She could feel Gillian's body as it became closer and then more distant as she rocked back and forth in front of her, the humming loud and then softer as she cradled Molly and the cries gradually began to subside into low sobs.

After a few moments of waiting for the tears to quell, Maggie spoke. 'Hey, Molly, do you know what I'm thinking about?'

There was no reply.

'A delicious creamy Welsh rarebit that I'm going to make for you as soon as we get home...'

The crying stopped and Molly's body twisted, her face turning up so that Maggie could feel her warm breath as she spoke.

'Really, Maggie?'

'Yes, really. I may even have some carrot cake left from Sunday, too.'

'Are you sure you'll have enough for us?'

'Is there enough Welsh rarebit for me?' Beatrice pleaded.

'Oh yes. And I have been trying out a new version with just the right amount of Colman's to turn the mixture a golden yellow, as bright as sunflowers. And there's just enough milk to make the bread moist and keep the topping crunchy.'

Then she lowered her voice even further. 'I was thinking of calling it *Churchill's rarebit* ... what do you think?'

She could hear the girls giggling in the dark.

'I think that your generous invitation has been accepted,' Gillian replied. 'Girls, what do you say to Maggie?'

'Oh yes, please,' they chorused.

The noise outside had faded and Maggie was no longer thinking about the carnage and charred wood; her thoughts were on the bubbling cheese and the smiles on the girls' dirt-smudged faces as they sat around the kitchen table.

As the door opened, a patch of moonlight flooded the shelter's entrance, transforming the anonymous dark soil into a ghostly carpet of white.

Her neighbours' silhouettes moved through the doorway, expelling the warmed air, the shelter's condensation mixing with the ribbons of smoke outside to create a low groundcover. Her shaking legs steadied enough so that she could climb the stairs as her eyes grew slowly accustomed to the light and her nose and throat to the sickening fumes.

The whine of the sirens was receding, the earth had at last given up its tremor and only muted whistles echoed in the remote emptying streets.

The bombs hadn't been close enough to hit

them; the danger was now a distant grumble. They were safe.

This time.

They had been lucky, but it was still unnerving to be making their way through the deserted streets, shepherding Mrs Brooks safely home, her neighbours drifting away with mumbled goodbyes, and Mr and Mrs Fox finally gone. Only moments now to see if the Victorian terrace was still standing and her landlady, Mrs Foster, unharmed. Then she would check on her cousin Rose, who lived not far away; Maggie hoped she had made it to the Tube in time.

The moon-touched streets emerged into view: first garden walls materialised, then hedges and porches, arbours of roses, low-pitched roofs and smokeless chimneys. Further on down the road, the Air Raid Precautions vehicles were parked outside St John's church, a short comforting convoy of dark green.

Ever since the paint factory in Silvertown had gone up last week, the radio factory where she worked had been on standby, expecting to be evacuated at a moment's notice. Their working hours were shortened so they could be home by nightfall, and the stone grey uniforms of the Home Guard were now a constant presence outside the gates.

She followed the progress of the ARP as they unloaded wooden crates from the backs of the trucks, passing the precious cargo from person to person. Maggie thought longingly of all the crates stowed safely deep inside the church, where there would be enough food and water for those lucky few who were sheltering there. For the rest of them it was a neighbour's Anderson shelter, where she had been, or risking the short distance to the Angel underground before the bombs started and the wardens padlocked the station gates.

Another crate was retrieved from the truck and she caught sight of the dark lettering on its side: WILSON & CO. She had been relieved by whispers that the first American lend-lease food aid shipments had arrived; there were supposed to be Canadian hams and bacons, orange juice and eggs, and other produce that had been difficult to get hold of.

Shivering, she pressed her hands deeper into her coat pockets and her fingers brushed against the pocket watch. She curled them around its smooth brass case, reassured by the solid cool of the metal and relieved that it was still there. Peter had given it to her on their engagement; he had said some time beforehand that he wasn't sentimental but then presented it to her, proudly declaring that it was a family heirloom and that he wanted to spend all his time with her, and the rest of his life. She was so intrigued by the old watch that she hadn't realised at first that Peter had proposed, until he started to apologise for the fact that it wasn't a ring, promising that he would buy her one as soon as he could afford to. She had known that would be years away – after the war ended, after their lives returned to normal – but she had been elated anyway; he wanted her to be his wife.

Head still bent in thought, she carried on

across the road.

'Maggie ... watch out!'

A hand reached out and pulled her onto the pavement as an ARP truck roared past.

It took a moment for her to catch her breath before she recognised the figure in front of her, covered as it was in dust, dark metal helmet pulled tightly down.

'Bill?'

'You alright, love?'

Bill Drummond, the warden, was barely recognisable. It was hard to believe he was only in his early thirties, his face was so worn looking. Now it was covered with dirt, too – except for his eyes, large and white like a barn owl's where he had been wearing a mask. Maggie's fingers unconsciously traced around her own eyes, then flicked through her chestnut hair, loosening the dust that had settled there.

'Thank you, Bill,' she said. 'I'm fine.'

'You were a million miles away,' he observed.

'Wish I was,' she said, watching as another truck accelerated by.

'It's been devastating, worst night by far – incendiaries and parachute mines. Lost a mum and her daughters on Highbury Station Road, two more houses over Liverpool Road too. Wiped out instantly, never stood a chance. But your street's fine. No damage.'

'Really?' she said, her relief mixed with guilt. 'What about Upper Street? Is Sutton Chambers okay?'

'Yes, Rose will be safe. Bloomin' miracle, but she'll find everything right as she left it. Wish St

Paul's had been as lucky. It's tragic, Maggie, really tragic. Parliament and the National Gallery too...' He sighed. 'Well, you'd best be getting yourself home. I expect your shift will be starting soon enough and they'll be needing good sustenance today.'

Maggie nodded. 'Bye then, Bill.'

'See you, love.'

Thinking about her boss hovering at the kitchen door, beady eyes watching until all the girls had arrived, she picked up her pace; for Mr Ferguson, not even the worst raid yet would be a good enough reason to be late.

But Mr Ferguson would just have to wait a bit longer. Right now Maggie had to collect the ingredients for Churchill's rarebit and make her way over to Gillian's house so that she could feed the girls before the older ones left for school. There was a small loaf in the pantry that she had been saving for tonight, she recalled, and enough cheddar for one – but that could be stretched for the three girls by mixing it with some milk and her last remaining egg. It would be good to give the girls this treat; this could be the last time Maggie saw them for a while, she knew, for Gillian was expecting the children to be evacuated again at a moment's notice. Gillian was so isolated without her husband and family that she welcomed any company and support Maggie could give her. Maggie understood how she felt, with her own father dead and her mother no longer around.

When she stepped inside her gate she had to duck beneath the old apple tree that dominated the small walled garden, its splayed branches home to dozens of young dew-speckled apples, now covered with soot. In just a few weeks she would be able to make a rich apple pie or something more adventurous that she would never have the chance to try at the canteen: pork stuffed with apple and sage, perhaps, or an apple charlotte. Maybe she should speak to Mr Ferguson today about a vegetable garden and then see if it might tempt him to introduce some new dishes; anything to improve the meals they were serving at the moment.

Approaching the house, she pulled the keys from her pocket.

The Victorian house was built at the same time as the rest of the houses in the street; solid brick walls, slate roofs that seemed to float above the buildings and meld with the grey of the dawning skies, windows tall enough to allow in the long reach of summer but small enough to keep out the drafts since the summers were never long enough. Only the front doors were unique, each one painted in a colour of the owner's choosing – at least, they had been until recently. If you had looked down the street twelve months ago you would have seen pops of bright red, cornflower blue, grey and green. Now they were all dark grey or black, military-issue colours for the blackout. Mrs Foster's door had been postbox red, a clear streak of which was now visible beneath the lock; her hand had been shaking so much that her key had missed the keyhole.

Maggie took a deep breath and waited for her hand to stop trembling before trying again. Pushing the door closed behind her, she leaned back against it, slipped the keys into her coat pocket and closed her eyes.

Her eyelids blinked open to see a small group of grazing cows, among them a number of calves suckling, the broad open fields flattening out around them and the hills rising up behind. The walls of the hallway were filled with her landlady's paintings, rich oils of pastoral scenes that Maggie would never have chosen herself but had grown accustomed to in the short time she had been here. These small rooms on the ground floor were her own private sanctuary and although they were furnished according to someone else's taste – velvet sofas from a previous era and curtains that would look better in a nursing home – this was her home for now and she felt relieved as she looked around, and grateful to Mrs Foster for accepting the low rent that was all Maggie could afford on her wage.

Her sense of relief was abruptly shattered by a noise – footsteps creaking across floorboards and an unexpected screech as a lock was wrenched, splintering the wood.

She tensed, unsure which way to run, not knowing whether the noise was coming from inside or out. But then she saw a dark fleeting outline that sent a shiver up her spine, causing every hair on her body to stand on end.

Her exhaustion and fear suddenly forgotten, Maggie rushed down the hallway and into the small kitchen, just in time to see a pair of shabby black boots disappear out the pantry window.

'Hey!' she cried. 'What are you doing? Come back here!'

The small kitchen had been ransacked; stone jars pulled from shelves, tins and pots upended, the contents spilled across the work-tops. The breadbin was empty, her weekly ration and home-made soda bread gone. She looked in the meat safe; the bacon was gone too. That was everything for the week; there was no way she could replace them now, nothing she could do. She could try to eat at work, but Mr Ferguson was so mean it was unlikely he'd allow it. She had the emergency larder concealed at the back of the pantry for safekeeping, although the small portions of flour, baked beans, coffee, evaporated milk and rice recommended by the Ministry of Food wouldn't last her long.

Standing a cream china pot upright and re-placing the lid, she reached to the back of the pantry. But there was an empty space where the emergency food pack should have been.

Her mouth fell open in dismay, then she raced for the back door.

Outside, she noted that Mrs Foster's prized hen, Matilda, was still in her coop. That was something to be grateful for, at least. The back gate was never locked so she easily pushed through and out into the back lane in time to see a nimble figure turn the corner into St Peter's Street.

Maggie ran for the corner and was soon sprinting down the tree-lined avenue, passing people as they straggled back to their homes from the Angel underground a few streets away. It was where she would have gone if they had been given more notice of the raid.

'Hey, miss, you okay?' an MP shouted after her.

25

'Yes,' she replied over her shoulder, realising how odd she must look, running so fast after the raid was over. 'I've got to catch my dinner...'

The figure seemed to be getting further ahead but, even though she was short of breath and her body still ached, she wasn't giving up. She had lived in Islington most of her life and knew it like the back of her hand; they were headed towards Regent's Canal, which was mostly deserted now, its residents long gone. There certainly wouldn't be many places to hide; the rats had moved in as soon as the men had left for war and the women and children for the countryside, but even the rats had now set their sights higher and were beginning to inhabit the crowded streets around her.

Across the road another Georgian terrace gave way to a landscape of rubble and earth and there was the thief, scaling a mound of debris with the confidence of a mountaineer on a bona fide expedition. Behind the rubble stood Maggie's old school, Noel Road primary, a three-storey Victorian building; proud sole survivor, erect and defiant.

She watched as the small figure disappeared inside.

As she squeezed through the temporary fencing, taking care not to snag her clothes, Maggie felt a lot calmer, her anger transformed into curiosity about this thief who had come all the way to Danbury Street to steal her food.

In the dim light of dawn she could see the school windows were boarded up. Signs warned DANGER: KEEP OUT and UNSTABLE

BUILDING and for a moment she hesitated; perhaps it was best just to let the culprit get away. But no – she was intrigued now, and so continued on, slipping under the rope that cordoned off the dilapidated building, stepping over the wreckage and edging around the larger fragments of fallen masonry, one of the building's once-elegant gargoyles staring up at her from the ground. Reaching the front door, she tugged at the brass handle. The door's bottom edge screeched across the stone floor. She stopped for a moment, listening.

There was only the whisper of wind down the long corridors and the banging of a forgotten window somewhere. She stepped inside.

The musty furniture, the faint chemical smells, damp books and lingering cooked lunches; she wasn't sure if they were real or imagined as memories of her own school days came flooding back. It occurred to her suddenly that the thief she had been chasing might be a child. Who else would hide in a school, know their way around, be small enough to fit through her window and daring enough to try? The thought of a child living here, scavenging for food, made her more determined to find him or her. But the school was vast; where should she begin to look? As she moved past the empty classrooms she thought about where she would hide – near a kitchen or toilet, somewhere with running water, if there was still any available.

Mrs Stoner's thick Scottish brogue echoed around her as she passed the home science rooms: *'Maggie Johnson, you will not handle the utensils before you have washed your hands.'* She

27

was the only teacher Maggie ever truly liked, the only reason that she finished school when so many of the other girls left before they were fifteen, and one of the reasons she had become a cook.

She moved past empty classrooms into the back part of the building, where hardly any light penetrated into the concrete rooms; the common rooms were here, she remembered, next to the kitchens. It was as if the intervening decade had vanished; she was looking at the same chipped wooden doorframes and breathing the same clouds of chalk dust, inhaling the same bitter smell of boiled cabbage. She was a schoolgirl again, struggling to swallow inedible meals. The only difference she could see was that the metal lockers and filing cabinets had gone – no doubt taken away to be melted down and reinvented as objects that might help in the war effort.

A shallow light flickered from under one of the doors; it was the entrance to one of the store-rooms. Her footsteps slowed: instinct told her that she was getting closer now, but she hadn't even considered what she was going to do when she confronted the intruder.

She flexed her fingers, suddenly aware that she was empty-handed, carried no weapon or tool with which to defend herself. Was this how Peter had felt before he was killed? She didn't even know if he'd had a chance to defend himself, the details of his death had been so vague. She pictured the telegram, its stained paper and the uneven typeface; ink thicker on one side of the letter than the other, the typewriter clearly damaged or the ribbon nearly at the end of its life, and she remembered thinking it a mark of disrespect to send notification in such a way. And then she had read the words:

It is my painful duty to inform you that a report has been received from the War Office notifying the death of Peter James Marshall. The report is to the effect that he was killed in action.

She had tried to find out more from the men he served with and from the ministry but it was pointless; the rest of the infantry were still drafted or convalescing, and the injured soldiers hadn't been able to help. Lieutenant Douglas Potter had been a friend but was either unable or unwilling to talk; he didn't reply to any of her letters and finally they had been returned unopened from the Surrey address where they had been sent. Peter's captain advised her that he was very sorry but he was unable to discuss the matter. And so she had been left to her own imaginings, in which he had endured hours, perhaps days, of unimaginable pain before suffering a violent and lonely death. Or perhaps he was in a prisoner of war camp somewhere, or recovering in a hospital here in England, but with no memory of who or where he was. She had read stories like this and heard reports on the radio of families being reunited when loved ones had long been given up for dead. Why not her, why not Peter?

She placed her hand on the doorknob, readying to turn it.

It was possible, after all, that these last eleven months had just been a terrible mistake. That somehow, somewhere, Peter was still alive. That one day, he might return.

Her heartbeat had settled, her breathing more regular now.

She turned the knob and eased open the door.

The momentary brightness faded and she could see a small figure sitting cross-legged on the floor in the centre of the room, scruffy black boots tucked beneath him. He was holding her bag of bread in one hand, while feeding himself with the other, only his big brown eyes moving as they flicked up and down her.

He was much younger than she had thought, only about eleven or twelve, but with a knowing look that was usually the reserve of an older child. His light brown hair was matted and longer than was the norm, his complexion pale except for a scattering of freckles. From his grubby hands and torn clothes she guessed he had been living rough for a while; the freckles could even be dirt.

He didn't stop eating, but carried on watching her as she looked around, scanning the room for signs of anyone else.

But there was no one else, she quickly realised, nor any signs of the storeroom it had been. Once textbooks and boxes of pencils and chalk had filled the floor-to-ceiling shelves that lined three walls of the room, but now carved wooden toys, metal cars and model planes, all made from discarded junk, had been carefully arranged so that they looked as if they were ready to take off or drive away. There were half a dozen flickering candles propped upright in glass jars beside them, giving the collection the appearance of a bizarre childish shrine.

'These are amazing,' Maggie said, momentarily forgetting what had brought her there. 'Did you make them?'

The boy shoved another handful of bread into his mouth.

'You by yourself?' he asked, still chewing.

She nodded. 'You're clearly very hungry, but why steal from me?'

'I've seen you,' he said, spraying crumbs. 'You work in the canteen.'

She was surprised. 'That's right.'

'Must have plenty of food over there. Figured a cook would be taking a bit extra home.'

'Well, you're wrong, and that food is supposed to last me. What are you doing here anyway? How old are you?'

'None of your business.'

'Where's your family?'

'That's none of your business either.'

He looked younger now, the bravado gone and the fullness of his stomach enabling him to relax as he leaned back against the legs of a chair.

'I could report you, you know. Stealing, breaking and entering – they're criminal offences. You could be in a lot of trouble...'

'You wouldn't,' he said, his bravado deserting him now.

Maggie raised an eyebrow. 'Wouldn't I?'

'They'd lock me up,' he said, looking panicked. He sat up straighter.

'It'd teach you a lesson. Come on, tell me

where your parents are and I might let you off.'

He said nothing, so she waited, moving over to pick up one of the model aeroplanes. It had beer bottle-top wheels, a crushed tin can body and its rough edges had been filed down, the intricate wires and clips that knitted it together crafted into shape. A tiny pair of pliers sat on the shelf below alongside another half-built machine.

'So you making your own private fleet?'

'That's a Spitfire,' he said, adding, 'One of ours.' He pushed the fringe out of his eyes.

'It's really good,' she said, rotating it in her hand, examining the detail of the tiny propeller and the small door at the back that opened for the imagined cargo it might hold.

The boy's gaze also stayed on the machine, the hint of a proud smile playing on his lips. He reminded her of Ernest; not just in his appearance but because her brother, too, had loved making things, building with his hands. One week a cubby house for them to play in, the next week a billycart to take up to the highest point of the heath and race, screeching and breathless, to the bottom. He had always been the one to invent the games and the one to break the rules, with Eddie and John constantly following in his wake, trying to repair the damage he left behind.

'Helps the nights go quicker – especially when there's a raid,' he said, rising and coming over to take the model from her, placing it carefully back on the shelf.

'Don't you go to the shelter?'

'Waste of time. Get blown up trying to get there. I'm better off just stayin' 'ere.'

'But what do you do for food ... when you're not stealing it?'

'There's good allotments round here, few hens for eggs too, if you know where to look. I get by.'

'When was the last time you had a proper meal ... a hot meal?'

He looked at her, the vague ghost of memory flickering across his face.

'Can't remember ... a few weeks ago, I suppose. Last time I had some meat, anyway.'

She considered him for a moment as he lowered himself stiffly back down to the floor.

'So you a real good cook then?' he asked.

Suddenly she was aware of the time passing. 'Do you know how late you've made me?' she demanded.

'What kind of things do you make?' he asked, as if he hadn't heard her.

'Lots of things, but the food at the factory is pretty simple; it's all soups and stews. Best thing when you're cooking for lots of people. Heaps of potatoes and vegetables makes it go further. Other than that, it's whatever we can get hold of.'

'You make shepherd's pie?'

'Of course.'

'What about scones, can you make them?'

She smiled. 'With my eyes closed.'

The boy's face had transformed, his expression dreamy – so like Ernest's when it came to food; she thought she could almost see his mouth watering.

He sighed. 'Here you are,' he said, holding out the emergency pack he had stolen from her.

Maggie reached for it, then let her hand drop to

33

her side. 'You keep it. You look like you need it more than I do.' She considered him for a moment. 'Tell you what, I've got to go to work now, but you know where I live. Come by tonight at half past six ... you tell me where your family are and I'll give you a good hot meal.'

He looked at her suspiciously. 'You mean it?'

'Yes. What's your favourite?'

His face lit up. 'Apple crumble and shepherd's pie ... no, hotpot ... no, wait, toad-in-the-hole.'

'I'll see what I can do,' Maggie said, turning to leave.

'But I like my pudding first – before the meal, that is.'

She raised her eyebrows in mock surprise. 'Yes, I bet you do. And your ma always serves your dinner like that, I suppose?'

His eyes twinkled. 'Of course.'

So he did have a mother then...

'What did you say your name was?' Maggie asked.

'I didn't.'

'I'm Maggie.'

'I know. I saw your mail.'

She was about to tell him off but changed her mind; it was more important to find out who he was, and why he was here on his own.

'Okay, but I can hardly have an anonymous dinner guest, can I?'

He relented. 'Robbie. My name is Robbie.'

She examined him again; yes, he looked like a Robbie.

'All right, Robbie, half past six then.' She walked to the door.

'Wait...'

Maggie turned.

'Can I bring Spoke?'

'Who is Spoke?'

He leaned towards a pile of hessian sacks that lay close to the shelves and lifted one of them. Underneath was the dark brown fur of a mongrel, little more than a pup, its sides extending and contracting like a pair of heavily drawn bellows as it slept soundly.

'Unusual name ... I don't suppose he talks?'

'That would be something.' Robbie grinned. 'No, he got run over, ended up caught in my bicycle wheel. Had to pull the spoke out of him myself. It's in that tank up there,' he said pointing at one of the larger, more complex models.

'Right. Well, in that case, Spoke is also welcome.'

'Great,' Robbie said, jumping up and brushing the crumbs from his jacket, catching a few of the larger ones and putting them into his mouth.

'We'll set off early then. He's got a bit of a limp.'

'Fine.' She smiled. 'Until tonight.'

'And Maggie?'

She sighed; she really was going to be terribly late.

'Yes, Robbie?'

'You're a lot prettier close up.'

Chapter Two

*There is no vegetable more useful than the homely
potato. It is a valuable yet cheap source of energy,
and one of the foods that help protect us from ill
health. It contains vitamin C as do oranges and
1-lb of potatoes daily will give half the amount
of this vitamin to prevent against fatigue
and help fight infection.*
Ministry of Food, War Cookery Leaflet No. 21

Mr Drummond's report of the local losses and
the incident with Robbie had unsettled Maggie;
it had left her with a queer feeling – relieved that
it wasn't her but also guilty for thinking as much
– and all wobbly too, like the jelly she'd be scrapping off the dripping when she got to work.
Perhaps it was because she was also breathless
from running, frustrated that she hadn't had
time to cook for Gillian and the girls like she'd
promised.

She slowed to a brisk walk across the gangway
and could see her supervisor, Mr Ferguson,
watching from behind the glass window above
the factory floor. Then an immense cloud of
smoke rose from one of the machines, obscuring
him from view.

'Morning, Maggie...'

She turned towards the muffled voice to see
two men in heavy metal masks struggling to push

a trolley towards the far end of the workshop where three covered lorries were parked.

'Hi, Tom,' she called, recognising the eyes just visible behind his protective visor. 'Roast joint today. You want me to save you some?'

Tom Washington had gone to school with her brothers and remained close right until they joined up, their friendship strengthened rather than weakened when he was found not medically fit to fight. She liked the fact that he was here now; seeing him regularly made her feel closer to them all somehow. And it reminded her of happier times, when they had all been together, when her father was still alive and before their mother left. When Tom could often be found at their kitchen table; she was feeding him even back then.

He took his hand off the side of the bucket to give her the thumbs up and it wavered precariously, looking as if it might tip. Tom quickly grabbed hold of the handle to steady it and he and his partner continued on towards the trucks, passing dozens of other workers in overalls and protective masks checking gauges on the growling machines, pulling levers and watching fixedly under the dull spluttering light of bare bulbs. Behind them, the factory's huge double doors stood fully open to let in much-needed light; the narrow strip of windows at the top of the building's brick walls were blackened from the dust of destruction outside and the stain of creation within.

She glanced up again to see Mr Ferguson's figure retreating. Then a thunderous crash below

37

made her jump, followed by another eruption of sound and an explosion of sparks a few yards away as a large piston bore down, forcing a piece of sheet metal into the radio casing mould before releasing it, the conveyer belt carrying it away. It had a hypnotic effect on her and she never tired of watching as the piston slammed down again and again. At the end of the row, a lever arm shifted upwards, tipping the conveyer belt and nudging the newly formed metal casings along, so that they clattered into a tray beneath. She had forgotten how noisy it was down here, and why the supervisors encouraged the canteen staff to take the other entrance and exit; she usually did when she wasn't late. Mounting the metal stairs as fast as she could, she was soon on the wide landing of the mezzanine, leaving the mechanical hum and the overpowering smell of oil and molten metal below.

She hesitated for a moment and then pulled back the double doors leading into a vast kitchen where geysers of steam sprang from the two banks of stoves that ran down the centre of the room. Amid the clinking and whirring of the machinery here, a dozen women in white aprons and matching headscarves were equally industrious, moving between benchtops and stoves, retrieving pots from cookers, whisking mixtures in bowls, washing vegetables and chopping food. As Maggie slipped past them, she wondered how different it might be in one of the British Restaurants she had read about a few weeks ago. The scheme sounded like such a good idea that it had played on her mind ever since.

She took off her overcoat, rolling it up and squashing it into one of the open shelves next to the door before smoothing down her crumpled white apron. No one seemed to notice her except Eliza, who appeared tired, grey eyes ringed with red; Maggie expected they would all be unnerved today, the raids having lasted so long.

'Sorry, I got caught up. I'll tell you about it later.'

'I told him you were in the ladies,' said Eliza. 'You're lucky he's not been back since.'

She could forgo the lecture for now; she knew he wouldn't be pleased, particularly since making her assistant supervisor while Janet was away after she'd petitioned so hard for it.

'Thank you. I owe you.'

Maggie and Eliza had been close since school and they always looked out for each other at work.

'You do look a bit ragged,' Eliza remarked. 'The veg is ready but you should probably go and do something about your hair...'

Maggie's fingers darted upwards; her hair always seemed to escape and she tucked away the stray wisps inside her snood. Eliza smiled at her and she finally relaxed for the first time since entering the shelter the previous night.

Then, thinking about Mr Ferguson and all that she had to do now she was running late, she grabbed a pair of thick oven gloves and bent low to retrieve a large metal tray from the oven. She groaned involuntarily as she placed the heavy load down onto a trolley already laden with several other trays of equal or larger size. Each held food for the early shift's lunch; a tray of pale creamy mashed potato, a pile of steaming shredded greens, thin slices of brown meat layered with rivers of gravy that trickled from the highest point to form a translucent grey lake at the base.

'Number three ready to go, Liza,' she shouted.

Eliza, her round youthful face pink from steam, banged the potato peeler down.

'Right you are, Maggie.'

Eliza grasped hold of the trolley and man-oeuvred it towards the closest set of double doors, butting them open to reveal the vast dining hall beyond.

There were ten long tables in the huge open space, men and women sitting side by side in oil-smeared overalls, the low clink of cutlery and hum of chatter echoing around them. Maggie saw Rafferty, the canteen cat, crouched under one of the tables waiting for scraps, occasionally stroked by a friendly hand. It made her think of Robbie and his gentle mongrel, and Robbie's poor mother – wherever she was – who was no doubt missing him.

Then the doors swung shut, and the momentary glimpse of the relative quiet of the dining hall was replaced by the noise and heat of the kitchen.

'Maggie?'

Maggie looked around to see Maeve, stirring wildly at a pot on the stove.

'Maggie, come here...'

She could smell the bittersweet aroma of burnt custard before she even reached the saucepan. Taking the spoon from the girl's hand she slid it through the yellow-brown liquid, feeling the resistance from the lumps as she did.

40

'Honestly, Maeve,' she said with a sigh. 'You've used too much powder again, and too high a heat.'

'I'm sorry, Maggie.'

'It's okay, but I've lost count of how many times I've shown you. We just can't afford the waste — it's a shilling each time you get through a packet of powder.'

The spoon scraped against the bottom of the pot, bringing up burnt and caramelised blobs of custard stuck as hard as barnacles to a ship.

'You start on a low flame, sieve the powder with a little water and then gradually stir in the rest.' Maggie carried on trying to mix out the lumps.

Maeve shook her head, eyes filling with tears. 'I'm sorry, I just can't seem to get the hang of it...'

'It's no good, I can't salvage it,' Maggie exclaimed. 'I don't know what we'll give them with the steamed pudding now.'

Then, seeing how upset the girl was, she turned off the flame, shunting the heavy pot to the back of the stove. Speaking more gently now, she said, 'Perhaps we should move you on to prep. Would that suit you better?'

Maeve nodded, pressing her lips together as she tried not to cry.

Maggie took her by the arm and led her through the maze of benches, noticing another girl on the other side of the room waving frantically at her.

'I'll be with you in a minute, Annie,' she called, relieved that the other cooks all seemed to be coping with their own areas.

She had shown them how to be organised in

the same way she had learned as a trainee at Battersea College, when cooking had been her life; before she and Peter had shared plans to open a restaurant of their own. Now all she wanted was for the war to be over so she could do something else, no longer be reminded daily of their lost dream.

'Okay, Maeve, you swap with Helen,' Maggie said when they reached two women in a quieter corner of the kitchen.

Here the smooth white ceramic tiles replaced the cold grey steel of the industrial cookers and created a brighter, calmer space.

She watched as Maeve took in the long trough sink that ran under the window from one end of the room to the other, where it was separated in four places by drainers, and where upturned cutlery and cooking utensils released tributaries of water that flowed back into the sinks and the branches of pipework below. Directly behind them, the parallel benchtop had been divided into separate stations with chopping boards and double bins underneath.

'That's your pig bin, the other is for general waste,' Maggie explained, picking up the peeler.

She began peeling a carrot, moving the blade away from her in long rhythmic strokes and then, taking a knife, she swiftly transformed carrots into miniature orange batons and the glistening courgettes into symmetrical discs.

'Come on, you have a go...'

Maeve picked out the correct vegetable knife and carefully sliced through a carrot creating unequal-sized sticks.

'That's a good start, but they need to be the same size so they cook evenly.'

Maeve's eyes were still wet with tears so Maggie decided to let her practise for a few minutes before telling her that she was going to need to really speed up too.

'Don't worry, you'll get quicker,' she said, 'and we're waiting on new peeling machines.'

Maeve summoned a smile but remained quiet, focusing all her attention on the carrot she held between her finger and thumb, gripping it so hard that her flesh began to turn white.

Maggie continued cutting on the board alongside her and with the regular, meditative beat of her knife against the solid wood of the board, her thoughts easily turned to Peter and their last drive into the country. They had fallen in love with a small country pub that had been advertised in *The Times* classified section. When they telephoned ahead first, the quavery old voice at the other end of the line left them in no doubt as to why the pub was up for sale. She felt guilty when they met the owner, though; his wife had passed away two years earlier and the burden of running the place on his own had left him as withered and gnarly as the old wisteria that clutched at the outside walls. She remembered her certainty that it was 'the one' the moment she put the phone down, and their excitement as they drove up to Hertfordshire. On their way through Barnet they had designed the pub's interior and by the time they were winding their way through the small villages they had planned the menus as well. It felt as if the borrowed Ford was gliding on air as it motored up the gentle inclines and she closed her eyes and imagined what the pub would look like as the hedges rose up either side of them. That day, everything lay ahead of them.

Their excitement was short-lived though; as the signs took them off the main road and they pulled into the unevenly paved car park in front of the pub, they were shocked by what they saw. Dozens of slates were missing from the roof, the once pale green window frames were faded and flaking, and the windows themselves were so dirty she could barely see through them into the dark interior. There were no roses climbing the black beams and peeling whitewashed render of the facade, no holidaymakers or travellers sitting on the garden's wooden benches, enjoying the summer sunshine and pub fare. Once inside, it had been no different; the tastes of a distant generation, the laziness of a more recent one...

'Maggie?'

She turned to Maeve.

'Ferguson.'

Maeve's eyes darted towards the dark-suited figure on the other side of the counter deep in conversation with the factory foreman.

'Lovely vegetables, Mags.' Eliza grinned as she walked past, oblivious to the presence of their boss on the other side of the support column.

'Yes, we're making vegetable pie,' Maggie said, remembering she was meant to be demonstrating for Maeve. 'Dice the vegetables and put them in a frying pan with dripping,' she said, looking back at Maeve to make sure she was paying attention. 'If you are going to use this mixture as a pie, you add oatmeal once the vegetables are cooked and wait for the liquid to be absorbed.'

'Oh...'

'What is it, Maeve?'

'Well, it's just, oatmeal doesn't really have any flavour.'

'Exactly, that's the point. The fact that it hasn't a distinctive flavour means it will take on the flavours of the other ingredients, while also making the dish go further.'

'I see, you mean like a sort of host?'

'Yes, I suppose so. And of course, it's very good for–'

'Lots of iron and vitamins,' Maeve finished.

'Exactly.'

'So is that why you divide the mixture in two?'

'That's right, you make a vegetable soup and a vegetable pie at the same time.'

She glanced up to see that Mr Ferguson was still there.

If Mr Ferguson were a dish, he would be a large tray of bland rubbery Yorkshire pudding, all flab and no flavour. She sneaked another glance; his triple chins spilled over his collar so that even though his shirt was clean and ironed, there was something unsavoury about him. She shuddered.

Bringing her chopping board up level with the deep-sided pot, she tipped it up and nudged the contents into the pan with her knife.

'Grab a wooden spoon and give it a stir, Maeve,' she said, wiping her hands on a cloth at the same time as moving after Mr Ferguson's retreating figure.

'Excuse me ... Mr Ferguson...' She had to raise

45

her voice to make herself heard over the sounds of grinding and sizzling. 'Do you have a moment?'

'I would have done if you had been here on time. Now you will have to wait until the end of your shift, Miss Johnson.'

'But, sir, I really need to get away today. This won't take long.'

'Very well,' he said, chin wobbling with each syllable. 'Come with me.'

She followed him out of the kitchen and down a bleak corridor to the door of his office. Once inside the large carpeted room, he gestured for her to sit and moved around to the other side of an antique wooden desk, where he lowered himself into the chair, wedging in his ample frame. He then began going through the documents on the desk in front of him, his pencil scrawling across paper the only sound in the room.

Maggie had been to his office a number of times before so was no longer overwhelmed by the double-height windows that provided a panorama of the street or impressed by the ornate carved bookshelves that were home to a vast collection of books, Her eyes skipped back to his desk and across the folders – INVENTORY, EMPLOYMENT RECORDS and SAFETY PROCEDURES – and came to rest back on his large round face and its overhanging chin. It was hard to believe that she could have been sitting in her own office now if Peter were still alive, going through their accounts and correspondence, making their own plans. Even though they had initially been disappointed with the pub they had recognised its potential. She could still see the flash of Peter's dark eyes as they looked around the bedrooms, realising that with a little work they could be comfortably let. With growing excitement they had moved from room to room, ducking beneath cobwebbed beams as Peter described how he would paint each one of them, her interrupting to explain what kind of curtains she could make, but then they had both stopped and looked at the bare wooden floorboards and knew they wouldn't have enough money to spend on carpets. He had smiled reassuringly. 'Don't worry, Mags, save that for tomorrow. We'll think of something.' And she had, straight away; there was an article in *Woman's Own* where they had painted the floorboards and arranged rugs across the floor. 'It's a very fashionable look, you know,' she had declared as she walked around the dusty old room.

They had gone back downstairs to the bar area and the small dining room that they knew needed a lot more work. 'A full restoration,' Peter had said, shaking his head. She opened the door to the kitchen cautiously, not knowing what she might find; a scrapheap of disused equipment and rusting cookers, a pile of rotting food and stained plates? But the room was quite clean, stark even, and the owner informed them that they hadn't cooked a meal there in a long time; not since his wife passed away. The bones of what she needed were there: large benches with plenty of work-space, a large range and a smaller wood-burning stove to keep the meals warm, and a room for cold storage. A double sink and draining racks were well placed close to the double doors through to the restaurant and a serving station ran the length of the room that would act as a pass to allow the dishes to be served and garnished. This was more like it; Maggie could picture them here now. Peter out front keeping the customers happy and the bar well stocked and running smoothly. Her in here, doing what she loved best.

There was a strange rasping noise, and she was startled from her recollections by Mr Ferguson clearing his throat and looking up at her.

'Well, what is it, Miss Johnson?' he asked, placing one chubby hand on top of the other.

'I've been doing a bit of research, sir...'

'Oh?'

'And I've found that some of the other factory canteens are growing their own produce. They can get hold of more fruit and vegetables that way, and it gives them a bit more variety.'

'And?'

'Well, I thought it might be something we could do too. Highbury Fields is not so far away, and we've got some keen gardeners here who are ready to help.'

'And how exactly would that work?'

'Well, we'd only need a few pounds, just to get started – we'd have to buy some seed and tools – but after that it will be just a question of time and we can work out a roster or something...'

As her voice trailed off, his expression softened.

'I appreciate your resourcefulness, Miss Johnson, but I think our time is better spent doing what we are supposed to here and getting on with providing hot meals for the workers. I don't think you need concern yourself with "variety"; sticking to the menus and following the recipes we have been given by the ministry will suffice.'

She knew he was referring to the few occasions recently when she had made changes to the set dishes; changes that had been appreciated by the workers but had met with her supervisor's disapproval. How could he be so narrow-minded when everyone else was going to such lengths to help each other? she fumed. She had been naive to think he would let them grow their own vegetables and she should have known it would be pointless asking. Perhaps she should apply for the British Restaurant scheme after all; she knew there was far more she could do to help overcome the food shortages if only she were given the chance.

'Thank you for your time, sir,' she said, rising from her chair, but her courtesy was wasted; his attention was already back on his work and he didn't bother to raise his head.

After running so late, the shift passed quickly and Maggie didn't get the chance to talk to Eliza again until the end of the day.

'So?' Eliza said, following her down the aisle towards the preparation area. 'How did it go?'

'Don't ask,' Maggie replied, scanning the tops to check each utensil had been put away and every surface wiped clean.

The clock showed five fifty; she only had ten minutes to get packed away, find some ingredients to make supper for Robbie and be on her way.

Eliza pulled herself up to sit on the benchtop,

legs crossed at the ankles. 'What do you think?' she asked. 'Shall we do it anyway?'

Maggie stared at her. 'You aren't serious?'

'Yes, I am.'

'And how do you propose we pay for it?'

'I don't know – you're the one with the brains. You'll think of something. I'm the manpower. It's what Woolton wants, remember: *The battle in the kitchen can't be won without help from the kitchen garden,*' she intoned in a deep masculine voice.

'Ferguson wouldn't even consider it,' Maggie said. 'Told me to stick to the menus and recipes we've been given.'

'Oh well, it was worth a try, Mags.'

'Not really.'

'Of course it was. He knows now that you can do more – that you want to do more. When they realise Janet isn't coming back he'll look to you as her permanent replacement.'

'I don't want to be supervisor anymore.'

'What? I thought it was what you had always wanted?'

'Yes, I thought so too.'

Maggie reached into her apron pocket and pulled out a piece of folded newspaper.

'Read this,' she said, passing it to Eliza.

'*The Times!*' Eliza exclaimed. 'When did you start reading *The Times?*'

'Very funny. Seriously, this is important. I first read about it a few weeks ago and it seems as if it's really going ahead.'

She pointed to the headline: EMERGENCY FEEDING OF THE PUBLIC: CATERING INDUSTRY'S PART. Then, checking that Mr

50

Ferguson wasn't nearby and that the other girls had left already, she returned to the article. 'It says here that more than two hundred and eighty new British Restaurants have been approved by the ministry. And there are some one hundred and forty-seven London meals centres carried out by the London County Council.' She glanced up to see if she had Eliza's attention. 'There's also two hundred and fifty British Restaurants which were taken over by the Ministry of Food from the Ministry of Health. That's more than eighty-two thousand meals a day they are serving!'

When she looked up Eliza was frowning.

'So, what do you think?' Maggie asked.

'I think it sounds like a lot of food.'

'But they are looking for people to run them. Look...' She pointed to a small printed box at the bottom of the page instructing interested applicants to send a letter of interest together with full curriculum vitae and references.

'So, are you going to apply?'

'I was going to, but now I'm not so sure.' She hesitated. 'I haven't stopped thinking about it, but then Mr Ferguson has a way of making me feel so hopeless about everything.'

'Well,' Eliza said as she carried on reading the article, 'I think you'd be as mad as a coot not to. Your chance to get away from Ferguson, cook what you want...'

'I don't think you can do that – you still have to cook what the ministry says – but, as you say, at least it would be better than being stuck here with old Ferguson stopping us from doing anything vaguely useful.'

'So why haven't you applied already?'

'I've already told you: I don't know if I can do it alone.'

The air seemed to flow out of her, her body slumping back against the bench. 'It would have been different if I'd been doing it with Peter...'

'Oh, Mags.'

'I don't know if I can do it without him.'

'Of course you can ... I know you can.'

Maggie looked at the clock again; it was nearly five fifty-five; she needed to be on her way.

'Just forget it,' she said, untying her apron. 'I should never have said anything.'

'No,' Eliza said, grasping hold of Maggie's arm, stopping her from moving away. 'Wait. Don't you remember those pictures of the King and Queen at that school in Peckham? That was a communal feeding centre, wasn't it? And they were giving meals to people who had lost their homes. Londoners need these centres. They need more British Restaurants, Maggie.' Eliza's eyes were stern, challenging her.

'I have to go,' Maggie said.

Her friend refolded the article and tucked it into Maggie's palm. 'I don't doubt that you can do it.'

'Thank you,' she said, squeezing Eliza's hand. 'I really do have to go though.'

Maggie ran her fingers across the cool scrubbed worktop as she walked, thinking about Robbie knocking on her door and leaving when no one answered, or perhaps just letting himself in as he had before.

Maggie was already half regretting inviting him;

what did she actually know about him anyway, apart from the fact that he was far too young to be on his own, that he was very clever with his hands and that he was a thief? Perhaps she had been too sentimental because of Ernest. Robbie had reminded Maggie of her brother the instant she saw him, and while her head knew that helping Robbie wouldn't bring Ernest back, that it wouldn't change what had happened, her heart was telling her something else. In any case, she had made a promise and she had to keep it, so she walked over to the pantry and pulled open the meat safe to see what was left. An end of bacon, that was all, until the deliveries arrived the next morning – and Ferguson would notice if it went missing; he always did a stocktake at the end of each day. Robbie had requested apple crumble and toad-in-the-hole, but they'd run out of sausages at lunchtime and the flour was riddled with weevils so it had been thrown away. On the floor by her feet, two sacks of potatoes leaned against each other; maybe she wouldn't be able to give Robbie what he had asked for, but she was sure he would be perfectly happy with a filled jacket potato, melted butter drizzling down the side and tasty cheddar crumbled on the top. She could never resist a baked potato when she was young, especially on 5 November, Guy Fawkes Day. She and her brothers had anticipated the potatoes as eagerly as the burning of the Guy Fawkes dummy and the fireworks. (Imagine that, she thought to herself: a time when there was delight not horror when fire lit up their skies.) Her father would prod and turn the parcels in the spitting bonfire until they were ready, and then came the ritual of handing them out: a relay of hot potatoes until they each had one. Maggie would try to make each mouthful last longer than the one before, but the first one was always the best; when the bitterness of the slightly burnt skin gave way to the sweet powdery flesh that dissolved on her tongue. No potato had ever tasted as good as her dad's on bonfire night.

She brushed the dried mud off the surface of two potatoes and slid them into her pocket. On a nearby shelf a small wedge of cheddar rested alongside a whole new wheel. She hesitated for a moment, instinctively looking over her shoulder; seeing no one there, she slipped it into her other pocket and headed for the door.

The sun had only just dipped behind St Mary's church but Maggie could already feel the drop in temperature and the shift in the sounds of the streets; the vehicles on Upper Street seemed to be driving faster than usual, pedestrians more hurried, their footsteps quick. And there was a great shadow above her as the starlings wheeled overhead, their evening song just beginning.

Simple piano notes spilled from a first-floor window; the unexpected sound of a child practising, the smell of cooking accompanying the notes as they drifted out onto the street, just as crisp and clear. She had always enjoyed walking home with Peter, guessing what different households were having for dinner based on the smells that collided in the dusk. Before the war they'd had time for lots of idle games.

As she turned into her street she caught sight of the brown hessian wall; she would never get used to seeing sandbags outside their homes, no matter how long this damned war went on. Outside public buildings was one thing, but here was quite another story and it always gave her a disquieting feeling. It didn't help that dusk was her least favourite time of day, the point when day transitioned into night, when she couldn't hide from the fact that her life would never be the same again; that she wouldn't have the husband she loved or the babies they planned for. And it was now that she missed Peter the most, wished he was alongside her, preparing their meal, sharing the details of their day.

By the time she was at home in her kitchen and had taken the potatoes from her pockets and washed them, she was beginning to feel more settled, soothed by the restorative act of cooking. The memory of Ferguson's stubbornness irritated her, and she still couldn't get the idea of running a British Restaurant out of her mind. She needed to though; she couldn't do it without Peter and she had no intention of being pushed into it, no matter what Eliza said. She also didn't want to be melancholy when Robbie arrived, so she forced her mind onto other things. In no time the potatoes were in the oven and she had prepared a small salad, but even though half past six had come and gone, there was no sign of Robbie. No matter, she decided. That would give her extra time to start on a mock cream to go with the apple charlotte. And perhaps she could make a gratin of leeks and mushrooms to use some of the cheese and breadcrumbs she had collected. It had been such a long time since the boy had had a hot meal, and who knew when he might have another? She would make this meal one to remember.

Cooking had always been her favourite distraction; growing up she cooked after Ernest had gone, and again while they waited and hoped for their mother to return. She had always diligently followed a recipe, making sure she used the correct technique and the best ingredients she could find in her parents' grocery store. She remembered the excitement she felt when using new things, ingredients she had barely heard of much less tried before. Her brothers and Tom wolfed down everything she made, even the dishes that didn't work, and were lavish in their praise.

The apple slices were beginning to brown so she picked them off the board and started layering them on the bottom of the cooked pastry case, neatly arranging them symmetrically around the base. The pale crescents were soon hidden by the smooth almond mixture, a handful of flaked almonds sprinkled over, landing on the surface and creating small indentations as they became embedded in the sweet doughy blend. She placed the tart on the top shelf of the oven, above the potatoes that had been moved right down to prevent them from crisping even more.

The glass ceiling light cast a warm honey glow around the room and her mood lightened as she continued her work on the table in its centre. She listened out for Robbie's footsteps but the only sound was the rhythmic tick of an old clock. She tried hard not to keep looking at it, but she couldn't help herself and finally glanced up. It was a whole five minutes since she'd last looked and a full fifty minutes since the boy should have been here. Perhaps he wasn't coming after all, or he had forgotten – or maybe it was never his intention to come in the first place. Her hands stopped fiddling with the cutlery and she placed the dessertspoons back in place above the forks. Everything was ready; the dish of leek gratin sat on a tablemat, the molten bubbling cheese releasing a sweet tangy steam. The apple charlotte, its pale brown crust studded with caramelised almonds, rested beside a glass bowl of mock cream, the silver serving spoon ready to deliver the smooth creamy pearls. She retrieved the two potatoes from the oven; they were overdone now, their insides probably claggy and dry.

It really didn't matter about the food; her land-lady was home so the meal wouldn't go to waste. She would understand if he had just changed his mind or got caught up with friends, but what if something had happened to him? He had seemed so sincere about wanting to come that she couldn't help but think that there might be something wrong.

Chapter Three

When arranging a salad, remember that a bright glean here and there in the greenery is tempting and where the eye leads, good digestion follows.
Ministry of Food, War Cookery Leaflet No. 5

Robbie had quickly learned that The Savoy's location near the banks of the River Thames ensured it wasn't just toffs and tourists who were able to enjoy the luxury; hungry mice and rats were regular visitors too, especially late in the day, when he too found that the best opportunities offered themselves. If he played it right, he could sneak into the kitchen and get something to take to Maggie's with time to spare.

It was despite the chefs' best efforts, and the fact that they fought as hard to keep the rats at bay as they did to hold on to the young apprentices they struggled to find, that the area was still overrun with vermin. Hours spent eavesdropping while waiting for the right moment to make his move had taught Robbie all manner of things involved in running the hotel's vast kitchens. Tonight was no exception; as he watched from behind the safety of a delivery van, a stern-faced chef oversaw the placement of baits at regular intervals along the grand stone perimeter. He had seen the kitchen hands engaged in the same ritual at other hotels and restaurants, but there was nowhere that did it as thoroughly as here. They even lay traps at the entrances and glue boards in the concealed spaces behind furniture and beside doorframes, where none of the hotel or restaurant guests would ever look. It was as unlikely that they would see the real workings of the hotel as he was to see inside the grand reception hall or opulent ballrooms at the front. His mum had been inside once to deliver an urgently mended evening gown to one of the guests. She had described the finely dressed valets and porters, the electric lift that had taken her up to one of the suites, and how the rooms dripped with velvet and brocade.

There was a shout from the left side of the building and a young man in his early twenties waved at another chef, who dutifully marched over with a hook and pole. Often the rats would eat the bait and crawl into the bushes or back down into the sewers to die, but Robbie had also seen how their gluttony would sometimes mean that they were unable to make it and their bodies would be left in the hotel grounds as bloated and rigid as a stuffed toy. The younger man made several clumsy attempts at transferring the body into the bag, causing more and more of his hair to spring from beneath his tall white hat, while the other one stood by shouting at him. Robbie took his chance; he tied Spoke to the railings and sneaked past. Just a quick detour and then he would make it to Maggie's in time for dinner and with a peace offering to show her how sorry he was for stealing her food that morning.

With a final glance to make sure that the coast

was clear, he ducked inside the delivery bay.

A steep descent led down to the wide mouth of a concrete entrance guarded by industrial-sized bins and double doors that led through to the hotel's kitchens and stores. Beyond the doorway there was a security guard smoking with the van driver as the vehicle's engine idled.

Robbie looked admiringly at the Bedford, its dark green lines and the larger recently re-modelled grille gleaming, its chrome headlights glinting as if they were winking at him. He had only built the Chevrolet Bolt 6 and hadn't yet managed to finish this new three-tonne van. He knew there were two types of wheelbase and guessed that this was the shorter one, at nine foot and three inches. He stared hard, trying to memorise the shape of the new cab and of the detailed indentation on the doors. He had tried to make this model a dozen times but could never get the axle and wheel space quite right. The deliverymen were deep in conversation, so he took his pencil and crumpled notebook out of his pocket and made a quick sketch. Drawing it now, he could see where he was going wrong; he had curved the wire too early and the width at the front of the truck was slightly less than the back, all things he could change now that he knew. His dad would have been able to show him; he was the best engineer that the navy had. That was the reason he couldn't come home for visits like the other sailors did, his mum had explained. But when he did come back, Robbie would show him all the models he had made and his dad would be proud of him.

Pushing the notebook and pencil back into his pocket, he checked once again that he wasn't being watched and then followed the delicious smells coming from deep inside the building. Crossing behind the van, he slipped silently past the bins and tiptoed through the open double doors into the great underbelly below.

He tried to identify the mouth-watering clash of sweet and sour smells, making out sugary sponge puddings, the familiar aroma of roast beef, the salty freshness of the sea, the floral fragrance of newly harvested honey. He knew that there were armies on the battlefields and on the farms here at home, but in the kitchen of The Savoy was an army of an altogether different kind; there were dozens of women in white uniforms ranging from one end of the huge underground kitchen to the other. And the noise was overwhelming too; only the roar of Jerry's planes overhead had ever seemed louder than the banging and clattering in here. It was a miracle that any of them could hear the head chef's orders, or the calls and requests from the waiters. He couldn't imagine this sort of racket at home; his mum just wouldn't stand for it from him and his two sisters!

Keeping close to the wall, he weaved in and out of the stacks of tables and piled-up chairs, watching those closest to him as they worked dizzyingly fast. He had only been inside here twice before, but from memory, the storerooms were on the left in between the four kitchens and the banquet room. It would be hard to find a way of sneaking through without being observed, even with his dad's lucky football cards in his pocket, but after

61

watching for a while he noticed that a bank of stoves on the right-hand side was unattended. Ducking down low so that no one could see his head above the top of the cookers, he slowly inched his way past, at last finding the storeroom door and disappearing inside.

The storeroom was even bigger than their house had been before the Luftwaffe had damaged it. There was also more food than he had ever seen before in his life; shelf after shelf held boxes and cartons of ingredients and the floor was lined with storage bins. There was not a bare wall in sight; every inch taken up with racks of wooden shelving. Only rather than looking like a giant pantry, it resembled his school library, with signs and arrows marking avenues of Dry Goods and Dairy, Tinned Foods and Oils. There was also another door at the far end of the room, and before he was able to pull the top off a storage bin and peer inside, the handle turned and the door swung open. He quickly looked around for somewhere to hide, at last squeezing beneath the shelving unit and pulling a storage bin in front of him, the lid clattering to the floor.

He tried to slow his breathing as footsteps approached but he could hear his own faint asthma wheeze, the air whistling in and out, and the next thing he knew a pair of chubby legs appeared.

'Bloody vermin!' the figure grumbled as it bent down and replaced the lid and then just as quickly marched away.

After a few minutes of banging and scraping the door opened and closed, and then there was silence.

Robbie let out a deep breath, and hastily pulled a thin hessian sack from his pocket. As always, he had come prepared. He knew which foods he should take – those that would last him the longest and be the easiest to store – but he did have an achingly sweet tooth. Spotting a sign for the Puddings section, he followed the arrow, hoping to find the sugar and dried fruit.

Once in the correct aisle, he couldn't believe his eyes; there were containers of dried figs as big as golf balls and jars of glacé cherries the size of king marbles. Imagine Maggie's face when he arrived at her place for supper with some of these!

He carried on filling up the sack with packets of tapioca and sugar before he came across the mixed peel he knew his ma used for making cakes; it would be the second Saturday of the month next week, the day he would make his monthly visit to the country near Bristol and the farm where his ma helped out while his younger sisters went to the local school. He knew his ma would have preferred it if he stayed with them, but then who would tell his dad where they were when he came home? Thank goodness she hadn't found out that their house had been boarded up and that he was camping out at the school, or else she would definitely be back to fetch him. Lucky for him that the post box hadn't been damaged and he still got her letters.

The sack was already heavy, but he took a second tin of bird's Custard Powder because it was his favourite, then he struggled towards the door.

He was startled to hear voices on the other side, and he had to wait an age till they faded and he was able to ease open the door and slip through.

He had only made it a few yards along the kitchen galley when he felt a hand on his shoulder. Turning, he found himself face to face with the young bait-layer.

'What you doing here, lad?'

'Delivery...'

His voice came out small and squeaky, not at all the confident tone he had rehearsed earlier when considering which disguise or excuse he could use without drawing attention. He was small and wiry like his dad, so he knew he looked too young for anyone to believe he was a kitchen hand or a trainee porter; the only thing he could possibly pass as was a delivery boy.

'So aren't you going in the wrong direction?'

Close up, the man looked much younger than Robbie had first thought, only about six or seven years older than him and with a face full of large crimson spots to prove it.

The young man nodded at Robbie's sack. 'What's in there?'

'Stuff was no good, chef said to replace it.'

'Oh,' the young man said, eyes narrowing. 'Better get on with it then.'

Robbie waited until his spotty face was well out of sight and swallowed hard as he carried on towards the entrance, a light breeze from outside already signalling his freedom. Just another few hundred yards...

Walking quickly with his head down, he avoided looking at any of the worktops he passed, ignoring the inviting smells and the dance of the utensils. Almost there ... almost...

Just before he reached the open doorway, a giant silhouette appeared, obscuring the light from the corridor beyond.

Robbie's eyes travelled across the dark grey clothing; not smart enough to be a uniform and definitely not police, so he must be hotel security. Robbie needed to act quickly and he only had two choices; he could run or he could summon up the courage to pretend he had every right to be there.

'Excuse me,' he said, attempting to step around the lofty figure.

'Not so fast – I know you. I've seen you here before.'

'Hey, let go of me,' Robbie yelped as the man grabbed hold of his upper arm, He tried to squirm free, but it just made the man tighten his grip as he dragged Robbie towards the exit and out into the open air.

One of the head chefs was standing talking to another even larger man in civilian clothes with a crop of wild blond hair. Their accents were strange, Robbie noticed; they sounded like the Polish men down at the docks where his father had worked.

They stopped talking as Robbie and his captor drew near.

'Hey, Bartek, you want to know why things keep disappearing? You can stop blaming the apprentices now.'

'What him?' The chef laughed. 'He doesn't look strong enough to lift a lid let alone carry anything out of here!'

The man's hand was like a tourniquet around Robbie's arm and he could feel the blood pulsing

65

either side of it. He considered bolting, just taking off and running as fast as his legs would carry him.

'You might want to look in here then,' the security guard suggested, holding up the bag that Robbie had filled.

Bartek came forward and took the sack, but Robbie didn't see his reaction as he peered inside; he was too busy watching the big man with the wild blond hair. His upper arms were nearly the size of Robbie's torso, and his chest looked strong enough to pull a plough. He didn't look like a chef, but Robbie was certain of one thing: his dad would have bet on him in the boxing ring. Then again, he didn't look like a boxer either; he wore a shirt but no tie and his jacket was slung over his left shoulder, while his hands were tucked deep inside the pockets of his dark trousers. At his feet was a large canvas bag, distorted by irregular bulging shapes, and Robbie leaned forward to see what was inside. He only caught a glimpse of wood and a flash of metal before the security guard tugged him away, but he had already imagined the worst; tools of torture and illegal weapons – perhaps these men weren't Polish after all, but German spies!

'There's only one thing to do with little thieves like you,' Bartek snarled at him 'I'm calling the police.'

'There is another way,' the blond man said.

'No, Janek,' Bartek replied. 'He has been here before. This has to stop now.'

'You do not need to involve the police,' the blond man insisted. 'I know how to keep him from coming back.'

Robbie looked at Janek, at the size of his arms compared to the other man's, at the fierceness of his expression, and suddenly the tightness of the grip on Robbie's arm and the gnawing hunger pangs in his belly seemed like the least of his problems.

Chapter Four

No country in the world grows vegetables better than we do, and probably no country in the world cooks them worse. For generations we have wasted our root vegetables by excessive peeling and overcooking, and boiled most of the goodness out of our green vegetables – only to pour it down the sink.
Ministry of Food, War Cookery Leaflet No. 1

He could see the boy was terrified, so as soon as they turned the corner and were out of sight of Bartek and the security guard, Janek loosened his grip.

'Where are you taking me?' the boy asked, pulling his arm free.

'You will see,' Janek replied, setting down the canvas bag and squatting down next to Spoke.

He scratched behind the dog's ears, burying his fingers into the wiry fur, and the dog responded by pushing himself up against Janek's legs.

'He likes you.'

'Well, that is good, because I do not think his

owner is so sure,' Janek replied, looking up at the boy. 'What is his name?'

'Spoke.'

'Spoke,' Janek repeated. 'And Spoke's owner – does he also have a name?'

'Robbie,' the boy said reluctantly, though Janek could tell that he was trying not to smile. Janek felt a rush of relief, it made him feel more comfortable knowing that the boy might trust him more now that his dog did.

'How do you manage to hide Spoke?'

Since he had first seen Spoke at the hotel, Janek had been wondering how the boy managed to keep the dog. Even though the English loved their pets, he knew that any animal that couldn't produce food or be eaten had to be put down.

'We don't get in anyone's way,' Robbie stated matter-of-factly. 'We don't mind them, they don't mind us.'

'What about this evening? That was not exactly minding your own business, was it?'

'That's different. We've all got to eat. I've got a right to take food wherever I can get it.'

'Is that what you really think?'

Robbie's gaze lingered on the ground a few moments too long.

'No, I didn't think so.'

'What's it to you, anyway?' Robbie said, crossing his arms indignantly.

Janek shrugged. 'It's nothing to me, but I would not like to see you in trouble. Who would look after your dog then?'

He could see that he had given Robbie something to think about as the boy went quiet, head bent over as he kicked his right foot back and forth across the pavement, as if toying with an imaginary football.

'I can swear in Polish,' Robbie said, looking up at him.

'Really?'

'Yes, *really*. There's loads of Polish men at the docks where my dad worked. They taught me how to say lots of things.'

'How do you say, "Hello, my name is Robbie"?'

'Aw, come on, they didn't teach me that kind of thing,' he said. 'I know how to say the "b" word.'

'If you were my son, I would not allow it.'

'Well, my father don't allow it either.'

'So how about I teach you the days of the week instead, or how to count?' Janek suggested. 'Something useful.'

'No, it's okay.'

As he carried on stroking Spoke, Janek's face drew level with Robbie's and he could see the goosebumps on the boy's pale skin and the blue veins of his neck as they disappeared into the thin grey fabric of his shirt.

'Come on, we can walk and talk,' he said, picking up the bag and checking both ways before stepping off the kerb, Spoke following close behind.

Janek led him across the Strand, up Wellington Street and along a deserted lane towards Covent Garden. The ground was still glistening from an earlier shower and Robbie deliberately splashed through the puddles that Janek tried to avoid.

'You still haven't said where we're going,' Robbie said, sidestepping a deep puddle that would have filled his boots.

'I thought children were supposed to like surprises.'

'Well, I don't, and my dad told me to never go with strangers.' Janek stopped walking and turned to him.

'Your *tata* is right, but I am no longer a stranger – we have known each other for at least twenty minutes. And I think that you do not have a choice; it is me or the police.'

'This isn't right, it's blackmail ... and anyway, I'm supposed to be somewhere.' Robbie thought of Maggie and the steaming hot meal waiting for him. She would be annoyed when he didn't show up.

'Well, I am afraid you are going to be late.'

'I'll come with you this time,' Robbie replied huffily, 'but it's only because Spoke wants to. Otherwise I most certainly would not.'

'That is fine with me. It is good enough reason.'

'How do you know your way around so well, anyway?' Robbie eyed him suspiciously. 'And your English is real good ... you some sort of spy?'

'These streets are not so difficult to learn when you have walked them many times.'

It had taken Janek only months to learn his way around the city, walking from the cobweb of historic monuments and buildings at its heart, through to the urban sprawl of mansion blocks and terraces that interrupted the skyline in every direction. He had been restless, unable to sit alone in the small hut that had become his home; a place where thoughts of his family constantly intruded, like the draughts that found their way through the cracks in the structure's irregular wooden boards. He tried to block out thoughts of them, think only of his brother and what he could do for him now, but helplessness gnawed at him. So he had walked for days, through the West End and the city, first tracing his way along the river and then into the outlying suburbs, exploring anywhere that wasn't closed off, avoiding streets with bombed-out sites and roads that were too difficult to navigate. Sometimes he followed maps or directions, other times he just went where his instinct took him; along commercial streets and residential avenues, recognising the well-known landmarks and features of the city but getting excited by none. After six months he had grown to know London as well as any Londoner and could find his way in the dark now as well as he could through any furrowed hill or dyke on his farm, but he thought no more of the city because of it. Attractions that tourists travelled across the Atlantic to see were of no interest to him; Buckingham Palace and Hyde Park were grand monoliths of little consequence. And while he felt saddened for the city's population at the sight of their scarred homes and palaces, he would happily trade all the royal parks and gardens for half an hour standing in a windswept field of Mazovia.

'Are we nearly there?' Robbie asked.

'No, we have about ten minutes to walk from here.'

He heard Robbie sigh impatiently.

They crossed the red-brick footpaths of Covent Garden and passed the neoclassical columns and glazed roofs of the piazza, which were now in full view, the tall Victorian buildings along the square's perimeter momentarily dwarfing them as he led Robbie through. He could see the appeal in their imposing design and the achievements of the architects and craftsmen of the day, just as he could with their stately Georgian houses and Regency crescents, but these buildings had not enchanted him the way they had generations of artists and writers – though he did admire Westminster Abbey, which reminded him of the gothic church in his hometown of Pultusk. He knew he should be grateful to be safe, to have found refuge here in London, but the truth was that he found the city claustrophobic. He felt suffocated by the immense buildings and the constant noise; he yearned for empty spaces, for nothing but birdsong and the feeling of standing apart from everything, only the wind running freely across him, the uncomplicated rub of nature.

Even in Warsaw, such a small city compared to London, he had not felt comfortable, but he knew that he had to get to know the Polish community here; to find out where his fellow exiles congregated, which backstreets were home to the refuges and Polish clubs. If there was any chance that he was to be of help or find his brother, he had to make himself known to the Polish resistance here. Bartek had told him that was how it worked. His plans hadn't included being sidetracked by a child, but Robbie reminded him so much of his nephew Roman; they had the same scrawny build, a tangle of constantly moving limbs. Even when the security guard had hold of him, Robbie had continued bouncing up and down nervously on his toes, arms and legs wriggling just as Roman would have done. Janek hadn't known Bartek for long, so it was a relief that he'd been able to persuade him not to involve the police.

They were approaching Bloomsbury Way when Robbie stopped dead.

'I really need to go now – someone's expecting me.'

'You have to come, it was the deal.'

'*I* didn't make the deal, it was *your* deal.'

'We can always go to police if you prefer?'

'Is it much further?' the boy asked again. 'I'm really tired.'

'It is very close, just around that corner.'

Janek pointed ahead to where the line of trees formed a semicircle of green before disappearing around the crescent.

'Alright, just a few more minutes,' he said grudgingly. 'It had better be worth it.'

Robbie may have been smaller than Roman but he was just as gutsy; *chutzpah* his mother would have called it. And as they turned the corner into Bloomsbury Square he saw Robbie's eyes widen at where a bomb crater in the centre had been transformed into victory gardens and where a scattering of people were tending the plots, weeding and watering even though it was nearly dusk.

'You brought me here for this?' Robbie said sullenly.

'Yes, you can help.'

'There are victory gardens everywhere ... I can go to one a lot nearer if I want to. What's so special about this one?'

'If you are patient, I will show you.'

The boy was right, there were lots of victory gardens – even the Tower of London had given over its moat for allotments – but Janek knew the men that came here. Some he had worked with at London and North Eastern Railway, and he knew that they would keep an eye on Robbie if he asked them to.

Robbie wandered ahead with Spoke, exploring the raised beds of recycled timber and the low brick walls.

'These are salvaged from the rubble, aren't they?'

'That's right,' Janek answered, glancing over at the other people in the garden, disappointed that Stefan and Josef weren't among them.

It was just five o'clock, so there were only a handful of people absorbed in their quiet industry before the office workers arrived. A woman in the dark grey dress and beret of the Women's Voluntary Service worked alongside a quick-moving figure that Janek recognised from his long black jacket and rows of shiny brass buttons to be a member of the Auxiliary Fire Service. He nodded as the man looked up. A few yards further on a group of young women talked and laughed as they worked; they could have been the image from one of the billboards advertising women in headscarves and dungarees digging for victory. Thankfully he could see that they had read their pamphlets and knew what they were doing, scraping the heavier soil away from the roots so that it didn't suffocate the growth.

Spoke sniffed the ground and pawed at the edge of a bed so Robbie tugged at his collar, pulling him away.

'Here, boy.'

The dog barked and then turned around a few times, looking for a moment as if he were chasing his own tail, and then he curled up, snout nuzzling into his paws, dark eyes looking back at Robbie.

'Good boy.' Robbie looked up at Janek. 'I'm still waiting,' he said. 'What *did* you bring me all the way here for?'

'I told you: there are some people I want you to meet.' Janek scanned the pavements around the square as he spoke, hoping to see his comrades, but there were only anonymous office workers. 'And I wanted to show you this,' he said, pointing to the gardens. 'If you ever feel tempted to go back to The Savoy, or any other hotel, then you should come here instead.'

'I can take stuff?'

'Only if you help to grow it.'

Janek scanned the gardens again. The light was beginning to fade; there was probably only half an hour of daylight left. It was annoying that the men hadn't shown; he needed to give them tools and he wanted to introduce them to Robbie so that they could look out for him. Then the boy could leave and it would be the last Janek would need to see of him.

'I suppose your friends don't like you very much either.'

Janek looked down at him, slumped across his dog; Robbie was barely double its size and clearly shivering.

'It's disappointing that you do not meet them.

It's what I had hoped for, but perhaps we try again another day.'

'Can I go then?'

'Not yet – first you come to the railyard with me. You can warm up and I will show you how to earn a meal.'

Chapter Five

HOW TO KEEP CHEESE:
Wrap in margarine or butter paper, hang in a piece
of muslin in a cool, airy place. This hardens the
cheese and makes it more economical in use. Use the
rind for flavouring sauces, etc., but remember to
remove it before serving the dish.
Ministry of Food, War Cookery Leaflet No. 12

As soon as she heard the dawn chorus Maggie was up and dressing, planning where she should look. The streets around the school were the first places to search, although she hoped to find Robbie in the school storeroom, tucked up in his blankets asleep, unaware of the concern that he had caused, Spoke snoring at his side.

She had spent most of the night awake, trying hard not to imagine the worst, her mind drifting between sleep and thoughts of where he might be; fallen down a shaft or caught stealing by the police and shivering in a freezing cell. She regretted not going to look for him last night. It didn't matter whether she had known him for a

76

year or a day; she should have tried to find him straight away.

Walking quickly south along Danbury Street, she glanced away when she heard a door open; she usually said hello to her neighbours, but today she didn't want to be distracted from her search. She hurried past the white Georgian townhouses, peering into their basements, just in case Robbie had decided to shelter there and gone to sleep. But the lower ground patios were empty and the blacked-out panes of glass in the large rectangle windows gave little clue as to what lay inside.

As she reached the end of the row and turned into Noel Road, the dark red brick of the school came into view, and for a brief moment she was surprised not to see children funnelling down the steps and through the doors, or playing games in the playground at the side. It only lasted a second, but the feeling that things were not as they had once been gave her a real physical jolt. She was accustomed to her job and had grown used to the all-female camaraderie that existed at work and almost everywhere else that she went now. Female workers populated the shops, the doctors' practices had been taken over by nurses' surgeries and, where schools still existed, female assistants had replaced the male teachers. She couldn't allow herself to dwell on how things once were, though, when the streets were filled with children, when their homes were not in rubble, and when the people who had been in her life only a year ago were still alive.

The cooing of pigeons on the ledge of a second-floor window brought her back to the present and, as she got closer, they took flight, lifting up and over the houses opposite to take refuge elsewhere. She watched for a moment, relieved that at least some creatures were able to get away. Her next breath made her feel lighter, more optimistic; perhaps it was the familiarity of her old school but she felt suddenly hopeful of finding Robbie again.

Once inside, though, the long corridors echoed only with the sounds of her footsteps, and when she called out his name hers was the only voice that came back. It took her ten minutes to search the whole school; he wasn't in the storeroom with Spoke; in fact, the room felt icily cold, as if no one had been there for a while.

Outside the sound of the morning traffic was beginning to build and she knew she couldn't be late for work again, but there was the canal at the back of the school still to search. She hadn't been near the canal since she was a child and Ernest had died – but it was a natural place to take Spoke for a walk and so she would have to look.

She hesitated at the top of the steps, her heart thumping loudly as her panic rose. The stone was damp and slippery from the foggy morning air and she took a deep breath, then descended, taking the steps slowly, before running down to the path that ran alongside the water. Her heart felt like it might burst from her chest; she had looked everywhere for Ernest but she hadn't found him in time. She hadn't seen the dark outline floating on the surface. If only she had; if only she'd looked harder, stayed longer.

There was a shallow mist rising from the water this morning, making it look even more ominous, and she pulled her coat tighter around her, feeling the cold creeping between the layers of her thin uniform. Beyond the low-lying fog she could just about make out the shapes of the buildings and the irregular outline of trees that lined the other side. There was no way of telling if Robbie was there; she would have to walk up and down both sides.

'Robbie!' she shouted.

A dog barked back at her and she turned in the direction of the bridge.

From under the archway a small mongrel trotted into view. Was it Spoke? He looked about the same size. But then a tall figure emerged, a lone dog walker; it was a man, not a boy.

Turning back along the path in the direction of Duncan Street, Maggie followed the canal around to where the lock separated the upper and lower levels, and where the powerful wooden barriers and metal winches stood idle. The buildings on either side, once primarily industry and offices, were now makeshift homes for the growing number of Londoners who had lost theirs. The wide covered doorway of the building nearest to her was boarded up but still allowed enough room for a mother and her children to shelter there.

'You got some food, love?' The woman's voice was a whisper as she extended her hands out towards Maggie.

A baby's head was just visible, a soft white dome poking out from under the layers of dark fabric wrapped around the woman's body. A boy a little younger than Robbie was slumped against the doorframe while a small girl, no more than a toddler, clung to her mother's legs.

'I'm sorry,' Maggie started.

'My little 'uns are real hungry.'

Then Maggie remembered the dried fruit in her pocket and pulled out the screwed-up brown paper bag. She had got into the habit of drying fruit recently to give to the canteen workers as a quick snack between meals.

'Thank you, love,' the woman said, almost snatching the bag from Maggie in her haste. 'What's your name?'

'Maggie.'

There were only a few pieces of pear left but it might as well have been a whole basket of fresh pears for the woman's reaction.

'Oh, thank you, Maggie. I'm really grateful to you...'

'Your children should enjoy them, they're juicy and sweet.'

The boy chewed and swallowed his instantly while the little girl concentrated hard as she held the fruit in her mouth. Maggie imagined the child pressing the rough skin against the roof of her mouth with her tongue as Maggie herself used to do, squeezing the flavour out of the sugary crystallised flesh.

'What about the feeding centre on Upper Street, have you been there?' Maggie asked. 'They'll surely give you something.'

'I haven't got a pram and this one can't walk far.'

Maggie moved closer, wanting to see the baby, but the girl huddled up to her mother, blocking her way.

'I could help if you like. I'm looking for someone now but I can come back.'

'Would you? Would you really do that?'

The woman sounded so desperate Maggie considered putting off her search for Robbie altogether and taking the woman and her children
right away, but then she thought about him being
out on the streets all night and alone.

'Yes, of course I will,' she promised. She was
about to leave when she thought to ask, 'You
haven't seen a boy, have you? He's about the
same size as your son, with brown hair and lots of
freckles.'

The woman shook her head.

'Never mind.' Maggie bit her lip. 'I'll come
back as soon as I've found him.'

The clamour of the kitchen came as a relief when
Maggie arrived later that morning, the rumble of
machinery and the potent smell of a warming
Irish stew a welcome contrast to the scorched
and dismantled streets outside. She hadn't been
able to find Robbie and there was an empty
doorway where the woman and her children had
sheltered when she returned to help. Now she
didn't know what had become of any of them.

Eliza came hurrying towards her.

'Maggie, watch out for–'

But before she had a chance to finish, Mr
Ferguson appeared behind her, index finger
summoning Maggie towards the cold store.

As soon as she entered she could feel the
atmosphere change, not just a result of the drop
in temperature and the strong smell of food

trapped in the stone floor beneath, but because of the cold glare coming from Mr Ferguson.

'What can you see, Miss Johnson?'

His eyebrows were raised but he didn't look around, so she had no clue what he was referring to.

She scanned the top shelf boxes of leeks and carrots at one end, the carton of eggs at the other. A large parcel wrapped in brown paper on the next shelf down, the wheel of cheese on the shelf below that.

'I can see carrots, leeks, bacon, eggs...' she replied hesitantly. 'What *should* I be looking for?'

'That's the point: you can't see it because it's no longer there!' he announced, almost triumphantly.

It was then that Maggie felt the first pang of regret. She had known in her heart of hearts that he would notice; he was too crafty and mean not to. And she knew that if she had asked him if she could take it, he would have said no. But she had taken it anyway, knowing it to be wrong yet thinking that for some reason it would be okay because of her good intentions – something he wouldn't understand. What she didn't know, though, was what to say to him now; she had never been a convincing liar.

'I'm sorry, Mr Ferguson, what is no longer there?'

'Come now, Miss Johnson – the cheese!'

'There's a new wheel of cheddar right there, Mr Ferguson,' she said, pointing.

'You know very well that I am not talking about the new wheel, but about the old piece that was there last night at the end of the shift but was not there when I came in this morning.'

'Oh, that small end piece?' Maggie said. 'I thought that it had gone far too hard and waxy to use. It hadn't been wrapped properly on account of us not having enough brown paper before the deliveries came today.'

'Waste, Miss Johnson.' He shook his head. 'It is not good enough. What are we responsible for now? Making do.' His face had become flushed and even the usually pale wobbly folds of his neck had taken on a rosy tinge. 'You could have used that in any number of sauces or gratins.'

Maggie's regret and fear at being found out were overtaken by an overwhelming impulse to laugh. She thought about the delicious leek gratin with the crisp cheese and breadcrumb topping that she and her landlady had shared.

'You're right, Mr Ferguson, point taken,' she managed to say. 'I won't let it happen again.'

'Good. That kind of waste is not what I expect from my supervisors, Miss Johnson. It demonstrates poor judgment and management skills.'

Maggie gaped at him, speechless, as she struggled to summon an appropriate response. Maybe she should tell him the truth; that she had taken it for Robbie, to give the child his first hot meal in weeks? No, she thought. That might do more harm than good.

'Is that all, Mr Ferguson?'

'Yes,' he said, straightening as if in a vain attempt to give himself more authority. 'But it's the last time I shall speak to you about such matters.'

Eliza was elbow deep in potato skins by the time Maggie rejoined her and began to help scoop the peelings into the pig bin.

'So what was that all about?' Eliza asked.

'He wanted to know what happened to the cheese.'

'Oh, Maggie, not the cheese again! I've told you it's high time those mice stood on their own four feet and began fending for themselves!' She giggled.

'It's not funny, he's serious this time. I think he'll sack me if he gets half a chance.'

'Well, you know what I think...'

'Yes, I do, thank you.'

'It should be you who's doing the hiring and firing, Maggie. Think about it: you'd be your own boss, no one to order you around.'

'Enough,' Maggie said, cutting her off. 'Best we just get on with this rather than give him any more reason to complain.'

Eliza's expression changed and she became serious. 'Okay, Maggie, just one more thing...'

'What is it?' she asked, looking up at her friend.

'Imagine Mr Ferguson came in to your restaurant ... you could ask him to leave!' And Eliza started to giggle again.

'Well, that would be something,' Maggie agreed, her good humour returning. 'How are you getting on with the lunches?' She was conscious that he would be on the warpath again if the meals were late.

'Fine. Gosh, that wind's got up again,' Eliza said, distracted by the branches battering the skylights.

'Eliza!'

'Sorry.'

'Now, Eleanor is mincing the salt beef so you just need to let her know when the potatoes are cool.'

'They won't be long,' Eliza replied. 'I've got the others soaking in cold water in buckets over there.'

'Good. I've asked Maeve to help prepare the vegetables for the soup. I think she should be able to cope with that alright.'

An alarm began to scream and they looked at each other; the bell only rang in an emergency, when there was an accident or fire. Maggie undertook a quick safety check of the kitchen, making sure the gas was turned off, but as the ringing continued the atmosphere changed; she could feel it through her connection with the floor. The building had its own rhythm, she could usually feel the vibrations from the machinery below, or from the movement of the counters and cookers where they worked, but now there was no mechanical pulse. The machines were all turned off.

A small crowd had gathered at the window overlooking the factory floor and she moved over to join them.

She expected to see a commotion and hear shouting but it was calm below and the steam was dissipating, revealing workers waiting calmly in groups next to dormant machines, except for a small crowd around one of the metal presses. Through the crush of figures Maggie could just make out a body bent forward, legs dangling, its torso locked into the great jaws of the machine.

Maggie shivered. She didn't want to think about what would happen when they lifted the press; there had been another accident just a few weeks ago, a young man who had slipped and lost his hand.

'Come on, back to work, everyone,' Mr Ferguson shouted as he walked through the kitchen towards them.

'Pray for the poor bugger, whoever it is,' Maeve murmured as she brushed past Maggie.

Whispers and a low mumbling grew as the women returned to their jobs, reluctantly turning back to the tasks they had left only moments earlier.

Eliza was still at the window so Maggie inched forward, following her gaze down to where ambulance men had parted the crowd, to where they were lifting a limp body onto a stretcher, and she saw that it was Tom.

Maggie was preoccupied as she walked home after her shift, her concern for Robbie and thoughts of Tom infiltrating as she tried to navigate the uneven roads in the dim light. Dust particles were suspended in the early evening damp, making it even more difficult to see and she stumbled on debris that crunched underfoot.

'Watch your step, miss,' one of the demolition gang shouted.

'Thank you,' she called back and began to cough; sore throats and coughs had been common since the bombings started and would probably only stop when the war was over and the air finally cleared.

Thinking of the bombings reminded her that she really should order a Morrison shelter so she didn't have to leave her home every time the air-raid sirens sounded. She also needed to pack a case of her precious things to put in her aunt's cellar for safekeeping at the weekend. She would go and visit Tom then too; the accident had been bad and even though the ambulance arrived in good time there had been no news since. Poor Tom: he had been so devastated to be told he was not fit enough to fight but now he was injured anyway.

Britannia Row was still sealed off so she took a shortcut down Packington Street. As she turned the corner she saw the warden, Bill Drummond, giving instructions to a family as they evacuated them from their home, the father piling furniture onto an already full handcart, carrying in his arms as much as he could manage. He disappeared back inside the brick facade, the only part of the home still standing, while the mother sat on the garden wall, comforting a small girl of four or five with a halo of golden curls. The woman watched Maggie's progress as she drew closer, until she was level with her on the opposite side of the road. She gave the woman a sincere smile and the woman smiled back but her expression was weak and drawn and the daughter just stared as she stood perfectly still, cocooned in her mother's arms.

Crossing into St Peter's Street, Maggie hurried towards home, grateful that she still had somewhere to go – but when she reached her gate there was a small dark shape slumped in the doorway.

'Robbie?'

The crumpled figure unfolded and stretched, still half asleep. 'Maggie?'

'Yes, it's me,' she said, crouching down. 'Are you alright?'

'I'm sorry I'm late.'

She felt a warm rush of relief. 'How long have you been here?'

'Since after school – it was light when I came.' He yawned, extending his arms above his head.

He looked tired, with dark circles beneath his eyes. He wore the same clothes as the previous day, but now they were even filthier.

'Where's Spoke?'

Robbie lifted his jacket and the dog's head bobbed up, his ears pricked as he heard his name.

She set down her bag and reached out and stroked him, feeling his strong wiry fur and smelling the earthy scent of damp dog.

'You know there's no toad-in-the-hole, don't you?'

'That's okay, a cup of Bovril will do.'

'Come on, then, let's see what we can find.'

She stood up and offered her hand to help him up. His weight was surprisingly light as she pulled him to his feet, and he stumbled slightly as he bent to scoop Spoke off the tiles.

'Are you sure you're okay?'

He nodded and they went inside, the drilling and hammering of the boarding-up fading behind them.

'It's straight through there to the kitchen,' she

said, pointing ahead. 'Oh, but you know that...'

He cast her a wounded look, and she instantly felt sorry.

'Why don't you come in here?' she suggested.

She led him through to the small parlour at the front of the house, the weak light from outside hinting at the comfort of the armchairs and sofa that were mere silhouettes in the room.

'Can I?'

'Yes, of course. Here, I'll turn on the light.'

She ducked in front of him and flicked the switch, the dull bulb fizzing on, painting the room in a low wash of white.

'How long have you been here?' he asked, gazing around.

'Almost a year,' she said, drawing the blackout curtains shut.

She had lived close by as a child, when her family owned a grocery store, so the neighbourhood wasn't new to her even though the house was. The three years she had spent working as a cook in the West Country had folded into the seams of time much like the great granite rocks of the Devon moors where she had spent much of her time.

He scanned the sofa and fireplace, eyes lingering on the half-finished puzzle on the coffee table, a panorama of London spread out before them; a half-constructed Buckingham Palace, sections of lions' heads without their plinths and the partially built fountains of Trafalgar Square. He pushed around a few pieces in the upturned lid and then picked out a piece and slotted it in to the corner of the jigsaw.

'And the lion gets his head...'

'Do you like puzzles?'

'Used to do them with my pa,' he answered as he carried on searching in the box.

'Hey, I've got something for you,' she said, indicating to her bag.

She led him down the dim hallway, Spoke obediently padding behind. When they reached the kitchen she turned on the light and offered him the bag.

He grinned as he heard the clink of metal, and when he looked, there were at least a dozen tins and bottle lids lying at the bottom. 'You collected these for me?' he said uncertainly.

'It would appear so.'

'I don't know what to say.'

'"Thank you" is usually a good starting point.'

'Oh, I've got something for you too,' he said, producing a tin of Bird's Custard Powder from underneath his jumper.

'Where did you get that?' she demanded.

'From a friend.'

Maggie narrowed her eyes at him. It was extremely unlikely he had friends who gave away tins of custard powder, she knew.

'I'm sorry I didn't come,' he said, setting the tin down on the table.

'I was worried about you,' she told him.

'I sort of bumped into someone,' he said. 'And then I went down to the docks; there was a big ship coming in.'

'Are you building ships now then?' She gestured for him to sit at the table as she filled the kettle.

'Oh, no, just the planes and cars. Actually, I was

looking for my dad.'

He was already sorting through the cans, holding up first one and then another as if assessing them for size and shape.

'Does he work there?' Maggie probed.

'No, he's in the navy. I've written to him – written to him loads – but I've not heard back.'

'I expect he'll write when he can. Must be difficult for him.'

'I know.'

He had finished going through the sack and sat watching as she moved about the kitchen.

'Where's your ma?'

He hesitated before answering. 'She's ... gone.'

She glanced at him but he was looking at the floor and wouldn't meet her eye.

'Oh, I'm sorry,' she said. 'Don't you have any other family you can stay with? It's not safe for you to be by yourself.'

'No, it's alright; Dad'll be back soon.'

'Hmm. How old are you, Robbie?'

'I'll be thirteen in December – you can bake me a cake if you like,' he said, grinning again.

'Do you want something to eat now?'

'Depends what you got.'

'Well, aren't you a fussy little bugger ... oops!' She placed the flat of her palm over her mouth.

'It's all right, I've heard worse.'

'I bet you have.'

'Made a few of my own up too.'

'Yes, well you can keep them to yourself,' she said, trying to hide a smile. 'Soup okay?'

'I'd prefer beef hash.'

'So would I, but I haven't got any.'

91

'Shepherd's pie?'

'No.'

'Hotpot?'

'No.' She laughed. 'I haven't got any of that either. I'm afraid soup is the star of the show tonight.'

Maggie lifted the pot of nettle soup onto the stove and then retrieved the bread from the larder, the cut-glass butter dish from the dresser, and set them on the table with bowls and glasses.

'So, what did you do at the docks?' she asked.

He was eyeing the bread.

'Go ahead.'

'Thanks.' He took a piece and jammed it in his mouth. 'There were a lot of hungry people there.'

'How do you know that?'

'There's no canteens or cafes down there. Plenty of people wanting some.'

'The dockyard would have its own canteen though.'

'Don't think so ... saw a couple of mobile ones but the roads were closed so I couldn't get through.'

The flame flickered as the gas burned noisily, its heat rousing the nettles from their cold stupor, releasing the sweet aroma. Maggie leaned over the pot, enjoying the hot steam on her face. After giving the soup a final stir, she ladled it into Robbie's bowl, scooping from the bottom to get the large chunks of vegetables.

Robbie didn't waste time waiting for it to cool; he scraped up a large spoonful, eating greedily.

'You should have your own restaurant,' he declared after he'd slurped a few mouthfuls.

'Thank you.'

'I mean it – this is really good.'

'It's a big thing opening your own place. More than just cooking meals.'

'Like what?'

'Well, it's not just about the food; you have to organise the setup, the staff, pay the bills...'

Before she knew it she was telling him all about the British Restaurants scheme and what it would entail; she described how to run a kitchen and the front of house and how it might feel to be your own boss, exciting and terrifying at the same time.

'See?' Robbie said. 'You know what you're talking about. I reckon you could do it and I could get you some stuff – you know, from the fancy hotels. You've got no idea how much food they have...'

'Really?'

'Yes, really,' Robbie replied. 'The Dorchester has meat straight from the country delivered fresh every morning and they have their own gardens where they grow things. I snuck around the kitchens, heard the chefs talking...'

The colour had returned to his cheeks now, and he reminded Maggie of Ernest more than ever; he had the same exuberance.

'And what do the chefs say?'

'They say how bloody greedy some of the toffs are!'

'And what do they say when they see you?'

'They don't. I take some bread or whatever is nearest the door and make a run for it.'

His eyes widened as soon as the words were out

of his mouth, as if realising his mistake too late.

'You shouldn't take what doesn't belong to you, Robbie,' Maggie scolded. 'It's stealing.'

'Robin Hood did and nobody seemed to mind.'

She tilted her spoon and sipped slowly. 'That's different – he was robbing the rich to give to the poor.'

'That's what I'm doing,' he pointed out.

'And what about the food you stole from me?' she ventured, but he looked away. 'Anyway, Robin Hood is only a story, he wasn't real.'

'Yes he was, just like Henry VIII or William the Conqueror. Ma read me.'

'And what happened to your ma, Robbie?'

Robbie dropped his spoon and it jangled noisily in the empty dish. 'It'll be alright when Dad gets back,' he said, avoiding her question. 'And I'm going to make sure I'm still here for him when he does.'

Not wanting to discourage him or dampen his hope, Maggie smiled and didn't say any more.

'So where's your fella then?' he asked.

'He went away too.'

'So you're like me then? You're waiting as well?'

'Yes, Robbie, I'm waiting too.'

The lock was stuck, the corroded metal sealing the suitcase firmly shut so that no matter how hard she pressed it, it still wouldn't budge. 'Damn!'

She flung it across the bed and dragged the chair towards the wardrobe, reaching for a brown leather suitcase just visible over the carved mahogany edge.

It had been a relief to find Robbie on the door-step and know that he was safe, and even though she hadn't managed to find out much about his family, once he started talking it had been difficult to get him to stop. She only managed to by promising to meet him after work the following week; he insisted there was somewhere he needed to show her and someone he wanted to her to meet. But once he left she found it difficult to settle and worried about him being alone again. As the night's silence closed in around her there seemed to be so much to think about and she lay awake as her conversation with Mr Ferguson, the woman in the doorway and the advertisement for the restaurant cooks played in a loop in her head. It was so frustrating, knowing how much she could help others if only she had her own restaurant. Once the idea took hold, she visualised the entire place; she equipped and decorated it, planned the meals, engaged the people that she would like to have work there and even the locals she knew as some of the customers they would serve. By then she was wide awake and decided she may as well pack her belongings to take to her aunt's on Sunday. Now the effort of trying to get the case open had drained her of all energy and she felt the sweep of tiredness at last.

She pulled the battered leather suitcase down and placed it in the middle of the bed. The locks glided easily but when the lid sprung open, she was taken aback by the musty smell and the state of the inside. The original sheen of the brown and cream silk lining had been replaced by the random flocked pattern of mildew. But it was the only working suitcase she had, so it would have to do.

In a drawer of the oak dresser she found the wooden jewellery box that she hadn't opened in a long time, cautiously lifting the lid as if unfamiliar with the contents. There was a thin silver necklace with a simple silver cross, unembellished except for a single line of floral engraving along one side. In the centre of the coiled chain lay two gold wedding bands, one larger and more solid than the other. She prodded the smaller ring with her wedding finger, gently nudging it on, twisting and turning it until it was nearly in place. Then she changed her mind, slipping it off quickly and placing it back in the box.

She snapped the lid shut and put the box in the bottom of the suitcase.

Returning to the wardrobe, she took hold of a hanger in a protective carrier, not noticing as the train of cream fabric trailed across the floor. She had promised that she wouldn't look at the dress again, not until she knew for sure that she would never be able to wear it.

On the bedside table two framed photographs caught her eye; a young couple on the steps of a church. The image wasn't clear, but its black-and-white contrast showed off the scalloped silk of her mother's wedding dress and the blunt cut of her short bobbed hair, her father's happiness evident through his proud youthful smile as he gazed at his new wife. Happier days, long before Ernest's death and her mother's depression had broken their family apart. She had always hoped her parents shared some happiness before then, but with her mother still missing and her father now dead, she would never know.

A second silver frame contained a more recent photograph; two smiling faces, hers pressed up against Peter's, eyes glistening.

She left the photograph on the table and picked up the one of her parents, wrapping it in a woollen shawl and placing it on top of the jewellery box. Then from the bottom of the wardrobe she retrieved a shoebox and was about to put it in the suitcase when she hesitated. Peeling back the tissue, she glimpsed the cream satin of the unworn wedding shoes, the light catching the silver thread of their brocade trim. At the side of the box, beneath another layer of tissue, the marcasite clasp of a small, embroidered bag came into view. Her fingers played across the thin silk strap; she had looked at lots of bags but this one had been perfect: just long enough that it hung from her wrist but not so big that it would get in the way of her posy of white roses.

She closed the lid of the shoebox, the reflected light in the sheen of the trim fading along with her smile.

Glancing around the room, she checked she hadn't missed anything and noticed the row of books arranged on the mantelpiece. She would keep them close by for now, she decided.

She fastened the suitcase and stood it by the door; now she was certain to be ready for Sunday when they would go through their usual routine and Aunt Mary would offer her tea. 'If there's any left in the pot,' was Maggie's standard reply, knowing that there would be, but that it would be weak and lukewarm. And that when she sipped it her aunt would say, 'Wet and warm, that's the way Gran used to like it. Wet and warm.' Only there was no way of knowing if her aunt would be in one of her sentimental moods or snapping at Rose as she often did.

Maggie remembered their gran saying it too. The ritual had become their way of acknowledging her; the perfect Devonshire tea complete with the polite teatime conversation, sticking to topics that she knew wouldn't invite harsh judgments from her aunt, scones with plump juicy sultanas and thick jam, but which she now made with carrots instead of fruit. It would all go well until, inevitably, Aunt Mary went too far; perhaps if Rose stood up to her mother more often Mary might not be so critical of her.

Maggie's attention was drawn back to the mantelpiece, caught by the gold embellishment on the side of a book, the brown-and-red-leather spine imprinted with gilt lettering: *Beeton's Household Management.* When she picked it up the cover felt dry and brittle and the first few pages crackled open. On the inside cover a neat black script read *Jane Beardmore, September 1874.* They had found the book at a church fete in Highgate and, much to his feigned annoyance, she hadn't allowed Peter to write inside, insisting the book still belonged to Jane Beardmore. Instead, Peter had bought her a bookmark and placed it inside.

Sitting on the bed, she flicked through the chapters, savouring the aged musty smell and the crispness of each page, and recognising familiar recipes she had made. Sometimes the recipes had sounded so old-fashioned and revolting that they had both laughed as she read them aloud. Then she came across the bookmark, the delicate colourful illustration of butterflies along one side, just as she remembered, and the inscription: *To my darling Maggie, Never forget the gift you have. Love always, Peter x*

She looked back at the framed photograph on the bedside table, at the promise of his dark eyes.

Was this his way of showing her what to do? She hadn't wanted to apply to the ministry because she didn't want to do it without him, but perhaps that was why she *should* do it now – because he no longer could.

Chapter Six

POTATOES SAVE SHIPPING:
Potatoes, which are home-grown, give us the same kind of energy-food as cereals, which are imported. Eat them in place of bread and other cereals wherever possible, and you help to save shipping space.
Ministry of Food, War Cookery Leaflet No. 3

Even though she had been waiting for nearly an hour, the strong smell of disinfectant barely concealed the institutionalised smell of the council offices. There were only two other women waiting on the benches of the long cheerless corridor, surrounded by the chorus of tapping from the typing pool at the far end and the click-clack of the secretary's heels. It was the fifth time the woman had passed by and Maggie couldn't help admiring her tailored grey wool suit and the black patent-leather shoes. Rose would love them; they looked expensive, perhaps from Dickins & Jones or one of the other department stores, not like the shoes they might buy from market stalls on their regular outings together.

Maggie smiled hopefully as the woman approached but she just smiled back and carried on into another office. She supposed the secretary was trying to be kind, but it just unnerved her and made her wonder all the more why the Food Officer was keeping the interviewees waiting so long. It was a good job she had told Mr Ferguson her medical appointment might take a few hours and had managed to get the whole morning off. She hadn't been for a job interview in years, not counting the quick twenty-minute discussion for the radio factory, and it seemed that even her stomach was growling in protest.

She looked at her watch again; nearly sixty-five minutes late now.

The grey-suited woman reappeared in the office doorway, folder in hand, and Maggie sat up, expectant.

'Miss McNulty?'

The young woman on the next bench followed the secretary into the office behind her.

Maggie sighed and shifted from side to side, trying to alleviate the low ache of her back, rolling her neck and wondering why on earth they had such grand hallways with high ceilings and ornate marble floors, and then such uncomfortable wooden benches to sit on.

Since she lived so close to the council offices on Upper Street, she had left home early and stopped at a cafe on the way, where she had been compelled to get out her notebook and make notes on things that she liked. The decor was far too twee, with lots of lace and brocade table lamps and pictures of the Virgin Mary on the walls. She wanted to create an environment where a man would feel as welcome as a woman – which meant no bone china teacups that he couldn't fit his fingers through. The doilies would have to go as well; way too fussy and extra clearing up. The cakes looked tasty though, displayed under great domes of glass...

'Miss Johnson?'

As the woman drew near, Maggie was able to see the detailed tailoring of her suit and the fine trim of its black grosgrain ribbon, and she self-consciously smoothed down the creases of her own skirt as she stood. She hadn't been able to bring herself to wear the only suit she owned, a dark blue crepe de chine skirt and tapered jacket meant for her going-away outfit. She had lost weight in the intervening months and her skirt hung loosely from her hips and the jacket made her look small and childlike, almost lost inside, so she had borrowed an outfit from a friend.

'Have you got your letter?'

'Yes, here you are...'

Maggie pulled the letter from her bundle of papers and handed it to the secretary, watching as she scanned the page.

'That's fine, come with me. Mr Boyle will be back shortly.'

The office was exactly as Maggie had expected it to be, a stuffy room that felt as if the walls, floors and ceiling were all the same size. Once the woman left, Maggie settled back into the chair and looked around for a family photo or a trophy, hoping to see something that would help break the ice, but there was nothing personal anywhere. The loud tick of a wall clock reminded her how long she had waited and butterflies began to flutter in her stomach. She had felt fine when she first arrived, ready to tell Mr Boyle why she would do a good job, that making supplies stretch further was already second nature to her. But now, sitting among all these folders marked CAPITAL EXPENDITURE, CONSUMABLES and MONTHLY ACCOUNTS, she realised that even though she had read every piece of paper she'd been sent, they didn't mean anything to her; all that really mattered was what ended up on the plate.

She could still hear the clicking of typewriters from the other end of the corridor and the intermittent whine of bus engines as they droned past. The office was airless and becoming even smaller and she was starting to feel breathless. She stood to leave but before she reached the doorway a man strode through.

'Miss Johnson?'

'Yes, I–'

'I'm so sorry to be late. Got held up on one of our new projects, school up on Canonbury. Anyway, please have a seat.'

He strode over to his side of the desk and Maggie lowered herself slowly into the chair opposite, clutching the folder in her lap.

'Well, Miss Johnson...' He glanced over the top of his spectacles, eyes flashing across her as if able to make an instant summation. Then he searched around his desk until he found the manila folder, flipped it open and spent a few minutes reading the information.

There was no wedding ring on his finger, even though he looked at least thirty, his dark hair smoothed down with Brylcreem camouflaging grey whiskers at the sides. His skin was rough and flaky, a prominent nose underlined by a pencil-straight moustache and small beard, his most distinguishing feature.

He abruptly closed the file and leaned forward. 'I don't have long, Miss Johnson, so let's get straight to it, if you don't mind.'

'Certainly.'

'So, what is it that appeals to you about running a British Restaurant?'

Maggie cleared her throat, straightening in the chair. 'It's like I said in my letter, Mr Boyle: I love cooking and I've been involved in mass catering for a few years now. I think I have the organisational skills required to run my own kitchen.'

'And you feel you have enough experience for this role?'

'Certainly, Mr Boyle. Otherwise I wouldn't have applied. I've worked in catering since I left school, worked my way up the ladder.'

She waited nervously for him to reply, hoping that he wouldn't quiz her on her time in Devon.

Even though she had put assistant cook on her curriculum vitae, she had exaggerated the role; it had only been when the chef was away or they were really busy or short-staffed.

'I see you have worked as deputy supervisor for the last six months. Have you ever been fully in charge?'

'Yes, sir. Our supervisor has been on maternity leave during that time so I've had sole responsibility for the kitchen.'

'I see.'

'I've never killed anyone,' she said, laughing nervously. 'What I mean is that people seem to like what I cook...'

'Health and hygiene are a serious matter, Miss Johnson. It is one of the most important parts of the job – probably *the* most important.'

'Yes, I know...'

'Did you read the memorandums on safety procedures that were sent to you?'

'I was joking; I didn't mean anything by it.'

'I am not worried, Miss Johnson; it is your suitability for the position that we are trying to ascertain.'

'Yes ... yes, of course. I did read the memorandums and we have the same procedures at work. It's very familiar to me – second nature, in fact.'

'Really?'

What a fool she had been, trying to be light-hearted; she should never have listened to Eliza. They had role-played a practice interview the day before, since she had not had one in such a long time and Eliza had been full of good ideas – at least they'd seemed so at the time. Make a few jokes, her friend had suggested, put him at ease – and don't be afraid to use your feminine charms if you need to.

'Yes, really,' she said enthusiastically. 'As you can see from my work history, I've learned about every aspect of running a kitchen...' She paused, waiting for a question, but none were forthcoming, so she continued: '...from cleanliness and hygiene through to food production and procurement.'

'And how have you coped with the rationed goods?'

'We have learned how to make do, make a tasty meal out of the trimmings, nettle soup instead of spinach, that sort of thing.'

He kept his gaze fixed on her mouth as she talked, as if he were lip-reading, then he picked up a piece of paper and handed it to her. 'Are you familiar with this?'

The letterhead was from the Ministry of Food: *Food Supplies, Rationed Commodities.*

'It doesn't look familiar,' she replied, even though all the memorandums had started to look the same by the time she had reached the twentieth one.

'That is because it's a new memorandum. Read it, please.'

She glanced down at the next paragraph:

THE PRIME MINISTER again desires to draw the attention of all Departments to the importance of brevity in all official minutes, memoranda, letters and telegrams. If more thought is given, very great savings of time will result to all concerned.

105

'Do you want me to read all of it?'

He nodded.

She took in the contents of the rationed commodities, the few ounces of bacon, the milk, sugar and butter they were allowed.

'We are working on similar rations at the moment, sir,' she commented.

'And what about the weekly accounts – are you familiar with those that require you to complete income and expenditure?'

His manner had become fiercer, his questions more officious.

'Yes,' Maggie replied and continued to read.

It is desired that accounts should be prepared monthly and should comprise (a) an Income and Expenditure Account and (b) a Balance sheet showing the amounts advanced by the Ministry and the manner in which they have been expended. Details of the number of meals served and other appropriate statistical information should also be kept.

'Will there be some accountancy training?' she enquired.

'Some, Miss Johnson. Do you envisage a problem?'

'No, of course not,' she said, scanning the rest of the page, her heart rate quickening.

And that these monthly accounts, certified by a competent official, together with such statistical information as is required should be sent to the Secretary, Ministry of Food, Neville House, London S.W.1.,

*marked 'Communal Feeding' as soon as possible, and
in any case within 28 days, after the end of the month
to which they relate.*

But she was struggling to breathe; she had
anticipated the accounts issue and even rehearsed
an answer, but now she couldn't remember it.
Her mind was a blank and all she could think
about was the delicate rhythm of the raindrops
outside and the spray of water from a bus as it
whooshed past, and wished she were on it.

'Would you find this area difficult then, Miss
Johnson?'

It felt as if her opportunity was slipping away, all
the hard work and reading and hoping vanishing.
Then she thought about Gillian and Robbie and
her newly homeless neighbours, and what Peter
would say if he were here, and she realised how
much she wanted it, that she knew how to do it –
and that she needed to prove it now.

'Not at all. I understand that there will be some
training involved for the role beforehand, and I
am sure that with a bit of guidance and support
I will be able to cope with the additional responsibilities and paperwork very well. You have my
references there.'

'Yes, I have. And you are aware of the number
of staff you will be responsible for?'

'Yes.'

'And the organisation of the kitchen, as mentioned in the earlier communication regarding
the British Restaurant scheme? In addition, the
capital expenditure will be reimbursed but you
will be responsible for the organisation of the

kitchen and adhering to the ministry's suggested layout and the daily menus.'

'I think the layouts they have suggested make perfect sense, Mr Boyle. I couldn't have designed them better myself.'

He regarded her for a moment, finger stroking his moustache, and then he closed the folder.

'Very well, I think that will be all for today, Miss Johnson. We will be in touch.'

He rose and came around the desk, but Maggie stayed seated.

'I have several other candidates to see...' he said pointedly.

'But did you want to see any of my menu plans?' she said, standing.

'Miss Johnson, you don't make menu plans; you cook what the ministry tells you to. We are feeding a nation of workers here, not catering a garden party.'

'Yes, of course.'

As he drew closer and shook her hand she noticed that he had no smell, not even the musty smell of other bachelors she had known: of damp clothes, homes where windows were never opened, of beds that were rarely made – it was the smell of emptiness, of rooms where flowers were never placed, gifts of cologne never given or clothes warm from sun-dried washing ever worn.

Chapter Seven

Reflect, whenever you indulge
It is not beautiful to bulge
A large, untidy corporation
Is far from helpful to the Nation
Marguerite Patten OBE,
Victory Cookbook: Nostalgic Food
and Facts from 1940–1954

Rose's shared rooms on Upper Street were only a
few streets away from Maggie's, and by the time
she had been home to change, and made her way
through the noisy evening traffic, she had already
imagined the first day and all that it would entail.
It had been two days since the interview but a formal letter from Mr Boyle had already arrived from
the ministry that morning. Ignoring his remon-
strations about only cooking food from the
ministry's menus, she'd spent the whole day con-
templating the meals she could make and thinking
about her inventory of classics; the intense creamy
aroma of her special leek and potato soup, then a
pigeon pie – but what about dessert? Fruit
crumble and custard? Perhaps she would have to
offer a set menu that changed each week, so there
would be some variety, with a daily special; she
knew from the factory that there was no knowing
from one day to the next what ingredients they
would be given.

She hurried past the closed shopfronts of Upper Street and closer to the tower and spire of St Mary's; it was all that remained of the church, its ancient walls now lying around it like the headstones in the graveyard where they had fallen. Sutton Dwellings was just past the church so Maggie always used it to guide her way and the clock on the tower to tell her how punctual she was. It was nearly seven and she was sure that Rose would be in, but when she rang the bell of the Art Deco apartment block there was no reply.

She was about to leave when the latch clicked and the door opened to reveal a woman a little older than herself whom Maggie recognised as one of her cousin's neighbours – only her complexion was so altered, skin the texture of pale paper with blotches of red and a spider's web of veins colouring her cheeks.

'Hello, love,' the woman said.

'I'm sorry,' Maggie said, 'I don't remember your name.'

'It's Irene.'

'You haven't seen Rose have you?'

'No, love, I haven't. Here, you're her cousin, aren't you?'

'Yes, I am.'

'Thought so.'

Irene's gas mask hung loosely around her neck and she took such great strides that it swung like a giant pendulum, even with the two heavy bags she carried weighing her down.

Maggie followed her back down the path. 'Can I give you a hand?'

'No, it's alright. Only going over to St Mary's.

We've got a card night ... bit of a fundraiser. Come if you like.'

'I'm sorry, I can't. I need to find Rose.'

'Never mind. Another time maybe.'

'Yes, that would be nice.'

'She'll probably be at the Angel.'

'Of course. Thank you.'

'It's where she usually goes these days. Not me, I'd rather save the money.'

Maggie felt silly for not remembering; Rose had mentioned how she was happier to pay for the ticket for the Tube and queue to get in, not just for safety but because she liked the camaraderie of being there.

'Don't you think it's safer to stay down there?' Maggie asked as she held open the gate.

Irene walked through and then swivelled, glancing back over her shoulder.

'When your number's up, your number's up.'

Making her way down Upper Street, Maggie was considering calling in to the school to check on Robbie when she found herself at the junction of Essex Road and across the street from her parents' old grocery store. The black-and-gold sign had lost its lustre but she could still see the words *Johnson & Sons* through the thick layer of grime. It had been many things since they left – a clothing store, an ironmonger's – but somehow the name had always stayed. The windows of the Victorian red-brick building wrapped around each side, affording a panorama of the street and of the people coming and going. There were only a few tonight; an elderly woman in a well-worn coat

111

crossed the road towards her, another in a head-scarf wrangled two small boys, one dragging a tricycle behind. Maggie and her brothers had used to race up and down this pavement on bikes or one of the contraptions that Ernest had fashioned from recycled parts, until she was called inside to help.

She waited for a delivery truck to pass and then crossed the road, coming to stand outside the shop. Now she was closer, she could see that it was as scarred and dirty as the buildings around it, with its chipped brickwork, broken windows and missing slates. Leaning in close to the glass, she saw that not much had changed inside; the same long wooden counter stretched across the back of the shop, shelves reaching right up to the ceiling behind. They were empty now but had once been as well stocked as any department store. If anyone asked for something their father didn't carry, he would order it in, and if there was a new product out, he would find it so he could offer it to his customers. Her mother had tempered him, reminding him that the days weren't just for working and the evenings not just for eating and doing accounts, but once she had gone he gave up and threw himself completely into his work.

'Shame it's not still open – might at least be able to get somethin' decent to eat round here.'

There was something familiar about the middle-aged woman standing next to Maggie, her stout figure enveloped in a brown wool coat, narrowing to a collar of light fur from which her head sprung, grey-blonde curls neatly pinned beneath a matching hat.

'Do I know you?' Maggie asked.

'I remember *you*,' the woman said. 'You're little Maggie Johnson. I knew your mum and dad.'

Maggie turned back to the window, seeing her own muddy reflection. She felt the instant prick of shame as if it were only yesterday. The people that came in and out of the store that day, speaking in whispers; the arrival of her aunt to 'help out'. She even remembered the floral scent when they had finally closed that night, and she poured away the water that had kept the flowers alive as surely as her mother's love should have kept her; she had willed every memory of her mother to wash away with it.

Maggie had finished school and helped her father and brothers but then, as soon as she was able, she left and took a job in Devon. She was happy there, distracted by the small talk of old ladies and ramblers, and for three years she had served cream teas to tourists and discovered her passion for cooking. Then she met Peter and had returned with him to London, the beginning of their romance and her formal training.

'I'm Margaret Evans from the dairy on Cross Street,' the woman was saying.

'I remember,' said Maggie. 'You delivered our milk.'

'Yes, that's right, pet. Such a hard worker, your dad, God rest his soul.'

Maggie smiled at her; an image of the horse and cart, their noisy rides bumping around with the pails in the back, came to her like a half-remembered dream. Yes, her father had worked hard to build up the business, even harder after their

113

mother had left him and their three children, and a host of unpaid bills. He opened the shop at seven in the morning and didn't close until nine at night, or when the last customer left. He'd tried to keep the rumours from them: that their mother had run away with the Canadian foreman from the local bread factory. In any event, Maggie had not wanted to know.

'How are your brothers, dear? Was it Eric?'

'Eddie ... Edward and John. They're coping as best they can – as most of the lads are. Ed's in the navy and John joined the army.'

'I was sorry to hear about your dad.'

'Thank you.'

Maggie had been in Devon when he died but she had seen him during his short illness. He told her that forgiving Agnes, their mother, was the only way he had been able to enjoy any happiness, but she knew it had come too late.

'Anyway, can't stop now,' Mrs Evans said, 'I'm in a bit of a hurry, but it was ever so nice seeing you again.'

'Yes, you too.'

'And good luck, love – it's a super site. Your old dad would've been so pleased.'

'About what?'

'At you opening it again.'

As Mrs Evans bustled away along the pavement towards the dairy, Maggie turned to gaze at the shop once more. Why hadn't she thought of it before?

The space was large enough, and it was empty, but it would be a big job; getting the shattered windows repaired as well as the plasterwork inside

114

that she knew had been shaken from the walls. But, yes: the site would make a perfect restaurant.

When her eyes had adjusted to the low light, Maggie could just make out the groups of people packed along the platform and on the track. If it wasn't for the fact that the air tasted so thick and dank and the tunnel walls curved overhead, she imagined they could be in an entertainment hall or one of London's prestige hotels. Three small square card tables were in use, while men and women crowded around heckling the players. Beyond that, there was a small makeshift library with a wooden bookshelf four rows deep, and a dozen or so readers poring over the pages of the books by lamplight.

She continued past to where the crowds thinned and a few figures were seated at the furthest end of the platform. They had created a small oasis in the confined space; a narrow table with a plain white cloth and a large brass crucifix, modest gold candlesticks on either side and small wicker chairs placed around in a semicircle. Maggie found herself drawn towards the unexpected shrine, imagining as the others must that something might be achieved by observing the religion that she had long since let go.

An older woman kneeled down in front of the makeshift altar and crossed herself with her right hand, her tight tweed coat straining with each movement. Maggie watched the woman's face as she murmured a prayer. She envied the woman's piety and wondered at what personal cost it had come.

Maggie looked away, turning back towards the swarm of people; Rose had to be here somewhere.

It was the first time she had been to the underground in months and the gates and barricades had been ripped away. Of course, not all the metalwork could be removed; the vast supporting beams continued to hold the tunnel roof in place and plates and studs as large as apples still remained. So too did the ornate cast-iron pillars that supported the great archways and metal staircases, too important to be melted down.

She had been a regular on the trains before the war, but it had been a long time since she had travelled by Tube; most of the stations had been closed for use as shelters. Back then the trains had pushed currents of air through the stations, but today the air was still and the odours from the mass of bodies mingled with the food smells that wafted from the mobile canteen.

Up ahead, she caught a glimpse of Rose's hair, golden pin curls still neatly in place, her cousin glancing around inquisitively as she often did, so that she looked lost even when she wasn't, and remained unaware of the male attention she usually attracted.

Maggie stretched her hand up to wave, and as soon as Rose saw her, she hurried through the crowd.

'Maggie!' Rose grasped both her hands.

'Gosh, your hands are cold,' Maggie said, pulling away.

'I know, I've got Gran's circulation. Need to eat more pepper.'

She rubbed her hands together. 'Anyway, what

are you doing here?'

'I was looking for you.'

'I thought we were meeting up tomorrow?'

'We were – I mean we are – but I wanted to see you. I've got some news.'

Rose gave Maggie the reaction she was hoping for, her eyes and mouth widening simultaneously. 'What is it? Tell me!'

Maggie's hair fell across her eyes as she dug around in her bag, searching for the letter. Around them the evening mood was lightening as people joined in the singing, snatches of the lyrics from 'You Are My Sunshine' filling the air.

'Come on, hurry up!' Rose urged.

Maggie gave up on her bag and reached into her coat pocket. 'Here it is.'

She opened the letter and handed it to Rose.

Dear Miss Johnson,

Following your interview relating to your application to open and operate a British Restaurant, we are pleased to inform you that you have been selected to run a premises in the Highbury and Islington area. You will be working directly with me on all matters relating to the setup and ongoing operation and supply of the establishment. I will be in touch with you shortly to arrange a meeting. Please do not hesitate to contact me in the meantime with any queries.

I look forward to a productive working relationship with you.

Yours sincerely,
W. G. Boyle
Regional Divisional Food Officer

117

'That's marvellous!' Rose squealed. Then she said, 'But why didn't you tell me what you were doing?'

'I'm sorry. I wasn't going to do it; I mean, I didn't think I could.'

'Why ever not?'

'I don't know...' She avoided Rose's gaze, instead turning to watch a young man as he climbed onto a low table nearby, preparing to sing to the enthusiastic crowd gathering around him.

'Really?' Rose prodded. 'So what changed?'

'I don't know...' Maggie crossed her arms defensively; she had never been able to hide anything from her cousin.

'Well?'

'Okay, Robbie happened, and Gillian and the girls. And Tom and Mr Ferguson... Well, it was a lot of things – and I just realised I could do something to help.'

Her cousin narrowed her eyes at her, as if she wasn't convinced. 'I see.'

'I thought I couldn't do it before, but I know now ... I can't *not* do it.'

'What do you mean?'

'If Peter was here, I wouldn't have thought twice about it, I would have applied straight away. But then I started to believe I couldn't do it without him. And that's just it ... I have to do it now because he can't.'

'So, when do you start?'

'Well, I have to do training first – even though I'm already working as a cook!'

The young man's singing had reached its

crescendo, his arm movements more exuberant as he stretched himself taller, wobbling precariously on the trestle table as he belted out the final chorus of 'You Are My Sunshine'. Most of the crowd had joined in and Rose and Maggie were jostled as the spectators grew more and more boisterous.

'And where will it be?'

'I don't know yet. What do you think – am I mad, Rose? Do you think I can even manage it?'

'I've no doubt you can do it, Maggie – and you'll be great! Think of the posters: USE SPADES NOT SHIPS, DIG FOR VICTORY – it's marvellous that you would want to help.'

'What?' Maggie struggled to hear above the din.

'I said it's marvellous you want to help,' her cousin repeated.

Rose's hands were clenched into fists by her sides and something in her tone made Maggie look at her more closely; Rose was on the verge of tears.

The singer hit his final note and the crowd erupted into cheers.

'I've not been engaged like you, Maggie,' Rose said, tears springing to her eyes. She began to sob. 'What if this is it? What if we go tomorrow? I'll die never knowing what it's like to be loved or to love someone as desperately as you loved Peter...'

Maggie put her arms around Rose and gently stroked her hair, just as she had when she was a child, when they had shared beds and secrets like sisters. With Aunt Mary grieving the death of her husband, they had become even closer after

Maggie's mother disappeared, all of them feeling the bitterness of betrayal.

'There, there, now, come on,' she said, feeling the shoulder of her dress growing damp. 'What's brought all this on?'

The man was lifted from the table by the cheering crowd and Rose waited for the noise to die down before continuing. 'I'll never meet anyone like Peter,' she said, still sniffing, 'because all the men are bloody well dying. There's no chance of getting a husband or a family now.'

'It's no good talking like that, Rose. There are still lots of men around and this war isn't going to go on forever. They'll come back. And when they do, you'll have the pick of the bunch.'

She pushed the damp strands of hair out of Rose's eyes. Her cousin didn't realise the effect she had on people, how one flash of those sapphire eyes could hypnotise.

'So what do you fancy then, a tall, dark handsome brute or one of those fair dashing types?'

Rose's crying ceased but she didn't respond to Maggie's teasing.

'I just feel so alone,' she said. 'And now you're leaving...'

'I'm not going anywhere,' Maggie protested. 'I'll still be here.'

'I'm really happy for you, Maggie, really I am...'

'Be happy for *us*,' Maggie scolded. 'You don't think I'd do it without you?'

'What?' Rose dabbed at her eyes with her blouse cuffs. 'But how can I help? I'm a shop assistant – I don't even know how to cook!'

'I'm going to teach you.'

'I thought you gave up on me years ago?'
'Well, I'll need waitresses and cashiers too.'
'You mean it?'
'Of course. And Rose?'
'Yes?'
'Just think about all the men you'll get to meet!'

Chapter Eight

Vegetables for you and your family every week of the year. Never a week without food from your garden or allotment. Vegetables all year round if you DIG WELL AND CROP WISELY.
Dig For Victory Leaflet No. 1

Robbie stepped lightly, his shadow sliding across the tunnel wall a few feet in front of Maggie's, guiding her forward. All he could make out against the liquorice skies were the outlines of abandoned machinery and equipment where the steam engines had once stood: engines that he had sometimes sketched by day and modelled by night. The metal engines and cargo trucks were now long gone, recycled for munitions, leaving only broken wooden remains, splintered skeletons at the edge of the track.

He glanced around to check that Maggie was still following and was relieved to see that she was. At first he thought she wasn't coming and had paced up and down outside the station with Spoke, disappointed that she had let him down.

Then he'd spotted her running towards him, all out of breath and apologetic. He didn't care that she was late; he was just glad that she turned up and he quickly made her promise not to ask too many questions, just to trust him. It would be a good surprise, he assured her, not a bad one. But now, as they picked their way through the darkening tunnel, Maggie was unusually quiet, as if she was having second thoughts.

'You okay?' he asked. His voice echoed off the damp bricks.

'Fine.' Her reply was little more than a whisper.

It was eerily quiet except for the intermittent whirr of engines as cars passed infrequently on the bridge overhead and he carried on the last few yards towards the tunnel's end where the ground was swallowed by shadows.

As he moved out into the open, the crunch of gravel underfoot changed as his boots met the thick grass, already heavy with the early-evening dew. He clutched his jacket with both hands, tugging the cloth tighter around him as the wind whipped his collar and he listened out for the familiar noise of the spade.

There it was, the steady tapping, and up ahead the solid outline of a figure as it rhythmically bent, pressed and tipped, bent, pressed and tipped.

If Maggie expected to see more broken equipment and a disused yard she was going to be surprised; here it was still a working track but there was also a flourishing garden, raised beds supported by old railway sleepers, wooden trellises trained with dark shoots and vines. Close by was a tub overflowing with new shrubs and boxes of seedlings on a low makeshift bench waiting to be planted. Robbie rubbed his gloved hands together and turned so he could see her reaction as she emerged from the tunnel.

He saw the small cloud of expelled air just before she appeared, her expression changing when she saw the allotment ahead.

'See, I told you it was a good surprise.'

She bent down, touching the fragile green fronds of carrots that swayed back and forth in the wind, running her fingers across the tough grainy outer layers of cabbages and scraping the soil from deep roots that probed the earth so she could take a better look.

'These are good quality ... how did you find this place?'

'Wait and see.'

He held out his hand, leading her on, past fractured pipes that sprouted weeds and through a path that widened to a laneway bordered with taller shrubs.

As they got closer the tapping stopped and the figure leaned on the spade, watching their approach.

'Janek,' Robbie shouted, letting go of Maggie's hand and running the rest of the way, Spoke trotting behind.

It had been difficult to get away, having given her notice and with Mr Ferguson keeping an especially close eye on her, but Maggie hadn't wanted to let Robbie down. It had been a real job getting through the barricades, too, and she'd had to hide from Bill Drummond when she saw him coming down Essex Road on his evening rounds. Whoever this person was that Robbie wanted her to meet, he was clearly very important to the boy.

By the time she reached the pair, Robbie was already chatting away. Turning to her, he said, '*Dobry wieczór* ... Janek's teaching me Polish.'

'Well, that's jolly good. What did you just say?'

'Good evening.'

'*Dob-ry wie-czór.*' She pronounced the words carefully, looking into the eyes of the mysterious gardener.

The eyes weren't set into a familiar oval or round face as she was used to seeing; instead it was angular, and appeared as strong and solid as the man's body. Even in the dark she could see that the pale blue eyes didn't seem at home in such a determined place; they were kind and uncertain.

'*Dobry wieczór*, Malgorzata.'

He offered her his right hand and so she extended hers, expecting him to shake it, but he bowed slightly, kissing her hand and clicking his heels together at the same time.

She gave a surprised laugh and then, embarrassed, covered her mouth.

'It is Polish custom. I am Janek. It is a pleasure to meet you.'

The sodden and frayed bottoms of his grey twill trousers looked like part of a uniform, but they were mismatched with a shirt with rolled-up sleeves and a thick brown knitted vest.

'It's nice to meet you too.'

She pushed away the strands of hair that whipped against her face and then slid both hands deep into her coat pockets, watching intently as the man and boy resumed talking again, curious about Robbie's unlikely new companion.

'*Jak sie masz?* That's "how do you do", isn't it?' Robbie translated before turning his attention back to Janek. 'I wanted to show Maggie the allotments. She has a special interest.'

'That's right, you told me – Malgorzata the cook. And who do you cook for?'

'At the moment I run the canteen at the radio factory. There are more than two hundred workers so it's like the radios themselves, more about assembly than cooking.'

'See this?' Robbie was pointing to the nearby beds. 'Janek planted all of it, everything you see.'

'It's very impressive. Who's it for?'

'The railway takes most of it for their canteens. The rest I sell at markets.'

It had started to rain and the wind stole the end off sentences that she was already struggling to understand. Raindrops stretched into long droplets as the shower grew heavier, splashing mud onto the lower leaves of plants and driving deep into the stalks and pockets of vines that wove around the nearby training frames.

'We don't have to stay here. Come.' He gestured towards an old signal box and she followed as he climbed the narrow wooden staircase, noticing how unsteady his walk was, how heavily he dragged one of his heavy boots up each splintered stair.

Once they were inside, Janek pulled the door closed behind them and struck a match, lighting an oil lamp before pulling the blackouts across two small windows. The meagre light flickered around the room, lengthening shadows and creating gigantic machines from small tools. An enormous elephant projected from the bulbous eyes and nosepiece of the gas mask that hung on its hook by the door. The inside of the building was the reverse of its outside; where the exterior walls were peeling paint and dirty splintered frames, the inside was clean and dry, its woodwork intact. The levers from the signals ran along the whole left side of the wall, a new workbench assembled directly over the top. A small table and folding chairs sat to the right, beneath a large station sign for Highbury & Islington. She could imagine Janek sitting here, planning what to plant next from the pile of trays that were stacked up on the bench, a few spread out in front with seedlings showing off their pale green shoots. There was a strong mix of mud and must, as if the old decaying plants were bound up with the new, like the tang of the earth when you first pitched your fork into it. It reminded her of weekends on her grandfather's allotment; when it was wet they would stay in the shed and she would watch and listen carefully as her grandfather grafted stems or nurtured seedlings until they were ready to plant outside. If the weather was good, she would be given a small trowel and would dig and plant alongside him until her mother sent one of her brothers to fetch her home.

Robbie was fidgeting excitedly. 'Do you like it?'

'Yes,' she said, 'it's very cosy.'

A camping stove sat in the corner and, after two failed attempts, Janek managed to get it to catch

126

and the blue circle of flame flickered to life.

'Not big enough for a three-course meal but we have some borscht. Will you take some?'

Maggie looked at Robbie, who nodded, indicating that she should say yes.

'Thank you.'

It looked as if the original paraphernalia from the signal box had been pushed into the corner, creating a heap of corroded metal and wooden batons, and Robbie made his way over to take a look.

'Is this the signaller?' he asked, turning the rusted metal equipment over, inspecting it from different angles.

'I think so. I have not looked properly.'

Janek's accent was thick, but he spoke in short sentences that Maggie found easy enough to understand. She took the mug he offered and squeezed into one of the frayed camping chairs placed either side of the door.

'Where are you from in Poland?'

'Mazovia ... it is in the north-west of the country.'

'Yes,' she said, warming her hands on the cup. 'I have seen it on the maps in the newspaper. It's close to Warsaw, isn't it?'

'That's right.' Janek nodded.

'How long have you been here?'

'In England – seventeen months and four days.'

She was surprised by his accuracy.

'And before that?'

'Before that I was in France. We left through Romania, before the border closed.'

She waited for him to say more but he turned

and removed his coat, hanging it on a hook on the back of the door. He glanced back and caught her looking at him, so she quickly looked away.

He reached into the breast pocket of his shirt and brought out a small rectangular tin. Leaning back against the benchtop, he flipped off the lid and retrieved a paper and a small pinch of tobacco, rolling it expertly between his thumb and forefinger to produce a miniature cigarette.

'And so now you are here?'

'I am one of the lucky ones, no?'

'Yes, I suppose so.'

'Luckier than many of my countrymen.'

Janek had seemed friendly at first but now she found him difficult to read, not sure if she had detected a note of resentment in his voice or just the intonation of a language that wasn't her natural tongue.

She sipped the purple liquid, savouring its warmth and the saltiness on her tongue. 'Borscht?'

'Yes, you have made this before?'

'Only a couple of times, but I don't add meat to mine. Is it hock?'

'Yes, we use wild boar at home but I have not seen any here.'

'No, I don't think a Wiltshire pig would taste quite the same,' she agreed.

'We also use beetroot leaves and shoots in our soup, but you English are too soft – you feed the best bits to your pigs!'

She laughed, relieved that he was proving to be friendlier than she had first thought. 'Yes, but then we eat the pigs too. Anyway, you will have to show me how to make it the proper way.'

'Of course.'

She quickly took another sip, allowing the rich earthy tang to spread across her tongue.

'Will you go back to Poland?'

'Not yet, but it is my plan.'

'Yes, of course. Eventually...'

'As soon as it is safe.'

'Are all your family there? I'm sorry ... I shouldn't ask so many questions.'

'It is fine. Robbie has spoken of you. You are not a stranger.'

'All the same...'

She noticed a small chess set on the crate nearby.

'Do you play?'

'All Poles play chess.'

'If the rain carries on for much longer, we shall have to have a game,' she suggested.

He looked surprised. 'You play?'

'Yes, I had three brothers – we played a lot of games.'

'And they are all fighting?'

She didn't want to talk about Ernest with a stranger; not even her brothers spoke about him much anymore.

'Ed joined the navy and John joined the army but he has bad asthma. He's doing his bit for the Home Guard down in Portsmouth now. Recently married, too, so I think he'll settle there.'

'They are lucky then.'

'How?'

'Because they fight for their country, it is not so easy for everyone.'

Maggie frowned. 'I don't understand.'

'You cannot understand. You have not had to leave your country. Once again the Polish people have to relinquish power to an invading nation.'

She didn't know how to respond. Janek's expression was serious again; clearly the time for jokes had passed.

He reached into his jacket pocket to replace the tobacco tin and a single card fell onto the floor near her feet. It was a picture of the Black Madonna, an image of the Virgin Mary masked in black. As she handed it back she noticed a large amount of handwritten text on the reverse side, and as he took it between his fingers, their eyes locked for the briefest moment before he looked away.

Robbie was still investigating the pile of junk when he came across a small piece of equipment at the back behind a tangle of cords and leads. It looked newer than the rest and more like a wireless or some kind of transmitter than a signaller, but when he turned to ask Janek what it was he was still talking.

He put on the headphones and fiddled with the dial. The silence turned into voices but they were faint, as if coming from down a very long corridor somewhere, and were only just audible above the low hum of the machine's own mechanics. It wasn't helped by the fact that he could still hear Janek and Maggie's muffled voices.

He removed the headphones and placed the instrument at the front of the shelf where he wouldn't forget it; it didn't matter that the instrument wasn't working properly because these metal rods at the base would make a great chassis for one of the new models he had just started, and the wooden outer shell could easily be fashioned into the deck of a miniature boat. He would ask Janek if he could spare it; he couldn't imagine that there would be anything else that Janek might need it for.

'What kind of farm was it?'

He could hear the interest in Maggie's voice so he went and sat on the folding chair next to hers.

'Cereals and grain mostly, also some cows to supply dairy to the hotels and restaurants in Warsaw.'

It was the opening Robbie had been waiting for. 'Maggie's going to open a restaurant,' he announced proudly. 'One of those ones the government are doing...'

'When is this?' Janek asked.

'Soon,' Robbie replied.

'Not that soon, it's not that straightforward,' Maggie said, grimacing at Robbie; she hadn't mentioned the issues with the site or that Mr Boyle had requested she attend a training course first.

'Some more?' Janek gestured towards the soup pot.

Maggie nodded and Janek ladled more soup into her mug and then refilled his own, but before he could hand it back to her, the floor began to vibrate, a noisy rumble that steadily built, rattling the pots and trays on the shelves, the sound of a train growing closer. Janek stopped moving and waited, trying to balance against the bench. Just when it seemed as if it couldn't get any louder, the

131

room shook violently and the carriages thundered past, air thrust like spears through every crack and joint in the timber walls and floors, sending the air and dust spinning around them. Then it receded, clanking and clattering into the distance, and the dust settled, the coal smell dissipated and all was still again.

'Whoa!' Robbie looked at them both and laughed.

'Not so funny in middle of the night,' Janek said lightly as he finally handed the mug back to Maggie. He returned to the subject of the restaurant. 'So, you will get there soon. There is nothing stopping you?'

Robbie blew onto his soup, liking the way it made furrows across the surface, and then he brought the mug up to his lips. He couldn't figure out what the sweet earthy smell reminded him of; it was like one of his dad's outdoor cook-ups, when he mixed the charcoal with apple wood or cherry wood so that it flavoured the meat.

'What is it?' Robbie scowled.

'Beetroot,' Janek replied.

'Never had beetroot soup before.'

'It's called "borscht" in Poland,' Maggie said.

'She's got the jitters,' Robbie told Janek. 'About the restaurant. She'll talk herself out of it if she's not careful. She needs to just get on with it.'

'No I won't – and you don't refer to people as *she* when they are in the same room with you!'

'You are right though, Robbie,' Janek said, his voice solemn. 'You cannot afford to waste time in wartime.'

'Why do you say that?' Maggie asked.

'In crisis we focus on what is real. What can be more real than providing people with their most basic need?'

Robbie knew that Janek was clever, he had felt it that first day they met and walked to Bloomsbury Square; he had shown Robbie things he had never noticed before, even though he had lived in London all his life. He looked at Maggie, wondering what she would say next.

'Perhaps you are right. But what if you are afraid you won't succeed?'

'Guilt and worry are worthless emotions – they don't help anyone. It is time to put your own thoughts of success and failure aside.'

Robbie saw her look away; she probably wouldn't approve of Janek's directness but she couldn't argue with plain good sense.

'I suppose now you are going to tell me that none of us know what is going to happen anyway?' she said.

'No, you know that already.'

Maybe it was because of the light but Janek's eyes looked dark, not as bright and clear as they had first appeared.

'Remind me: how did you two meet?' Maggie asked, looking at Robbie.

'Janek sort of rescued me,' he said, hoping that a white lie wouldn't count as much as a big full-blown one.

'Why, where were you?'

'I went out of town for the day, got a bit lost – Janek helped me.'

He could see how curious she still was so he

started to explain how Janek had been coming back from the countryside, that he grew vegetables there too since there wasn't nearly enough room in the city, and once he started talking he worked out that he couldn't really stop as Maggie would ask him another question, one for which he might not have a ready lie, so he ended up gabbling for ages. When he couldn't carry on any longer, he placed his mug on the bench and racked his brains for something to say to change the subject. He hadn't been lying about Janek rescuing him, and the bit about Janek growing stuff in the country was true too, but he couldn't bear it when people looked at him the way Maggie was looking at him now.

'That still doesn't explain what were you doing in the countryside.'

He tugged at his sleeves, stretching them until his hands disappeared completely and the ends looked like giant fabric belly buttons. He did want to tell her about his ma and the huge house that they were staying in, how there was a whole room just for the toilet and another one just for the bath. And about the huge green dinner table that they didn't even eat at, just kept for playing ball games on. Then he smiled as he remembered the hot-water bottles they took to bed at night that they were supposed to use to wash with the next morning, but how he emptied his out and weed in it because he got too scared to go to the bathroom.

'What's so funny?'

He looked at Maggie and feigned tiredness, stretching his arms and transforming his smirk into a wide yawn.

134

'All this talk of the countryside is making the boy sleepy,' Janek said.

Robbie pulled himself up slowly. 'You coming, Maggie?'

Janek looked disappointed. 'You cannot stay longer?'

'No, I really must go. I'm on the breakfast shift tomorrow so I have to be up nice and early. Can't afford to be late with Mr Ferguson.'

'Well, it was pleasure to meet you, Malgorzata.' He held out his hand.

'Is that Polish for Maggie?'

'For Margaret,' he explained.

'No one has called me that since I was a child.'

'It suits you.' He smiled.

'I prefer Maggie.'

Robbie was nearly at the door but turned just in time to see Janek bend to kiss Maggie's hand and click his heels, and this time Maggie turned nearly as red as the borscht.

Chapter Nine

ENEMIES OF VITAMINS:
AIR, WATER, HEAT. Too much of any of these
will destroy the vitamin C. Therefore, have your
vegetables as fresh as possible. Best of all,
grow them yourself.
Ministry of Food, War Cookery Leaflet No. 14

Robbie had stirred something in Janek, reminding him of his young nephew; he was quick-witted and assured, not afraid to take on authority, although that wouldn't have served Roman well under the German regime. All the more reason that he had to work faster, make contact as quickly as he could. There were cells of the Union for Armed Struggle all over the country; it was just a matter of time before he could join a network that would help him find his brother.

The train was late and he felt conspicuous standing astride the frayed sack on a platform full of strangers. Everyone was suspicious, and even with his identity card and papers in order he still felt out of place among their formal clothes and newspapers.

He cupped his hands together, blowing into the hollow and watching as the condensation escaped the other side, the image of Maggie vanishing and re-forming with it, just as it had ever since Robbie had brought her to the yard a few days before. She seemed different to the girls back home and he knew she was strong but she held back, choosing her words carefully, not necessarily saying what she meant. He hoped she would be more open the next time they met.

When the train arrived he waited for the other passengers to disembark and the rest of the commuters to board – not that anyone thanked him for the courtesy. Inside, the compartment was strong with the sour smell of brilliantine and tobacco, and the majority of the seats were taken by soldiers travelling out to camps and barracks in the Essex countryside. Bags and gas masks took up most of the space on the baggage rails so he stashed the sack under a seat and propped himself against the doorway. The train jolted from side to side, grinding slowly out of the station, only gathering speed once the larger buildings and warehouses were left behind. As they bore deeper into the countryside, he looked around at the soldiers; they had barely left boyhood, and he shuddered at the thought of what lay ahead of them.

He was relieved it was only a short journey; he alighted after a few stops and followed Josef's directions along a lane and down a secluded farm track. It felt good to be back in the countryside, taking great gulps of air so cold that they stung the back of his throat, but it was also disturbingly quiet. At home the grunt and bray of the animals sang them to sleep at night and saw them rise in the morning, but here all the livestock had made way for crops to feed more mouths.

The turf was slippery underfoot, not yet fully thawed from the night freeze, and around him trees and hedges had been taken hostage by a light frost so that the wind moved noiselessly through the branches. A few yards ahead, next to a rusted silo, he spotted a barn, a greying wooden structure with more planks missing than still intact. He stepped around the bicycles leaning next to the half-open door and slipped inside, setting the sack down.

The barn was eerily empty, a vast hollow space with wide-open pens where closed ones should have been, the ground scattered with dried mud and brown hay, and moss and lichen camouflaging the walls. At the back of the barn three figures huddled around a metal drum, warming their hands over a fire that flickered discreetly inside.

They watched silently as he approached.

The sun made a skeleton of the roof with its missing rafters and in the naked light he could see the wind-burnt faces of the men. Their clothes were a combination of working gear and old uniforms, not worn for necessity but as a measure of pride. One wore dungarees and an old sheepskin flying jacket, the other a blue jacket of the Polish air force and dark trousers, while the one closest to him had well-worn farming clothes.

The man in the flying jacket hurried towards him. 'Janek?'

'*Tak* – yes.'

'Welcome. I am Stefan.'

'*Tyr.*'

Stefan shook Janek's hand then embraced him and slapped his back, the customary welcome.

'This is Fryderyk and Filip...'

Janek greeted them both in the same way, feeling the rub of their calloused hands between his. Then, remembering the sack, he dragged it over. 'A gift for you.'

They ushered him towards a small table and upturned crates where a wooden chess set and shot glasses stood.

Stefan gave him a broad smile, revealing black and uneven teeth. 'We drink, then we talk.' He poured vodka into each of their glasses and raised his own.

'What should we drink to?' Janek asked.

Stefan nodded at him, his mouth twisting as if to suggest it was his choice.

'To Poland then ... and to freedom!'

'To Poland!'

'*Na zdrowie!*' they toasted.

The clink of glasses echoed loudly in the chill of the empty barn and as they sat down, Janek felt the weight of their expectation. He had recognised them instantly as his countrymen; broad noses that dominated their faces, ears so low down that even the Poles had a joke about themselves, but it was when he looked into their eyes that he saw the proof he needed. They had shared the same sorrows and loss. Now he needed to find out how far they would go to take back their freedom and their country.

'I'm from Pultusk, Mazovia,' he said, remembering his instructions. He rubbed his cold hands together and looked at Fryderyk. 'And you?'

'The north-east, Bialystok.'

'Near Lublin,' offered Filip.

Stefan moved his stool closer. 'I'm from Warsaw, but your contact would have told you that...'

Janek nodded and then made a careful assessment before asking something that had been bothering him since he had arrived. 'I thought there were supposed to be five?'

Stefan spoke in a hushed tone. 'You will meet Franciszek soon. Your contact would also have told you what we do here ... and why you should not put your trust in these ugly men.'

Janek eyed him for a moment, wondering if this was some sort of trap.

Then Stefan laughed and the others did too.

'They are both bad chess players,' he continued, 'not to mention lazy farmers!'

The conversation continued light-heartedly, avoiding any talk of why they were there; instead they shared their dislike of English cooking and agreed that the British were terrible singers, and then they talked of politics. Janek was eager for any news from home and listened patiently as they described how the Russians had taken over Polish schools and universities, how they had introduced the Cyrillic script and were still confiscating farms and livestock belonging to the peasants. He heard how the Soviets were leading propaganda marches in the streets, setting up loudspeakers and mobile film projectors and chanting slogans to the Poles.

'We are expected to use roubles and pray in private,' Fryderyk spat.

'And if you disagree or refuse Soviet citizenship you are sent to Siberia!' Filip added.

Janek twisted his hands together, not for warmth but out of frustration. He hadn't wanted to talk of his own family but paid attention as the others spoke of how their families were taken hostage. Finally they turned to him: it was his turn to speak. He knew if he didn't it would only make them suspicious, so he talked of his own escape through Romania and the journey on through Syria and into France – no different to some of theirs – and he watched as their rings of smoke stained the air. When he had finished Stefan filled their glasses again and then stood as he prepared to toast, so they did the same.

'We give our lives to Poland knowing that she

will give us back ours!'

'But how?' Janek had been patient but now he wanted to know how to get back to France and find the brother he had left behind.

'There is nothing for the time being, except ... the contacts you have made working at the rail-yard and the markets – you are in a good position. You must pass on any information you think important.'

'How?'

'We will come to that.' Stefan waved his hands to silence Janek. 'I know you are eager but our priority is intelligence. Any access to the resistance overseas will only come after you have proved yourself or under specific order. Is that understood?'

He nodded.

'The Madonna,' Stefan announced.

'The Madonna,' they chorused.

As they drained their glasses, Janek recognised something new in Stefan's eyes; it was a familiar resolve, the same one he saw when he looked into the mirror. He had found the compatriots he had hoped for, not just to sing old folk songs with and reminisce, but to find a way back home.

Chapter Ten

Dig for your dinner
When salvage is all that remains of the joint
And there isn't a tin and you haven't a 'point'
Instead of creating a dance and a ballad
Just raid the allotment and dig up a salad!
Marguerite Patten OBE,
Victory Cookbook: Nostalgic Food and
Facts from 1940–1954

Maggie stopped running and tried to catch her breath; it was another few hundred yards to her aunt's house and she was already late. At least she could see the short distance uphill to the lamppost that stood directly outside, its iron branches curling around where the light globe should have been, but still a beacon for her now.

It had been a relief that the number 137 came when it did, and that she had been able to climb on board and find a seat where she could huddle close to the heat of the engine. The street warden warned her against coming to Clapham, told her that the roads had been closed for days after Tuesday's raid. She had seen the damage; half-carcasses of entire apartment blocks, gaping holes where walls should have been, glass blasted from windows, rooms uninhabitable except for the curtains still hanging, fluttering in the breeze. As they had passed along Queenstown Road she saw

142

how fire had engulfed the homes, and thought of Bill Drummond's brother, who lived in the area, and of the whole families he knew who had been killed. She shivered; they had been lucky so far, none of them losing their home, and even though her aunt's moods were unpredictable, Maggie knew how fortunate she was to have some family left with whom to celebrate important occasions. And perhaps Rose's surprise meal would finally earn her some praise from her mother. Maggie set off again, buoyed by the thought.

'What on earth are all those for?' Rose had asked when they had sneaked into the factory kitchen a few days earlier.

Her cousin was bewildered by the row of tarnished metal spoons on the worktop, larger ones at one end tapering down to one barely any bigger than a fingernail at the other.

'Serving spoon, tablespoon, soup spoon, dessert-spoon, teaspoon, measuring spoon,' Maggie replied as she pointed at each one. 'But you don't need to worry about that yet. We're doing savoury first.'

There had never been occasion for Rose to learn to cook; until recently she had still lived at home, where her mother looked after her far better than she could ever look after herself. And when Maggie had been in the kitchen with Rose for family get-togethers – birthdays and Christmases and the like – everyone just took it for granted that Maggie would be the one to cook. But as she tried to find another clear surface to move the ingredients and mixing bowls onto, she felt a deep pang of regret for not having taught Rose any of the basics sooner. It didn't seem to be coming naturally to her cousin; she made soup without too much trouble, but stewing fruit ready for the dessert and making the stock had been a long slow process with a lot of waste and no small measure of first aid required. At least the canteen kitchen was still empty, and with no one due for another hour, she should be able to get on to the main dish.

'This is your mum's favourite casserole so remember it well. It's also the kind of dish where you can double or triple the quantities and it still tastes good.'

'What, you mean you can't do that for all recipes?'

'Of course not. Different food groups require certain active ingredients to do their job properly.'

She had taught more difficult pupils than Rose in the past, so if she could just summon a little more patience, and Rose could concentrate a little harder, surely they'd get there.

Rose tucked her bottom lip behind her teeth and looked even more perplexed.

'Introducing larger quantities sometimes means they react differently. It changes cooking time, not to mention the colour and even the texture of the food. You don't want some ingredients staying hard while others are too soft, do you?'

'I suppose not...'

'Don't worry, that's domestic science. You don't really need to know all that; it's just useful. Here, follow what I'm doing.'

Maggie took hold of a sharp knife and with quick, precise movements, she halved a leek, then ran the blade through the white bulb, dicing it in seconds. She pushed the small pieces forward with the front of the knife so they fell into the nearby pan. Next she topped and tailed the carrots and cut them lengthwise before running the knife along them horizontally, sectioning them into semicircles. The potatoes had already been peeled, along with part of Rose's index finger, and now they were halved and quartered in one swift move, the blade barely leaving the wooden board.

Maggie was on autopilot now, moving from one ingredient to the next, explaining how she was cutting them into appropriate sizes so that they would cook to the right texture with the other ingredients, become the correct consistency for the dish: the vegetables not too soft, the meat tender enough to eat. Not that most of the meat she cooked these days was ever that tender; they were poor cuts of mutton or beef that needed cooking for hours before they were the least bit palatable. She could still taste her last piece of sirloin, over a year ago now; it had been for Peter's birthday, which they celebrated in the Green Man. The meat was succulent, the new potatoes crowned with a sprinkling of fresh mint and a robe of melting butter, and then there was the chocolate tart they had shared afterwards, with thick whipped cream that oozed down the sides.

'You make it look so easy,' Rose complained.

'It won't take you long to get the hang of it, it's just practice.'

'I'm not sure I'd enjoy it as much as you do...'

She *was* enjoying herself, sharing the craft that enabled her to create dishes from nothing, tips and tricks that she hoped she would be able to pass on. It didn't come naturally to everyone; recognising the right combination of tastes, producing a blend of colours and textures, being able to step up a gear in the kitchen while everyone around you panicked.

'There are a lot of things you need to know, but the most important is getting the timing right.'

'How do you mean?'

'When everything you have been doing comes together at the same time, that's the best feeling. It means you've got it right.'

She pushed *Mrs Peel's Victory Cookbook* across the counter towards her cousin.

'You had better hurry, we haven't got long. Find something you want to make for pudding.'

Rose flicked through the pages, scanning recipes with a furrowed brow as if trying to decipher a foreign language. She banged the book shut and pushed it away.

Don't look so worried,' Maggie said. 'It's only us as guinea pigs – it's not as if you're going to be cooking for strangers.'

'Yes, but can you imagine what Mum is going to be like?'

'So,' she said, pushing the cookery book towards Rose again. 'Just choose something. Anything you make will be special – it is her birthday.'

Rose opened the book again and the pages fell open at the honey and walnut pudding. 'Oh, she'll love this. Can I have a go?'

'Of course. Can you get the ingredients ready?'

'Yes, are they in the store?'

Maggie skimmed the ingredient list, trying to

ignore the nagging question of what she would say to Mr Ferguson when he arrived, which was likely to happen at any moment.

'Should be...'

Rose returned quickly, carrying only flour and sugar. 'I think the honey and walnuts could be a problem,' she said. 'Shall I choose something else?'

'No, don't worry. I know someone who can help.'

'Not black market is it?'

'Of course not! It's someone Robbie introduced me to.'

'You've been seeing a lot of young Robbie lately.'

'I know. We've been trying to get a response from the navy – he wants to contact his dad. It's a bit tricky, though, without Robbie having a proper address to send information to.'

'I still don't understand why he hasn't been billeted or isn't staying with a proper foster family.'

'Of course he should be, but he doesn't want to. It's no use forcing him, he won't listen.'

'Sounds like someone else I know...'

Arriving at her aunt's house, Maggie knocked on the door and turned to admire the view over the common, noticing how quiet the street was; there were hardly any cars on the road and even the usually busy common was devoid of its Sunday walkers and picnicking families. She couldn't even hear the customary quacking of ducks as the children chased them around the pond.

The door creaked and she swivelled around to see her aunt's overly made-up face break into a smile.

'Maggie, at last. We've been waiting for you, pet.'

'Happy birthday, Aunt Mary. These are for you.' Maggie held out the small pink-and-white posy she'd been clutching.

'They're lovely. Thank you, dear.'

Her aunt offered up her cheek and Maggie stooped forward, obediently planting a kiss, the smell of her aunt's face powder and scent mingling in a sickly sweet combination.

'You are a clever girl,' Aunt Mary said, admiring the flowers. 'Wherever did you manage to find them?'

Her aunt's face was a shade darker than usual, and the thick foundation had collected around her jawline, transforming her soft white skin into a stiff mask of beige.

'The florist's near the station,' Maggie said, following her into the hallway. 'They didn't have too much left, but I know how you love your peonies. How are you?'

'Old – but grateful for it. Can't moan, can I?' Her aunt sighed.

'Rose here?'

'Locked in the kitchen; been in there all morning. And she won't let me in. Dread to think what she's up to, banging around like nobody's business.'

It was typical of her aunt to complain when someone was doing something for her. She had been born for wartime, when she could grumble about the food shortages, hoard everything and darn already recycled clothes; to Aunt Mary, even her sandbag was half empty, not half full.

'Would you like me to take a look? I can put those in water for you...'

'I suppose so,' her aunt said, reluctantly relinquishing the flowers.

Maggie hung her coat over the end of the banisters as she passed and knocked on the kitchen door.

There was a muffled voice accompanied by crashing and the sound of the oven door being slammed.

'Rose?' she called.

'Go away!'

'It's me – Maggie.'

The door flew open and an arm grabbed her and pulled her inside. 'Thank God you're here!'

'Why, what's going on?'

The kitchen looked worse than hers did the day she found it ransacked; open packets and jars were scattered across the worktop around a large mixing bowl rimmed with an inch of flour, the tiny particles still suspended in the air.

'It's okay, you don't need to answer that,' she said, taking in her cousin's startling appearance. Rose looked as if she had been wrestling with the ingredients. 'What are you making now? I thought you had cooked everything yesterday.'

'I changed my mind. I remembered how she always used to make a roast and a jam roly-poly when we were kids, and I thought she'd like it if I made that for her – but now it's all burnt!'

Rose opened the oven door.

Maggie bent down to look and was blasted by a heat that nearly sealed her eyelids shut. She coughed as the acrid smoke hit the back of her throat. 'Blimey, Rose, I think you've got it on a bit high,' she said.

'You never told me what temperature to put it at!'

'It's in the recipe!'

At the back of the middle shelf sat a baking dish with a small brown log in it, shrivelled and burnt.

'Mutton end is really a boiling meat,' Maggie said. 'You can also use it for stock...'

'Now you tell me! What shall I do?'

Maggie took the oven gloves from her and retrieved the baking dish, placing it on the stovetop.

'Mmm,' she said, thinking. 'What vegetables have you got?'

Rose pointed towards the pan at the back of the stove where green leafy kale had transformed into pale green slivers that floated like lily pads on a pond.

'I was going to use the water for gravy, just like you showed me.'

'Do you have any more?'

'Some boiled potatoes and there's raw carrots and some red cabbage over there.'

The vegetable tray next to the back door held a few misshapen carrots, a handful of soil-covered potatoes and a medium-sized marrow with pitted skin.

'Have you got any Bisto?'

Rose rummaged around in the cupboard and then handed her a packet.

'What are we going to do?'

She looked so desperate that Maggie knew she couldn't suggest that they should throw it all away and start again. Rose had so wanted to cook her mother's birthday lunch, but she was sure that this meal would only invite criticism – although it really would take a miracle to salvage something edible from this lot.

'Go and tell her that lunch will be ready in fifteen minutes. And Rose?'

'Yes?'

'Go tidy yourself up – you look like Potato Pete!'

It was a great relief that lunch wasn't such a disaster after all; Maggie managed to shred a small amount of meat from the joint and was able to make a confit of lamb, and after grating carrots and red cabbage and sautéing them with onion and apple, she assembled the fastest Woolton pie that she had ever made. Even the mashed potato topping she had recycled from Rose's over-boiled potatoes had crisped up nicely under the grill with the last of the butter and cheese ration.

'Another sherry?'

'No, ducks,' her aunt replied. She was already listing slightly as she balanced plates in one hand while trying to turn the doorknob with the other. 'Better not. Want to leave some room for that birthday cake. Rose has been making such a song and dance about it. Besides, I want to hear more about this restaurant of yours and all the wonderful things you are going to make.'

Hardly, Maggie thought, but she wasn't about to spoil the celebrations. After her initial excitement over Mr Boyle's letter she read the paper-work and was surprised by the Ministry of Food's Allowance of Rationed Foods to British Restaurants; in fact, it had left her feeling decidedly anxious. If she had thought it was hard for an individual to get hold of food, she had been woefully wrong. That was nothing compared to the meagre portions supplied for each patron of a British Restaurant. She'd had to put the papers aside to get ready for her visit to Clapham, but when she got back she would need to think carefully about how they would be able to make the suggested menus with such small portions. With a quarter of an ounce of butter or margarine, an eighth of an ounce of jam and a pennyworth of meat per person, they would hardly be able to make the hearty meals that she'd intended. Even the beans, lentils and split peas she usually bulked the meals out with were rationed now. The specimen menus had also been disappointing; there was far too much sago and tapioca for her liking, and recipes that would not fill the bellies of men who laboured for ten hours a day and then worked as volunteers at night, too.

With her mother out the room, Rose came and sat on the sofa next to Maggie.

'She loved it. Thank you. She has no idea how close it came to going in the pig bin.'

'Don't be daft. You did a great job.' Maggie turned to face her cousin. 'I was thinking, how about you come and work at the restaurant straight away, not wait like we talked about?'

'Really?'

'Yes, we'll need kitchen hands and staff for the dining hall.'

'But I've no experience of restaurants. You'll need people that can help you, Maggie, not hinder you.'

'There will be training,' Maggie replied.

'I don't want you to choose me just because I'm family – I want to be selected because I can do the job.'

'I'm going to need all the help I can get, Rose. Where on earth I am going to find enough food for the two hundred and fifty meals we're expected to make? It's impossible!'

'That bad?'

'Worse.'

Maggie ran her hands down her legs, smoothing out imaginary stockings.

'So what do you plan to do?' Rose asked.

'Wait and see. What else can I do?'

'Do about what?' Aunt Mary enquired as she arrived with the tea tray.

She set the tray down unsteadily, the three bone china teacups rattling on their saucers, the matching floral teapot losing a little of its pale brown liquid.

'Maggie was just talking about the restaurant.'

'Yes, dear, and I want to hear all about it – but first get yourselves some mending out of the basket over there. There's never a moment to spare for some industry.'

Rose rolled her eyes at Maggie. 'Yes, Mum, idle hands cost lives...'

'You can mock, my girl, but our WVS group has made dozens of blankets for the Red Cross. Anyone who can't knit or sew needs to learn how.'

'As if people aren't tired enough already, Mum. Everyone needs to rest sometime.'

'I don't doubt that, but you young ones should have enough energy not to sit idle at night.'

Maggie knew the conversation could soon escalate into an argument so she took a ball of wool and some knitting needles from the basket and cast on.

'There were a lot of worn-looking faces at work last week, Aunt Mary, but you know we had a charity knit-in for the Motor Ambulance Fund and raised a tidy sum. One shilling and six for tea and biscuits, as well as money from the raffle.'

'That's good of you, Maggie. See, Rose? You could manage a few of these initiatives if you put your mind to it.'

Maggie looked over at her cousin and winked, knowing that she must be longing to tell her mother she was leaving the shoe shop where she worked.

'Rose will surprise us all, Aunt Mary, you wait and see.'

'And what's become of that nice young man who got injured ... Tom, is it?'

'He's going to be okay – they had to amputate his arm though.'

Aunt Mary shook her head and mumbled into the yellow blanket spreading across her lap like a field of ripening corn, growing at a much faster rate than Maggie's small square.

'I was actually going to see if he wanted to come and help at the restaurant.'

'What?' her aunt spluttered. 'How could he

help with only one arm?'

Maggie shrugged. 'There's plenty of jobs that a one-handed person can do just as well as a two-handed.'

A few moments of quiet followed with only the clicking of needles and the occasional twitter from the budgerigars, until Aunt Mary looked up from her knitting.

'You know your mother was always very resourceful. She took after Dad that way, always thought of a way round things. Not like me – I'd always get stuck right in the middle, one mess after another.'

Maggie grimaced, hoping that her aunt would stop and not dig up old wounds but she carried on.

'You're just like her in that way, Maggie, and a good cook too. Do you still have that enormous cooking encyclopaedia she gave you for your eleventh birthday?' Her aunt was becoming even more animated. 'I can't believe the things you used to make, and you were just a slip of a girl. Do you remember?'

She didn't usually mind taking a trip down memory lane with her aunt, but she really didn't want to think about her mother today.

'Yes I do. It was *The Gentle Art of Cookery* by Mrs C. F. Leyel & Miss Olga Hartley. I made a treacle tart for Dad's birthday.'

'Did you? Fancy that, Rose, and you only just learning to cook now.' Aunt Mary laughed.

'I'm surprised you remember that,' Maggie said, trying to distract her aunt's attention from Rose's supposed shortcomings.

155

'And what about that ghastly meal you made for us one Christmas, Maggie? Sausages and kidneys with rice, I think it was. Don't know what possessed you to choose such a thing!'

'I think it was something about the shapes that appealed to me. I certainly didn't realise how difficult it would be to make.'

Maggie dropped a stitch and twisted her needle around to pick it up. She'd thought her aunt wanted to talk about the restaurant, not her cooking failures.

'Do you remember helping your mum decorate the birthday cakes? You always had a talent for it. How about that soccer boot you made for Ernest...'

'Eliza's going to do the desserts, Mum,' Rose said; she knew how Maggie hated to talk about her brother. 'And trained cooks will do the actual cooking. Maggie will be running the place.'

'Yes, yes, of course.'

'Actually, Rose will be helping out too,' Maggie announced.

A smirk crossed her aunt's lips. 'Is this true, Rose?'

'Yes, Maggie said I can help out front on the servery – get some experience before training in the kitchen,' Rose said hesitantly, glancing at Maggie and then back at her mother. 'I'm good with the public, you've said so yourself.'

'One charity case is quite enough, Maggie; you don't need to help Rose too, you know.'

Maggie stood up, winding the wool around the needles and placing the knitting back in the basket.

'Which reminds me,' Maggie lied, 'I need to go and meet Eliza. We have a few things to talk over...'

'Oh, can't you stay a bit longer? What about the cake?'

Her aunt looked genuinely disappointed but Maggie needed to get away; she had been so certain that she could do this, that she was the right person to run a restaurant, but now that her aunt had reminded her of her failures, she was having second thoughts.

She remembered Mr Ferguson's face when she had given him her letter of resignation, how her explanation had turned into an apology as he read it. But his response had surprised her. Instead of bristling, his manner had softened. 'I can see that you won't be satisfied unless you can be making a difference. Good luck to you, lass.' Now she wondered if she had been too hasty about handing in her notice.

'I'm sorry,' she said, bending to kiss her aunt's cheek. 'I really do need to go. Save me a piece for next time.'

Rose stood too. 'I'll see you out.'

At the door, Maggie gave her a long hug. 'Are you okay?'

'Yes, good job I've grown a thick skin.'

'I'm sorry I said anything. I would have waited if I'd known she would react like that.'

'Don't worry, it's fine. You've enough on your plate.'

How could Rose remain so sweet when her mother undermined her so? Maggie wondered, not for the first time.

She was about to leave when she remembered something.

'Rose, did you get your mum that new Pan-Cake foundation for her birthday?'

'Yes.'

'Thought so ... let's hope she wears it to her next WVS meeting!'

When Rose closed the door behind her, they were both still giggling.

Needing time to clear her head, Maggie crossed the road to the common, walking west towards the sun that was sinking over the rooftops of the Victorian mansion blocks opposite. Night had started to close in and she would need to walk swiftly to beat the curfew or risk being stranded on the other side of London, her gas mask and tin hat still hanging on the coat stand by the front door.

Following the path that she hoped would take her towards Clapham North and a bus back to the city, she pushed her hands deep into her pockets and picked up her pace.

Her aunt's mention of Ernest had made her think of Robbie. They had hoped that Ed's contacts in the navy might be able to help find the boy's father, but the past few weeks had sped by and they'd still had no word. And each time she saw Robbie it was like looking at her brother, the same wide brown eyes pleading for any news. She wasn't sure what to do next; it was getting too dangerous for Robbie to stay at the school, each fresh blast making the foundations even more unstable. And on top of her anxiety about the boy, there was the restaurant. She had been so sure that this was what she wanted, but the task before her seemed overwhelming. If only Peter were here; he could help her with all the documents that needed to be read, the government guidelines that needed to be followed, the paperwork she would have to complete.

The common was nearly empty now and she began to walk even faster. As she passed a small grove of elm trees she noticed a couple kissing beneath.

The young man nodded when he noticed her. ''Night, miss.'

'Goodnight.'

Maggie smiled at the pretty blonde girl, knowing how she must feel; even in the dimming light Maggie could see the young man's uniform, the buttons bright and shiny, not yet used.

Chapter Eleven

HOW TO MAKE SHORT PASTRY:
UTENSILS REQUIRED
A pastry board or any cold smooth surface, such as an enamel-topped table or a marble slab; a mixing bowl or basin, wide enough to get both hands in, for rubbing fat; a flour sifter or sieve; kitchen knife; rolling pin; a jug of water and a pair of kitchen scales or a half-pint measure.
Ministry of Food, War Cookery Leaflet No. 26

The large sinewy organ slithered onto the plate,

159

wobbling for a few seconds before relaxing in porcelain comfort. Maggie looked at the smooth surface of the viscera cocooned in a network of grey and red capillaries and then up at the other girls' faces; they clearly felt just as queasy.

Her memory of school domestic science was nothing compared to the experiences of the past few days; she had decapitated a chicken, gutted a fish and boiled for brawn parts of a pig that she hadn't even known were edible. All their prior knowledge had been challenged when they had been shown how to use every part of an animal's body and which parts were the most nutritious. Now, standing around the table watching the instructor demonstrate how to make shortcrust pastry, she finally was on more familiar ground.

'Remember, ladies, the most important thing in a large kitchen is to be organised and efficient. Have your utensils ready and your ingredients to hand. For pastry you need a cold smooth surface, a mixing bowl, a flour sifter or sieve, a kitchen knife, a rolling pin, scales and a measuring jug.'

Miss Barker tapped each of the items named as she spoke.

Maggie wished that Eliza were here; the two of them would have had a hoot at Miss Barker's expense. She had all their most hated traits rolled into one and, as far as Maggie could make out, no redeeming features. She had no patience and no sense of humour either, she wasn't inspiring and even managed to make all the new things that Maggie was learning sound dull. She could just imagine Eliza's impersonation of her; the annoying mannerisms and habit of fiddling with

160

anything her hands came into contact with. She was nothing like Mrs Stoner, her favourite domestic science teacher from school, who always had an encouraging remark and a smile. Miss Barker may have been at least a decade younger than Mrs Stoner but she hadn't worked in a proper restaurant her whole life, only taught cookery, and it struck Maggie that she wasn't necessarily the right person to be giving them advice. Still, Mr Boyle had insisted so here she was, and in only five more hours her training would be complete and she would be free to go.

She tried to concentrate on Miss Barker's instructions, but her mind kept drifting off. Anyway, she knew exactly how to make pastry and it was nearly lunchtime and she was hungry. They would already have to wait until the kitchen maids ate the pies they made earlier before she and her fellow pupils could eat. Then they would replicate the dish again and at last the moment Maggie had been waiting for would arrive, and they would serve their dishes to the general public at the busy college restaurant.

'The perfect pie is one of the basics that all good cooks should have as part of their repertoire,' Miss Barker continued in clipped tones.

The kitchen was converted from a grand room in one of Westminster's oldest buildings and at their introductory session at the start of the week the course director proudly told them that the facilities were equal to those of any of the larger London restaurants and hotels. Maggie had thought he looked rather out of place, like a giant summer pudding, skin all red and blotchy and

161

with a peculiar habit of continually smoothing down his hair; it seemed rather undignified, not to mention unhygienic, for a man in his position. He was right though; the soaring windows would match those of any stately home, and there were solid brass doors that kept the draughts out and the moist heat from the ovens in. The cupboards were well equipped with every possible domestic appliance and a set of Kitway scales for each of them. The larders were stocked with rationed foods that Maggie hadn't seen for months, including, much to their collective excitement, quantities of Bournville cocoa. Wide enamel-topped benches were evenly punctuated with marble slabs, one for each of the twelve pupil-cooks attending the course.

'Right, now, one of you girls ... Maggie, you show us how much water you need for this quantity.'

'You need just sufficient to bind the mixture together, miss.'

'And?'

'And you use a knife...'

'But what if you add too much water?'

Maggie glanced around at the faces of the other pupils, growing crosser with herself by the minute. *Oh, come on, Maggie, this is basic.*

When Mr Boyle had first told her she would need to attend the National Training College for formal training she had reminded him that she wasn't a novice, but still he insisted. Maybe he had been right; if she knew so much, why couldn't she think of the correct answer now?

She stared at the group of ingredients on the

counter but all she could think about was how the packets of Dyson's self-raising flour looked so different; it was the same flour but the packaging had changed so much over recent months in order to save waste that they bore no resemblance to the ones she was used to. It wasn't just the flour, either, it was everything: breakfast cereals, tinned goods – austerity measures affected all the food they ate and the clothes they wore; Hitler's evil fingers stealing from every part of their lives.

'It goes tough.'

Her voice was a little too loud but she was so relieved to remember.

'That's right. Perhaps you would like to take us through the next stages.'

As she moved around to where Miss Barker stood and took hold of the basin, Emily gave her an encouraging smile. They had got used to the hands-on approach this week and most of it had produced good results, except for when Emily had been asked to make a jelly and used insufficient gelatine. It took them ages to get the sticky syrup off the cupboards and floor after she had lifted the mould from the platter and the jelly collapsed, liquid rivers running like lava down the sides of the bench.

The mixture in the basin was the consistency of breadcrumbs, and Maggie grasped the knife and stirred until it came together in a large ball of pale dough. Then she dusted the marble board and rolling pin with flour and began to press and roll.

'What are the important things to remember at this point, does anybody know?'

Maggie was surprised when Sally furtively

raised her hand; the young woman from Tooting had lost her parents during the March blitz and had barely said a word.

'You have to remember not to handle the dough too much.'

'Why, Sally?'

'Because overhandling can make it hard too.'

'Yes, that's right. And when you gather the trimmings together after, you must roll these lightly too. Remember, nothing wasted.'

'How do you know, though, if you've over-rolled it?' Sally asked.

'That's a very good question. Does anyone know the answer?'

They all looked back at her blankly.

'It will become very elastic and springy. If that happens, you can put it aside for half an hour before baking and it will improve. Some things just take time.'

Maggie thought that was the most sensible thing she had ever heard Miss Barker say.

By the afternoon she knew their pies were a success; blind baking the cases had ensured the pastry stayed crisp when the filling was added and the pie was returned to the oven. And the salads they had created from the edible flowers and herbs complemented the devilled fish perfectly. Maggie had occasionally made lavender shortbread, but her salad was now dotted with red and yellow rose petals, violet buds and brightly coloured geraniums and she couldn't wait to show Eliza. But first they would serve their dishes to the public and she would be able to experience what it was

164

like to present food in a proper setting, just like she would in her own restaurant.

Miss Barker was fussing around behind them as they loaded their trolleys, adding last-minute garnishes and forgotten serving spoons. Maggie looked at her own dishes: the crisp golden pastry of the offal pie topped with delicate vines of sweet pea, the bright red and orange of the turnip top salad, the steam rising from the glistening dark crown of her chocolate sponge pudding. And it all smelled so good! She knew that she didn't need to add anything else; only the silver warmers that they had spent most of the afternoon polishing were missing.

Miss Barker appeared behind her and placed the lids down over her dishes.

'Ready then, girls? Remember, this is the paying public – we don't want anything sent back...' Then she smiled and pulled open the wide brass doors.

For a moment Maggie was disorientated, blinded by the unexpected brightness pouring through the expansive windows and the light that reflected off the silver domes on her trolley.

She took a deep breath – *Alright, Peter, I can do this* – and, bracing herself, she grasped hold of the trolley and pushed it into the room.

Chapter Twelve

A GOOD BREAKFAST EVERY DAY IS THE FIRST RULE IN THE BOOK OF GOOD HEALTH:

Get up early enough to enjoy breakfast without hurry. A cup of tea and a morsel of toast gulped down with one eye on the clock is no use to anyone. Breakfast is an important meal for all of us, but especially important for growing school children and young factory workers.
Ministry of Food, War Cookery Leaflet No. 33

AUGUST 1941

A procession of trucks continued to arrive throughout the morning, clogging the streets and snaring the interest of curious locals and passers-by. Robbie sat cross-legged on the brick wall, intrigued by the trucks and the cargo being delivered. First, pipework and pots of paint were unloaded and quickly dispersed inside. Then a second, larger lorry with only one driver had arrived to offload kitchen equipment so big Robbie thought it would never fit through the doors. The driver took ages to manoeuvre the bulky machines along the path that ran up the side of the building, jimmying and shuffling it as he went.

Robbie couldn't believe his luck when Maggie told him where the new premises would be; not at her parents' old shop, like she had hoped, but at the disused bicycle repair workshop on Essex Road – the workshop itself needing more repair than any bicycle. He had come with her to look around before the heavy work began, and had trawled the workbenches and floors, gathering a handful of discarded tools that he had already fixed and put to good use. It was a large space with windows the colour of plum jam and skylights blistered and uneven like pork crackling, but Maggie had explained how the offices at the back would be converted into kitchens and food storage as she had given him a special tour. The whole place had been filled with a heady mix of oil that reminded him of the dockyards, and grime so thick that he wasn't sure how she was ever going to get the place clean enough to cook in, let alone have anyone eat there. But in the few weeks since he had last seen it, the place had been transformed. It was like when he found the housing for one of his models; he knew that with the right parts added, and some adjustments here and there, something incredible could take shape. Even so, he was surprised how quickly the inside of the workshop had changed and the walls had gone up to make the new kitchen and an office for Maggie.

He was supposed to be cleaning the glass on the front door, removing the crust of dirt in exchange for some treacle tart that Eliza was testing out, when another truck pulled up. The driver jumped down and began loosening ties from around a giant cylinder, his overalls and hands as black as the rubber of the truck's tyres.

A long gash on his forearm glistened red and made him wince as he moved but still he smiled at Robbie.

'Hey, kid. Anyone inside to give us a hand?'

'Sure, I'll get them.'

Robbie dashed inside, scanning the room in search of the foreman and hearing his voice booming from the back. Spoke waited obediently as Robbie nimbly dodged past a team of carpenters sawing wood on trestle tables, ducking under stepladders where painters stretched their rollers skywards. When he reached the kitchen entrance, he found Janek was hauling planks, stacking them against the wall of the storage rooms. Robbie realised he wasn't the only one watching him; Rose and three kitchen assistants were learning about some of the new cooking equipment, and while they watched Maggie's demonstration, he noticed them darting glances at Janek. Robbie was proud he had introduced Maggie to Janek and had already overheard her telling the foreman how invaluable Janek's help had been, that they would never have been able to come this far in only a few short weeks without him.

'Janek, you got a minute?' Robbie yelled over the noise of construction.

'What is it?'

'They need your help out front.'

Janek propped up the plank he was holding and followed Robbie back through the dining hall, his face red from exertion and tiny beads of sweat visible on his brow.

One of the cylinders was already off the truck by the time they reached the entrance and Janek made light work of hauling it up the alley and into the kitchen.

'Come on, Robbie – don't just stand there looking lazy,' he teased.

Robbie lifted lengths of pipework off the truck and shadowed Janek up the side of the building, pleased that the materials were light enough for him to carry and that he was able to help.

Maggie grimaced at her distorted reflection in the side of the copper cylinder and took a step backwards. She couldn't imagine the volume of water they needed to fill the cylinders, or the amount of gas to heat them, but at least they were here now and the last of the kitchen equipment to be installed. It was taking shape, although the painting of the dining hall was yet to be completed and the backyard was still a bulldozed mess. Still, the kitchen was just how she'd imagined it would be. And although most of the ovens and cookers were reconditioned or on loan, they had scrubbed and polished them until they were as good as new. The broilers shimmered, the worktops gleamed and the network of pipes and extraction fans seemed to form a lifeline connecting them with the outside world. There was a palpable buzz and it wasn't just the bald-headed plumber and electrician's apprentice talking constantly as they had all morning, but ruddy-faced cooks already producing quantities of food as they practised sample menus. The kitchens were well organised; ingredients placed systematically across counters, cooling racks and equipment emerging efficiently from cupboards, and a batch of bread pulled straight

169

from the oven produced an inviting yeasty smell.

Eliza's head and shoulders suddenly appeared above the worktop as she brought out another tray between gloved hands, crusts perfectly baked, crowns like golden honeycomb.

'I hope you've got enough butter to go with those,' Maggie said, catching her eye. 'You know that smell makes everyone hungry!'

'Well, why don't you go and have a look in cold storage then, Miss Bossy-boots!' Eliza said, shaking her head as if she were talking to a five-year-old.

Maggie laughed; there was an excitement in knowing they were nearly ready, but there was the exhaustion of the work and the trepidation of opening too. She was sure that if she hadn't had Eliza to distract her, she would have gone quite mad by now. Especially with Mr Boyle here, pedantically running through everything with her, checking every condition was met and every directive adhered to, second-guessing her every decision when she hadn't followed procedure to the letter. He had installed himself at one of the kitchen worktops earlier that morning and hadn't moved since, beadily observing the cooks and kitchen hands, questioning the workmen, and eyeing Janek and Robbie suspiciously, even though they had every right to be there.

Maggie rolled her eyes at Eliza as she went back to join him, reading over the latest memorandum and mentally ticking off the conditions they had completed.

They had already been through the plans and the estimate of the costs had been approved along with the schedule, but the area that seemed to be giving them the most trouble was the staff list; they appeared to be understaffed and yet over budget already and couldn't agree on where the changes should be made.

Maggie wearily rubbed her eyes in an attempt to fend off an emerging headache. 'We've been going over this for hours. Don't you think it's time for a tea break?' she suggested.

He looked at her as if she had just made an improper proposal.

'You only have one week, Miss Johnson. Are you sure you have time for tea breaks?'

'Time for tea breaks? Of course, Mr Boyle. It is why we are here, is it not? To provide refreshments for people – and I am desperately in need of some refreshing.'

'Very well, Miss Johnson. I'm going to take a short stroll. I will see you back here in fifteen minutes.'

'Don't you want to join me for some tea?'

'I can go without until our work is complete. It's what we are trained for, Miss Johnson: strength and vigour. I intend to maintain my strength for as long as my country needs me.'

'I assure you, there is no question as to the robustness of my team,' Maggie said, glancing around at Eliza, Maeve and the other cooks.

'I hope so, Miss Johnson, but we shall see.'

Maggie put down her papers and stood up. 'Very well, Mr Boyle. Enjoy your stroll.'

It was all she could do not to stomp through to the staffroom where Rose was pinning film posters across the bare walls. Not even Gracie Fields's smile was enough to distract her from Mr Boyle's maddening comments.

'You know what it is, Rose?' she said, banging the kettle down on the stovetop.

'What *what* is?'

Rose stepped back to admire the triptych of female heroines she had collected from *Picturegoer Weekly* – which was still called *Weekly* even though issues were only published fortnightly now.

'Do you know what the problem is with Mr Boyle?'

'No, although I'm sure you are going to tell me...'

'He can't bear the fact that I'm a woman,' Maggie declared.

'Don't be silly. He probably loves the fact you are a woman!'

'No, really – he's one of those men who can't accept that we are doing their jobs. We're equals now; they've got to accept it and stop treating us as subordinates.'

She really had Rose's attention now.

'I don't know, Maggie, maybe. You think that's why he talks the way he does?'

'Yes, I do. And I'll bet that's why we're opening here. The grocery shop would have been far more suitable, but he just didn't like the fact that I suggested it. Or that I might be right!'

'You sure you're not just being paranoid? You know, with the pressure of opening and everything?'

'Of course I'm sure.'

It really would have been so much easier and quicker to take her parents' old grocery shop. Yet

Mr Boyle maintained that it wasn't suitable: 'Not enough room for safe evacuation,' he'd insisted. But he was wrong; she had grown up there, and knew that there were two separate doors to the outside. There would have been no problem evacuating a large group of people, and the spacious storeroom at the back of the shop could easily have been converted into a kitchen. To this, Mr Boyle had said that the costs 'were too prohibitive', claiming that this disused bicycle workshop was ideal and had been empty for years. It certainly felt like it when Maggie first saw it; mould clung to the walls and decorated them with an irregular brown pattern. The paintwork was yellow and the ceiling sagged as if it had just lost the will to cling there any longer and no amount of paint or plinths could encourage it to.

'I really think you need that cup of tea,' Rose said, nibbling the edge of her fingernail.

'I know. I've just about got time for one before he's back.'

'Would you mind if I head off soon? Mum's having one of her neuralgia episodes so I said I'd pop in.' Rose grimaced. 'I'm sorry, I know you're up to your eyes in it...'

'It's fine. Give her my love, tell her I hope she feels better.'

Maggie took her cup of tea outside where she could take gulps of clean air, away from the dust and fumes of the building work and the heat of the ovens.

The yard was crowded with building tools and debris, and she could only just keep track of who all the workmen were that came and went, so was relieved when she saw a familiar face. She had only seen Janek fleetingly since Robbie had taken her to the railyard allotment and there had not been that many occasions for them to speak over the busy weeks of demolition, so now he somehow looked different. Perhaps it was the daylight; the contours of his face appeared less sharp, features softer than the hard lines that she remembered from when they first met.

'That's it – the last piece of equipment, Malgorzata,' he said as he rolled and butted a huge cylinder towards the back door.

'So there's no going back now?' she said, only half joking.

'You don't need to, Malgorzata. You are ready for this.'

She looked up at the heavy skies, memories of the last few weeks scuttling as fast as the clouds; there had been leaking pipes and badly burnt hands, cooks that she'd had to let go after first shifts, sacks of ingredients ruined by weevils. Mr Boyle had been scrupulous about approving every stage and there had been enough papework to sink a battleship – but Janek was right: it felt like time.

'Yes, Janek. I think I am.'

Chapter Thirteen

*Two classes of people will suffer if we make full use of
our vegetable crops. First, the vendors of patent
medicines, whose wares will be less in demand.
Second, the makers of too highly-seasoned sauces,
because our palates, once accustomed to good eating,
will be content with the delicate flavour of
well-cooked vegetables.*
Ministry of Food, War Cookery Leaflet No. 6

Plumes of smoke billowed skywards and drifted
east on a bitter morning wind, spreading the
smell of freshly baked bread across the streets
and avenues of the north London suburb. The
industrial chimneys had been difficult to install
but now they sat atop the squat brick building
like candles on a giant birthday cake.

Maggie leaned forward to peer through the
newly polished windowpanes into the restaurant,
the room stretching away to the vast kitchen at
the back, broad skylights allowing the summer
sun to drench the long benches and tables of the
dining room below. Rose appeared at the kitchen
doorway then walked quickly through into the
dining hall, the tray she held releasing a coronet
of steam. Two more cooks followed behind her,
also in kitchen whites with arms bent under the
strain of their heavy loads, their slow progress
reflected in the chrome servery, making the din-

ing space appear even larger than it already was.

Maggie's chest heaved and she instinctively brought up her hand, swallowing hard; there was something about seeing her cousin carrying their first meal that took her by surprise. It had been the same earlier, when they had unpacked the crockery the customers would eat from and arranged the furniture at which they would dine. So much had changed, her life was so completely altered, and now it felt as if her insides had been rearranged too; her heart beating much higher up than it should, her stomach as if it had shifted to a different place as well.

As she pulled back from the window she noticed a woman standing next to her, smartly dressed in a navy crepe suit and hat, her gaze fixed on the dresser inside. Its four shelves were stacked with the cakes and desserts that Eliza had made: stands of pale crumbly shortbread, a sticky ginger sponge, chocolate puddings still plump from steam and individual bright yellow tarts, sweet with the tang of homemade lemon curd. They looked good and she knew they tasted far better than any of the cakes at the Marks and Spencer cafe where her friends and neighbours were already using their ration tokens to buy food.

'They look delicious!' the woman said.

'Yes, I think we'll be able to give Lyons a run for its money,' Maggie replied, admiring Eliza's handiwork.

The cakes were not on the list of recommended recipes that Mr Boyle had given her but she hadn't wanted to waste the chance to feed the hungry trade between breakfast and lunchtime, or the skills that Eliza had to offer.

'Are you open yet?'

'Not quite, but if you come back in half an hour you can be my first customer.'

'Oh dear, I'm going to meet my friend Pam up the road.' The woman looked disappointed.

'Never mind, maybe next time.' Maggie extended her hand. 'I'm Maggie.'

'Mary – Mary Bevan. Pleased to meet you.'

They shook hands.

'I'll tell you what, Maggie,' the woman said, brightening, 'I'm going to meet Pam and bring her straight back here.'

'Well, you know, Mrs Bevan, the first customer gets a free pot of tea.'

'You don't have to do that, dear.'

'I know, but today is a bit of a practice run for us anyway.'

'Well, thank you. I'll see you soon then, Maggie. And don't forget to save us one of those cakes.'

As Mrs Bevan strolled away Maggie followed her progress across the road as she turned the corner into Gaskin Street and disappeared. It wasn't yet seven o'clock and the streets were already filling with people on their way to work so she knew they had to hurry to be ready for the busy breakfast trade.

Eliza came outside to find her. 'Ready?' she asked.

'I think so...'

Eliza put her arm around Maggie's waist and gave her a squeeze. 'You got opening-night nerves?'

'Yes, I think I have,' Maggie confessed.

Eliza pulled a face. 'You're serious?'

Maggie nodded vigorously.

'I'm surprised.'

'Don't be. Everyone gets nervous, Liza – even you.'

'No, not me. Never been nervous before in my life!'

'Really? Not even before your first date with Johnny Wilkins?'

'No, not even then.' Eliza smirked. 'Anyway, we're not talking about me. Look–' she said, pointing up to where the sign-writer was painting the sign. 'It says "Maggie's Kitchen", not "Eliza's Kitchen".'

'Alright, yes, I am nervous, but can we stop talking about it? You're only making me feel worse.'

'Sure,' Eliza said, stepping away. 'Although I fail to see how you can feel nervous. Everything looks, well ... everything looks perfect.'

Maggie took in the newly cleaned brickwork, the fresh black paint of the window frames and door. It wasn't quite what she and Peter had envisaged for their place; the outside wasn't painted white because of the blackout and the inside had to be painted with pale enamel paint because of the condensation from the cookers, but it looked appealing nonetheless.

'Well, are you going to stand here all day or are we going to get this place open?'

Maggie looked at her friend's face; there wasn't even a flicker of the doubt and nerves that she felt and she was overwhelmingly grateful for it.

She grasped Eliza's hand. 'Thank you, Liza. I couldn't have done it without you.'

'You could do anything you set your mind to, Maggie Johnson,' her friend remonstrated.

'I mean it,' said Maggie. 'And look here,' she sniffed, as tears welled in her eyes. 'Now I'm making a fool of myself!'

'So, are you going to turn the sign or just stand here blubbing?'

'No, we should wait until exactly seven – it might be bad luck otherwise,' she said, walking backwards and into a ladder.

The sign-writer, six feet off the ground, wobbled slightly and the two women grabbed the ladder.

Eliza giggled. 'That wasn't very clever.'

'I'm so sorry, are you alright?' Maggie asked, looking up at him.

His paintbrush was poised just above the 'e' of *Kitchen* and he waited until the ladder ceased to shake.

'Yes, fine, thank you, miss.'

'Oh, look...' Maggie had noticed a dark speck of paint on the glass. She took out the duster from where it was loosely tucked in the top of her apron and rubbed hard at the mark. She would never get rid of the city's constant blanket of grime but at least for her opening day she would like to see the windows clean.

There was a pull on her sleeve as Eliza grabbed her arm.

'Come on, let's get inside. Everybody's waiting for you.'

'Yes, you're right. I can do this later.'

'What time did you say that Mr Boyle was coming?'

'I didn't, he could be here any moment.' She

179

moved her face close to Eliza's and spoke very slowly. 'With the cook adviser for the whole of the London region!'

Inside, Rose was kneeling down, hurriedly writing the day's meals on the blackboard, Tom was giving instructions to two of the girls on how the customers needed to queue and pay, and the serving staff were checking the equipment and filling the bains-marie with boiling water. It was five minutes to seven.

'Can I have everyone's attention, please?'

Her voice sounded small in the cavernous dining hall. She waited a few moments as the rest of the staff came to join the dozen cooks and kitchen hands that waited on benches. The group looked more like nurses in their white smocks and aprons, hair tucked neatly beneath their snoods. She had wanted to thank them all for their hard work, talk to them about the important role they would be playing in the war effort, give a rousing and inspirational speech – but now, faced with the vastness of the room and the challenges that lay ahead, she had forgotten what she intended to say.

'Thank you, this won't take long. We've got a lot to get through this morning but I just wanted to say welcome aboard to everyone–' she glanced around to see them all listening intently '–and thank you for getting everything ready in time. The restaurant looks ... well, it looks amazing.'

Tom and Eliza began clapping and the others joined in. It took Maggie by surprise, but, buoyed by their enthusiasm, she carried on more confidently than before.

'We've got a few challenges ahead – some that most of you probably know about – but we've also got some aces up our sleeve. Our wonderful pastry chef, Eliza...'

There was another round of applause.

'And our talented new cashier, Tom.'

The gathering turned towards the only male in the room and Tom bowed theatrically, bending his right arm under his waist as he tilted forward, the empty sleeve of his left arm pinned into his jacket's left pocket. The applause subsided and he turned and smiled at Maggie.

'I'm pleased to say we also have a new server, too.'

She looked to where Gillian sat, slightly away from the rest of the group.

With the girls now billeted in the countryside, Maggie had been sure Gillian would jump at the chance of a job, knowing how unhappy she was at the factory where she worked. As she continued to look round at the other familiar faces – some friends, others people she had recruited from the factory canteen – she realised how great her responsibility had become. She was used to managing a team but this was very different; they were all relying on her now.

Then she noticed Robbie leaning against a pillar to one side; he had been a great help over recent weeks too, making tea, doing small jobs and lightening the mood with his continual good humour. He deserved to be sitting up here with them now instead of hiding away in the shadows.

Maggie waited for the clapping to subside before taking a step towards Robbie, motioning with her hand for him to come closer. He grinned and shook his head, staying firmly rooted to the spot, trying to conceal Spoke who hid between his legs.

'You will also have got used to seeing Robbie and his dog in recent weeks. We owe a big thank you to Robbie for the endless supply of tea and jokes – and we are looking forward to seeing more of him but, unfortunately, Spoke will have to remain outside.'

Tom gave a good-natured groan.

'Well, we had better get on with business; just a quick recap in case any of you missed anything – I know there's been a lot to learn. The day's meals are all on the blackboard until our printed signs come in.' She pointed to the board on the wall where Rose had written the dishes of the day in chalk.

'The hot breakfast with bread or toast and tea is two shillings and six, but you don't need to worry about the prices – either Tom or the cashier that is covering for him will take the money.'

'What about lunch?'

'There are always two choices daily. Today's is lentil or pea soup to start, then Lancashire hotpot or fish and tomato bake with cabbage and boiled potatoes. Our desserts are steamed rice and apple pudding or date pudding. All meals are three and sixpence and include a mug of tea. Any questions?'

'Do the desserts come with anything?'

'They are all served with custard.'

She waited for another question but there weren't any.

'Okay, if that's all, let's get on with it. And good luck, everyone.'

The women began to move away, most through into the kitchen, a domestic regiment falling out, Gillian and Rose taking up their positions.

Maggie followed them over.

'Have you checked the temperature of the bains-marie?'

'Yes, they're nearly there,' Gillian answered, nudging the dial a little higher.

'Good, the scrambled eggs will be ready soon so you keep on number one and shout through when the tray gets to less than a quarter full.'

'Right you are, Maggie.'

'And both of you remember to use the right serving spoons. We need the portions to be exact; we'll run out if the servings are too large.'

'Do you want us to try and give a bit less then?'

'No, Rose, we serve a square honest meal. If we run out, they'll have to have something else.'

'Alright,' Rose replied.

'And it's half a pint of porridge per person – less for children but more for the men. You'll have to use your judgment to make sure it balances out.'

Maggie smiled reassuringly and was quickly on the move again.

The morning passed quickly and the lunchtime rush came and went with surprisingly few hiccups; they managed to keep the food hot, the portion control worked out and even Mr Boyle's visit went without a hitch. All that was left for the afternoon was to get the cooking and prep ready for the following day.

Maggie strode through the kitchen, already accustomed to the rich woody nose of the meat stock and the rattle and clack of utensils, but despite the large wall grilles that ventilated the area and the air ducts over the cookers, the hot cooking fog still hit her. Their cotton dresses and aprons were warm enough for the cooler months, but it had been a scorching August day and she already knew that the conditions were too hot. Two six-foot-long hot closets and salamanders directly in front of her shielded her from the intense heat of the roasting ovens as their doors were opened and trays of fruit cobbler were loaded in, the apples and cinnamon giving off a tantalising syrupy tang. The industrial steamers weren't turned off yet and a cloud of condensation lingered over Maeve where she stood stirring a copper pot at the central stove.

Maggie turned to survey the blackboard on the wall just inside the kitchen, examining the lists of the next day's meals and the preparation checklist. The board had been divided into two columns showing morning duties and afternoon duties so she could easily look around and see what had been done and where extra help was required. The whole week's menus hung on a bulldog clip underneath with the staff schedules and delivery charts, easily accessible in case she wasn't there. She didn't intend to run her kitchen like Mr Ferguson, never giving any of her staff the chance to learn and grow.

Taking the papers off the hook, she walked through the kitchen towards Eliza, past the noisy clatter of the peeling machines.

184

'Have you measured out the ingredients for the rissoles tomorrow?'

'Yes, Mags, and the gravy – but do you really think we're going to do this many covers every day?'

'That's what I've been told. Besides, we didn't have any left today.'

'But how? It's not like anyone even knows we're here yet.'

'Remember those other feeding centres that I told you about?'

Eliza wrinkled her nose, uncertain.

'You know – there's one on Hanover Street, and one at Canonbury Road School up near Highbury Corner.'

'Oh, yes.'

'Well, they're run by the Londoners' Meals Service and Mr Boyle says they sell out every day.'

'Blimey.'

'We need enough for one hundred covers for breakfast and two hundred and fifty for lunch.'

'It does seem like rather a lot.'

'Well, he said he was going to put an advert in the *Highbury & Islington Gazette* so we'll see. I have to say, though, I'm a bit disappointed with the menus.'

'Why?'

'Listen to this: Monday, minced meat, cabbage or meat pudding and boiled potatoes; Tuesday, rissoles and gravy; Wednesday, shepherd's pie; Thursday, Lancashire hotpot ... Friday looks a bit better: toad-in-the-hole. Honestly, I think we were making better meals at the factory. And you'll have had a gutful of roly-polys by the end of the week, too, by the look of this.'

Eliza groaned. 'Do we really have to stick to the ministry's menus?'

'We've got no choice,' Maggie said, pressing her lips together and looking over the sheets again. 'It's all centralised: all the ordering, the allocations... We get the same ingredients as the other British Restaurants and the exact amount to make each dish.'

'I suppose you are officially stuck then, Mags.'

'What's wrong with a bit of imagination? Fish casserole, steak and kidney pudding – stuffed marrow even!'

'Come to think of it, a bit of marmalade for the toast in the morning would be nice.'

'Are you saying something's wrong with my carrot jam?' Maggie asked in mock alarm.

'Well, don't be too hard on yourself,' Eliza counselled. 'The poor buggers are going to be pleased with whatever they get.'

'I know. And maybe it will get better. You know, tomorrow's delivery still hasn't arrived yet. Do you think the driver has got lost or something?'

'I doubt it, but I do hope it turns up soon. You know that I would do anything for you, Mags, but even I can't conjure bread and cakes out of thin air!'

'It will work it out,' Maggie assured her.

'How?'

Maggie took her by the shoulders and looked her straight in the eye. 'Trust me, Liza, worse things have happened.'

'Tell you what,' Eliza replied. 'You can show off your culinary skills later and make Robbie and me something special for dinner.'

'Very funny.'

'Well, we should celebrate ... first day and all.'

'Perhaps,' Maggie conceded. She was satisfied by their first day but tired, too, and not sure she felt up to a celebration. 'Where *is* Robbie?' she asked.

'He was in the yard last time I looked.'

The late-afternoon light spilled through the crack of the half-open doors as Maggie slipped through.

Outside, the ground was still covered with rubble, disused pipes and the tools needed for the unfinished work. Adjoining the back fence, broken gates were propped open leaving a clear view through to the lane behind, and just inside, Robbie sat on an upturned crate throwing a ball for Spoke. His shoulders were hunched and there was something about him that stopped her from disturbing him. His trousers and shirt were the same ones she had washed and ironed more than a week ago and it didn't look as if he had changed them since. Even Spoke looked forlorn, half-heartedly retrieving the ball.

She watched for a while as he threw the ball over and over, until he noticed her and forced a smile.

'You okay?' she said, walking over to sit beside him.

'Yep.'

'You sure?'

'I said so, didn't I? What about you? How was your first day?'

'We sold out at lunchtime, had just about

187

enough for the teatime rush and only one stove is broken. I think you would say pretty good all things considered.' She nudged him playfully.

He continued throwing the ball, looking straight ahead. 'You hungry?'

He shook his head.

'No? I've never known you turn down food before.'

Robbie shrugged.

'How was school?'

'Fine.'

'What's wrong, then?'

'Nothing...'

'Robbie, *nothing* means *something* – and you not being hungry definitely means something.'

'Okay, but if I tell you, you won't tell me I have to go?' He carried on throwing the ball, not looking at her.

'No, I won't, but you can't sleep here again. Last night was a one-off – there are so many other people around now, someone might see you.'

'I know.'

He continued passing the ball from hand to hand.

'There's been a letter from the navy,' he said at last. 'They finally replied.'

'And?'

He held the ball in one hand and inspected its torn dirty surface.

'They say there's nothing else they can do. They've "exhausted every avenue".'

'Oh, Robbie, I'm sorry...'

Maggie knew what it felt like to lose hope, but she had to tell him that he shouldn't, that there was always a chance; that he should never give up. But she couldn't bring herself to say the words because she also knew that it meant he would have to leave. There was no reason for him to stay now; she had done what she promised and helped him look for his dad, but now she needed to contact the authorities so they could find him a foster home or a billet in the country. She needed to let him go.

She reached out and took his hand and they sat for a while, listening to the sparrows chirruping and watching the clouds scatter their dreams across the skies.

Chapter Fourteen

Even if you have no garden, you can have
fresh-picked parsley or mustard and cress, for these
both grow well in window-boxes or flower-pots.
Or mustard and cress can be grown on a damp
flannel. Remember – the fresher the better
for you – and the better the flavour!
Ministry of Food, War Cookery Leaflet No. 14

The silver blade sliced down through the flesh, carving tissue from the bone, sinew and skin pulling away in a long, lean pink strip. Maggie quickly looked away as Janek pushed the knife deeper into the tiny leg and there was a sickening crunch of bone.

From the corner of her eye, she could see the

189

blade of the other metal tools leaning against the wooden fence – each one, she had discovered, with its own unique purpose in the business of slaughtering and dissecting bodies. She allowed her gaze to settle for a moment on the pile of wood stacked against the restaurant's back wall before forcing her attention back to the animal.

'I don't think I'm going to be able to do this.'

'You'll get used to it … it just takes time.'

'No.' She swallowed hard. 'I really don't think I can.'

'You do it for chickens.'

'That's only plucking, it's different. Anyway–' she grimaced at the rabbit's fur lying on the ground like a discarded coat '–we didn't have chickens when I was a child, but we had pet rabbits.'

'You cannot afford to be cowardly.'

She watched numbly as he picked the pelt up off the ground and hung it over the clothesline that stretched across the yard, already sagging under the weight of other skins.

'None of us can.'

Holding out the deep metal tray, she forced herself to look as he placed the small pink body inside, as gently as one would lay a newborn in a crib, and no different in size. She bit down hard on her bottom lip, hoping it might stop the burn of bile that rose in her throat.

He was right, and she cursed herself for being so feeble, so squeamish, when hundreds of thousands were having to put up with much worse.

'What should I do now?'

'I'll finish here. You go in.'

Maggie went inside, relieved that she had been given a reprieve this time but knowing that next time when the rabbits were delivered freshly killed she would have to help skin and bone them herself.

The other kitchen staff were arriving and she hurried through, looking forward to seeing Rose and Eliza, but their stations were empty, aprons still hanging on hooks on the back door. There'd be no gossip for the time being, no talk of Mrs Harraday's new grandson, or Mary Thomas taking in another infant. Maggie would have to wait to hear Eliza's animated recount of her night out, as well as all the intoxicating details of the latest bar or club that she had gone to. She had grown used to the girls' company in the past few weeks, finding it more difficult now to be alone than she ever had before; they might all travel the same scarred and shattered streets on their way to work, but once they entered Maggie's Kitchen, it was somehow as if the rest of the world didn't exist.

Remembering that the rabbit stew would need dumplings, and that Eliza would be starting on the puddings as soon as she arrived, Maggie went through to the storeroom to get the ingredients they would need.

She measured out four cups of flour and sieved them into a large bowl.

By the time Janek appeared, she was rubbing lard into the flour with her fingertips. She watched as he slid the rabbit meat straight off the tray and into a pot standing ready on the stove.

'I will have to go now,' he said, rinsing his hands at the sink. 'Do you need anything else?'

191

She didn't want him to leave yet, but she couldn't think of a reason to keep him there.

'I'll be fine, thank you,' she said. She hesitated, hands hovering over the mixing bowl. 'Eliza and Rose are late. Do you think they're okay?'

'Of course, it's probably closed roads.'

'Yes. Perhaps. There was a closure last night on Holloway Road. Cars crashed at the crossroads. I wonder when people will realise it's safer to walk than drive without lights?'

She was aware of his closeness beside her, of the faint tinge of tobacco intermingled with his own scent.

'Well, if you do really have another five minutes to spare...' She paused for him to object, and when he didn't she continued, 'Do you know how to make croutons? Yesterday's bread is just over there.'

He selected a sharp knife from the block and began dicing the bread into small cubes.

'Nothing goes to waste; stale bread is perfect for the croutons with today's soup.'

She was cross at herself for her pitiful performance earlier and was putting on a show to prove she knew what she was doing, but by the time she looked up he was already pushing neat squares onto a baking tray and spreading them out in an even layer. He caught her eye and she realised he was watching her closely too, following each movement, and his silent glances were unsettling.

'What is it, Janek?' she asked finally.

'Why did you want to open a restaurant, Malgorzata?'

'Well, it's obvious, isn't it?' she said, flushing.

'You've seen the streets: there's nowhere to eat. People don't have time to wait in mile-long ration queues.'

'Is that all?'

'Isn't that enough?'

'Yes, of course it is, but is it the only reason?'

'Well, no. It's because I love to cook ... that's why I can do it.'

'And would you eat those dumplings?'

Her eyes narrowed. 'Well, no, but that's because I don't like them.'

'Why?' He was smiling now.

'Because they don't really taste of anything.'

'Exactly, and that is what makes the difference between a good cook and a great cook.'

She was surprised at the mischief on his face; she had never seen him like this before.

'You should never expect other people to eat what you would not. Ask yourself what you can do to give them flavour.'

He reached for the flour packet and measured some out into a bowl, then added a cupful of dark marbled fat. He plunged both hands into the bowl, his large fingers and thumbs moving nimbly. He sprinkled salt and poured water and the mixture began to take shape, the dry powder transforming into elastic dough.

'Now, to eat like this would taste ... urgh.'

'It doesn't look very appetising,' Maggie agreed, smiling. 'So what did you have in mind?'

'In Poland we add herbs and spices to our dumplings that give extra flavour to the dish.'

'So do we sometimes – but there aren't many herb gardens left.'

'Yes, but you must make room ... in a window box, on a small scrap of land, even in an old bucket. Thyme, parsley, rosemary – any of these will do, and then you will want to eat the dumplings as well as the stew.'

'Very well then.' She bent down and plucked a spindly sprig of thyme from the shelf beneath the kitchen block. 'I do have my secret supply, for very special occasions.' She held it out.

His hand brushed against hers as he took the sprig from her. Holding the stalk in one hand, he pulled the leaves back with the other so that the tiny fronds fell onto the board.

'Thyme has one of the strongest flavours of all the herbs so you need only a small amount.'

'Thank you, Janek, I do know that.'

'I'm sorry.'

He chopped the small leaves finely and pushed them into the bowl with the edge of his knife, then he worked them carefully into the mixture until they were distributed evenly throughout.

'Shouldn't you add the herbs to the mixture while it is still dry, before the water?'

'Whichever you prefer ... everyone has different methods.'

He had made her cross at first, alerting her to her own failings, but the feeling ebbed as she recalled the pleasure of cooking with someone else.

'Alright, what are you going to show me now?'

A door banged and they both looked up as Eliza burst into the kitchen.

'Is someone going to give me a hand? In case you two hadn't noticed, there's a huge queue out there!'

Maggie looked at the clock; it was already eight! She had lost half the morning somehow.

'I didn't realise it was so late. Where have you been?'

'The bus broke down. I had to walk all the way from Farringdon. Seemed like a good idea at the time.'

'Well, at least you're here now,' Maggie said, throwing an apron at her. 'You go and help on the serveries, I'll get the hot food out.'

Maggie had her head down carrying a heavy tray when she reached the doorway through to the restaurant, but she could hear the crowds before she saw them. Not just the regulars and local office workers who had become familiar faces over the past few weeks, but men in overalls and uniforms, women in finer clothes who probably lived in even finer houses in suburbs miles from here; a queue stretching from the servery all the way to the door. For a moment it didn't seem real, as if she was really there in her very own restaurant, with a queue of people down the street. Then she was back in the room, making her way to the counter, unloading the trays into the heated bains-marie.

On the other side of the dining hall, Rose had arrived and was looking pink and flustered as she squeezed her way through the customers.

Even though Maggie was in a rush, she couldn't help noticing a woman at the counter staring at her, and felt even more uncomfortable when she glanced up and the woman quickly looked away. Stranger still since she was next in line to get served that the woman should replace her tray and hurry towards the door. There was something about her, about the way she moved, and even though her hat cast a shadow across her face, its shape was familiar: the smallness of the nose, the deep hollow of her cheekbones...

'Maggie? Maggie!' It was Rose, summoning her to the registers.

When Maggie turned back to look at the woman again, she had already closed the door behind her, disappearing onto the crowded street.

Chapter Fifteen

Once upon a time cooks used to think a good soup needed 3 or 4 hours cooking, and that to be nourishing it must be made from meat and bones. Today we know better. We know that, although meat and bone stocks are tasty, they have very little food value because only the flavour of the meat comes out in the soup. We know, too, that tasty soups can be made quickly using vegetables and vegetable water or stock from meat cubes or vegetables extract.
Ministry of Food, War Cookery Leaflet No. 15

By the end of the first month, Maggie had forgotten all about the jammed storeroom door and the spilled oil drum, or that some of the walls still hadn't been painted. They had been forced to close early on one occasion when they had run out of food, which had made the customers most unhappy, but recently she noticed the same

196

people returning day after day – not just the office and factory workers, but the local women too. And Tom was always there to greet them with his signature cheeriness.

'How are you, Tom?'

He looked up from the register where he was counting the change. 'Twenty-four, twenty-five... I'm well, Maggie. How are you?'

'Very well. So you're managing then?'

'Better... The arm's a bit stiff of a morning, but it's alright once I get going.'

'Well, let me know if you need a break.'

'It's fine, I have a word with Rose and Gillian to slow things down if they send them through too quickly.'

'Good – so we won't need to get that second cashier after all!'

'No,' Tom agreed, 'we'll be just fine.'

Once in the kitchen, she didn't check on the cooks individually like she usually did, making sure their stations were all cleared and prep for the next day complete, but went straight through to the storeroom.

The metal shelves were nearly bare: only a few tins of Bird's Custard Powder and a random selection of well-worn packets remained. She took the lid off one of the storage bins on the floor and found that was empty too. The refrigeration cupboards were just as bad, with barely enough cartons of bacon and dried eggs for the next few days. They wouldn't be able to stick to Friday's menu at this rate, let alone their meal of last resort: mutton stew and a spotted dick that you could play spot-the-sultana with. She couldn't believe that it had come to this, but they might have to close the doors again.

Threading her way back past the cooks, she hurried into the small room that had been converted into an office. It was barely large enough for her desk, which took up the whole of the back wall, but she had made good use of the space by putting shelving above it where a line of files and stacks of paperwork now sat. The wireless was in here, too, ready for mornings at 8.15am when *The Kitchen Front* was broadcast and they listened to the imaginative and hilarious recipes that were sent in.

Hoping that she wouldn't be interrupted, she sat down and pulled the chair in as far as it would go, jamming her legs up against the Morrison shelter that the desk had been fashioned from, complete with a rubber camping bed. It had been a good idea to make the shelter work as a desk, particularly as two of them could take refuge inside if there was a raid, three at a push. Any more, though, and they would have to take their chances with the diners, squeezing under the reinforced wooden tables in the dining hall. It was one of the things the authorities had insisted on – making sure all the furniture was capable of protecting the patrons in the event of an attack – but she had seen enough bombsites to know that a table with a metal surface wouldn't do much to protect them from a five-pound bomb.

Spread across her desk were documents and forms that she needed to complete, but after staring at them thoughtfully for several minutes, she made her decision and picked up the phone.

After several shrill rings the secretary picked up and she waited while her call was transferred.

'Hello, Mr Boyle? It's Maggie Johnson here again. I said I'd call back today if we hadn't received our allocation and we still haven't.'

Her statement was met with silence and she wasn't sure if she had been disconnected.

'Hello? Mr Boyle?'

'Yes, I'm here, but I don't understand why you haven't received your food stocks. Are you sure there's not been some kind of mix-up?' His voice sounded terse.

'I don't know,' Maggie replied, struggling to keep the exasperation from her voice. 'All I know is that it's the end of the day and we haven't had the delivery. I know exactly what we're expecting...' She reached towards the pile of folders in front of her and pulled one out. 'I have the form right here.'

'Miss Johnson, I have five other establishments to visit tomorrow. Afterwards, I will look into it and get back to you.'

'But can't you do anything in the meantime?'

'No, Miss Johnson, you were given your full allocation at the beginning of the week. Perhaps the supplies for this coming week are just not available yet.'

'How can that be? We didn't get our full allocation last week. It says here that we should get a penny's worth of meat per main meal, a quarter of an ounce of bacon, a quarter of an ounce of butter per person...' Her finger ran down the list on the signed memorandum.

'I know what it says, Miss Johnson,' he interrupted. 'I helped draw up the document. But if it's not available, it's not available.'

'So all we can do is wait?'

'Exactly.'

There was nothing for it; if their allocation didn't arrive by morning, she wouldn't be able to open the doors.

When Maggie went through to the dining hall after her call, the last customer was just leaving.

'Goodnight, Mrs Bevan.'

'Mary, please,' the other woman said, turning towards her.

After returning with her friend on the first day, Mrs Bevan had been back every day since, choosing to sit at the exact same table and enjoy the same tea and scones with homemade rhubarb jam.

'Alright. Goodnight, Mary.'

'Goodnight, dear.'

Maggie locked the door and leaned back against it; she could swear it was the first time she had stood still all day. Not that she would be able to stay still for long – the dining hall was a mess; chairs askew, cups and plates piled up on tables, and crumbs and spills everywhere. She would be lucky to get out of here within the hour again tonight, especially since everyone else seemed to have disappeared.

She dragged herself back towards the kitchen, conscious of the heaviness of her limbs and the soreness of her feet; even her head felt foggy with tiredness. She had fallen into bed after eleven every night this week, reeking of food and cleaning products, and then been up again at five to start all over again.

She would check the kitchen first, she decided, make sure the stations had been cleaned and re-stocked. But when she pushed open the double doors, she found the area was completely spotless, pots and pans all put away and the surfaces clear. Rose and Eliza had their backs to her but they had already changed into their own clothes and were jostling each other to get a look in the mirror.

'What's going on?'

'We're going to celebrate,' Eliza said as she turned, a piece of raw beetroot clenched in her hand, her lower lip a deeper shade of red.

On the bench beside her stood an open tin of Bisto.

Maggie glanced down at their blotchy brown legs. 'Do you want me to give you a hand? You look like a couple of Jerseys!'

'Thanks,' Eliza muttered through tight lips as she continued rubbing beetroot across them, darkening her upper lip until it was also a deep maroon.

'Where are you going?' Maggie asked.

'You mean where are *we* going?' Rose said.

'We? Oh no.' Maggie shook her head. 'I'm not going anywhere. I'm exhausted.'

She slumped against the bench to emphasise her point.

'You'll be fine once you're out. Come on, Maggie – you did it. You opened your restaurant. We need to celebrate!'

Rose was wearing an outfit Maggie had last seen at a cousin's wedding; clearly she meant business.

'It's a lovely idea and I think we should – but not tonight. Maybe next week, or the week after...'

'Or the week after that. Exactly, that's why we have to go tonight. If we don't, we'll never go.'

'We will,' Maggie promised weakly.

Eliza narrowed her eyes. 'Will not. When was the last time you went out for the evening?'

Maggie couldn't remember; not since Peter went away, she knew.

'See?' Rose said smugly. 'You can't remember.'

Maggie sighed. She really wasn't in the mood. It had been an exhausting month and she knew that she wouldn't be good company with so much on her mind. But as she looked from her cousin to her friend, she didn't have the heart to disappoint them.

'Okay, but can I at least go home first and get changed?'

'Absolutely not! If you do, you'll never come back!' Eliza turned and picked up a bag. 'That's why we bought you these...'

Eliza indicated that Maggie should open it, so she reached inside. The fabric was liquid soft between her fingers and when she lifted it out, it was a silk dress in a delicate shade of teal.

'You got this for me?' she gasped.

'Of course. You don't think it would fit either of us, do you?'

'But where did you get it? It's beautiful...'

'The charity shop. It's Jaeger though. And it's in perfect condition.'

Maggie didn't know what to say; she felt both guilty that she didn't really want to go out and overwhelmed by their generosity. The bag still wasn't empty and, reaching in again, she found a pair of nearly new black high-heeled shoes with grey suede edging and a bow.

'Golly, they look expensive!' Her smile faded. 'You haven't used your coupons, have you?'

'It's fine, we don't need anything,' Rose said proudly.

'That's right, we're in whites all the time now anyway,' Eliza added, smoothing down a crimson dress that was stretching at the seams. 'Anyway, you wouldn't catch me dead in those ugly utility clothes.'

'Eliza!' Rose gasped. 'You can't say that.'

'Of course I can, you silly old thing – don't be so pious!'

Maggie was still admiring the clothes, holding on to the worktop as she slipped off her work shoes and pulled the new ones on.

'I don't know what to say...' She kept her head down, hoping they wouldn't notice, but it was too late.

'Oh, Mags – you can't cry,' Eliza said. 'It's meant to be a celebration!'

'I know, I'm sorry. It's just been such a busy time, and I really haven't been sleeping well...'

'I know,' Rose said, looking as if she might cry too. 'We'll open up tomorrow ... you come in later.'

Eliza interrupted to say, 'Hurry, Mags, the bus is in ten minutes,' and ushered her through to her office to change.

Maggie knew there was no point objecting now. 'So where are we going?'

Eliza looked at Rose and then they chorused,

'The Putney Palais, of course!'

Once out of her stained work clothes Maggie
didn't have time to feel tired, because even
though she was sure she must be trailing the smell
of meat and boiled cabbage, she let them whisk
her out the door and down to the bus stop just as
the number 19 bus was pulling in. They settled in
for the short ride to Piccadilly and then made a
quick change to the number 14 for Putney.

Maggie hadn't been to the West End for months
and was distracted by the changed streetscape;
shops that were once familiar to her were now
boarded up with oversized wooden planks. It
wasn't just the shopfronts that had borne the
brunt of the damage but the upper levels too, the
higher storeys of once-elegant buildings singed
and broken.

As the bus made its way through the stream of
early-evening traffic on Oxford Street, Eliza
shared salacious gossip about one of their customers and the postman's wife, and Rose surprised them both by revealing that there was
someone she had a crush on; irritatingly, though,
she wouldn't say who. Maggie had noticed a
change in her recently, she realised: a growing
inner confidence, and a distractedness too.

They passed a gothic mansion block on the
corner of New Bond Street and Maggie glanced in
at the window parallel to hers, coming face to face
with a gargoyle that was missing its nose. It was as
if someone had taken a chisel and used it to chip
away at the intricate stone detail of the facades.

'Don't look now, Mags, you'll want to cry,'

Rose said, squeezing her cousin's forearm.

Selfridges was just coming up on their right-hand side and Maggie had heard about the damage from a friend who had wept as she described how the great stone columns had fallen concertina-like onto the pavements.

'Do you remember the fashion show we went to for your birthday?'

Maggie instantly recalled the day they had watched models parading across the spectacular rooftop gardens and then had afternoon tea as they enjoyed the majestic views over the city. She shuddered to think what London would look like now if she were to stand in exactly the same place; the panorama would be completely changed, the nation's capital disfigured.

She squeezed her eyes tightly shut, wanting to remember it how it had been.

Maybe it was the dwindling light, or the memory of shopping trips with Peter, but now she wanted the journey to be over, to leave the naked mannequins and empty storefronts behind.

It was completely dark by the time they arrived at Putney High Street, but it took only a short time to reach the corner of Putney Bridge Road and the parade of shops and milk bar above which the dance hall sat.

The carpeted stairwell up to the grand double doors was teeming with young women, hair pinned perfectly, lips gleaming like strawberry jelly. As they joined the queue she looked at the two girls in front of her; they wore tight-fitting dresses and high heels, their hair in elaborate coils pinned back off their faces. Then she looked down at her own pale thin legs, and at the same time noticed Rose's; her calves were now white, the gravy powder smudged by the bus ride and a rude contrast to the deep brown of her shins.

'What's wrong with you?' Rose frowned.

'Nothing ... I'm famished.'

'Me too,' Eliza said. 'Don't worry, you can have tea and cake between dances.'

They reached the top of the stairs and were drawing closer to the entrance, the music becoming clearer, the ground vibrating.

Rose and Eliza looked at each other, eyes widening as their excitement grew.

'Who is that?' Rose said, bouncing on her toes.

'Not sure who the orchestra is but I know the song,' Maggie replied recognising the lyrics. 'It's "All or Nothing at All".'

A few minutes later the suited doorman was opening the elegant brass doors and ushering them through. There was a squeal of excitement from behind and they felt the swell of the crowd as the surge forced them along a narrow red-carpeted corridor and out into the hall. Here the music was even louder, the thundering of hundreds of feet across the wooden floor sending vibrations from the soles of her feet, up through her body. Apart from those seated at small round tables around the dance floor, heads leaning close as they strained to listen and be heard, everyone was moving.

Eliza grasped hold of Maggie's wrist and pulled her into the crowd, weaving through the tangle of outstretched hands and tapping feet towards the longer tables pressed against the walls. They were laid with cups and saucers, tea urns and jugs of milk, and small plates of half-eaten cakes and broken biscuits.

Rose screwed up her nose. 'Looks like we are a bit late...'

'I don't care ... I'm hungry,' Eliza said, scooping up a handful of broken wafers and jamming them into her mouth.

'Me too.' Maggie reached for a slice of the crumbled fruitcake but Eliza put out a hand to stop her.

'You can't eat before you dance. Look around you ... there's six girls to every man here. You want to waste your time eating?'

Maggie laughed. 'You're serious?'

'Of course I am!'

And before she had a chance to react Eliza grabbed the cake and ate it.

'Ha! Had you then!'

'Very funny!' Maggie narrowed her eyes. 'And I thought we were here to dance.'

'I thought you wanted to talk – have a conversation about something other than pig swill you said.'

'That would be nice!' Maggie replied.

There were many more girls than men but they were taking it in turns to twirl each other around, hands gripping, bodies bumping, feet stamping.

'I've never seen anyone jive like that,' Maggie said, leaning close to Eliza to make herself heard and pointing at a couple close by.

'Quite something, isn't it?'

'Are you going to have a go?' Rose asked.

'Maybe. Are you asking?' Eliza smiled.

'What – you and her, do that?' Maggie laughed.

Eliza placed her arms out in front of her in the dance position. 'Why not? We're on our feet all day. Pretty agile, I reckon. Come on, Rose. Let's give it a try...'

'You go, I fancy a cigarette,' Rose said and tapped the end of the packet until one came out. She placed the soft tip between her lips.

'Hang on to these then, will you?' Eliza said, thrusting their gas masks at her. Then she grasped Maggie by the hand and pulled her onto the dance floor.

The lights were low, only two grand chandeliers at either end of the dance hall and the small glass wall-sconces filtering a pale warm light, diffusing the clouds of smoke that twisted and swirled with the dancers.

At first Maggie felt awkward, her muscles so tense that she couldn't will her limbs to do as she wanted, making her movements feel jerky and forced. Then Eliza started mucking around, trying to catch the eye of an American GI who danced with another girl, batting her eyelids at him when he looked around. Maggie knew that Eliza's talent for flirting was as notable as her talent for baking so it wasn't long before he gave her a friendly wink and kept glancing back.

As soon as the song ended he came over.

'I'm Mike,' he said, holding out his hand. 'You two make a fine pair of dancers.'

'Thank you. Not the same though, is it?' Eliza smiled brazenly as she took hold of his hand.

'No, it certainly isn't.'

'I'm Eliza, this is my friend Maggie.'

208

'I'd dance with both of you, but I don't want to be greedy. How about I introduce Greg?'

He let go of Eliza's hand.

'No, I'm fine – happy to watch, in fact,' Maggie replied. 'Besides, our friend is over there on her own.'

'That's swell, I'll introduce you to Patrick too then.'

And he raised his arms, trying to get their attention.

'Don't be so antisocial,' Eliza whispered. 'You can't come here and not dance!'

Maggie smiled at Mike. 'You're very thoughtful, thank you.'

There was barely time for an introduction, just a quick exchange of pleasantries, of which she only heard brief snatches. Greg was from Minnesota and worked for the engineers, and was a corporal no less. His thick dark hair and broad features gave him a boyish air, so even though she hadn't wanted to dance with him initially she couldn't help but respond to his friendliness. And she needn't have worried about not knowing the songs or being able to dance, either; as soon as she heard the orchestra playing 'Lullaby of Broadway', her movements became involuntarily. 'Let There Be Love' merged through to 'Blue Champagne' and more Jimmy Dorsey numbers followed. At first the six of them danced in a group but as the songs started to slow and the big band tunes gave way to soothing vocals, she found herself dancing slowly with Greg. He was a lot taller than her so she had to hold her hands uncomfortably high, his left hand lightly around hers, his right hand resting on her waist. But it was the closest she had come to relaxing in months, being swished gently around the dance floor, nestled against the warmth of another human being; an intimacy she hadn't known in a long time.

Rose and Patrick remained talking and smoking close by, while Mike and Eliza danced alongside, Mike's hand pressing into the small of Eliza's back, her arm encircling his neck. She looked graceful in a way that Maggie had never noticed before; she was always usually the practical one, ready to pitch in and get her hands dirty. It felt as if she was intruding so she looked away, her attention falling to the brass badges pinned to Greg's lapel. If it had not been so loud, she would have asked him what they were for. There were quite a number of them for such a young man; perhaps there was more to Greg than met the eye.

The room was now jammed with people, the crowd nearly doubled in size, and even the dancers were squeezed in, pushing up against the spectators' tables and chairs. Subdued light and ribbons of smoke created a haze and screened the edges of the room so that she couldn't even make out where the dancers ended anymore.

Her breathing became uneven, her chest rising and falling as her heart worked faster. And then she began to feel dizzy.

Fighting the instinct to close her eyes, she looked up to where the smoke curled towards the painted roses and cornices of the ceiling. Seeing the crowd pushing against the balustrades on the mezzanine above made her feel worse, as if the crush of people was closing in on her. The room started to spin. She needed to get outside … away from all these people … so many uniforms but none of them Peter … too hot and smoky … and she couldn't see Rose anymore, only Eliza and Mike twirling around and around and around … and then she was falling … but there were hands there to catch her, holding her tightly.

'Are you all right, Maggie? Are you okay?'

But when her eyes blinked open it wasn't Peter.

'Yes. Yes, I think so…'

'Let's get you outside.'

Greg escorted her through the crowd, which parted in front of them, faces turning to stare as they passed.

Once downstairs and on the street, Maggie leaned against the wall.

'How are you feeling?' Greg asked.

She drew a deep breath and felt the oxygen flow through her body and her strength returning.

'Much better,' she said.

'You still look a little out of it, if you don't mind me saying so,' Greg observed. 'Do you live far from here?'

'Yes, unfortunately. But I came with Eliza and Rose. They can help me home … if I can find them.'

He bent closer, his face looking more mature as it took on a concerned expression. 'Do you really think you'll be able to make it back inside?'

She nodded.

'I could help you home if you like.' His southern American drawl was soft and reassuring.

'That's kind of you, but it's best if I go with them.'

'Really? I'm leaving now anyway...'

She had been glad of his help but now she just wanted to get home, sink into bed and feel the pillow beneath her head.

'It's fine. You've done enough. Do you remember what Eliza looks like?'

'She's the pretty blonde, the one dancing with Mike?'

'Yes ... would you mind fetching her for me?'

'You'll be okay on your own?'

'I'll be fine.'

'Okay then. Don't go anywhere...'

'No, I won't – and thank you,' she said, forcing a smile.

He strode away, and for a moment she felt a twinge of regret; maybe she should have let him walk her to the bus or see her home. Part of her would have liked to talk with him some more; there was an easiness between them – or perhaps it was just the concern of a man in uniform that felt familiar. It reminded her of the times she and Peter had walked along the nearby embankment, stopping at the Star and Garter to have a drink and watch the rise or fall of the river. She considered walking to the end of the street on her own, standing on the bridge and looking down into the inky water, letting the gentle motion of the tide wash away her tiredness. Her legs were still a little shaky, though, so she opened her bag, took out a small compact and handkerchief, and pressed it to the sides of her nose where tiny beads of perspiration had formed.

There was no clock to see what time it was, but it felt as if Greg had been gone for ages. What if he couldn't find Eliza, or they decided they didn't want to leave? she fretted. Then she heard her name being called and forced her eyes open as Eliza and Rose hurried towards her.

'Are you alright?' Eliza asked.

'I think so ... I just need to get to bed.'

'What happened?' Rose said, taking off her jacket and placing it around Maggie's shoulders.

'One minute I was dancing with Greg, the next I was dizzy and passed out. Trust me to make a fool of myself on my first night out!'

'See?' Rose said, looking at Eliza. 'I told you she wouldn't have just gone outside with him.'

Eliza had been trying to pair Maggie up ever since the restaurant opened, pointing out any handsome man who walked through the door, asking the other girls if they had any brothers and interrogating the poor unsuspecting delivery men. Even Mr Boyle had been under consideration until she realised what an annoying man he really was.

'Well, at least he knows where to find you,' Eliza said triumphantly.

'What?'

Eliza bit her lip and looked at Rose.

'She told him where the restaurant is,' Rose explained. 'He said he wanted to call in on you tomorrow, to check that you're okay.'

'If we see you onto the bus, do you think you'll be able to make it home on your own?' Eliza asked.

'Eliza!' said Rose.

'What?'

'How can you even suggest it? We can't leave

her like this.'

'But what about Mike?' Eliza said.

'She's right, I'll be fine,' Maggie assured her cousin. 'Just walk me to the bus stop.'

Rose glared at Eliza. 'So, were you planning on letting Mike take you home then?'

'Why not? You know what they say.' Eliza grinned.

'What do they say?'

'Never pass up an opportunity!'

'What about you, Rose?' Maggie asked. 'You and Patrick seemed to be getting along quite well.'

'He is nice, but I told you – there's someone else.'

But when they pressed her to reveal a name, she shook her head stubbornly and refused to answer.

Chapter Sixteen

When tomatoes are available the wise housewife will preserve some for use in the winter. They are valuable then, not only for the colour and flavour they give to dishes, but also for the protective vitamins they contain. Don't forget that you get more food value from bottled tomatoes if they are eaten 'straight from the jar', since further cooking destroys their vitamins.
Ministry of Food, War Cookery Leaflet No. 24

Mr Boyle would be there at any moment to go

over the accounts and Maggie wanted to be ready for him; there was a whole list of things she needed to sort out, including the supplies and reviewing the menus. She had been going over the paperwork for hours and according to Mr Boyle's calculations, and the information in front of her, there should be more machinery. They were at least a dough machine and a mincer short, and Eliza never let her hear the end of the fact that she still had to mix most of the bread and cakes by hand. Meanwhile, six weeks after opening the deliveries were still erratic. Maggie had spent the whole morning trying to work out if there was anything she had missed, making sure she had entered the right amounts in the correct columns, checking and rechecking her sums. Maths had never been her strong point at school, arithmetic even less so, but Mr Boyle had told her that the sooner she showed a profit the sooner she would receive the capital expenditure grants. But she couldn't see any way to make more cuts; surely Mr Boyle couldn't expect the restaurant to operate with any less staff.

Just as she was about to make the calculation a fourth time there was a light knock at the office door and Rose stuck her head round.

'He's here.'

'Oh, blimey! Just offer him a cup of tea, will you? I'll be there in a tick.'

She needed to remember what Eliza had said; flatter him first, tell him what he wanted to hear, then go in hard with her requests. Their recent conversations had been fraught with tension because of the erratic food supplies and she couldn't afford to let personal prejudice get in the way; the restaurant had to stay open.

She closed the ledger, replaced the pen in the desk tidy and scanned the office. It was neat and clean, the accounts were in order – well as much as they were ever going to be – and they had thoroughly cleaned all the areas of the restaurant he would want to inspect.

She was still worried as she left her office, but once in the kitchen she felt a sweep of pride at what she saw, an impressive range of equipment operated by a skilled team in smart kitchen whites. Having been drilled about the visit they had all responded positively, volunteering to stay back the night before and help with extra jobs. She wasn't too worried about the restaurant; they had settled into a good rhythm, everyone seeming to work well together, functioning strongly as a team. There was a steady amount of customers and a growing number of regulars among the locals and workers from the nearby factories and dairies. Only last week they had held their first 'knit and natter night'; her landlady, Mrs Foster, was a member of the local WVS and she had asked Maggie if they might use the restaurant as a venue for their monthly knit-in. She was overwhelmed by the response, and the one hundred squares they produced for the Red Cross blankets over multiple cups of tea and buttered brazils. Thank goodness all remnants of the wool and laughter and gossip had now gone; somehow she didn't think that Mr Boyle would approve. In fact, she had even told Robbie to keep a low profile today rather than playing in the backyard as he had taken to doing, popping his head in between gardening jobs for a chat and the chance of something to eat No, she wasn't concerned about the restaurant; it was the shortage of food-stuffs that she needed to address.

She checked her hair in the small wall mirror, parted her lips to make sure there was no trace of lipstick on her teeth and strode confidently into the dining hall.

Maggie couldn't see him at first, scanning the tables for sight of his small dark bearded face, but then she saw Eliza showing him around, arms swinging enthusiastically as she pointed things out to him.

Maggie went to join them.

'Good morning, Mr Boyle.'

'Hello, Miss Johnson. How are you?'

He shook her hand vigorously and gave her what was surely his first genuine smile.

'The restaurant looks very pleasant, Miss Johnson, very pleasant indeed. It is more than adequate.' He nodded his head approvingly as he looked around, taking in the painted walls and the already significant queue of people that had built up since they had been standing there.

'As you know, it was a bit of a challenge given the short timeframe,' Maggie replied, 'but the decorating has been completed since your last visit and I am very happy with the results.'

'"And for all this nature is never spent,"' Mr Boyle replied.

'Sorry?'

'God's Grandeur...'

'I'm sorry, I don't follow.'

217

'It's Hopkins, you know, the poet. Gerald Manley Hopkins...'

'No, I don't actually. I'm more of a Wodehouse fan myself,' she said, forcing herself to be polite. 'Anyway, I'm sure you must be pressed for time so I'll show you around and then we can go into the office.' She started towards the kitchen.

'As you like.'

'Well, everyone knows that's Shakespeare,' she said glancing back at him over her shoulder.

'Very good, Miss Johnson. Oh touché.'

Maggie grimaced; it was one of the irksome things about him that she had noticed during their meetings, his peculiar habit of making quotes. She knew why: he had dropped into conversation once that he had been a classics teacher at university before being seconded to the ministry. It became obvious to see then that he carried his snobbery around with him like a stuffy old briefcase, but his pretensions were quite wasted on her, she had no appreciation for the quotes and had a sneaking idea that they were his misguided way of impressing her. Or perhaps she was wrong and maybe it was just that he would rather be talking about anything other than flour deliveries and the shortage of bains-marie.

After a brief inspection of the restaurant and kitchen, during which she patiently answered his pedantic questions, she showed him through to the small office, intending to raise the issue of the deliveries.

'I see that you are doing the full two hundred and fifty covers a day,' he said, glancing up from his own paperwork. 'That's quite impressive for a new establishment. Quite impressive indeed.'

'Yes, we're getting there, but I really do need to speak to you about the stock deliveries...'

He glanced around for a chair to sit in.

'I'm sorry, I don't have a spare chair, but please, take mine and I can show you the accounts. There are a number of items that I haven't been able to reconcile...'

'I'm not here to go through accounts, Miss Johnson – I expect those to be sent to my office fortnightly as requested. I wish to talk to you about the mobile canteens, and I thought there were pressing matters you wanted to discuss?'

'Yes, there are ... the shortages. The last fortnight and the one before, we didn't receive some of the items on the purchase orders. Items it says we have received.'

He took a cursory glance at the forms.

'If you're not getting your requested proportion of stocks, it's because you are already operating a deficit, Miss Johnson, and you aren't able to pay for them yet.'

'I thought you said it was because there wasn't enough supply?'

'That may be the case too, although there are the ministry's emergency stores; those can be accessed in extreme circumstances, but you first need to demonstrate that you are able to balance the books, so to speak.'

'But that's not going to happen for weeks, maybe months what with the initial outlays – especially if we don't have enough meals to sell because we can't get the ingredients we need to make them!'

'And therein lies the conundrum, Miss Johnson.'

'Well, is there anything you can do?'

'An allowance has been made for the adaptation of buildings and installation of equipment, and these costs are amortised over a specific period...'

'How long?'

'That hasn't been determined yet.'

'Then how do you know how well the restaurant is doing, if you haven't set the time period for repayment?'

'We have procedures, Miss Johnson; we have to follow them.'

'So,' Maggie said, taking a deep breath, a warm flush creeping up her neck to her cheeks, 'are you saying that you can't give me any more stock because I can't afford to pay for it because I'm paying back costs?'

'It's not quite that simple; you have a grant for capital and that can be repaid at a later date, but, yes, effectively the setup costs must be paid out of your first income.'

'So in the meantime what – the restaurant closes and the community have nowhere to eat?'

He took a deep breath and stood up, and for a moment she thought she had gone too far.

'I know it seems frustrating, but it's not going to come to that. And there's no use getting cross – not with me, anyway.'

'Well, who should I get cross with then, Mr Boyle? What do the other restaurants do? They must be facing the same problem.'

'No, I'm certain that your situation is quite

unique. The other restaurants have all been slow burners, so to speak, serving small numbers at first so they have not had such a high demand for ingredients.'

'It doesn't make sense, any of it, I would never have...' She stopped.

'You would never have what, Miss Johnson?'

She didn't want him to know that she would never have taken it on if she'd known how frustrating it would be dealing with his bureaucracy, and all the time she would spend stuck in her office dealing with his damned forms and circulars.

'I'm sure you are doing your best,' she said and smiled.

'As soon as there's an operating surplus, I'm sure you'll find that there will be no problem getting the stock.'

'That is rather ridiculous, though. How am I supposed to make a surplus when there's not enough to sell?'

'You have shown yourself to be a very resourceful young woman, I am sure your talents won't let you down.' He moved to the door, then turned back abruptly.

'And about the boy, Miss Johnson?'

'What boy?'

'You know very well which boy – the one who has been sleeping here. The authorities have been notified, so you'd do well to warn him that it's high time he went home. It would be better for everyone, especially you, if they didn't find him here.'

For the rest of the day, Maggie went over the conversation again and again in her mind. What had

221

Mr Boyle meant by her 'resourcefulness'? Was he suggesting that she should get supplies elsewhere – the black market even? Surely the uptight Mr Boyle would never consider such a proposition. And there was the matter of emergency training for the staff. She had called a staff meeting for that afternoon, and would explain to them what was going on. And then there was Robbie; 'It's high time he went home,' Mr Boyle had said. If only he had a home! But he didn't, so she had to help find him one. But how? If she contacted the London County Council, who knew where he might be sent: hundreds of miles away, maybe even to Scotland or overseas. He would never forgive her if that happened, she knew.

By the time she reached the dining hall for the staff meeting, everyone was already waiting for her.

'The reason I have asked you to stay behind is because there has been a development: the ministry has requested that all British Restaurants and communal feeding staff should be trained to operate emergency meal centres and mobile canteens.'

The women looked at each other and began to whisper, and Maeve's hand shot up.

'Is that as well as working here?'

'Not for the time being, no, but it looks as though it could end up that way.'

'How can we do that?'

She took in the sea of worried faces and realised that getting them used to the idea of the emergency meals centres and mobile canteens, and trained in how to operate them, might be more difficult than she had thought.

'Look, I know that many of you're already working with the Women's Voluntary Services or the Auxiliary Fire Service, and this won't affect you, but for everyone else there will be a requirement.'

She waited for the murmuring to subside.

'They are drawing up guidelines as we speak, so that could change, but in any event, emergency feeding will take priority over the restaurant so you will need to be prepared...'

Gillian raised a hand. 'Who's going to train us?'

'That'll be the responsibility of the ministry. I'm not sure yet how they are organising it, but it will involve learning how to use the emergency cooking equipment'

'Like what?' Eliza interrupted. 'An invisible fire that Jerry won't see?'

A half-hearted ripple of laughter went through the room.

'Not invisible, but fires, yes. Has anyone here used the trench system or braziers, maybe in the Girl Guides?'

There was a small show of hands.

'Well, those of you who haven't will be taught how to set up a campfire for cooking with bricks to provide draught channels and a tripod to support a roasting spit.'

'Doesn't sound too difficult,' Rose said, glancing round at the others.

'Well, it is,' Maggie responded firmly. 'A field kitchen is one of the toughest environments you can work in. There are all sorts of issues to deal with: safety, the weather, cracking plates from the direct heat, burns...'

There were a lot of questions that she didn't

have answers for, but she had told them enough for now. It was best not to share too much detail yet or tell them how difficult it could be working in the field, soaking dried vegetables for hours before they could be used, or how they would need to serve everything extra hot because of the increased risk of food poisoning. And no point telling them about the painstakingly long time it took cutting small portions so that one serve was readily available for a child but could be doubled or trebled for an adult. Or even how hard it was to manage the crowds, telling them not to rush their meals but encouraging them to be quick enough so that they could serve more people. She would wait to tell them about the difficulties because, for now, she had more pressing problems to deal with: how she was going to get more supplies for her own kitchen, for example, and finding a home for Robbie.

Chapter Seventeen

...soups may be made nourishing and sustaining by adding body building food such as milk, cheese, eggs, fish and meat. Broth is a soup of this kind and is popular with the North Country housewife who prefers to cook some of her meat ration in this way and serve it in place of a meat dish.
Ministry of Food, War Cookery Leaflet No. 15

The three students from the local art college

224

arrived promptly at five o'clock as arranged; two girls and a boy, conspicuously young and happily chain-smoking as they carried their own paint-brushes and equipment through the emptying restaurant. Workers from the council had in-conveniently left the ladders and scaffolding clut-tering up the backyard much earlier in the day.

'Don't forget to leave the key under the brick,' Maggie repeated again when six o'clock came and went and, reluctantly, she had to leave.

Their blasé response hadn't given her much confidence but she had promised Mr Boyle that she would help with some issues at a nearby mobile canteen. It had niggled at her for the last couple of hours; should she stay and keep an eye on the painters and risk upsetting him or just leave them to get on with it? She finally decided that currying favour with Mr Boyle was more important, especially since they had been forced to close their doors again the previous week when they had run out of food. Even though it had taken her weeks to arrange the painting, and days to decide what she would like them to paint, she had eventually left them to it.

She entered the restaurant the next morning to find that the plain white walls were now decorated with a mural that took up the entire left side of the dining hall. It was a streetscape of London and its major attractions from before the war, when they had taken for granted the great spires and domes of their city. The two stone towers of Tower Bridge, the dome of St Paul's, Nelson's column, the Houses of Parliament and Buckingham

Palace, spreading out from the banks of the river that now threaded across the wall. She had been to exhibitions and galleries before but had never seen anything that had made her feel quite like this. Goosebumps pricked her skin and a lump formed in her throat.

'Makes you feel lucky to live here, doesn't it?'

Maggie glanced around at Tom and then back at the mural, noticing tiny details she hadn't seen at first: the statues of lions on the columns, the fine spray of water from the fountains.

'Certainly does.'

'Did you tell them what to paint?'

'Only on this wall.' She indicated the wall behind her, where a panorama of the English countryside spread before them. 'I thought it would be calming, since most of us don't get out to the country anymore.'

'They both look terrific.'

'Yes, they do, don't they? And you can choose what you want to look at depending on the mood you are in...'

Tom looked amused. 'I think I'll go out of town this afternoon,' he mused. 'Maybe take a picnic. Would you like to join me?'

'Well, yes, thank you,' said Maggie, playing along. 'I don't mind if I do.'

'What's in the picnic basket?' he asked.

'Oh, well, now you're talking ... we've got some roast beef sandwiches – silverside, I believe. And some salmon quiches. Fresh oranges and, of course, your favourite chocolate mousse cake.'

'I heard a rumour that there is a talented young cook here who makes a terrific game pie...'

'She does, and she has access to an enviable pantry. All sorts of goodies.'

She was a young girl again and they were back in one of Ernest and Tom's games; Maggie slipped her arm through Tom's as they carried on the pretence, laughing at their expanding haul as they encouraged each other to rampage greedily through an imaginary larder. For a while, their make-believe world was a delicious distraction and they even agreed on the perfect picnic spot: a small village in the Sussex countryside that they had both visited as children. There was a pond with ducks, a cricket green and a small teashop on the miniature high street, where – if they should, God forbid, run out of goodies – they would go for a cream tea. Afterwards, they would walk the cobbled streets, peering through the tiny windows of white Georgian terraces until they came to the antique shop whose small doorway they would bend to fit through. There they wouldn't have to hurry; there wouldn't be any meals to prepare or stock to order or schedules to write. They wouldn't need ration books, they wouldn't have to rub castor oil into their cracked and peeling hands. Yes, that was just the sort of afternoon Maggie would like to have – but it seemed to belong to a distant past. Who knew if it would ever be possible to recapture it?

'I think it's working,' Tom said, disturbing her melancholy reflections.

'I think you're right.'

'We could spend hours here...'

'I know; I hadn't thought about that. I just thought it would be nice for the customers – but we don't want them to stay too long. It is a bit of a distraction.'

'A good distraction though.'

She smiled at him; typical Tom, always looking on the bright side. How good it was to have him around again.

She had turned down the posters that were offered under the ministry's decoration policy. The works that were going to be supplied were of ships and planes; the air force and navy's finest machines to invoke a collective national pride. Maggie thought the last thing people would want to look at over lunch were machines of destruction. So she got in touch with the British Institute for Adult Education and they supplied the local art students – now she couldn't help but feel pleased that her resourcefulness had paid off.

'You know, there are some restaurants in Westminster that have got pictures from the Royal Collection,' she said, admiring the detail and colour of the birds' feathers.

'Do you expect the King will lend us one?'

'Oh no, definitely not. The conditions need to be exceptional – no condensation, for a start. Imagine telling Eliza she isn't allowed to make any steam!'

'Impossible!'

The early-morning sun spilled through the skylights bringing the rich tones of the mural to life, illuminating the undulating countryside. Maggie closed her eyes, imagining being outdoors with the warmth of the sun on her skin. She wondered what Janek would make of the mural; whether the images would be a welcome reminder of where he grew up, or whether it would be a disturbing memory of a home that he might never see again. He had finally talked about his home the night before, when he'd stayed to help with the liver and sausage hotpot that now had a permanent place on the lunchtime menu. The ministry wanted it baked or stewed and served with potatoes and cabbage or boiled rice. She hadn't much experience making sausages, as they had always been delivered straight from the butchers, but since they now had to use every last scrap and sinew, she had asked Janek to show her how to make them herself. He had begun by washing pigs' intestines and rinsing them with salted water, arranging them in a long coil so that the lengths could be cut as needed. Then he had minced pork shoulder and combined them with herbs and sugar, adding plenty of salt and pepper. He had then forced the mixture through a nozzle to fill the intestine with sausage meat, his powerful hands and arms able to turn the grinder's handles far quicker than she was able. In lieu of a smokehouse, they used one of the disused sheds at the back. Afterwards, she and Janek had sat under the night sky talking and eating his homemade Polish pancakes as they waited until the sausages were ready.

'You alright, Maggie?' Tom interrupted.

Maggie returned to the present with a start. 'I'm fine. Just tired.'

'Been burning the candles at both ends?'

'No, that's Liza you're thinking of.' She managed a smile. It had been a good few weeks since their night out at the Palais and even though she tried to get enough sleep there was always something to do and she was constantly weary. It didn't seem to stop Eliza, though, who had seen Mike several times since. Greg had appeared at the restaurant the day after her dizzy spell and asked her out again, Maggie had politely declined, and he hadn't asked again. 'What about you, Tom? Are you alright?'

'I'm fine. No concerns here.'

'You know, you've made quite an impression on Maeve...'

'Yes, well, best not talk about that now.'

'Tom Washington, I do believe you are blushing!'

'Come on, Maggie, give it a rest.'

'Sorry,' she murmured. It was strange for Tom to be so sensitive, she thought; he was usually ready to shrug things off.

'I'm enjoying myself here, Maggie. I really do appreciate you giving me a chance. It's good to still be useful.'

Just then the door opened and Maggie turned to greet their first customer only to see that it was Maeve.

Maggie glanced at Tom.

He didn't return her look, but as he turned to leave Maggie noticed how he brought up his hand, self-consciously running his fingers through his blond wavy hair.

It was well into the lunchtime rush and Robbie sat on a bench eyeing the line of men and women as they shuffled towards the servery; men with hats pulled down tightly over their heads, women wrapped in thick dark coats, the fabric of their uniforms or overalls poking out beneath. It amazed him that they could be so patient, stay in such an orderly queue, when they were so close to the source of those delicious smells!

There had been a queue when he arrived nearly an hour ago and it wasn't showing any sign of abating. No wonder Maggie was always so busy these days. He had no idea where she was now. He'd stuck his head into the kitchen when he first arrived, and she wasn't there; nor was she here in the dining hall. But he really needed to find her; he had been to the country to see his ma again and he knew it was time to tell Maggie about her. The lying was becoming a bit of a strain; he was sure he would let something slip, and he was feeling really guilty about deceiving her now that he had got to know her well. She had been so good to him, giving him food, helping him look for his dad – and she had even got him interested in school again.

He tore off his jacket and dropped it on the bench beside him; it was warm and busy here, quite unlike the quiet damp of the school storeroom where he returned when he wasn't allowed to sleep at the restaurant. And there was food – lots of it! Maggie had told him he could have one meal a day but he had eaten it already and still had a gnawing in his belly. What was more, the corned beef with cabbage had reminded him of his ma's; there were loads of spuds in it, just like hers. The only problem was the steamed jam pudding; there wasn't nearly enough jam. He'd had to press the sponge against the roof of his mouth to extract every last tiny drop, and when he had sucked that out, the doughy sponge hadn't melted on his tongue like it was supposed to but stayed there in a thick floury wedge.

He dragged his finger across his empty plate for the umpteenth time until there wasn't a single speck of gravy left on it. The line of waiting customers was growing, snaking right back to the door, and the noisy lunchtime conversations drowned out the clattering from the kitchen and the drone of traffic outside.

Right, if that bald bloke in the brown coat can get to the counter by the time the clock reaches twelve forty-five, then I can go up for more.

Robbie licked his lips and waited, watching intently and then sliding along the bench with each step that the man moved closer to the counter.

When he had visited his mum and sisters at the weekend, they had spent the whole day out in the fields and orchards picking fruit before the real harvesters began, and when his sisters had gone to bed, he helped his mum with the peeling and slicing. They had made a gigantic pot of sweet sticky jam from the apples and plums into which he had dipped great springy doorsteps of bread smothered in local butter. A big blob of jam – that's what Eliza's pudding needed – so that when he pressed the pudding to the roof of his mouth, all the jam squished out the sides!

The man was only a few feet away from the counter now; it looked as if it might be his lucky day. But then he caught sight of Tom looking in his direction. Robbie ducked down out of sight, shifting along the seat again until he could go no further.

There were now only two people in front of his man and only three minutes to go on the clock so he swivelled his legs over the bench and headed towards the gap that had just opened up. Tom wasn't looking anymore and two men he recognised from the dairy were turned to face each other, locked in conversation so they hadn't noticed the advance of the queue.

He slipped quietly in front of them.

'I'd be fed up too, if I were you,' one of them was saying. 'You shouldn't have to do it if the others don't.'

'That's my point,' the other replied. 'What's good for the goose should be good for the gander ... that's what my missus is always telling me. Different when the boot's on the other foot, isn't it!'

The man in the brown coat stepped up to the counter. *Hooray!* Robbie cheered silently. *Roast potatoes and treacle tart here I come!*

Luckily, Gillian had gone on a break and her replacement hadn't seen him come around once already. He held out his plate while she piled on a large portion of roast meat and vegetables.

'Bit extra for kiddies,' she said, winking as she added another potato.

He dodged around Tom and headed straight for the cutlery stand, already casting his eyes around for a place to sit. The dining hall was full except for a space where a group of market-sellers were leaving, so he squeezed in between two businessmen and a couple of old ladies.

'You look like you're enjoying that,' the younger

233

businessman observed as Robbie shovelled food into his mouth.

'It's good,' he spluttered, swallowing in a hurry.

'Can we take your photo?'

The other man pointed towards a flashy-looking camera on the bench beside him.

'Why?'

They looked decent enough, both wearing trilby hats and posh-looking suits, but why on earth did they want his picture?

'We're from the *Highbury & Islington Gazette*,' the first man explained, 'and we're doing a piece on the place. Seems like it's a bit of a hit with the locals. You have to be a regular or very patient to get a seat here.'

'Yeah, but people been coming from all over too,' Robbie said, 'even outside London. Maggie had to turn some of them away.' He dragged a roast potato through the stream of gravy. 'You serious about the picture?'

'Of course we are – get your face alongside the mayor's.'

'I dunno...'

He didn't want to draw any more attention to himself than he needed to, but then again, if he got his picture in the paper, his dad might see it.

'Alright then.' He grinned. 'I'll do it.'

'Good. Just wait right here, our photographer should be back any minute.'

Robbie finished his last mouthful, pushed his plate away and asked the man, 'Why can't *you* take the picture?'

'I'm a reporter – typewriter's the tool of my trade.'

'So you'll write the piece then?'

'Yes, I'll review the food and interview a few people before I leave so I can get some quotes.'

'Will you interview Maggie?'

'Yes, of course, but we've got to come back later for that.'

The reporter had a really soothing voice, one that Robbie thought people wouldn't mind answering questions to; that he might ask them anything and they couldn't help but tell the truth.

'What else do you write about?' Robbie wanted to know.

'Other stuff that goes on around here mostly, but sometimes we go up the West End.'

'So what's the worst thing you've ever seen?'

'Well, that depends,' he replied, raising an eyebrow.

'Depends on what?'

The reporter leaned forward conspiratorially. 'Depends on whether you are talking about murder or kidnapping.'

Robbie sat back abruptly, deciding a change of subject was in order. 'Will you print something I say, then?'

'Yes, we'll put the quote with your picture. What would you say about Maggie's Kitchen?'

Robbie grinned. 'Best nosh in the whole of London!'

When the photographer still hadn't arrived a few minutes later, Robbie started to get restless. Excusing himself, he went to find Maggie; he needed to tell her about his ma before he lost his nerve. So when he couldn't find her in the kitchen or the backyard, where he had tied Spoke, he headed through to the office.

He could hear raised voices before he reached the door, and even though he knew he shouldn't listen, he couldn't help himself. He had never heard her so angry before.

'I'm not sure how he expects us to operate on thin air! What am I to tell everyone?'

'It'll be alright, you'll see...'

He recognised Eliza's voice and could see a strip of her uniform through the crack in the door.

'Really? Are you going to tell them we won't be opening, then? That there's not enough for the regular meal service?'

'It's not come to that, has it? It's going to look bad on him...'

Eliza seemed to be trying to calm Maggie down, but it didn't appear to be working.

'It *has* come to that, Eliza. I've got to go close the doors again!'

'Really?'

'I just wish I could look him in the eye and ask how this has happened again.'

'Is it anything to do with the Private Caterers Association? I've seen them in the papers, complaining we get allocations that they don't.'

'I know; it doesn't help... Perhaps he has been giving them our rations to keep them happy and persuade them to stay out of the news? Goodness knows, Eliza – but we need to do something...'

'Maybe we're going about it the wrong way,' Eliza suggested. 'Rather than keep telling him why it's a problem, you should just *show* him why we need more supplies. Why don't you invite him for lunch so he can see for himself?'

Robbie heard Maggie sigh.

'I just don't want to let everyone down,' she said quietly.

'I know, Mags, I know.'

Robbie knew it too, and he wished there was something he could do to help.

Chapter Eighteen

Dishes using cooked vegetables should, as far as possible, be served with a fresh salad, or a serving of freshly-cooked greens to make up for the vitamin C lost in cooking and re-heating.
Ministry of Food, War Cookery Leaflet No. 11

When she arrived at the restaurant a few days later, Maggie was greeted by an unfamiliar scraping noise coming from the backyard – not the light scratching that Spoke often made, but the sound of metal hitting against a stony surface. It was still too early for deliveries so she cautiously tiptoed towards the back door and stretched to peer out the window.

Although they were only silhouettes in the dim morning light, she recognised the solid outline of Janek gracefully bending and hoeing, and the smaller figure of Robbie, quick and jerky alongside.

The metal bolts on the back door screeched as she pulled them across and they both looked up.

'Morning, Maggie,' Robbie smiled cheerily.

'What are you doing here? I thought you were supposed to be staying away?'

'Yeah, well, I couldn't.'

Janek put down his hoe and came towards her, the dull fingers of light creeping across his face, accentuating the hollows and contours. She could see how handsome he must have been as a younger man; how impressive his features still were despite the lines that stress and loss had etched onto his skin.

'Robbie said that you needed some help.'

'I do,' she said, still surprised, 'but I never expected *him* to do anything about it – especially something like this!'

'This is the best way – now you will have your own supply.'

'Yes, I suppose we will.'

She stepped forward, taking care not to tread on any of the freshly turned grooves and paced to the fence and back, exploring their work. With two small hoes they had managed to turn most of the yard, transforming the pale stony soil into a rich deep brown earth. There were trays of seedlings on the ground, huge logs and piles of wood stacked against the wall, and a newly rigged-up outside tap and hose.

'I don't know what to say...' she said, glancing fondly at Robbie.

'Don't say anything then,' Janek offered.

'Bit of breakfast wouldn't go amiss,' Robbie interrupted.

'It's the least I can do,' she said, ruffling his hair. 'What can I get you, Janek?'

'Nothing, I will eat when I finish.'

It seemed such an obvious thing to do that she couldn't believe she hadn't thought about doing it herself – although this way was much better; she would get to see more of Janek. The unexpected direction of her thoughts surprised her and she turned her face away.

'How long have you been here?' she asked. 'You must have started when it was still dark.'

'We have been working quickly. You will be the one who needs patience while it grows.'

'What have you planted?'

'Just carrots and potatoes for now, but you will be able to grow most things – sprouts, kale, beetroot.'

'That's wonderful.' Maggie had seen enough potatoes to last a lifetime and had learned entirely new things to do with carrots – she had created pies and pasties, cobblers and casseroles, she had made war-and-peace pudding, croquettes and curries. Some different dishes would be a real treat.

Mr Boyle wouldn't like it, and she wasn't sure how she would deal with him, but he had praised her resourcefulness, so it was time she put that quality to good use!

It was late in the afternoon by the time Janek and Robbie had prepared the soil, built the supporting beds and established the seedlings. Janek offered to return after work for a few days to help with watering, and said he had showed Robbie how to rig up a device that would scare away the birds. He told Maggie an amusing story of how he had designed one back home but, far from discouraging the birds, they seemed to like the light musical sound it made when the wind lifted the tins and banged them against the wooden posts. The one he designed for her was different though; it had to be dark, for a start, and non-reflective. He was far more talkative than usual, buoyed by news of the Atlantic Charter and the joint proclamation that Roosevelt and Churchill had made, declaring that they were fighting to 'ensure life, liberty, independence and religious freedom and to preserve the rights of man and justice'. Maggie wasn't sure exactly how this was going to change things, but Janek seemed to think it was a breakthrough, and one in the eye for Hitler.

Back in her office afterwards she found a basket full of black-painted tin cans and a length of string on the floor, a hand-drawn sketch of Janek's apparatus lying discarded beside it. Not much of it had been completed and Robbie lay open-mouthed and snoring on a mattress inside the Morrison shelter with Spoke, one of the cans modelled into a cylindrical engine ready for his next aircraft resting by his side.

Maggie kneeled down and gently shook him awake. 'You can't sleep here. You know that.'

He blinked at her sleepily. 'Just this once,' he pleaded.

'Come on, Robbie, I mean it. You know what'll happen if Mr Boyle finds out.'

'You're just like Ma,' he grumbled. 'You worry too much.'

There he went again, talking about his ma. Maggie had intentionally avoided asking about his mother for fear of upsetting him, but he had brought her up in conversation several times recently and not with any appearance of grief. She was about to pursue the subject when she heard Janek calling his farewells, his voice echoing through the empty kitchen. By the time she reached the back door, he had finished packing his tools and was about to leave.

'I was hoping to catch you,' she said, resting her hand on his arm, her eyes now level with his. 'I want to thank you properly. I've been meaning to say something to you all day...'

The intensity of his gaze was so distracting that she wanted to look away but she needed to say what she had planned.

'I can't tell you how grateful I am to you for this. And even though I can't pay you for it now, I will, sometime soon.'

'I told you, there is no charge.'

'I insist. Why should you do this for me?'

'It is for the community, Malgorzata; it is what we do for each other in Poland.'

'Well, it's very generous. You must eat here, whenever you want.'

'That is kind, but the money you gave me for the seeds is more than enough.'

'Even so, your time...'

'That is one thing I do have to spare.'

There was a note of sadness in his voice and she wanted to ask him what he meant, but he was already hauling the large canvas tool bags across his body, the straps crisscrossing his torso and making him look every bit the soldier she knew he wished he could be.

'Goodbye, Malgorzata.'

'Goodbye.'

She watched as he went through the gate into the back lane, listening to his footsteps as they took him away towards the canal and his shortcut back home. Perhaps if she could find out more about where he went and what he did, she could help him just as he had helped her.

In the shadows she hadn't been able to make out if his expression held the same anticipation she felt, or whether it had been altered by a sense of duty. Whatever it was, as she turned back into the yard her body felt charged, a sensation that was at once familiar and unknown; and with it came a nervous tremor, as if something new and exciting had been set in motion.

Chapter Nineteen

SALADS:

There is hardly a root or green vegetable that does not deserve a place in a salad. Use them raw whenever you can. A good mixed salad with wheatmeal bread and a little grated cheese makes a complete meal. So serve and enjoy a salad or raw vegetable sandwich every day.

Ministry of Food, War Cookery Leaflet No. 5

Although it had been Eliza's idea to invite Mr Boyle for a special luncheon, Maggie insisted that some of the locals should be there too, so he could meet those whose lives were most directly affected by the shortages. Maggie had made Woolton pie as a special – it had been named after the Minister of Food himself – and she had managed to broach the disruptions in supply and felt quietly confident at his response. In fact, the whole luncheon was proving to be quite a success.

Mrs Foster was wearing her Sunday best, and Mr and Mrs Cross and the warden Bill Drummond and his wife Janey had all mingled well, but Mr Boyle had talked with Mrs Bevan for most of the lunch. Maggie really couldn't imagine how they could have so much in common and was trying hard to listen in on their conversation.

'What a clever man you are,' Mrs Bevan said with a sigh. 'And what a splendid job you are doing under such difficult circumstances.'

Maggie could hardly believe her ears; she couldn't have wished for more sincere flattery if she had given Mrs Bevan the script herself, and she had never seen him looking so relaxed. It was hardly surprising that they remained fixed where they were and requested more Pathfinder pudding, but she had to refuse simply because there wasn't any left.

At quarter past two, Maggie rose from her seat and, murmuring her excuses, left the table.

Rose was filling in as cashier for Tom and browsing through the *Daily Express* when Maggie approached.

'I've got to go out for a while, Rose; there's another mobile canteen I need to check on. But I want you to make sure he leaves here happy. It's really important.'

243

'Of course,' Rose replied, still scanning the pages for the horoscopes. 'I'll make sure he has everything he needs – although maybe just leaving him with Mrs Bevan would be a better idea...'

'I know, quite the surprise, isn't she?' Maggie looked over her shoulder at the pair. Mrs Bevan had evidently said something amusing and they were both laughing. 'She seems to have quite charmed him.'

'Dark horse,' Rose said.

'She's certainly one to cherish,' Maggie replied.

When Maggie had left, Rose turned her attention back to her horoscope.

A day to assert yourself. Make up your own mind.

When she next glanced up, Mr Boyle was standing over Mrs Bevan and offering her his hand.

Rose had always seen him buttoned-up and officious, giving out orders, but now his disposition seemed completely changed; there was a chink in his armour.

Staring again at the words from the horoscope, an idea took hold.

She didn't know exactly what she was going to say, but she had overheard Maggie and Eliza talking about how he might be diverting their supplies, giving them to private establishments because of all the fuss in the newspapers about British Restaurants having an unfair advantage. She knew that it was her chance to help Maggie; an opportunity to repay her cousin's faith in her. She would open Mr Boyle's eyes to how important Maggie's Kitchen really was.

Mr Boyle was shaking Mrs Bevan's hand.

Rose made her move, reaching the door just ahead of him.

'Must you leave now?' she asked.

'I'm afraid so; work beckons,' he said, wriggling fingers into black gloves, his other hand stretching the leather firmly as he teased out the wrinkles. 'Please thank Miss Johnson, though, it has been a very pleasant afternoon.'

'Maggie – surely you can call her Maggie by now.'

'Where is your sense of propriety? Should I address all my work colleagues by their first name? And you...'

'I am Rose Barnard, but you can call me Rose.'

'And I'm sure many people do; you are well-named, Miss Barnard.' He gave her an insincere smile. 'But if you don't mind, I really need to go now.'

The dining hall was hushed, the lunchtime diners trickling back to offices and factories nearby, and it felt as if the few who remained were watching them. And then she heard the words again: *A day to assert yourself. Make up your own mind.*

She clasped her hands together and stepped closer. 'Mr Boyle, I know that you and Maggie haven't always seen eye to eye...'

He looked up at her briefly and then returned his attention to his gloves.

'It won't be the same, if we have to keep closing,' she continued. 'People won't come back, and Maggie can't bear to let them down. Why can't

245

you make sure we get the supplies we need?'

'I appreciate your loyalty, Miss Barnard, and your idealism, but unfortunately I am merely an instrument of the government and our government works in its own way, particularly in wartime. Miss Johnson knew this when she took on the restaurant, and may I remind you that she applied to us; we did not recruit her.'

Maggie was right – the man was maddening. She had said once that he was a man of rigid principles and a harsh disposition; that he would not be tolerant of kindness shown to others that he could not dispense himself. Rose had seen his weakness, though; had caught a glimpse of the man he could be. She was sure there must be some way of appealing to him.

'What will you do when the war is over, Mr Boyle?'

His eyes flickered but gave nothing away.

'Do you know, Miss Barnard, I really haven't given it much thought. I am far too busy concerning myself with living from one day to the next.'

'You are an unusual man, Mr Boyle. Most folk that come in here, well, that's all they ever talk of – what they are going to do when the war is over. They are full of plans of where they will go when their family is back together and their loved ones are home again.'

His eyes were cold now; whatever emotion he felt was masked.

'Is there no one waiting for you, Mr Boyle?'

'What sort of question is that?' he snapped.

'Have you ever lost anyone?'

246

'You are either very naive or unaware that your questions are quite impertinent, Miss Barnard.'

He moved towards the door.

Rose walked ahead of him, stopping in front of him so that he was forced to look at her.

'I imagine that it might not be so easy for you to lay these conditions on others if you had someone waiting for you. Someone you had made plans with.'

'I'm not sure I understand your point,' he said stiffly.

'Maggie had someone and they had plans. Nothing can come of those plans now, but look at what she has still managed to do, Mr Boyle. Look at all that she's achieved...'

Rose raised her arms, gesturing around her.

'How can you risk all this? Think about what you are taking from everyone; it's not the food from their plates – it's hope. That's what people come here for, Mr Boyle; the chance to talk about their futures. Because unlike you, they have dreams of one.'

But if Mr Boyle was moved by her words, he gave no sign of it. His face was stony as he stalked past her to the door.

As it closed behind him, Rose considered Maggie's parting words: *I want you to make sure he leaves here happy. It's very important.* It was possible, she thought with a sinking feeling, that she had gone too far.

Chapter Twenty

YOUR CHILDREN'S FOOD IN WARTIME:
You want your children to be healthy and happy,
of course; and to grow up strong and sturdy.
Do you know that all depends very largely
upon the food you give them now, and the
food habits you help them to form?
Ministry of Food, War Cookery Leaflet No. 10

Maggie had been distracted for days but Robbie thought he knew what was wrong. He had overheard her telling Eliza that she had seen the woman again, the same one who had stared at her and then slipped out of the restaurant before she could find out who she was or what she wanted. Surely that wasn't why Maggie was still behaving so oddly, though, the reason that she hadn't even noticed him come in. Or maybe she had found out about his mum? He knew he had to tell her about his family before she found out from anyone else. It was on the tip of his tongue each and every time he saw her, but then he just chickened out. He didn't want to leave London yet; he liked being around Maggie and the restaurant. Then again, he didn't like lying either, especially after all she had done for him. He clutched the paper bag tighter. So this was it: he would tell her today, and hopefully she would accept the peace offering he had brought her.

248

'Boo!' he said, jumping out, thinking she would laugh.

'Blimey, Robbie, you nearly gave me a heart attack!'

'Sorry.'

'What are you doing here, anyway? School's not out yet ... and you know I can't allow him in here,' she said, glaring at Spoke.

'I know.'

He ushered the dog outside and closed the door quickly before Spoke could push his snout back through.

'Good surprise first or bad?' he offered.

'Well, it's usual to have the bad first...'

'Okay, let's go with the good this time then.'

'I thought it was my choice?'

'I've got something that's going to put a big smile on that long face of yours.'

'Robbie!'

'So, do you want to know what it is or not?'

'No, not really.'

She walked over to the blackboard and began checking through the day's schedule.

He tried to contain himself, knowing she didn't mean it. He counted silently in his head. *One, two, three, four, five...*

'Oh, alright then,' she said, relenting.

He rushed over and thrust out the bag. 'Here you are!'

'Gosh, it smells awful. What is it?'

'Open it and see.'

She tipped it onto the bench top and a small dark object rolled out, its irregular-shaped sides bringing it to a stop. He could smell it from where he stood; a strong earthy smell and vaguely familiar, like damp mushrooms that were on the turn.

'Gordon Bennett, that's ugly!' Eliza said, coming over to see what all the fuss was about. 'What is it, animal or vegetable?'

Rose, never one to be left out, made her way over too.

'Looks like one of your ex-boyfriends, Liza.'

'Thanks, Rose!'

Maggie shook her head. 'It looks like a mushroom with warts. Honestly, Robbie, what on earth is it?'

'Worth more than gold, that is,' he announced proudly.

Maggie looked from him to the object and back again. 'I find that hard to believe!'

'It's a truffle ... the chef said it comes from this place in France and it's really rare. And now it's even more difficult to get hold of because of the war.'

Eliza prodded it with her index finger. 'But what do you do with it?'

'I don't know ... I forgot to ask.'

'What do you mean you forgot to ask? Where did you get it?'

'The chef at The Savoy gave it to me.'

'Really? So he just gave it to you, this "more valuable than gold" truffle?' Maggie asked.

Robbie nodded then dropped his gaze.

'What, you were just wandering past The Savoy and thought, *I know, I'll just pop in and have a cuppa and grab myself some truffle while I'm here?*' she said using a mock hoity-toity voice.

'Alright, no need to be like that. I thought you'd be pleased.'

She narrowed her eyes at him. 'I'll be pleased when you tell me how you got it.'

'I remember now,' Robbie said, hoping to distract her. 'You put it in omelettes, or in scrambled eggs ... somethin' like that.'

'Ask Janek,' Eliza suggested. 'You seem to go to him for most things these days.'

'That's a good idea,' Maggie agreed, ignoring her friend's sarcasm. 'He's coming here after work. Stop by after school, Robbie, and you can be the one to ask him.'

'It's okay,' Robbie said, trying to grab the truffle and missing.

'Go on – scarper,' Maggie said, pushing the truffle back into the bag. 'We've got work to do.'

Robbie hung around the doorway; it looked as if their conversation about his mother would have to wait. He was half excited at the prospect of showing Janek the prized truffle, but also dreading what Janek would say when he found out Robbie had been back to The Savoy.

When Janek finally appeared late that afternoon, he seemed to be in a good mood.

'I'll bet he'll know what to do with it,' Robbie whispered to Maggie. 'Anyway, if you don't want it I can go and sell it somewhere else for a *lot* of money.'

'I'm glad you're here, Janek,' Maggie said. 'You can help solve a little mystery for us.' She prodded Robbie. 'Go on then, show him.'

When Robbie opened his palm to reveal the

truffle, Janek's eyes narrowed and his brows met in an angry scowl.

'Where did you get that?'

'I told Maggie – a friend gave it to me.'

'Well, you need to give it back.'

'Why?' Robbie protested, pouting.

'Men are dying because of them.'

'What do you mean?'

'They risk their lives going into regions where they grow, areas that are dangerous, because of the ridiculous price people will pay.'

'I'm sorry, Janek, I – I didn't know,' Robbie stammered. He tried to stop his voice from shaking but he had never seen Janek so angry before.

'It's okay, Robbie, you weren't to know,' Maggie said, placing an arm around his shoulders.

'Yes, but he does now.' Janek, clearly furious, pulled on his cap and was gone before Robbie or Maggie had a chance to react.

For a brief moment all they could do was look at each other, then Maggie said, 'Why don't you take it back? Or, better still, let's just throw it away. If what Janek says is true, I wouldn't be happy making anything with it and I don't imagine any of our customers would be happy eating it.'

'They wouldn't even know,' Robbie objected.

'Robbie!'

'I know, you're right – I just thought you'd be pleased,' he said, disappointed all over again.

'I am pleased ... well, sort of. Look, I'm grateful to you but I've told you before, I don't want you getting into any trouble. You know I also don't want anything in my kitchen that has not been

252

acquired by honest means, don't you?'

'Yes, but you said that the menus were dull; I thought that something like this, like the hotels up the West End have...'

'We're not up the West End though, Robbie; we're serving simple meals to hungry people. I know what you thought, but perhaps you could stick to helping us in the vegetable garden – that would mean a lot more to me.'

'Alright, if you say so...' He edged towards the door and then stopped. 'You could just try one of those omelettes, though. It'd be a shame to waste it.'

'Goodbye, Robbie!'

He scurried out, closing the door behind him.

When Robbie had gone, Rose nudged Maggie. 'Don't be angry with him, he's only trying to please you.'

Maggie sighed. 'I know, but I can't encourage dishonesty though.' She quickly walked over to the blackboard and began checking through the order forms.

'I don't know,' Eliza said. 'It's not as if the rich can't afford to lose a truffle or two. Remember that protest?'

On an outing to the Strand earlier in the year, the three of them had run into a protest at The Savoy; angry women with empty shopping baskets were waving banners reading: FEED THE WORKERS, RATION THE RICH. They had also handed out flyers accusing the government of providing 'one ration for the Rich and another for the Poor'. The protestors' chants demanded increased rations and complained that there were no eggs for their children but omelettes at The Savoy.

Rose nodded in agreement then reminded Maggie, 'And it's not as if Robbie's mum and dad are around to guide him.'

'Forget about Robbie,' Eliza interrupted. 'What about Janek? What on earth got into him?'

'He's got good reason to be upset,' Rose replied. 'We've not had to leave our homes or country.'

'Not yet, but we've lost loved ones too, he's not the only one. You know that better than anyone!'

Rose glared at Eliza, but she wasn't stopping.

'If you ask me, he's getting a bit too big for his boots, making himself right at home around here too.'

But Maggie's thoughts weren't on Janek; she was still thinking about Robbie. Maybe she had been a little hard on him. But she didn't want him to get into trouble again; they had already had two visits from a constable over reports of stolen vegetables from a nearby allotment. She hadn't asked Robbie directly but he had arrived last week with leafy gifts that he couldn't account for.

'I don't know,' Maggie sighed. 'Maybe we do need to be a little more patient with each other.'

Rose was right; Robbie was just a boy trying to help in the only way he knew how and it made Maggie feel quite anxious thinking about him on his own, spending the rest of the afternoon feeling bad about what had happened. And Janek had surprised them all becoming so angry. Was it to do with his brother? Or perhaps he just hated to be reminded of the destructiveness of the war and his frustration at not being able to do anything about it. She knew she hadn't done anything wrong but nevertheless she felt complicit, as though she was somehow responsible.

Placing the papers back on the hook, she went out to the backyard, but there was no one to be seen, and no sound of Robbie's incessant chatter, or Janek's Polish folk songs.

Weaving between the raised beds, she checked for any sign of them but the only murmur came from the foliage as the wind rustled through. She made her way to the back gate and out into the laneway. There was a small figure retreating down the street, leaping from one doorstep to the next, jumping up and energetically spinning around in mid-air before landing back down and launching off again, Spoke keeping pace alongside. Maggie smiled to herself. She didn't need to worry about having upset Robbie, at least.

The spire was just ahead, only a few hundred yards away, and hopefully he would find Stefan and the others inside. If not, at least he would be in a familiar place, somewhere to pull himself together and focus his mind. He had to stop thinking about Maggie and the boy and get on with finding his comrades.

He wasn't a regular at mass, but he knew that the other Poles worshipped here. And he was just in time; he had sensed the wind change on his way here, bringing strong gusts from the east and with it large spots of rain. Now he wouldn't feel bad that he hadn't watered Maggie's plants as he'd promised he would. He knew he shouldn't have stormed off like that, but the incident with Robbie had shaken him. It had taken him back to a place he had worked hard to move on from; even now the growl of traffic was as loud and invasive as the artillery had been, and he could taste the choking fumes. It wasn't the physical discomfort, though, he could cope with that; it was the wrenching pain and helplessness of losing his family and leaving his brother behind.

He reached for his collar, quickly unbuttoning his shirt as he hurried up the portico steps.

Inside the cool nave, he immediately felt calmer as he inhaled the comforting smell of frankincense and candle wax. He crossed the stone floor, transformed a deep ruby, blue and gold by the weak light through stained glass, and he scanned the pews for anyone he recognised. There were only a few well-wrapped figures scattered in the middle rows; an elderly couple kneeling in the second row and a soldier who rose to light a candle close to the altar where the priest prayed aloud. Churches here were never very full like the ones back home, but St Paul's was one of the oldest in Islington, and easily as old as the gothic church and basilica at home where he had attended all the important family occasions: his brother had married Lila there, Roman and Krystina were baptised there, and their grandparents were buried in the graveyard alongside their ancestors. It was one of the things that angered him the most, not to be able to bury the rest of his family in their rightful resting place.

He kneeled behind the elderly couple and removed his prayer book, opening it at the place marked by his prayer card, the dark skin of the Black Madonna appearing even darker in the shadows. The priest's words were rhythmic, like a soothing chant, but still he couldn't concentrate. He had to find his comrades; he needed to know how much longer he would have to wait. Trying to gain intelligence in his local area had reaped nothing; there wasn't anything out of the ordinary to report. He was certain of it, despite the distraction and all thoughts returning to Maggie. He closed his eyes and bent his head to pray, but each small sound was an intrusion; the closing of a car door outside, the creak of the church's door opening and the soft padding of footsteps that grew closer until they were alongside him, accompanied by a strong floral scent.

He crossed himself and looked up as a woman passed with a large bouquet. It could have been his mother or Lila; they used to take flowers from their gardens for the church every week, even more often in summer when Roman and Krystina collected the petals that had fallen for his mother's rose petal jam. The recipe was a family favourite; he had told Maggie about it and she was eager to try it when they were able to grow flowers again.

The woman placed the bouquet on the altar and rearranged it, her dark hair falling around her shoulders in soft curls, just like Maggie's did. He was spending too much time at the restaurant, thoughts of her increasingly distracting him. He had let his guard down and it was a mistake; that same night she had asked about his past and he had said too much. She had a way of making him

257

talk when he didn't intend to. They had been waiting in the backyard for the sausages to smoke, and although he was unable to see her clearly in the dark, he could feel her close beside him.

'I had an uncle who visited Poland before the war,' she said. 'He told me you have as many stately houses as here.'

'Yes, every duke built himself a castle.'

'You must feel at home here then?'

He didn't want to offend her by telling her how her country could never compare to Poland, so he chose his words carefully. 'There is much to like here, and much here like home.'

'What do you miss the most?'

'My family.'

'Where are they?'

How could he tell her the truth? That they had hidden his parents under the farmhouse with his older brother and his brother's wife and children. Of how he and his younger brother had fled to the fields when there was no more room. Of what happened next...

Instead he simply told her that they had been killed.

'I'm so sorry,' she said.

They were simple words, spoken with genuine emotion, but they took him by surprise, moved him in a way he hadn't expected. But the truth was that no one could ever be as sorry as him. If only he had gone down first, if only he had made them squeeze in further, if only he hadn't left them behind. They had examined the hiding place a dozen times, agreeing it was safer to hide there than in any of the lofts and spaces of the vast farmhouse's stables and barns. They practised the drill, always improving their speed. He could picture the children now, just as they had looked the last time he saw them, before he had pulled the boards over their heads to conceal them; pink and white dressing gown flapping around Lilla's skinny legs and Roman crouching down in his oversized uniform, all ready for school.

'I imagine Peter is still with me sometimes,' Maggie said softly.

It was the first time she had spoken of her fiancé and it had weakened him so that he had been unable to stop and told her the whole story of his escape; how he and his brother had fled, staying clear of the river and train lines, hiding only in the hedges and undergrowth that they had explored as boys. How when they reached Pultusk the market square was covered with bodies, its cobbled streets running red with blood.

By the time he had finished talking he felt numb; deadened by the thought of never seeing his parents again, the brothers he had grown up with, and the niece and nephew who were like his own.

Then he felt the warmth of her touch as Maggie placed her hand on his, her voice a gentle whisper.

'You must miss them terribly...'

A silence fell between them and she didn't try to make conversation, which he was grateful for.

'Do you think Robbie's father is a prisoner?' she said at last.

'I think if he is, he will wish he were dead.' He moved his hand away. 'My younger brother,

259

Dimitri, he was captured in France. He is a prisoner now.'

'I expect it means everything to him that you are free.'

It might seem that way to her, yet he felt trapped, helpless; knowing that his brother was a prisoner and not being able to do anything about it.

'I may be here, Maggie, but I am not free.'

'At least you are helping people. You couldn't have done that if you had been captured.'

He dropped his head, rubbing each wrist as if trying to prise off imaginary handcuffs. 'I am sorry ... I should not be talking like this...'

'It's fine; I mean, I want you to.'

He turned to look at her then, large eyes glistening against her pale smooth skin, and he had wanted to reach out and touch her. 'You shouldn't be blaming yourself. For anything.'

'I know you are trying to make me feel better, but there's no need. I know what I have to do.'

The priest stopped talking and Janek watched as he lit another candle. He had nothing to confess today, nothing that the priest hadn't heard before. In any event, the priest's words didn't help.

Since the others hadn't shown he would go to the allotment and get on with his work; it was best to keep busy.

As he rose to leave, the priest noticed and came towards his pew.

'Hello, Father.'

'Janek, I'm glad you are here. Your two friends have been looking for you.'

'Who was it? Do you know?'

'Stefan and Filip. They said that it was important.'

'And did they say where I could find them?'

The priest patted his shoulder. 'They said they would find you.'

Chapter Twenty-one

MAKING THE MOST OF FAT RATION:
Always scrape the butter, margarine and cooking fat
papers with a knife so as not to waste a scrap.
Save the paper to use for greasing cake tins
and pudding basins and for covers for steamed
puddings and dishes baked in the oven.
Ministry of Food, War Cookery Leaflet

Mr Dummond had given them the bare facts: the bomb had been a six-pounder and the dairy would have been wiped out instantly. In fact, it was a miracle that only seven were killed. 'A hole the size of St Paul's,' had been the warden's parting words. It hadn't helped and everyone was walking around looking pale and shocked. Maggie was trying to put on a brave face and stay strong for the others, but at the sight of Gillian's red and blotchy complexion and swollen eyes, Maggie felt her own face crumple.

'I know, I know,' she said, feeling the full weight of Gillian's body press against hers.

'And what about those poor animals? No one spares a thought for them...'

'Of course they do, but we've got to think about the rest of the workers,' Maggie said briskly, wiping away her tears. 'They'll need a good deal of sympathy with their tea, not tears. And the rescue crews are going to need to eat.'

She would miss Mrs Evans; the woman could talk like no one else Maggie had ever known, and while she never waited to be invited into the kitchen, she strode through it with the charm of her lyrical monologues gathering force behind her until no one could help but take notice.

Maggie shook her head; with the dairy and the pub next to it now gone, that brought to seven the number of neighbouring buildings and businesses destroyed: the pub on Pleasant Row, the Home & Colonial Store on Essex Road, St Stephen's church on Canonbury Road, Daniel Gregg's bakery, The Prince of Brunswick on Barnsbury Road, and not forgetting the Carlton Cinema late last year, its beautiful Art Deco facade reduced to crumbled pillars and fractured mosaics.

Meanwhile, for the rest of them it was business as usual; Essex Road Station still had its customary throng of commuters, the Northern District Post Office its stubborn queue of customers, and she and her staff needed to carry on cooking, making sure they could sustain the customers for as long as possible – or until Jerry gave them another nasty surprise.

'It could have been us...' Gillian's voice sounded hollow.

'Well, it wasn't, and you're not even here at night so that's enough of that.'

'I'm sorry. I never used to expect the worst ...

262

you do know that, don't you?'

Maggie couldn't ignore the desperation in her voice. 'I do, and you mustn't expect it now, either. Come on, go and clean up and let the customers see that beautiful smile.'

When Maggie reached the kitchen Rose was greasing baking tins while Eliza kneaded pastry, thick arms pressing up and down like an athlete doing push-ups. She was surrounded by tins in which the dough was already beginning to rise and blind-baked pastry cases waiting to be filled, but the fine film of dust on the surfaces could not be mistaken for flour.

'Liza! What did I tell you about keeping the windows closed?'

Maggie rushed over to close the latch on the first window.

'Well, what do you expect me to do? The fans still aren't working properly. If we close the windows it steams up and we can't see a bloomin' thing. And the cakes and sponges get spoiled!'

'I know, I know, I'm sorry.'

'Me too.' Eliza sighed. 'I suppose we're all a bit on edge. You been round to see old Evans yet?'

'No, I am going but I need to make a call first.'

'It's dreadful, can't believe it,' Rose said in a hushed tone, shaking her head. 'Maisy and George...'

'I know, both of them,' Maggie replied.

Maggie scanned the kitchen. 'You haven't seen Robbie, have you?'

He hadn't been around for a few days and having a bomb drop so close to home had made her realise how vulnerable he was, living on the streets alone. It made up her mind; as soon as she had spoken to Mr Boyle, she would call the education officer. She didn't know where they would send him, but London was just too dangerous.

Eliza had paused in her kneading and was looking at her closely. 'Here, you're not looking that special this morning, Mags. You alright?'

'I'm fine. Well, no, actually...' She took a newspaper clipping out of her pocket. 'Did either of you see this?'

'Haven't got time to read papers. Honestly, next you'll be suggesting we take a day off!' Eliza scoffed. 'What do you say Rose, fancy a day trip to Eastbourne?'

'What does it say?' Rose asked, ignoring her.

'I'll tell you what it says – that we've been driving ourselves mad for nothing. Listen to this.' She read the headline aloud: *'Food reserves in London bigger than during the past twelve months...'* She paused to look at them.

'Go on then,' Eliza urged. 'I'm all ears.'

'Mr. W G. Boyle, London Divisional Food Officer, speaking at the opening of a British Restaurant at Edmonton yesterday, said: "I can assure you most definitely and sincerely that the stocks of food in London are larger today than they have been during the past 12 months."'

Eliza's mouth fell open. 'What a wretch!'

'Wait, there's more,' Maggie said. *'"In addition to the usual stocks, I have under my control six of the most important commodities that will provide rations, and in some cases double rations, for one hundred per cent of the population for two weeks in any emergency."'*

264

Maggie folded the article and looked at them both for their reaction.

'So what do you think he's playing at then?' asked Rose.

'I don't know, but I'm going to find out. If I can't get him on the phone I'm going to go down there.'

'Do you want me to go instead?' Rose said, her cheeks flushing unusually red.

Maggie was surprised by the offer, but she needed to sort this out herself, the luncheon had seemed to go so well, yet there had been no improvement in their supply of foodstuffs. It was time to have it out with Mr Boyle.

'It's okay,' she told Rose. 'I think it's best that I go on my own.' She was about to leave but hesitated.

'Oh, and Rose? If Janek turns up, could you ask him to come and find me?'

'I'd like to, but I'm not sure that Eliza would approve!' Rose replied.

'Why, what is it?' Maggie asked. Turning to her cousin, she saw Rose's eyes were fixed on Eliza.

'It's nothing,' Rose said.

'Come on, Rose. What's going on?'

'Well, Eliza's got some stupid idea about Janek.'

'It's not stupid,' Eliza said, narrowing her eyes. 'I don't think it's right and I'm not just going to stand by and say nothing.'

'Say nothing about what?'

'You're ridiculous!' Rose said. 'Just because he's foreign,' she explained to Maggie, 'she thinks he's some kind of spy!'

'What?' Maggie exclaimed.

'And you would know that he's not how, exactly?' Eliza jabbed her right hand at Rose, the pastry cutter she still held stabbing the air. 'Just because you've fallen for him don't let it cloud your judgment!'

Rose blushed bright scarlet and she put her head down, turning her attention back to washing the vegetables, albeit much more vigorously than before.

Eliza fell silent and went back to pumping the dough, also with a little more force than was really necessary.

'Would one of you mind telling me what is going on?' Maggie asked after a few moments of silence.

Eliza and Rose looked at each other.

Maggie crossed her arms in front of her. 'Rose?'

'Well...' Rose took a deep breath. 'Eliza has some rather strange ideas about Janek that she is considering sharing with the Home Guard. I told her that if she has any suspicions about him she should just come right out and ask him herself.'

The room was steaming up, the stockpots simmering noisily.

'What kind of suspicions?'

'Go on then, Eliza, tell her.' Rose nodded at Maggie. 'Tell her how you've been spying on him.'

'I haven't been spying on him. It's just a coincidence that I sometimes pass near the railyard on my way home.'

Maggie had thought at first that this was some petty squabble between Eliza and Rose, but now she realised it was something much more serious.

'And what have you seen?' she asked.

Eliza avoided eye contact, looking down as she picked at the rapidly drying pastry that stuck to her hands and fell away in thick claggy flakes.

'But I'm going to ruin my pastry,' she muttered.

'Liza!'

'Alright, alright. There's a group of them that meet under the railway track. At the allotment there.'

'There's nothing suspicious about that,' Maggie interrupted. 'That's where he works and sleeps. They're probably just helping out.'

'Well, no. That's what I thought at first, but they don't stay outside, they go in the hut and, well, they talk.'

'That's hardly illegal! They must be friends of his.'

'Have you ever heard him talk about friends before? No...'

Eliza moved closer to Maggie, glancing at the girls on the other side of the kitchen, voice lowering to a whisper as if someone were spying on her right now.

'I saw them last night. Heard them talking but couldn't make out what they were saying because it was all ... *foreign.*'

Maggie was exasperated. 'You mean you followed him and you spied on him?'

Eliza nodded slowly.

'But that's so rude – and foolish.' She glanced at Rose, who was nodding her head in agreement. 'Not to mention possibly dangerous!'

'So you agree he's up to no good, then?' Eliza replied.

'No! No, I don't think that at all. I was referring to you wandering around in the dark at night, on your own.'

'See? I told you she was being ridiculous,' Rose said.

'You've really no right, Liza. Janek is our friend.'

'She's been listening to Mike,' Rose said. 'He's filling her head with all sorts of rubbish.'

'That's not fair. You don't even know Mike – anyway he knows more about what's going on with this war than you do!'

Maggie had never seen them so at odds with one another. Rose looked furious and Eliza's cheeks were even pinker than usual.

'Come on, you two, this is so unnecessary. Especially on top of everything else today...'

'She started it!' Rose muttered.

'Please, if you want to continue this conversation – although I strongly suggest you don't – can you do so after work?'

Maggie looked over at the other side of the kitchen where their heated conversation was arousing the interest of the rest of the staff.

'Now, are you two alright?'

They both nodded, although Eliza a little more slowly than Rose.

'I don't want a hostile atmosphere in my kitchen, so whatever differences you have, when you're here you put them aside.'

The morning flew by as emergency workers came and went, and everyone wanted to stop and talk about the dairy. By the time Maggie returned to the kitchen the flans were cooked, several sponges had been steamed, and the conversation about Janek had been shelved, at least for the time being.

She escaped into the yard and leaned back against the wall, taking a deep breath as she watched a blackbird drill its beak into the soil searching for worms. She hadn't known a morning like it; all the problems with Mr Boyle and the orders, Eliza's ridiculous suspicions about Janek, and now Rose and Eliza were at each other. What on earth had made her think that she could run a restaurant without Peter? She clearly wasn't making a very good job of it. And it was really niggling her that she hadn't noticed what had been going on with Rose – although come to think of it, she had been behaving oddly. She was spending much more time in the garden, offering to water or weed rather than refilling the salt and pepper pots or doing one of the dozens of other jobs waiting indoors. It was obvious; Rose was attracted to Janek. Her shy young cousin, who was always going on about being left on the shelf, was smitten.

As the bird tugged its victim from the ground and flew onto a nearby branch, the glimmer of warmth she felt at Rose's joy rapidly faded as Maggie realised what it would mean for her; that she would have to set aside her own feelings and try to avoid Janek whenever he visited. It would be hard – his visits had grown into a daily occurrence and she had come to rely on him – but she also knew that she could not stand in the way of Rose's happiness.

Chapter Twenty-two

ENERGY FOODS:
We need energy to live and work. The human body,
like any engine, needs fuel. Appetite is a good guide
to our needs of these energy foods and,
if we take more than we require,
we generally store the surplus as fat.
Ministry of Food, Foods for Fitness

It promised to be a fine October day without the usual autumnal clouds scudding across the sky, threatening to sabotage their trip. Maggie was secretly disappointed as she had mixed feelings about going; on the one hand she was anxious about leaving the restaurant, but on the other she was relieved not to be there when Janek came by. She didn't want to see him until she had figured out what she was going to say and here she had the perfect excuse to get away. It had been her idea to go to the country to see if she could deal directly with the rabbit clubs that Mike had told her about. Although it did mean spending a whole morning with Eliza's beau; while he had grown on her a little, she feared it wasn't as much as Eliza had hoped for. She didn't really understand what Eliza saw in him. She wanted to ask him what he'd told Eliza about Janek to make her so suspicious, but decided it would be prudent to wait and approach the topic discreetly.

As they slowed at the traffic lights he glanced across at her and smiled. 'Comfortable?'

'Yes, very. Thank you.'

He had boasted that the car he had borrowed was a splendid new model and would get them to the farm in no time. He'd also insisted on wrapping woollen blankets around her legs to block out the draughts.

'Don't worry, they'll be fine without you,' he said, as if reading her mind.

She had gone into the restaurant early to make sure everything was ready before he picked her up and it had felt strange leaving. It was the first time she had left her staff alone for any length of time and she wasn't certain how they would manage. Maeve had volunteered to run things while she was away and Maggie was pleased to give her the chance; while she had shown she could get by in the kitchen, it was at the organisation that she excelled and it was good to have another supervisor to help.

'Makes you want to climb up and ride them right out of here, don't it?' Mike said as they passed Clapham Junction and the barrage balloons that guided them south.

'Not especially,' she replied, peering at the great amorphous shapes that dominated the skyline. 'They give me the creeps, actually.'

It wasn't long before they were on the A23 and the drab grey buildings gave way to the undulating green of meadows and woods. The outskirts of the city hadn't altered much, the only noticeable changes being the barbed wire running along the side of the railway tracks and the impromptu sculptures created by irregular sandbags.

Thin spears of rain began to slice the wind-shield, temporarily obscuring the road from view. Mike flicked on the wipers, which screeched noisily across the glass, making a stippled fan pattern from the dirt.

'Which road are you taking?' Maggie asked.

'We turn off at the A272 towards Cowfold, then onto Henfield – the 281. Do you know it?' He glanced over.

'Yes, I do, actually. We used to go there as children.'

'Smoke?' he said, slipping a packet from his breast pocket and tipping it towards her.

'No, thank you.'

'You mind if I do?'

'No, of course not.'

She watched as he fumbled with the packet and the lighter while keeping his eyes on the road ahead, which disappeared around a narrow bend.

'Say, I don't suppose you could light it for me?'

He handed her the packet and she took a cigarette, resting it between her lips and inhaling as she flicked the lighter.

'Thanks,' he replied, his smile showing off perfect teeth.

It was because of his good looks that she hadn't taken to him initially, his thatch of dark hair and the kind of grin she could tell had snared a dozen girls before Eliza.

'Eliza says you were engaged once,' he remarked.

'Yes. He died.'

'I'm sorry. Must have been one hell of a–'

'Yes, he was.' She didn't want to talk about Peter, especially with someone she barely knew. 'What about you, is there anyone special back home?'

He took a long sideways glance at her. 'You don't think much of me, do you?'

She was embarrassed; all this time she thought she had hidden her true feelings and she clearly hadn't.

'It's not that,' she said awkwardly.

'It's okay, I get it. Eliza's your friend and I'm some jerk who's going to break her heart. Well, if you must know, there was someone back home, but she married someone else.'

'Oh, I'm sorry. That must have been hard.'

'Not really.' He smiled. 'If she hadn't, I would never have met Eliza.'

Maggie quickly changed the subject – perhaps she had judged him too quickly – and they spent the rest of the journey talking about the places he had visited, from the Rocky Mountains to various states in America that sounded so wild and interesting she decided against sharing stories of her family holidays to Brighton, which didn't seem quite so adventurous anymore.

It was nearly an hour later that the white-painted sign for Henfield flashed past, reminding her of their annual trips, the countryside itself so familiar, changing from its calming patchwork of green to the great bluffs of the South Downs, showing no clue to the grey-pebbled beaches that lay beyond. As children she and her brothers had spent their days swimming, shrimping and exploring the pier with its carousel and amusement arcades. They took it in turns but she always chose

273

to sit in the great iridescent nautilus shell or astride a galloping sea horse, stroking its long, colourful mane. They wouldn't go back to their bed and breakfast until late, choosing instead to eat fish and chips out of newspaper, the sour vinegar and steam warming their faces. Or if the wind had started roaring off the Channel as it often did, they would sit below the canopy of one of the many restaurants under the stone arches. Typically, the music and the rattle-and-ching of money from the nearby amusement arcades would summon them inside and they would stand for ages watching their father shoving change into the machines. When he was lucky enough to have a win he would divide it between them and they would reach up and feed their tightly gripped coins into the slots, watching as the small symbols spun round, clasping their hands together and hoping for the bulging sacks of gold. The noise and chaos of the arcades, which had scared her at first, soon became part of their holiday ritual. Eventually, covered in her own salty brine with disobedient hair set into crisp strands, she would wearily lead them along the promenade towards Kemp Town, where the cheaper holiday flats and boarding houses stood in the town's dilapidated terraces and Regency crescents. Once her mother left they stopped going, and none of them had mentioned Brighton again, as though it was part of a life they needed to leave behind.

'Okay, this is us,' Mike said, slowing the car and turning off the road.

Maggie gripped the side of her seat as they bumped up a long rutted track, farm buildings coming into view and a small gathering of cows congregated around a water trough. The farmhouse was half hidden by orchards that rose with the land to low hills in the east and fields that dipped to a valley on the left.

As they jolted to a stop she could see the uneven roofs, broken windows and exposed walls, a sign of the disrepair that meant they would offer little shelter to any cattle or stored feed. There was an assemblage of battered machinery off to one side and her heart sank at the thought of a wasted journey.

'Who did you say the place belongs to?'

'The Taylors – it's been in the family four generations.'

'That's right, I remember now. How do you know them?'

'We use the fields at the back of those hills for training. One of the Land Army gals said the locals had a strong rabbit club here, so I asked around.'

'Well, let's go then,' she said, fixing a smile on her face as she stepped out of the car.

A ruddy-faced man in his fifties in dirty overalls and a woollen hat appeared at the barn doors.

'You folks here to see where the real work is done, eh?' he said, coming to greet them.

'On the contrary. Terrance, this is Maggie, the young lady I was telling you about.'

'Pleased to meet you, Miss...?' He rubbed his hand on his trousers before extending it towards her.

'It's Johnson, but call me Maggie.'

'I certainly will, Maggie. Any friend of Mike's is

275

a friend of ours.'

'Is that so?'

'Certainly is. Don't know what we'd do without these boys.'

'That's good to know.' She glanced at Mike. 'Mike says you have a rabbit club here?'

'I suppose you're wanting to see some, but there's not too much to show you right now – rabbits are caught at night mostly. We put the traps out last thing and normally catch a good amount. We've kept some for you in the back of the barn.'

'Can we take a look?' Mike asked.

The barn was a vast warehouse of splintered boards and sodden hay, but towards the back, underneath a section of roofing that still looked intact, a pen of roughly ten yards long was home to a dozen rabbits, snuggled together, ears flicking, noses twitching.

'We've got sties out the back. Is it pigs you're interested in too?'

'I don't think we'd have the cold storage for them,' she said, thinking quickly; a few rabbits was one thing but whopping great pigs to butcher and cook was something else. Mr Boyle would have a conniption.

But she didn't want to appear ungrateful either so she followed him through the farmyard and out behind the farmhouse.

An enormous female pig lay on her side, pink bristled belly exposed where six small piglets lay suckling. At the rear of the pen a lone piglet lay motionless.

'Don't fancy his chances, poor little runt,' Mike said, following her gaze.

Terrance opened the gate and walked to the back of the sty. 'Best get him out of here before the others have him...'

He bent down and scooped the little body up, laying it across his opened hand. ''Ere, he's still warm.' He rubbed the piglet's stomach with his hand, gently at first and then more vigorously. Its body jerked and then the piglet opened its eyes. 'Lazy little blighter was just having a nap,' Terrance laughed. 'There you go, you get stuck in there.' He lowered him onto the hay next to his siblings and it looked as if it was about to go back to sleep, so Terrance gave it a prod with his boot and the piglet latched on and began to suckle.

They stepped back outside. The leaves on the trees were a golden brown and they snapped underfoot as Maggie strolled around, breathing in the smell of ripe apples and blackberries, of fields ready for harvest. Not even the beautiful murals that the students had painted could conjure the smells and sights of the fruit that hung on the branches right in front of her. These would be mid-season apples and all the more juicy and flavoursome for it.

She reached out and pulled one from its branch, turning it around in her hand.

'Best for cider those ones,' Terrance remarked, grasping one for himself and biting into it with a loud crunch.

Maggie smiled and bit into hers.

'I should get my wife to give you the recipe for her cobbler. She makes the best cobbler in the whole of Sussex!'

After exploring the orchard and fields and meeting some of the Land Army girls, Maggie realised it wasn't that the farm was not well kept, but that all the Taylors' time and money was being re-invested; like the rest of the country, every waking hour was devoted to producing more, growing more and wasting less, so there was little time to spend on maintenance and repairs. That's why the farmer was so obliged to Mike and his fellow soldiers for the help they gave.

With her apprehension about the day gone and her worries about Mike too, she felt ashamed that she had allowed herself to be influenced by first impressions. Whatever small morsels of concern Mike had fed Eliza about Janek, he hadn't repeated them to her and she suspected that Eliza might have misunderstood. By the time they got back in the car after Terrance had insisted they stay for lunch, she could feel the tingle of her sun-warmed skin and the familiar pull of tiredness only associated with spending a long day out-doors. She had become so focused on the restaur-ant and the problems of those around her that she had forgotten there was life outside of N1. What was more, Terrance turned out to be a riotous storyteller and had them in fits of laughter with accounts of the predicaments that they had found themselves in over the years: sheep stuck in fences, cows in neighbours' houses. By the time they began the journey home, she had the promise of a delivery of rabbits in the next few weeks, some new recipes from Mrs Taylor, and a good idea of what to do about Robbie.

Now all she had to do was broach the subject of the rabbits with Mr Boyle...

Chapter Twenty-three

*Honey and syrup can be used to replace up to half
the sugar used in jam and marmalade. For example,
if the recipe needs 3lb. sugar you could use instead
1½lb. sugar and 1½lb. honey or syrup. Make sure
the fruit is thoroughly cooked before the sugar and
honey or syrup are added. This is important as if
long boiling takes place afterwards sugar
crystals may separate out.*
Ministry of Food, War Cookery Leaflet No. 21

Rose slumped onto the kitchen stool and kicked
off her shoes, pulling her right foot up across her
left knee and rubbing the sole with both thumbs.

'That Mrs Devereux's a right haughty one!
Anyone would think the old bag was the Duchess
of Kent the way she swans about the place,
making all sorts of special requests.'

'Like what?' Maggie asked, amused.

'Like: *Could I have cold milk on the side? Can I
have my scones toasted? Would it be possible to have
fadge instead of mash?* Where does she think she is,
the Ritz?'

'She probably has dined there,' Maggie said.
'She certainly has the wardrobe for it.'

Mrs Devereux's suits, though well worn, looked
expensive, as did the rather mottled and moth-
eaten fox stole around her shoulders.

'You don't mean that old thing she wears come

rain or shine? I'm convinced it's still alive – it's just found a comfortable resting place!'

'Listen to you two, you're just like Gert and Daisy off *Workers' Playtime* – you'll have your own radio show before you know it!' Eliza said with a sniff.

'Not bloomin' likely,' Maggie replied as she lifted a box onto the counter. 'Goodness, that's heavy!'

Eliza glanced at her. 'Got any more eggs?'

'No delivery yet, and Mrs Foster's Matilda didn't lay anything this morning. She was so terrified last night I was tempted to give her an aspirin when Mrs Foster took one.'

Rose looked shocked. 'Is it okay to give them to animals?'

'Must be. Mrs Foster used to give them to her dog. Poor thing was a nervous wreck otherwise.'

'Who, the dog or Mrs Foster?'

'Both!'

As their laughter subsided, Maggie heard a soft meowing coming from near the cookers. 'That's strange. It sounds like...' She bent to look. Underneath the stove, black and white paws were tucked beneath a familiar whiskered face. 'Rafferty!'

Maggie looked at Rose, who shrugged, so she turned her attention to Eliza. 'Liza?'

'Nothing to do with me,' Liza said, though a crimson flush was spreading across her face. 'Well, okay then, but he is the best mouse-catcher, you have to admit.'

Maggie bent down and tickled his ears, listening to the deep purring as she stroked along the length of his back, then grabbed him up and headed for the back door.

'He does need to stay outside, though – at least during the day, when there's a chance Mr Boyle or someone from the ministry might come. We'll let him in at night.'

When she returned, Maggie swapped her coat for an apron and moved over to the small wall mirror near the doorway to the dining room. She knotted her headscarf, tucking in stray pieces of hair and looking past her own reflection to Rose, already dressed head to toe in white and moving around the kitchen. It was such a relief that her cousin and Eliza seemed to have forgotten their argument about Janek.

She moved over to the bench and took the lid off the box, then sifted through the contents. The fruit and vegetables were from their own garden, and there were some herbs that she'd picked from the communal gardens on her way to work. The carrots were small and the potatoes knobbly but it didn't matter; she had it in mind to make a beef broth and barley soup, so the size and shape of the vegetables wouldn't be noticed, only the rich flavour.

'Mr Boyle hasn't been able to get any more supplies then?' Rose asked, looking at the meagre provisions.

'Funny, I was just thinking about him.'

'Oh, really, should I be worried?'

'Of course not – but honestly...' Maggie pursed her lips. 'I don't think he's trying very hard.'

'Here, you lot, listen to this,' Eliza said, folding back the newspaper so Maggie could see the headline: MRS CHURCHILL'S TOUR OF MEALS CENTRES.

She read aloud, adopting a clipped upper-crust accent. '*Mrs Winston Churchill, accompanied by Mr Charles Latham, leader of the LCC, made a tour of British Restaurants in London yesterday–*' she glanced up to make sure they were still listening '*–and at one of them in Fulham had a meal consisting of cold pressed beef and potato salad, syrup pudding, and a coffee at a cost of elevenpence.*'

'So, do you think she'll come here?' Rose asked excitedly.

Maggie shrugged. 'I don't know. But why are they charging tuppence more for their meals than we're allowed to?'

'Different borough, isn't it?' Eliza replied. 'Everything costs more in Fulham.'

Just then Maeve's head appeared in the doorway. 'Maggie?'

'Yes, Maeve?'

'Mr Boyle is here. And he seems in quite a fluster.'

'Better show him through to my office then. I'll be there in a tick.'

Eliza raised her eyebrows. 'Talk of the devil!'

'What do you suppose he wants?' Rose asked anxiously.

'Be charming but firm,' Eliza said. 'Don't stand any nonsense.'

'Perhaps you should go and see him for me...' Maggie suggested, only half joking.

'Maybe, but I wouldn't be as nice as you. You want to risk it?'

'Probably not.'

'Thought as much,' Eliza said, smiling. 'Remember, you're the boss here, not him.'

282

Maggie was barely inside the office before Mr Boyle leaped to his feet and thrust the *Highbury & Islington Gazette* at her.

'Do you have any idea of the problems you have caused?' he demanded.

Maggie stared at him in surprise. 'What? How?'

'I don't know what you were thinking, Miss Johnson. We have had the police involved, the National Caterers Federation, the Wartime Meals Division – even the Hotels and Restaurants Association have damned well had their say!'

'But what have I done?' Maggie asked, bewildered.

'Do you mean apart from serving meals of your own choosing and securing ingredients from questionable sources? Oh, wait, have I left anything out? Oh yes, employing illegal immigrants and underage workers!'

Since he put it like that, Maggie could see how he might be a little angry, but he was still overreacting. After all, they had read about other British Restaurants producing their own vegetables, and they'd thought it would be good publicity to write about what Maggie's Kitchen was serving. The regulars clearly liked it; the queues were longer than ever and the article had attracted new customers keen to try out some of the more unusual fare. As for Janek, there was nothing illegal about him, and she had spoken to the Taylors about Robbie and they were more than happy to have a spare pair of hands to help out on the farm. So now, with a safe place to stay, Mr Boyle could hardly accuse him of being in the way.

'You told me to be resourceful.' She crossed her arms defiantly.

'I did not give you carte blanche to beg, borrow and steal what you needed!'

'Well, where else did you expect me to find the extra food we needed?'

'I admit that there may have been one or two problems with supply, but really, Miss Johnson – engaging in criminal activity!'

'I have done no such thing, Mr Boyle. Nor have any of my staff, I can vouch for all of them. And I take great offence at any suggestion otherwise.'

'I think you'll find, Miss Johnson, that a few members of your staff have been key in securing these foodstuffs.'

'Yes, through reputable sources.'

'And you have receipts to support this?'

'Well, no.'

'I had hoped we might sort this out calmly and reasonably, but it appears not.' He handed her an envelope. 'I'm sorry, Miss Johnson, but you've left me no choice.'

Her fingers were trembling as she tore open the flap and pulled out the pages.

MINISTRY OF FOOD
NEVILLE HOUSE, PAGE STREET, LONDON
S.W.1
NOTICE

Dear Miss Johnson,
I am authorised by the Minister of Food to serve notice to you on this, 7th November 1941, that unless you adhere by the conditions set out in the agreement

signed under the Establishment of Communal Kitchens, and operate your centre in keeping with the terms therein, that the Ministry shall have no option but to close the premise or replace you with a new operator in 6 weeks. This is in direct relation to failure to comply with item 9. Of those terms wherein you have given to abide by providing:

These monthly accounts, certified by a competent official, together with such statistical information as is required should be sent to the Secretary, Ministry of Food, Neville House, London S.W.1., marked 'Communal Feeding' as soon as possible, and in any case within 28 days, after the end of the month to which they relate.

Her mouth had gone completely dry and the letters were blurring into each other.

The notice went on for three pages and she skimmed its contents. She knew that her accounts were fine, but as they couldn't come out and accuse her of stealing, she supposed this was their way of finding a reasonable excuse to put her on notice.

'But you can see for yourself,' she protested. 'Go out to the yard! You've seen the gardens, you know we've been growing our own vegetables – not just here, but at the railyard and at the allotment too. We haven't taken anything that we weren't entitled to.'

'Even if that were the case, Miss Johnson, what were you thinking serving what you bloody well pleased? Borscht and Polish sausage – what sort of message is that sending? We need to be serving traditional British food, not food that's closer to

German cuisine than our own. Surely you can see that, Miss Johnson?'

Maggie glared at him. 'My main concern has been providing enough food for our customers, and if that involves cooking dishes we aren't used to, then so be it. Better experiment than starve!'

'That may be your position, Miss Johnson, but it's not one the ministry shares; so unless you re-align your thinking, I am afraid Maggie's Kitchen may soon become someone else's kitchen.'

He gathered his coat and hat.

'Wait,' Maggie said. 'Does this mean that we will be getting our full allocation of foodstuffs from now on?'

'No, Miss Johnson, read the letter. It means you are on formal probation. You have six weeks to turn things around and abide by the terms of your agreement or you will be replaced. And, if a suitable replacement cannot be found, the restaurant will be closed.'

Chapter Twenty-four

MAKING THE MOST OF SUGAR:
The best way of stretching the sugar ration is by making full use of other sweetenings such as saccharin, honey, syrup or treacle, jam, marmalade, sweetened condensed milk and dried fruit.
Ministry of Food, War Cookery Leaflet No. 21

Robbie was starving as he followed his nose to the

286

kitchen, guessing at the origins of the rich syrupy aroma that had magically transported him from the pavement outside. It could be gingerbread or treacle pudding, neither of which he would refuse, but as he got closer, he heard his name. His ma always said that no good would come of listening in on other people's conversations, but he couldn't help himself, he wanted to know what they were saying. Besides, it would be rude to walk in now and interrupt. He peered through the gap in the doorframe. He had just the right angle to afford him a narrow view of the bench where Maggie stood and where small shreds of carrot scattered from her steel grater, contributing to a growing pile on the chopping board.

'We don't have much longer, he's going to be here at four,' she was saying loudly.

'You'd think we were expecting the bloomin' King and Queen for tea, not a thirteen-year-old boy. Honestly, Mags!' Eliza was holding a bowl, whisking its contents so fast that her whole body jiggled as it joined in.

'You only turn thirteen once,' Maggie insisted.

'Imagine if Mr Boyle turns up again. He'll want to know where this lot has come from.'

'And I'll tell him the truth: that it's come from the allotments and my own rations.'

'I know, but don't you think you're overdoing it a bit? It was only a few weeks ago we couldn't even get enough carrots for stews and now you're making carrot cookies!'

'Doesn't matter if it's on a stick or in a bowl, Doctor Carrot won't mind,' Maggie sang spontaneously.

'Good Lord, those radio advertisements are

really getting to you!'

'It's not that, Liza, he's a teenager. Don't you remember turning thirteen?'

Robbie couldn't help but smile; she looked as excited as his sisters Emily and Beth would have been if they were here.

'Yes, well, I think I got sixpence to keep out of the way on my birthday,' Eliza grumbled.

'Even more reason you should make sure someone else enjoys theirs then.'

'So are you going to let me take you to the Palais again next month?'

'Next month ... why?'

'For *your* birthday, of course.'

'Mmm, well, that's different. It doesn't count once you get to twenty-five.' She swiped her finger across the side of the bowl and licked it.

It was almost more than Robbie could bear; the smells were far too tempting. He craned his neck to peer further into the room ... and couldn't believe what he saw. The kitchen was decorated with paper garlands, and red, white and blue bunting was strewn from each corner, crossing over in the middle where a large handmade sign was suspended. Cut out cardboard letters were wound with different-coloured wools, each letter a contrast to the next, spelling HAPPY BIRTH-DAY, ROBBIE.

'Robbie!'

Maeve had appeared out of nowhere and stood right behind him with her arms crossed.

'I suppose you had better come with me...'

Robbie's mouth gaped when he saw what lay on the table beneath the decorations: a handful of presents wrapped in newspaper and tied with kitchen string, and a feast the likes of which he had never seen – a large metal tray sizzled with toad-in-the-hole, and next to it a plate of crisp-coated Scotch eggs sat in a nest of chopped green leaves, alongside two lots of sandwiches cut into the neatest triangles. In the centre of the table was a trifle, the multi-coloured layers promising sponge, fruit, custard and jam. Last but not least, a large porcelain platter was arranged with mouth-watering biscuits and smiling jammy faces arranged around a chocolate birthday cake, glossy dark icing still dribbling down the sides.

When he finally looked up they were all staring at him: Maggie and Rose and Eliza, and even the kitchen hands had stopped work and come to watch. His mind whirled at the thought of what to eat first

'*Happy birthday to you, happy birthday to you...*'

Maggie started and the others joined in, the chorus building.

'*Happy birthday, dear Robbie, happy birthday to you!*'

And then they were all crowding around him and Gillian was wishing him a happy birthday and Tom was shaking his hand and making him feel fifteen already instead of thirteen. He kept looking out for Maggie but it was Rose who reached over and hugged him and just when it seemed as though Maggie would never get through, at last her face appeared beside him.

'How does it feel?' she asked.

'Same as yesterday, and the day before that.'

'Come on, you must feel a bit different. I can

remember being your age.'

He couldn't imagine her being thirteen.

'Why, it's not like I can do anything different, is it? I can't leave school yet or drive a car or have a drink at the pub.'

'You're on your way to being a young man though. And you've lived more than a whole decade.' She said this as if it was something he should be proud of.

'Where's Janek?' Robbie asked, looking around. He had hoped Janek might finally give him the old transmitter he had been dropping hints about for weeks.

She shrugged. 'Perhaps he couldn't get away. Anyway, he told us the Polish celebrate their name day not their birthday, remember.' She handed him a present. 'Here you are. Happy birthday, Robbie.'

'What is it?'

'Open it and find out.'

He ripped through the newspaper to reveal a biscuit tin decorated with pictures of a family and fairground rides, just like the fair that used to come to Highbury Fields before the war. She nodded for him to carry on, so he lifted the cold metal lid to find a set of miniature tools: a pair of pliers, a file, a screwdriver and tiny tweezers.

'Brilliant!' Robbie exclaimed. 'They're exactly what I need. Where did you find them?'

Maggie winked at Tom. 'Friends in high places...'

'And this,' he said, lifting his gaze to stare at the food. 'It's really grand...'

Maggie hadn't liked making excuses for Janek but she knew that Robbie would be disappointed if he didn't come. When the party was nearly over and he still hadn't arrived, she led Robbie through to the backyard where Spoke waited, eager to see them. She sat Robbie on the wall of a garden bed and produced a large orange as theatrically as if she were a conjurer performing a magic trick.

'One catch – you have to share it with me.'

Her nails pierced the skin, releasing a strong citrus tang.

'It's okay, you have it,' Robbie said.

'No, it's for you.'

'I'll just have a couple of segments,' he said earnestly. 'You have the rest.'

'I was only joking. You have as much as you want.'

They huddled together on the wall, sucking at the sweet, sharp juice as the wind picked up, bringing cool gusts that lifted the leaves and swirled them around in the chill night air.

It had been good to have the distraction of the party, and even though it had been a struggle to keep it a secret, it was worth it for the look on Robbie's face. It was a tonic for everyone after the difficulty of the past few weeks. She had been fully intending to tell the staff about Mr Boyle's visit and the notice period since it was halfway through with only another three weeks left, but then there was more news overnight of big casualties and somehow the fate of one little restaurant didn't seem to matter so much any-more. Their enemy's progress into the East was

291

not the news they had expected; it was another victory for Hitler. She didn't follow every twist and turn of events – she hadn't the time – but she knew that it would be difficult for the Allies to recover from this latest setback. It also meant that there was less chance of Eddie's planned visit home. Even so, she had to put on a brave face; after all, they had to protect the children. It was also why she was going to tell Robbie about the temporary arrangements she had made; it really would be for the best.

'Robbie...' she began.

'You know, it was nearly a perfect birthday,' he interrupted.

'Really? What would have made it perfect?'

'If Dad was here. He loves birthdays more than any of us. Always makes a real big day of it. An outing or a picnic...'

'That sounds like fun. Your dad sounds like fun.'

'He is. You wouldn't want to be near him when he's angry, though; he's mad as a wild pig when he gets cross. Even Ma's scared of him then.'

'Robbie, you remember when I went to Sussex, to the farm? You would have really enjoyed it.'

Robbie didn't seem to be listening. 'Maggie,' he said 'I need to tell you something.'

'Wait, let me finish. There's so much to do there ... and there's room for you to go and help if you want to. The Taylors are a really kind couple and they've had children of their own.'

'What?'

'There would be school, of course, and helping out on the farm, but there's plenty of Land Army girls for company and some rather cute piglets.'

'But I can't go to Sussex!'

'You have to, Robbie. You can't stay here any-more – it's not safe. It would just be temporary, until they find you a real foster home.'

'But I have a home, Maggie, and a family.'

'Yes, Robbie, I know, and we'll miss you too, but it really is for the best. When I think about what you could be doing ... and your dad will find you whether you are here or in Sussex.'

'You don't understand – I don't need a foster home.'

Maggie hadn't expected him to agree straight away, but she felt a growing sense of urgency about his situation. London was just too danger-ous. But it seemed a shame to ruin his birthday with talk of his going away.

'Well, let's talk about it tomorrow,' she said.

'No, Maggie...'

'Come on, Robbie,' she insisted. 'Today we're celebrating.'

'Alright – thank you, Maggie. I've had the best day.'

'It's a pleasure.' She elbowed him playfully. 'I bet you're glad you had some of that orange. Delicious, isn't it?'

'Bit ripe,' he said. 'Eliza should have made mar-malade out of it.'

'Is that right?'

'Yeah, I miss marmalade.' He sat up straight on the wall. 'You know what you should do? You should start a competition, with prizes and every-thing, just like the ones you had at the village fetes.'

Maggie had told him about the annual church fetes they attended as children, when they would collapse into piles, exhausted and giggling after competing in games, and when her grandfather would unfailingly win the horticultural prize. And her grandmother's proud smile as he shook hands with the judges – the long evenings spent at the allotment weeding and watering seemed worth it in that one afternoon.

'Do you think enough people would enter?' Maggie said doubtfully.

'Anyone who has a garden is growing something.'

'I suppose you're right.'

'We could make a poster – you know, like the Dig for Victory ones. It could be Dig for Prizes.'

'And what would the prizes be?'

'Meal for two at Maggie's Kitchen for the first prize and then smaller prizes for second and third.'

'Maybe it's not such a bad idea. Who would we have as the judges?'

'I don't know, maybe Mr Boyle for one, seeing as you're always trying to get him to come here. And then Eliza, I suppose.'

'Only two? There are usually three judges on a panel.'

'What about Janek?'

'Of course,' she said. 'He'd be the ideal judge.'

'Well, that's that then,' Robbie said, jumping up and wiping his sticky hands down the front of his trousers. 'I'll go to the railyard and tell him.'

'But don't you think we should wait?'

'What for?'

She had got caught up in the idea and hadn't really thought about the work it would involve, but it was too late to stop Robbie now. She had missed Janek's company and had tried her best to avoid him, but it was just making her think of him even more.

'Yes, you're right. You should ask him.'

'And what about you?'

'What about me?'

'Are you going to ask Mr Boyle?'

For a short while Robbie's birthday had been a distraction; she had been able to put thoughts of Mr Boyle and the notice out of her mind, but now she knew that she couldn't put it off any longer.

'Yes, Robbie. You leave Mr Boyle to me.'

Chapter Twenty-five

BEDTIME STORY:
Once upon a time there were five housewives. Their names were Lady Peel-potatoes, the Hon. Mrs Waste-fuel, Miss Pour-the-vegetable-water-down-the-sink, Mrs Don't-like-uncooked vegetables, and Mrs Won't-eat-carrots. Don't let one of them put a nose in your kitchen.
Marguerite Patten OBE,
Victory Cookbook Nostalgic Food and Facts from 1940–1954

A noisy hiss of brakes announced the arrival of a

large vehicle in the back lane and Maggie rushed out to greet it, calling for Rose to accompany her. She rubbed her arms with her hands, trying to keep warm as she waited impatiently for the driver to open the heavy metal doors. Inside were the promised rabbit carcasses, and she could tell instantly from their smell that the box of black-berries Terrance had also sent were overripe; per-haps because the delivery was three weeks late.

'So, are you taking them or not?' the driver said. 'I've got four more drops to do before I head back.'

'Thank you,' Maggie said firmly. 'We'll defin-itely be taking them.' Rose was looking less cer-tain. 'How do you pick them up?'

'Like this...' Maggie took two rabbits by their hind legs, grasping one in each hand, eyes averted.

As they ferried the thirty small carcasses into the shed, she wished that Janek had been there to help as he'd said he would. She dreaded the thought of having to skin and debone all the rab-bits by herself, and keeping Rafferty out of the way while she did.

Once they'd finished unloading, she was sur-prised to find two men in the kitchen talking to Gillian.

'Oh, Maggie. Thank goodness you're here.' Gillian was looking flustered.

Maggie's heartbeat quickened. Were they here about the rabbits? How could they have found out so quickly? She hastily tried to work out how she would explain the barter system she had used to pay for them; they weren't black market but it'd take someone with an open mind to see that.

'I'm Mr Chambers and this is my colleague Mr Davies,' said one of the officers. 'I believe you know Robert Saunders?'

'Robbie? Yes. Why? Is he alright?'

'We hope so, but we do need to find him before the police do.'

'You mean you're not from the police?'

'No, we're from the Board of Education – but the police are looking for him in connection with a theft. Do you know where he is?'

'No, I haven't seen him today.'

This wasn't strictly true since he had slept in the Morrison shelter under her desk overnight and left early in the morning to find Janek. 'Yesterday?'

She caught sight of the remnants of the birthday banners and bunting out of the corner of her eye.

'Well, yes. He came by at teatime, had something to eat and then left. Can I ask what sort of theft?'

'The taking-things-that-don't-belong-to-you sort,' Mr Davies said.

His colleague scowled at him.

'What I meant is, where did he steal from?'

'Why, has he done this sort of thing before?'

'No, not at all, it's just – oh, never mind...' She didn't want to get him into any more trouble.

'The theft was from a hotel, if you must know,' Mr Chambers said, looking around. 'Are you sure he's not here? It's a big place, plenty of room for a little fella to hide.'

While Mr Chambers continued talking to Maggie, his colleague walked around poking his nose into cupboards and storerooms.

'Sorry, where did you say you were from?' she asked.

'Local council. We received a report that a boy is sleeping here. You have heard of Operation Pied Piper, haven't you, Miss Johnson? You do know that our children are safer out of the city?'

She was relieved they hadn't come about the rabbits but her heart was still pounding and it was because she knew he was right.

Once they realised that Robbie wasn't there, they left with a request that she contact them as soon as he turned up.

'Phew! What was all that about?' Eliza asked.

'Someone has reported Robbie and now they want to send him away.'

'Oh dear,' Eliza mumbled, turning her attention back to a custard that was refusing to thicken. 'Isn't it for the best, though, Mags? They'll help him find somewhere to go. Really, it's probably better if it's official, don't you think?'

'I suppose so. That's not what worries me, though. It's the fact that the police are looking for him. I think he'll be with Janek; Robbie said this morning he was going to look for him at the railyard. One of us should go and find him...'

'I'll go,' Rose offered quickly.

Maggie knew what Eliza would be thinking and willed her not to say anything, not to start trouble now, when Robbie's safety was at stake.

'You know how to get there?'

'Yes,' Rose said, adding for Eliza's benefit: 'I've been there before.'

'Maybe it's you the police should be investigating,' Eliza muttered.

'Hurry up and get your coat then, Rose. Tell Robbie not to come back here until he hears from me. It's not safe for him here anymore.'

The figure standing in the doorway was slightly removed from the rest of the queue that snaked back to the entrance.

'Excuse me, sir, you aren't allowed to stand here – it's a fire exit.'

'Bossing people around as usual...'

'Eddie! Is it really you?' Maggie flung her arms around him.

'Hey.' He pulled away. 'You'll do more damage than Jerry if you carry on like that.'

'I'm sorry. But why didn't you tell me you were coming? I would have come and met you at the station.'

'Well, I'm here now.' He took hold of her hand and looked around at the room pulsing with chatter. 'I think I must have come to the right place, too.'

'Let me look at you...' She took a step back.

His trousers sat loosely around his hips, and his jacket seemed too large for his slight frame. His skin had a dull tinge; rather than the ruddy complexion she would have expected from being outdoors, his skin seemed blanched as though he had seen very little natural light. It made her feel wretched to see him like this, but he was still her Edward. And he was alive.

She swallowed back tears and forced a smile. 'Come on, let's get you something to eat.'

'Any news of John and Maureen?'

'Yes, just last week actually; I'll show you her letter when we get home. He's still on invalid leave. Maureen says he's not too down. You are staying, aren't you?'

'I've only got two days. Thought I'd stay here and then head down to Portsmouth tomorrow to see them.'

'They're doing well,' she assured him. 'The cinema went up though. Maureen was on her way and changed her mind, thank God. Thirteen killed. Anyway, come and sit next to me...'

She gestured for him to sit in one of the only empty seats at the end of a long table.

'You stay here and I'll fetch some food.'

He grasped her wrist, preventing her from moving away.

'Not yet, Maggie. I want to hear about you first Lunch can wait.'

She faltered; she had longed to talk to him about her problems, but now that he was here she was reluctant to worry him.

Taking a deep breath, she smiled. 'You might be able to wait, young man, but my kitchen can't. You need to eat what you can before it runs out. There'll be no more until tomorrow once this lot's gone.'

She hurried away, returning some minutes later with a tray on which was a large plate of cod casserole and vegetables, a steaming hot mug of tea and a double helping of bread and margarine.

'I want you to tell me everything, but first things first...'

'I tried for you, Maggie.'

She reached out and squeezed his hand. 'I know

300

you did.'

When she had reached a dead end with her enquiries about Peter, she had asked Eddie for help, knowing that he was limited as to what he could do, but she'd been so desperate to find out how Peter died. Predictably, it had led nowhere.

He ate slowly, nodding when she asked him a question and listening as she talked about the last frenzied few months and all the wonderful people she had met.

'And what about you, Maggie? How are you?'

It only took one of his looks and the tears began to roll. She found herself telling him about how difficult it had been with Rose and how helpful Janek had proven to be, recalling how stressful it was trying to make the ingredients stretch to make the necessary meals. She shared her suspicions about how Mr Boyle seemed to have it in for her and had been diverting their supplies, and now there was the awful threat of the notice period. Finally, she told him about all the problems with Robbie and the police.

'So you're worried he's going to get into trouble if they find him first?'

'Of course. They'll probably put him in an orphanage if they can't find a foster home – or worse still, if they can prove he stole anything, they could lock him up. Surely he's too young, though, isn't he?'

'I don't know, Maggie. I'm really not clear where the law stands on juveniles. But if he's a thief, are you sure you want this kid hanging around? How do you know he's not stealing from you right now?'

301

'Oh no, he's not like that. He's a great boy; he's really helped me. I'd love for you to meet him. He – he reminds me of Ernest.'

'Maggie...'

'It's okay, he's just got the same cheeky monkey in him.'

She liked to remember the good things about Ernest; his mischief and how much he made them all laugh. She didn't only want to feel the immense gnawing loss; the never-ending guilt. She was supposed to be keeping an eye on him; instead, she had let him go ahead on his own. It had only taken a few minutes, a slip on the canal path, and he was gone. And she knew that was part of the reason their mother had left too.

'Tell you what, why don't you show me around and then we could take a walk. Look around the neighbourhood, places he might be.'

She reached across and put her hand on his arm. 'Oh, Eddie, it's so good to see you.'

He smiled as he scooped up a forkful of fish and vegetables.

'Eddie...' she said hesitantly.

'Yes?'

'Do you ever think about Mum?'

'Sure I do. Not a lot, but occasionally.'

'Me too. Do you think she's still alive?'

'I don't know,' he said, pushing away his plate.

'There's a woman I've seen in here a couple of times – there's something about her. It's odd...'

'Odd in what way?'

'I don't know. Forget it, I'm just being silly.'

She didn't want to admit to her daydreaming, that sometimes she believed her mother had come back to find her.

'You've been working too hard, sis – you're seeing things!'

'I know.' She laughed, flicking him with her cloth.

The lunchtime rush was nearly over and the dining hall was emptying, the staff setting up for the afternoon. She was going to call Tom over but she changed her mind; she wasn't ready to share Eddie with anyone yet.

'Do I get the guided tour now?'

'Well, if you mean what you said about looking for Robbie, I could give you a quick tour first and then we could go – but don't you want to get some rest?'

'Course not. I've only got forty-eight hours' leave. Plenty of time for sleeping when I'm dead.'

She looked at him in dismay. 'Eddie, don't say such things.'

'Oh, come on, don't give me that.'

She shook her head, trying not to smile. 'You go and say hello to Rose and Tom while I finish up.'

By the time she was ready to go, Eddie had caught up with Rose and Tom and she was pleased to see that some colour had returned to his cheeks.

'Where to first?' he asked.

'The depot at Islington Green – it's where all the emergency services have a base. I'll have a word with Bill in case he's seen Robbie. Let's go this way, I'll show you our kitchen garden on the way out.'

Once outside she could tell that he was impressed and there was good reason to be; despite the cold snap, the warm Indian summer had extended the life of most of the plants and there was still rich foliage flowing across the trellises and canes.

It wasn't until they reached the centre of the garden that Maggie heard footsteps on the path and realised that they weren't alone.

She glanced at Eddie and then made her way slowly around the corner.

'Janek!'

'I'm sorry to interrupt. I cannot come here for the next few days so I wanted to check on things.'

'That's fine. It's good to see you.'

'You are busy,' he said, glancing at Eddie.

'This is my brother Edward.'

'Welcome home.' Janek shook Eddie's hand firmly.

'It's good to meet you,' Eddie responded. 'I've been hearing a lot about you and the help you've given Maggie. It's made all the difference.'

'Thank you, but it is Maggie who is responsible for all of this.'

'We're still looking for Robbie,' she interrupted, embarrassed. 'Have you seen him?'

'No. He hasn't been to the railyard, and Rose and I looked along the canal and in the school,' Janek said. 'I don't know where else to try.'

He looked tired, she thought, noticing the dark rings circling his pale eyes.

'Well, I suppose we had better just keep on.'

'I am glad that you are here, Maggie. I wanted to ask you something.'

'Yes?'

'I...' He glanced at Eddie, who immediately took the hint.

'I'm just going to say goodbye to Tom and Rose,' he said. 'I'll see you out front, sis. Good to meet you, Janek.'

'Yes, you too.'

When Eddie had gone, Janek said, 'We have been invited to The Savoy for dinner tomorrow evening. The chef is a friend of mine.'

'That is very kind of him, but why?' Maggie asked, surprised.

'He has read about Maggie's Kitchen and he would like to meet you.'

'Really?'

'Yes, really.'

She hadn't been out for months and the thought of dinner at The Savoy, and with Janek, was very tempting. But how would she get away? There would be the two shifts to organise, not to mention Rose's feelings to consider – and how could she go with Robbie still missing?

'I shall have to think about it. Can I let you know in the morning?'

'Yes, of course.' He looked disappointed.

'I shouldn't be able to enjoy a meal without knowing what has happened to Robbie,' she explained.

'I understand. We will find him.'

Even though she was excited by Janek's offer, the fruitless search for Robbie followed by saying goodbye to her brother, not knowing when she'd see him again, had left Maggie quite worn out.

'I really don't think I should go' she sighed as she slumped against the kitchen counter the following morning.

'I should think not,' Eliza huffed. 'You can't mix with spies!'

'For goodness' sake, Eliza, not that again.'

'Yes, that again – and again and again. And for as long as it takes for you to realise that you shouldn't trust him.'

Rose, who had been silent up until then, said, 'I'll go if you don't want to.'

'I'm sure you would,' Eliza muttered, dragging pots noisily across the stove.

'It would be nice if we could all go,' Maggie said, glowering at Eliza, 'but it was a personal invitation from the chef. Sorry, Rose. Perhaps we could have an evening out next month? Danny Kaye is on at the Albert Hall over Christmas.'

'That's a great idea, Maggie; a Christmas outing.'

But Maggie wasn't listening; she was staring into space.

'What? What is it?' Rose asked.

'Maybe you will have to go after all...'

'Why, whatever is the matter?'

'I gave away the clothes and shoes you bought me for the Ambulance Fund. I don't have anything to wear!'

'Maggie, I'm surprised at you. Some without a coat to put on their back and you worrying about what to wear for a night out!' Eliza scolded.

'Well, I do have to wear something – I can't very well wear this!' she said, hands lifting up the stained white skirt of her uniform.

'It's good enough for most folks,' Rose replied. 'Maybe you could ask Mrs Devereux if you can borrow one of her old furs?'

306

'Rose Barnard,' Eliza scoffed, 'I do believe you are jealous!'

Maggie placed an affectionate arm around her cousin but Rose shrugged it off.

It was true, Maggie realised, studying the sulky expression on Rose's face. This was more than a crush; Rose had really fallen for Janek.

'Perhaps you should go, Rose,' Maggie offered. 'The invitation was for me, but we are a team...'

Rose's eyes brightened. 'Really? Would you really let me go in your place?'

'Why not? Be sure to remember everything about the meal and the ingredients. And you must take note of the other details, anything we can learn from, like the decor and how the waiting staff do things.'

'What do you mean?'

'Well, like: what condiments do they use? What are the substitutions they make? That sort of thing...'

Rose's face had clouded again. 'It's thoughtful of you to suggest I go, Maggie, but it really has to be you. It's important for the restaurant that you see these things for yourself.'

'Well, I suppose so,' Maggie said. 'But only if you're sure.'

'Good, that's settled then,' Eliza said.

Maggie was relieved; the possibility of Rose going in her place had also made her realise just how much she really wanted to spend an evening in Janek's company herself. She would let him know that she would be pleased to accept his invitation.

Chapter Twenty-six

WHAT'S LEFT IN THE LARDER: SOME GENERAL TIPS

Food which has already been cooked only needs to be re-heated and is spoiled if cooked too much a second time. This is especially important to remember when using up left-over meat, fish and vegetables.
Ministry of Food, War Cookery Leaflet No. 11

He could see Maggie and Eliza on their way out the door, so he pushed Spoke's head down and shrank lower, staying out of sight until they were gone; he knew he would be for it if she saw him. He had hidden out before the police finally caught up with him, which they'd only done by luring Spoke with some food. Luckily he had got off with a warning: 'You're alright this time, lad, but next time you'll be seeing the inside of a cell,' the spotty young one had sneered as he pressed his face close to Robbie's.

He stretched his woollen mittens further up his hands; until recently they had covered most of his fingers, but now they were frayed right back to his knuckles. His jacket felt tight too, so that even when he pulled it snug around his belly, he couldn't do the buttons up anymore. It wasn't just his clothes; his shoes pinched and he was hungrier than ever. Whenever he saw his ma she said how much he had grown; maybe she was right.

No one seemed to take any notice of him as he dashed through to the dining hall to see Tom. The cashier was deep in conversation with Maeve, although he stopped when he caught sight of Robbie.

'Robbie! Where've you been? Maggie's been looking all over for you...'

'Well, I'm here now.' He shrugged casually.

'You've had us all worried sick, especially Maggie.'

'What a shame, you just missed her too,' Maeve said. 'Although she'll be back in a while.'

'Best stop here till she gets back,' Tom said, winking at him. 'It'll take a load off her mind knowing you're alright. Here, you want something to eat while you're waiting?'

'What you got?' Robbie said, lifting his nose towards the food trays.

The couple in the queue behind were getting restless so Maeve pulled him to one side.

'How about some rabbit curry? I just made it...'

Tom looked at her and smiled. 'Maeve's been selected by the Wartime Meals Division to do training at Vaughan College in Leicester.'

'Will she be learning to cook properly then?'

'Better.' Tom beamed. 'She'll become a cook adviser.'

'Sounds fancy...'

Robbie had no idea what it meant but he could tell that Tom was impressed. And the way Maeve was grinning back at him, he could see she felt the same way about Tom.

'She your sweetheart now?' Robbie asked.

'None of your business,' Tom retorted. 'Here, Maeve, reckon the lad needs to find something to keep his mouth occupied. You'd better take him out the back to eat.'

Robbie followed Maeve through to the kitchen and watched as she spooned the curry into a bowl.

'Big portion, please,' he said.

'First batch from the country, these rabbits are. You're a lucky young man.'

He wished she wouldn't take so long fussing around with vegetables and making it look nice and just give it to him.

'If it's not ready yet, I'll just go and fetch some dessert first...'

'Oh no, you wait here. Besides, who eats their pudding before their main course?'

'I do. Always.'

'Really?'

'Yes,' he said, trying to sound convincing. 'My ma always said it was alright.'

What his mother really said was that if you couldn't find anything else to eat, then it was okay to eat sweet things if they were available, but Maeve didn't need to know that.

'Well, I only know what Maggie says and that's different.'

'Look, I'm a growing boy,' he said, forcing his stomach out as far as it would go.

'Oh, that doesn't look quite right. I reckon you might have worms'

'When did you say you were off to Leicester?'

Eliza had Maggie by the elbow and was dragging

310

her along Upper Street, ignoring the bewildered looks of passers-by.

'I really shouldn't go, you don't understand,' Maggie told her.

'Of course I do, but you can't let principles stand between you and a four-star meal!'

'But what about all that you've said about him?'

'Forget what I said until after you've been!'

'I can't just put on a happy face and pretend everything is fine when I know that Rose wants to be sitting in my place!'

'Yes, you can – it's called wine ... wine, sherry and port.' Eliza stopped and put her face close to Maggie's. 'You have enough then you'll be pretending he's Frank Sinatra – but don't have *too* much or you'll tell him everything, so just watch yourself.'

Maggie shook her head.

'Come on,' Eliza said, taking her arm again. 'We'll go to Marks and Spencer. If we're going to find anything suitable, it'll be there.'

'It's a waste of time – they'll only have utility clothes. I don't want something with big pockets and buttons; I want to be able to take my coat off!'

'I don't know what's got into you, Maggie. I hope all this press attention hasn't gone to your head. The Maggie Johnson I knew would have been grateful for hand-me-downs!'

'Don't be ridiculous. Why shouldn't I want to look like I fit in with the people around me? Anyway, you know better than most that I can find a nice outfit at a fraction of the cost of one from Marks and Spencer.'

'Where?'

'The charity shop, of course – not the same one you got my lovely outfit from, I suspect, but it's one that I've found some good bargains before!'

A cheer went up as a wedding party stepped out onto the steps of the town hall and a photographer set about arranging the group, lowering the bride's hands, instructing the soldier to stand taller, separating the two young fidgeting bridesmaids. At last they were all in position, framed between the columns of the entrance, only for the bride's veil to be swept away by the wind. The groom took off after it.

Eliza and Maggie looked at each other and giggled.

'Come on, it's just up here,' Maggie said, pulling her friend along.

Inside, she began flicking through a rail of ladies' suits.

'Hey, Maggie,' Eliza shouted from the other side of the shop. 'Look at this...'

She stepped out from behind a rack holding up a dark grey double-breasted suit jacket, the trousers dangling beneath.

'I said I wanted to fit in, not look like I was there to do the cabaret!'

'It's not for you, silly – it's for Janek.'

Maggie thought she must have misheard her for a moment, then it registered.

'Oh, Eliza. Why didn't I think of that? What a marvellous idea.'

She took the hanger and flipped the jacket open; the lining was still intact and the buttons all attached. Only the sleeves looked a little worn but that wouldn't be noticed once it was on.

'Do you think it's the right size?' she asked.

'I think so,' Eliza said, tilting her head to one side.

By the time they left the shop half an hour later, they'd found a white dress shirt with a patch under the arm (they decided this wouldn't be noticed if he didn't take his jacket off), and a grey-and-red striped tie. Maggie had tried on three outfits: a brown wool suit that fitted well but, as her friend pointed out, was the colour of wet moss; a pretty silk dress with a small floral print that they both liked; and a red silk dress that set off the rich chestnut tone of her hair. It not only looked the best, but it had the smallest price tag too, at only ten shillings, so she allowed herself to look through the small basket of jewellery and trinkets on the counter, where she found a leaf-shaped brooch that completed the outfit perfectly.

As she stepped out onto the busy main road, shopping bag in hand, Maggie felt a rush of excitement at the prospect of an evening out with Janek. It had been a long time since she'd anticipated anything so much.

Chapter Twenty-seven

HERRINGS

"Of all the fish that swim in the sea" runs the old saying, "the herring is the king." Certainly whether it is a question of flavour, food value or cheapness, we have to agree that the herring is worthy of his crown.
Ministry of Food, War Cookery Leaflet No. 9

She had only been past The Savoy before during daytime and hadn't expected it to have such a startling effect on her, but as they turned off the Strand and Maggie saw its gleaming steel facade and the black-and-white swirl of the marbled Art Deco entrance, it quite took her breath away. And the doorman displayed all the theatricality that she had expected too, from his top hat and tails right down to the way he bowed his head as he gripped the elaborate gilt scroll of the door handle. Once inside she instantly forgot about the dreary wet streets and her problems with the notice period. Eight majestic chandeliers, at least as large as any of her kitchen stoves, created a waterfall of coloured light in the entrance. A bell-boy pushed a shiny brass trolley past them in one direction while porters guided a group of guests in the other, and behind the carved wooden reception desk well-groomed personnel attended to the exquisitely dressed patrons with practised efficiency. She was still staring when she felt Janek's hand take hers and guide her across the lobby.

She was used to seeing him in his work clothes and was surprised at how different he looked – and at how differently she felt. The suit fitted him well, the jacket stretching across his broad chest, the trousers tapering down so that they sat at just the right place on his shoes, the white shirt snug but not too tight around his neck; if only he would stop fiddling with his shirt cuffs.

The atmosphere in the Grill was subdued compared to the bustling lobby they had left behind, even though there were many diners at the white linen-covered tables.

The maitre d' stepped out from behind the chrome podium and swooped to greet them.

'Good evening, madam, sir.'

Maggie inclined her head. 'Good evening.'

'May I take your coat, madam?'

'Yes, of course. Thank you.'

She felt Janek's eyes on her as she unbuttoned her coat and handed it to the maître d'.

He leaned forward to whisper, 'You look very beautiful.'

'Thank you,' she whispered back. 'So do you.'

She had known as soon as she tried the dress on that it flattered her slim build; the skirt covered her knees but showed off the curve of her legs, the low scoop of the V-neck revealing just a little of her perfumed skin. Her face was bare except for the smallest dab of lipstick that she had also quickly applied to her cheeks after noticing their paleness.

'The name, sir?'

'Raczynski.'

'Sir, madam, would you like to come this way?'

They followed him to a small round table, cocooned by a black velvet booth where they could sit side by side, just close enough to the piano to hear the music without their conversation being drowned out. It was all Maggie could do to stop herself from burying her fingers in the soft fabric of the seat as she leaned back. Everything was so luxurious, right down to the exquisitely embroidered napkins and the intricate pattern of the cutlery; it seemed extravagant but she felt a spark of satisfaction that even in wartime The Savoy had managed to keep its silverware.

Most of the other diners were men in uniform and women in fine clothes and furs, well-off sorts who probably made a habit of dining here. But there were a few tables of people she guessed were just like them – in their Sunday best, here for a special occasion, a birthday or perhaps even a marriage proposal. The wall nearest to them was hung with black-and-white framed photographs: Charlie Chaplin, Errol Flynn, Marlene Dietrich and other distinguished faces she couldn't put a name to but reminded her of the esteemed company that had dined here. Noel Coward and Oscar Wilde were once regulars, she knew, and Winston Churchill frequently brought his cabinet here for lunch. The closest she had come to meeting anyone famous was when the mayor had stopped by the restaurant for a cup of tea after attending a local funeral.

Three waiters with white jackets and bow ties stood with their backs to the wood-panelled walls, but a dozen of them were reflected back in the bevelled mirrors that hung between the columns and windows.

'It's such an elegant room,' Maggie said, awed.

'Yes. It reminds me of a hotel in Warsaw.'

'You miss it?'

'I do, but as you keep telling me, I am lucky to be here.'

'I'm sorry, that must sound so terribly flippant. I don't mean to be.'

'I know.'

He had that distant look she had seen many times before.

'Tell me about Warsaw. What's it like?'

'If you don't mind, can we talk about something else?'

'Of course, whatever you want.'

'I want to just enjoy being here, with you...'

A woman at the next table surveyed the two of them, smiling as if she approved, and Maggie felt a jolt of exhilaration as she realised that the woman probably thought they were a couple.

She glanced up at Janek; he looked perfectly at ease, as if he dined here all the time. Perhaps, like her, he felt that being out together tonight seemed completely natural.

'Is it true that the chef here invented Peach Melba?'

'It is one of Bartek's favourite stories, how Escoffier created Peach Melba for the famous Australian.'

'Who was he?'

'She – Nellie Melba. She was an opera singer.'

'Tell me about Bartek. He's one of the chefs

317

here, isn't he?'

'Yes, one of many, but we are his guests today. Lucky for us you impressed him.'

'Really? I thought you were joking.'

'No, not all, he has told many people about Maggie's Kitchen, so many that you will soon have to move to bigger premises.'

His smile spread across his face and she knew that she had to trust her own instincts rather than Eliza's stories. How could she feel anything other than grateful for the friendship of a man who always had her best interests at heart, who spent so much time helping others? When he arrived he had nothing, no possessions of any kind, and she had been suspicious because of it. Now she knew it wasn't because he was a man who had run away, but because he had fled with all that he needed, and the only thing of value to him – his life.

'Madam, may I?'

The waiter hovered, white linen napkin in hand.

'Thank you,' she said, lifting her arms so he could lay it across her lap with a flourish.

'Would madam care for an aperitif?'

It had been so long since she had been out for a meal that she had quite forgotten what drink she should order.

As if sensing her hesitance, the waiter suggested, 'Perhaps the house cocktail, the Kir Royal?'

'Yes, of course. That would be lovely.'

'And sir?'

'Vodka.'

'Certainly. With...?'

'Ice.'

318

'Very good. The salmon has been replaced with a lemon sole,' he informed them. 'Do you have any questions about the menu?'

'Can we have a few minutes?'

'Certainly, madam.'

Her eyes flicked across gold lettering and she couldn't help but think of Robbie, scouring the hotel's vast kitchens for ingredients he could forage.

BILL OF FARE FOR THE DAY
Empire port
Muscat wine
★

Hors d'oeuvres
Turtle soup
★

Jugged hare
Stewed tripe with peas and onion
Salmon with boiled potatoes and salad
★

Peach Melba
Stewed cherries and custard
★

Tea or Coffee

'Oh look, they've got Peach Melba! What are you going to have?' Maggie asked.

'I haven't decided. What about you?'

'I'm not sure either,' she replied.

'Why are you whispering?'

'Am I?'

'Yes.' He smiled. 'We are supposed to be here, remember.'

'I know...'

She looked away, embarrassed; she could hardly believe they *were* there, and despite their second-hand clothes, she certainly felt the part.

'I can't tell you how much I'm looking forward to this,' she said. 'Do you know how long it's been since I've eaten a meal that somebody else has cooked?'

'Let's hurry up and choose then.'

'I'll guess what you are going to have. You tell me if I'm right.'

'If you like...'

'You think it's foolish?'

'Of course not. Go ahead.'

'Right,' she said, looking back at the menu. 'You are going to have the turtle soup – no, make it the hors d'oeuvres – and then ... the jugged hare. Am I right?'

'What about dessert?'

'The Peach Melba of course!'

'Two out of three isn't bad.'

'Which one did I get wrong?'

'The dessert. Stewed cherries are a favourite.'

'Never mind – it's your turn now.'

'Definitely the hors d'oeuvres, then the lemon sole ... and of course, the Peach Melba.'

'Very good, you win – although you did have a bit of help on the last one.'

'It's a draw then. Is that fair?'

'It's okay, I'm not a sore loser.'

'That's good to hear. I'd hate to have to leave before we have even begun the meal, that would be an awful waste.'

'Of the evening or the food?'

'Both.'

As Janek placed their order with the waiter, she looked at him, at his thick blond hair and the strong curve of his nose, and she realised why she had been so nervous about coming tonight. It wasn't because of Eliza's suspicions or her fear of upsetting Rose; it was because of her own feelings. Until now she hadn't admitted how she watched out for him at the end of each day, how she listened for the click of the gate to signal his arrival and how her heart sank when she saw he had gone. She had recently taken to creating small jobs for him to do and questioned him on things she already knew the answers to, just to keep him around.

The meal was served at just the right pace, the starter coming soon enough to satisfy their hunger but leaving enough time between the main course and the dessert to ensure they were not too full and had plenty of time to talk. And she was surprised by how much they had to talk about; they spoke of the food and how they would make things differently (he insisted her stewed cherries were superior). She secretly wished she could hold each mouthful longer, relishing the taste and texture; the fresh snap of asparagus, the rich velvety lemon butter which coated and refreshed her tongue at the same time, the sweet tartness of the raspberries with the cold smoothness of the ice-cream. After the years of austerity and rationing, she wanted the flavours to linger on her palate, to smell and feel each morsel.

As well as discussing the meal, they speculated

about the origins of the other diners, which prompted them to talk about the places they one day hoped to visit. They paid little attention to the war and the limits it placed on them, behaving as if it were merely a temporary situation and any day now the borders would disappear and they would be free to travel wherever they pleased. Maggie journeyed by boat from Paris down to the French Riviera and then by train up to the Italian Lakes, visiting famous churches and palaces she had read about in magazines. Janek was drawn to the wild savannahs of Africa and the animals he would see there.

It was ten thirty by the time the pianist retired and they looked up to see that they were the only ones left in the dining room.

'Are we able to see Bartek?' Maggie asked when the waiter approached with her coat. 'I'd like to say thank you.'

'I'm sorry, madam, he sends his apologies but there is a matter he is attending to. He hopes that you have enjoyed your evening.'

It had been wonderful, but it was a world away from the stress and shortages of living one day to the next; it wasn't a world that she was part of, or Janek.

'We did, thank you very much. Please tell him that he must come into Maggie's any time; he is most welcome there.'

'Of course.'

As the waiter helped her into her coat and she slipped her hand inside the pocket, it brushed against the pocket watch and she realised that her thoughts had not turned to Peter all night.

Janek watched from the end of the path until the light flickered off in the hallway and Maggie closed the front door behind her. He hadn't expected to be invited in but he would have had to refuse anyway; during dinner the waiter had slipped him a message from Bartek asking Janek to meet him at the Polish Club. It was the first time he had received such a request. Ognisko Polskie had barely been open a year but it had become a primary meeting point for Polish officers and exiled Poles. An invitation to meet there could only mean one thing – that the Union for Armed Struggle wanted him to do something.

He was able to get the bus most of the way and walk the last part through the near-deserted streets of South Kensington, barely noticing the empty shopfronts and offices, pausing only to look at a corner block dominated by a giant billboard with Churchill pointing at him and demanding that he DESERVE VICTORY and LEND TO DEFEND. He picked up his pace and hurried past the white stucco-fronted buildings towards 55 Exhibition Road.

Two Polish guards standing on either side of the imposing columns took his papers and left him alone for several minutes, so he shrank back into the shadows of the portico watching uniformed officers as they entered, rubbing his hands together to keep warm.

At last they waved him inside and he was greeted by the raucous conversation of his native tongue. It was just as well he was wearing a suit, he realised, otherwise he would have drawn attention among the uniformed officers as he looked for Bartek.

The crowded room led through to a much larger main salon that looked strangely shabby for such a stately house. He hadn't been into any of these residences before but had expected the interiors to be as elegant as the outsides. Here, though, only the marble fireplaces and the cornicing of the ceiling and doors hinted at its grand Georgian origins. The rest of the decoration was more akin to the clubs back home; a mix of worn sofas and tables partnered with an assortment of chairs and stools. The walls were hung with muted oils of rural landscapes and portraits of prominent Polish military men and politicians, so that even the room, hazy with smoke and noisy with heated discussion, felt rousingly familiar.

'Janek!'

At first he couldn't make out where the voice was coming from, but then he saw Stefan waving at him from a doorway on the other side of the room.

He greeted him briskly and Janek took his altered manner to mean that this was the meeting he had been waiting for, so he followed the other man without question.

Stefan led him down a dim musty stairwell into the basement, the voices and laughter fading as the narrow corridor took them much further than the length of the rooms of the club upstairs. The odour of stale nicotine and beer was overtaken by an intense briny smell, and as they passed the kitchen he caught a glint of silver scales as a chef plunged a fish into a pot of boiling water.

They passed open storerooms on the left and closed doors on their right, until the air seemed to vanish altogether and they were at the end of the corridor.

Stefan opened the door ahead of him and motioned for Janek to enter.

It was some kind of storeroom, with racks of shelving and upturned crates. He could see Filip and Fryderyk sitting together with another man he didn't recognise; there was no sign of Bartek.

Stefan addressed the stranger.

'Franciszek, you have not yet met Janek...'

The storeroom was claustrophobic with low ceilings, and Janek had to bend down to shake Franciszek's hand, dispensing with their usual formal greeting. The low lighting made grim caricatures of his comrades; unshaven, dark circles beneath their eyes and mouths set firm. Under any other circumstances he wouldn't want to trust any of them, but he knew better now; he knew that these were brave men.

There were only upturned crates to serve as table and chairs, so Janek lowered himself onto one of them and waited for Stefan to speak. 'You had some trouble getting in?'

'They took my papers. They said they would return them on the way out.'

'That is good. It will be for your identification – all you need now are photographs.'

He didn't know what Stefan was referring to, but had learned that it was best not to ask too many questions; the last time they had met, after the message Janek had received while at church, he had become frustrated, told them that they were running out of time. But Stefan had warned him that he would be replaced if he wasn't patient.

'We have a delivery coming,' Stefan said now, without preamble, 'and we need you to meet it.'

'What is it?'

'You don't need to know.'

'What do I have to do?'

'The delivery needs to be stored for a few days. At the restaurant.'

'What?' Janek hadn't known what to expect but it certainly wasn't this. 'I'm not sure that is such a good idea.'

'Why? You and this woman are lovers, are you not?'

'No, we are friends – but that's not it. She would want to know what it was... I would have to lie.'

'What are you saying, Janek? Are you not willing to help? Is this woman more important to you than your countrymen now, more important than Dimitri?' Stefan's eyes had become cold.

'Of course not. It's the authorities that are the problem. There are constant inspections and visits from the local government – it's too risky.'

Stefan stood up and paced for a few moments; this clearly wasn't the response he had anticipated.

'You are sure?' he asked.

Janek nodded.

He'd barely had time to consider his response, and it surprised even him; despite his denial, he *was* putting Maggie first – but it couldn't be any other way.

Stefan was looking at him now, his eyes calculating.

Janek held the other man's stare; he was committed to the Union for Armed Struggle and all that the Polish resistance stood for, but he had let the people he loved down once before and would never let it happen again. After tonight, he was certain that Maggie shared his feelings; he would not put at risk all that she had worked for.

Stefan finally looked back at the other men.

'The Germans have captured Kerch and the Panzers are advancing on Moscow; it could be only a matter of days before it is under German control.'

Stefan had been talking to all of them but now he focused his attention on Janek and spoke very slowly.

'Nobody really knows how the new Polish army will fare in the Soviet Union... I think you would agree that our army deserves our support.'

'We can use the railyard,' Janek replied. 'The access there is easier, the road wider and more discreet.'

'Yes, we considered this, but there are some places that are more easily observed than others. You must find a way to make the restaurant work. We are all depending on you, Janek. Especially your brother.'

Chapter Twenty-eight

GOOD FOOD LEADS TO GOOD HEALTH:
It is very important that we should understand the
part that food plays in our lives and so be able
to choose an adequate diet from the foods
that are available.
Ministry of Food, Foods for Fitness

She lay awake most of the night, watching the moonlight dance across the wall and ceiling, and listening to the footsteps of the ARP warden on his rounds. She replayed the evening in her mind, thoughts quickly returning to the naturalness of it and the ease of their conversation. The effect of his physical presence had surprised her; sitting close to him for hours as they had never done before, legs occasionally brushing, their bodies only inches apart; it had been exhilarating but she had also been excited when he suggested things that they could do together in the future, places they could go. Now she felt quite certain that his feelings were as strong as hers.

Eventually, she threw back the eiderdown and dressed, so early that even Matilda wasn't awake when she left, the coop uncharacteristically quiet and free of the familiar scratching noise.

It was still dark as she crossed Essex Road and the wind thrashed branches against neighbouring buildings, sending dead twigs and leaves spiralling to the ground.

She had to force the restaurant door closed against the wind and only then realised how weak her arms felt and how little energy she had left. It had been her habit to get to the restaurant at five in the morning and leave at eight at night, but now, with only two weeks of her notice left, she couldn't leave anything to chance. The paperwork needed to be up to date, the inventories complete, accounts all filed and the kitchen hygiene faultless. Then there were also the mobile canteens that she had to staff and supply, and while she had adhered to every condition of the notice so far, she wanted to make sure there was nothing that Mr Boyle could catch her out on.

Even though the kitchen was empty, the smell of roasted meats and syrupy puddings lingered and the bare worktops gleamed as if they knew how prized they were. She could still hear the cook assistants' voices, the unguarded laughter and the shouting when the pressure was on, and she could picture Eliza standing against the worktop she so coveted, the one right near the end with a view directly through to the restaurant so that she didn't miss a thing.

Maggie was walking towards her office, her mind on the paperwork that awaited her, when a noise made her stop.

It was a scratching sound, coming from the other side of the wall, like a dog trying to find a bone.

She waited but there was no further sound so she carried on to her office and settled at her desk.

'Three hundred and twenty-four...'

It had always helped her calculations to count out loud, but there was the scratching noise again; another quick burst and then nothing.

Goosebumps pricked her skin as she thought of the rats they waged a constant battle against that had proved too large for poor Rafferty.

The noise seemed to be coming from the storage cupboard, so she tiptoed slowly towards the doorway, then stopped to listen, hoping that it wouldn't come again. But there it was, louder than before; too loud to be a rat.

A sliver of dawn light crept through the window, reflecting off the blades in the knife rack. She reached for the long carving knife and stepped softly back across the floor.

She took a deep breath; she was probably being silly. At worst it would be a large trapped rat; more likely it would be one of Tom's practical jokes. She leaned forward and wrenched open the door.

Slumped on the floor, partly hidden by a dark oversized coat, lay a small, distorted shape. Light from the doorway fell across a barely recognisable face, features contorted and covered in tiny beads of sweat, eyes rolled upwards in the grip of fever. His breathing became more rapid as he pulled his feet up towards his stomach, gripping his knees and groaning.

'Robbie?' she gasped.

She dropped down beside him, pushing damp hair from his eyes, moving the coat away to reveal the sodden clothes beneath. Not just his shirt and jumper but the blanket that he was lying on were wet.

'What is it, Robbie? What's wrong?'

His answer came quickly as he vomited in several violent heaves. Maggie stroked his back until eventually he slumped exhausted to the floor.

She needed wet towels to wipe his face and rags to clean the floor where he lay. More than that, he needed a doctor. But when she moved to leave, he reached for her.

'Please. Don't go.'

'I need to get help, Robbie. You're very ill.'

'Don't leave me,' he whispered.

'Alright, I won't go anywhere.' So she stayed kneeling beside him, stroking his head, until he closed his eyes and all she could hear were small whimpering sounds. 'Is there anything you need?' she said after a short time.

'Can you fetch Ma?' he whispered.

'What do you mean?'

His eyelids flickered, half-opening.

'I'm sorry, Maggie – I lied to you...'

'But you're sick, Robbie. You're not making any sense.'

He twisted round to look at her, his eyes finding her in the dim light 'I have a ma, and two sisters – they're staying near Bristol. I just lied because I wanted to be here for Dad, and for you, Maggie. It was good being here – feeling part of things.'

'But, Robbie, how could you? How could you not have told me about your mother – does she even know where you are?'

'Yes,' his voice was weaker now and he laid his head down across her lap. 'I write to her most weeks ... visit each month...'

Typical Robbie, trying to justify his behaviour, but this was unforgivable and hurtful. How could he have kept this from her – didn't he care about the worry he had caused? But then she remembered their conversation in the garden after his birthday – hadn't he been trying to tell her something about his family then?

'She thinks I'm still at our old house, that the neighbours are looking out for me.'

Poor Robbie, and she felt partly to blame. How terribly wrong she had been to turn a blind eye, to let him remain on the streets, to help him evade the authorities and the police. She should have insisted they find him a home, forbid him from helping at the restaurant, and she never should have let him stay here.

'I'm sorry, Robbie,' she murmured. 'I'm so sorry...'

Chapter Twenty-nine

The Ministry of Food dried egg is pure fresh egg with no additions and nothing but moisture taken away. It is pure egg, spray dried. Eggs are a highly concentrated form of food. They contain first-class body building material. They also help us to resist colds and other infection because of their high protective properties.
Ministry of Food, War Cookery Leaflet No. 11

As Eliza slid another batch of gingerbread from

332

the oven, the mixed spice mingled with treacle and ginger, producing a fleeting memory of Christmas. The comforting smell had always reminded Maggie of her mother's recipe, and she hadn't made it for years because of it. Pushing the thought to the back of her mind, she went in search of Maeve.

After the morning's downpour the dining hall was still empty, and with a gale forecast for the afternoon, it would be an ideal opportunity to continue her training. The transformation in Maeve had been quite unexpected, from being quite hopeless in the kitchen when Maggie had first met her at the radio factory, she was now working faster and more proficiently than any of them, and these days Maggie relied on her to help bring all the new kitchen hands up to speed and train them for the mobile canteens. In their quest to keep the cupboards stocked, Maggie had shown Maeve how to preserve – bottling fruits and vegetables, making sauces and ketchups, pickles and chutneys. There was no waste and hardly anything made it into the pig bin anymore thanks to Maeve's exacting eye. It was the other reason Maggie had put her forward for the training scheme; while she had been reluctant to lose Maeve for a week, she couldn't ignore the fact that the notice period was nearly up. If he wasn't satisfied with what he found, Mr Boyle wouldn't be giving her a second chance. At least with Maeve trained and ready, he wouldn't need to look far for a replacement. It had not been without problems though; she had left the gas on overnight and Maggie had to go to great lengths to show her the safety routines – a gas explosion would be devastating.

Not that Maeve was perfect, of course; she had been responsible for the food-poisoning incident, since she had been the one to cook and store the rabbit curry that had felled Robbie – luckily it hadn't been served to any customers. Poor Robbie, though, had been hospitalised before being sent home to his mother and sisters who were alive and well and living near Bristol.

She had felt so hurt and vulnerable that it was then that she decided to tell Eliza about Mr Boyle and the notice period. In the end it had proved to be a relief; Eliza was extraordinarily helpful, making sure she did everything to the letter and keeping the others in order without giving anything away. Maggie was still feeling terribly upset and a little angry with Robbie, despite remembering his trying to tell her that he didn't need a new family, when her aunt arrived, unannounced and dripping wet.

'It's bitter out there, really bitter.' She patted her coat down, sending droplets flying.

'Aunt Mary, this is a surprise.'

'Hope you don't mind me just dropping in like this, but it couldn't wait.'

'Of course not. Here ... sit down.'

'Well, I'm just going to come straight out with it, if you don't mind – no point beating around the bush. I don't want you to think I'm ungrateful after all you have done for Rose, but I don't think she should work here anymore.'

'What? Why ever not?'

'Don't you know, really?'

'No, I don't think I do.'

'Come on, Maggie, you know what I'm talking about. Poor Rose is heartsick over this fella, and I hear you've been out with him yourself – to The Savoy no less.'

'Do you mean Janek? Yes, I did go to dinner with him, but it was a professional outing; we'd had an invitation from the chef there.'

'Still, couldn't you have let Rose go? You'll have no trouble getting another fellow, Maggie, and Rose has really fallen for this one.'

Maggie didn't know what to say. And to make matters worse, she hadn't seen or heard from Janek since that evening. She was beginning to think she had imagined the whole thing!

'That may be true, Aunt Mary, but there's nothing I can do – not if he doesn't feel the same way about Rose.'

'It's not just that, though, is it?'

'What do you mean?'

'Well, first you lure Rose away from a perfectly good job, a job that suited her well and with reasonable money, and you promised to teach her to cook. Then, after keeping her as a waitress and kitchen hand – a skivvy, for all intents and purposes – she then gets passed over for training in favour of someone else.' Her aunt reached for her handkerchief and began dabbing at her eyes. 'Are you not looking out for your cousin at all?'

Maggie couldn't look at her aunt; she had nothing to be guilty about, she had done nothing wrong, yet she felt ashamed.

'What do you want me to do, Aunt Mary?'

'If you care anything for Rose – and for me –

you'll give up any designs you have on this fella and leave him for Rose.'

Once her aunt had gone, Maggie went in search of Rose. She found her flicking through *Picture-goer Weekly* in the staffroom and she didn't raise her head when Maggie entered.

'Rose, I'm sorry you missed out on the training scheme this time,' Maggie said, 'but they will be offering it again. I'll try my hardest to make sure your skills are up to scratch by then.'

Rose ignored her and continued leafing through the magazine.

'You know what a valuable job you do here, don't you?' Maggie asked.

Finally Rose looked up at her. 'I think I was better off at the shoe shop! I know you can't treat me differently because I'm family, but you are harder on me than anyone else.'

'That's not true,' Maggie cried.

'It is, Maggie. And I never thought it before, but I do now: you are cruel. You know that you could have anyone, so why Janek? Why him?' Her lower lip was trembling, just as it had when she was a child.

Maggie she sat down in the seat opposite and reached for her cousin's hands.

Rose pulled away.

Maggie sighed. 'I don't want to upset you, Rose, but I don't know what you want me to do.'

Rose pouted. 'Do you always have to be the one to spend time with him? Isn't there something he and I could work on together?'

Maggie thought of how naturally her days over-

336

lapped with Janek's, of the interests they shared, the instinct for all things natural and a passion to succeed in what they were doing; she saw it in him and she knew he recognised the same qualities in her. She couldn't imagine Rose being an equal to Janek in the same way, but she would never have the heart to say so.

'What do you have in mind, Rose?'

'I don't know. Could I be put in charge of the gardens maybe?' She was animated at last. 'I could look after them when he's not here and help him when he is.'

'What about the roster? Everyone likes an excuse to get outside and help.'

'Fine, don't help me then – but I think I would rather be lonely my whole life than see him come and go all the time and never be with him!'

Chapter Thirty

A good high tea or supper should include either a raw salad or a correctly cooked vegetable dish and one of the body-building foods such as cheese, egg, bacon, meat or fish.
Ministry of Food, War Cookery Leaflet No. 7

He could hear his own breathing, the push and pull of his chest muscles, the air whistling in and out his nostrils; with his telephone conversation finished it felt too quiet – he needed to hurry up and leave before Maggie found him here. Quickly wiping the condensation from the receiver, he replaced the handset and folded the paper into his pocket.

Stefan had been to see him twice since their meeting at the Polish Club and had finally given him an ultimatum: tomorrow was when they wanted to make the drop. The layout of the restaurant hadn't been a problem, he knew it like the back of his hand, but they hadn't been satisfied with his diagrams and he had to come back to double-check they were right. There were only a few more details that he needed to give them and then he would have delivered on his promise. Then he was going to tell Maggie everything; he would tell her what happened to his family and he would explain what Stefan had asked him to do. He would promise her that it was only a few days and then the goods would be gone. Then he would ask her to go out again, regularly.

He checked the desk, making sure that nothing was out of place, pushing the papers back where she had left them, when he caught her reflection in the glass of a picture frame.

'What are you doing here?'

When he turned, her expression was so pained that it made him want to tell her everything right away.

'I'm sorry, I should have asked...'

'Yes, you should.'

But he couldn't tell her anything now; he needed to get away, make sure the rest of the arrangements were in place, leave her before he lost his resolve, but the small room trapped them together and he was unable to pass.

'Who were you calling?'

She was only inches away and, distracted by the scent of her skin, at first he couldn't answer.

'My cousin; we are trying to find out what happened to his brother. No one will give us answers.'

He couldn't look into her eyes, not like he had at dinner. And he couldn't lie to her either.

'Maggie, I have to tell you something...'

'No, let me go first.'

'You need to let me tell you how I feel.'

Only one side of her face was illuminated, as if it were only a fragment of her that was really there.

'No, listen to me,' she insisted. 'I want you to know that I couldn't have done this without you. I haven't said it before but you helping me ... having you here, means more than you will ever know...' Her voice cracked and he heard her swallow as she paused. 'But I have to ask you to leave now. Please don't ask why.'

He didn't believe her; maybe he hadn't heard right.

'I'm sorry, Janek – you can't come here anymore.'

After all he had planned, the decision he had made; she was going to come first in everything.

He moved closer, forcing her to look at him.

'I have my reasons.'

Rain battered the roof and he hoped he had misheard but she repeated the words.

'I'm sorry – you have to go.'

He tried to look at himself through her eyes, at the man who ran from his responsibilities; he had feared this day would come, when she would see him for the coward that he really was. It was the only explanation. But why now, after their evening together, when he was more certain of how she felt than he had ever been?

'What have I done wrong? Please tell me.'

She turned her head away; he couldn't even read her face anymore but he saw her body tremble.

'It's nothing to do with you, Janek. It's me.'

He waited for more but she didn't say anything, so he took the Bible from his pocket and removed the prayer card. The picture of the Black Madonna facing upwards, benevolent eyes turned towards his, and on the back the inscription:

True love requires courage and triumphs in the friendship it brings.

'I will do what you ask of me, Maggie, but please ... remember these words.'

And he pressed the prayer card into her hand.

It wasn't hard to fill the days after Janek left; she had to make sure everything was up to scratch for the ministry's last inspection barely more than a week away, and she threw herself into training to keep up morale. It had become routine for the women to start the morning around one of the warming stoves, listening to the news service on the wireless, hands cradling mugs of steaming tea with the whole of the day's sugar ration in it. Just in the last week the weather had turned even more bitter and she noticed it was taking them longer to get back to work, particularly now with events worsening in the East. Each day there was news of Japan's belligerence and threats and it felt as if it would surely only be a matter of days before an announcement came of their attack. She had managed to keep going as if nothing were wrong, but she couldn't help glancing up every time there was a knock at her office door, or when she heard the groan of the back gate or someone called her name. She'd thought Janek would come back, but he hadn't.

'Come on, Maggie, you've not even touched your tea this morning.'

'No, I'm fine, really. Thank you, Tom.'

Standing around drinking tea wasn't going to solve any of her problems, or theirs. The energy to feign cheerfulness had deserted her and it was an effort to join in the conversation. It was an unusually excited exchange, with everyone huddled around Maeve, congratulating her on passing her cook's test, but Maggie struggled to feel pleased for her and felt worse because of it. She couldn't help herself; as Maeve received a letter confirming her future as a cook adviser, Maggie was waiting for one to confirm whether she could even continue working as a cook. Robbie was recovering with his mother in the countryside, there was no more Janek and soon there may be no more restaurant; everything that she had cared about was gone.

She slipped out into the garden, where the sight of tiny shoots poking from the earth and new buds usually cheered her, but now there was only the cold white glare of frost. The plot was barren where once fruits and vegetables had thrived, and with no Janek or Robbie to maintain it, the weeds would soon take over. Even the glow of sunrise looked menacing rather than being a friendly reminder of a new day. The noise of buses on their commute down Upper Street intruded but she had lost interest in the people on them or in providing sustenance to them as she once had.

After a short while she heard the door close and Eliza's voice behind her.

'Penny for your thoughts...'

'You don't want to know, I assure you!'

Maggie turned her face away so that her friend couldn't see the tears that never seemed to stop falling of late.

'I know it's a strain, Mags, but you've got to keep going. We all must.'

'What's wrong with me, Eliza? I can't even find two kind words to say to Maeve. I'm not the same person anymore.'

'There's nothing wrong with you. You've had a lot to deal with, huge pressures. You're the only woman I know who could have held it together and come this far; others would have crumbled months ago.'

'I don't feel anything though, Liza. It's worse than feeling jealous or angry; I just feel numb. What's wrong with me?'

Eliza pushed the stray strands of hair from Maggie's face and tucked them behind her ear.

'There is nothing wrong with you. You've just realised that Maggie Johnson is human too, that's all.'

But it wasn't just that. She hadn't even been that kind to Eliza and Mike when they had announced their engagement, instead wondering how they could have been so selfish and done it at a time like this. It wasn't just the restaurant; she had lost Peter and now she had lost the only other people she cared about and who had made her want to carry on.

She looked into her friend's eyes. 'I should never have done it, Eliza. I told you I couldn't.'

'Don't be silly.'

'It's true – look at the damage I've done: Robbie nearly poisoned, Rose is miserable and hates me, I drove Janek away and now I'm going to let down everyone who relies on me for a job, customers who depend on us for their meals. We could be closed down this time next week and then where will they all go?'

'You are overreacting now. No one is going to close us down – and as for Rose and Robbie and Janek, they're all fine. They'll be back, you'll see.'

But Maggie couldn't. As far as she was concerned, she had driven them all away. Everyone she had ever cared about had been harmed or had left: Ernest, her mother, Peter, and now Janek and Robbie. Mr Boyle was right all along: she wasn't capable of running her own kitchen, and the sooner they took it away from her the better.

Chapter Thirty-one

Puddings and sweets are a delightful addition to a main meal but should only be regarded as such. Children particularly should be encouraged to eat their first course of meat, fish or cheese, etc., potatoes,

vegetables or salad before they are
allowed the sweet course.
Ministry of Food, War Cookery Leaflet No. 13

According to Robbie his sisters always wore their long blonde hair in pigtails and his mother was one of the shortest people you were ever likely to meet, but as Maggie blew onto her gloved hands, she wasn't sure she would recognise any of them in the swell of passengers that pushed past.

For nearly an hour she had watched keenly as each train arrived, as the platform emptied and refilled, and the crowds funnelled through the gates and onto the concourse behind her, but there was no sign of Robbie and his family.

There were no guards around to ask, and since departures and arrivals were no longer advertised at stations, she could only hope that nothing had happened and that the train would arrive soon, otherwise she would have to go back to the restaurant.

Two female ticket collectors stood near the gates, long black coats and hats making them quite indistinguishable from the suited businessmen and women that swarmed the platforms. And just inside the barrier, a small group of shivering children clutched their gas masks and suitcases. One of the helpers bent to attach a London Evacuation Scheme label to the coat of a girl whose arms were wrapped around an overstuffed teddy bear. On the other side of the barricade the mothers watched, their faces half hidden by handkerchiefs clutched tightly between fingers. Maggie was still crying at the slightest thing and

344

the sight of them made her eyes well up; she couldn't imagine how these poor women felt. She had seen Gillian fall apart when the girls went away, and how she still missed them now. Each new letter that arrived was read aloud in the staffroom and carried around in Gillian's apron pocket until the next one came, the change in each new handwritten letter or numeral analysed, the improvements praised. And she talked about them endlessly, never an opportunity missed to footnote a conversation with: 'Shepherd's pie is Molly's favourite', or 'Beatrice tried making scones once', or 'I can never get Alex to eat cabbage'.

Maggie made her way over to a small kiosk that nestled between a newspaper stand and a mobile kitchen selling tea and sandwiches. The kiosk displayed a collection of goodies that she could see from where she stood; packets of Parma violets and lemon bonbons, small bags of wrapped Fruit Salad sweets and Black Jacks, which were Robbie's favourite.

She took a shilling from her pocket and picked up a packet of Parma violets for herself and a bag of Black Jacks for Robbie.

'Excuse me, you wouldn't happen to know which platform the Bristol Temple Meads trains come in at?' she asked the vendor.

'That one over there.' He took the coin she proffered and pointed to a platform that was already choked with thick white clouds from the arriving train.

'Thank you,' she said, pushing the sweets into her pocket and setting off in the direction of the platform.

The carriage doors were barely visible but she could hear them slam as the passengers disembarked and began to throng along the platform. It was only a short time that Robbie had been gone but it felt as though there was so much to tell him, so much he had missed. He would be as surprised as they had been by Mike and Eliza's engagement and at Maeve's new appointment, but she still hadn't worked out what to tell him about Janek. She knew how much Robbie would miss him and how upset he would be that Janek hadn't said goodbye. For now, she would just stick to news of Mrs Foster's new chicken and the Hitchcock film playing at the Screen on the Green.

She pictured Janek emerging from the steam, striding down the platform towards her, head and shoulders above everyone else, but as the air cleared and the crowd thinned there was only a short woman holding a carpetbag in one hand and a brown suitcase nearly as big as her in the other. Two young girls either side of her wore plaits, just as Robbie had described, and a few feet behind was Robbie himself, struggling under the weight of two cases even larger than the first. He looked as though he had grown; even his face seemed altered, the shape and features elongated so they were not all crammed into the centre anymore. Her instinct was to rush over to help, but there was something about seeing him here with his mother that made her hold back.

Then he noticed her and broke into his lopsided grin. Dropping the bags, he ran towards her and threw his arms around her waist.

'My, look at you ... I think you must have grown at least two inches,' she said, standing back and straightening herself up. 'I told you the country air would do you good.'

'You can breathe it easy enough, but you'd die of boredom if you stayed in it too long!'

'So you must be Maggie?'

Robbie's mother moved to stand next to him. She was the mirror image of Robbie, with her features set in exactly the same way; not too close together or too far apart. Her nose was slightly too pointed, but the long lashes framing her dark eyes made feminine an otherwise plain face.

'I'm Nancy. It's lovely to meet you – I've heard so much about you,' she said, grasping Maggie's hand. 'Thank you for looking out for him.'

'I haven't, really. He's been helping me.'

'I know what you've done for him. He's told me. He couldn't've stayed here if it wasn't for you. And I know what a little bugger he can be, so it's no mean feat keeping him out of strife.'

'He's been no problem,' Maggie assured her. She dared not mention the stolen truffle or the black market foods and hiding from the police.

'It's meant so much for him to be here for his dad.'

'Is there any news of your husband?'

'No, no news, but we've made the decision that we're all going to be together from now on.'

'Oh, is Robbie staying in Bristol?'

'No. We're all coming back.'

Nancy leaned over and patted the smallest girl's head. 'Beth, this is Maggie. Say hello.'

'Hello, Maggie.'

The little girl gave a gap-toothed smile and Maggie kneeled down so that she was eye level with her.

'You have the most beautiful hair I have ever seen. Is it real gold?'

Beth giggled.

Nancy pushed the other girl forward. 'And this is my older girl, Emily.'

'Hello, Emily,' said Maggie. 'How old are you?'

'I'm seven and Beth is only four.'

'Well, she is lucky to have you. I only had brothers.' Maggie stood up. 'And how was your journey?' she asked Nancy.

'It was good; these two slept and Robbie and I played I Spy, didn't we? Kept beating me though!' She leaned over and planted a big kiss on Robbie's cheek.

The effect of this simple maternal gesture on Maggie surprised her. She had never tried to fill Robbie's mother's shoes, but the relationship they had formed was the closest thing to motherhood she had ever known and felt she was ever likely to. They had been through a lot in the last few months, but as she watched him now she realised that things would be different; he would be permanently back at school and unable to visit so often. And he had his mother back.

As if reading her mind, he pulled away from his mother and threaded his hand through Maggie's.

'I'll be starting school again on Monday, but I'm going to come and help every afternoon when I finish.'

'Now, Robbie...' his mother cautioned.

'It's fine, Ma, I'll manage.'

348

'You'll have homework to do.'

'It's okay, I can do both.'

'We'll see,' said Maggie. 'You should listen to your mother, Robbie.'

'It'll work out,' he said confidently. 'Anyway, where else am I going to get a decent meal!'

His mother tapped his head lightly and laughed, and Maggie twisted the top around the bag of sweets and pushed it down deep inside her pocket.

Chapter Thirty-two

COOKING FOR ONE:
Eke out the bacon ration by serving it with fried, mashed or sliced potato; mixing a little chopped cooked bacon with mashed potatoes and form into cakes before frying or grilling; adding bacon to scrambled egg.
Ministry of Food, War Cookery Leaflet No. 31

From early on Rose had understood what was meant by the clap and roll of thunder, and as she sheltered under an awning, smoking, she contemplated making a dash for it, hoping that she wouldn't get hit as the sky flashed and thunder bowled around her. As a child she knew a boy who was hit by lightning; the whole of her primary school attended his funeral and she had seldom ventured out in a storm since if she could avoid it.

There was another flash and, moments later, an angry burst, as loud as any day in the kitchen with Eliza banging around, and the echo carried for miles. It felt as if the city was trapped again, only captive to the weather instead of enemy fire, and she worried that people would be hurrying home; only she had to catch Mr Boyle before he left. She had spent most of the night awake, guilty about what was to become of Maggie and the restaurant, and determined that she should try and put things right. She hadn't known about the notice period until Eliza had exploded at her yesterday, or how much worse she may have made things by insulting Mr Boyle after the luncheon. So, with the council offices only a few hundred yards further on, she trod on her cigarette, pulled her mackintosh hood over her head and ran across Canonbury Lane, striding along Upper Street until she was at Compton Terrace Gardens.

A noisy group, banners aloft, was crowded onto the steps, shuffling to get out of the rain. She crossed the road and followed them inside, where the foyer too was clogged with men and women bearing placards. They were filing into a hall where a sign read: HOTEL & CATERERS ASSOCIATION AGM.

She shook off the raindrops and pushed her way through the throng and into a hall with a small wooden stage on which sat four speakers: two women and a man whom Rose didn't recognise, and Mr Boyle. One of the women was trying to respond to a question from a seated member of the audience, but heckling from the sides of the hall and the balcony above became increasingly loud, making it difficult for her to be heard. She paused for a moment, waiting for the barracking to subside.

'I will say it once again. The policy is quite clear on this and the minister has stated it a number of times: if the local catering trade can demonstrate that there are enough catering establishments, and that they are adequate in capacity and price, then the government will see no need to set up a British Restaurant.'

The audience erupted in disagreement.

'Well, why have they set up four new ones in the past six months then?' a young woman shouted.

Rose was aware there had been a lot written in the press about the catering industry's objections to British Restaurants, of the growing resentment because their access to supplies gave them an unfair advantage, but she'd had no idea that tensions were running so high.

Before the speaker had a chance to respond, Mr Boyle spoke up.

'If you refer back to Circular CMF49, you will see that if there is any contention we are happy for an inspector to investigate. That has also been made very clear from the beginning.'

He had barely finished speaking when the same woman responded: 'So even more money to be spent by the council and taken away from private caterers!'

Mr Boyle didn't look in the least agitated but Rose certainly was; all this anti-British Restaurant sentiment didn't bode at all well for Maggie, or the decision Mr Boyle was due to make.

'Yes, inquiries are expensive and as such will

351

only be undertaken with consent from both parties, the ministry and the local authority, *if* the local catering association apply for one. But we will not be changing our policy at this stage as we have already had an extensive consultation period with the Hotel and Caterers Association.'

It was unlikely there was going to be a chance to talk to him now, and the crowd was so agitated that she wanted to leave, but Rose knew she had to try. She thought about Maggie and Eliza finishing off back at the restaurant and at her own feeble attempts to bake the daily special – of her embarrassment at the Frankenstein date and walnut pudding she had created. To make things worse she had used the Primus oil cooker and got muddled with the temperature and overcooked it, which only added to its diabolical look and flavour. It would make all the difference if she apologised to Mr Boyle, but it didn't look as if it would be easy. Her only opportunity might be to catch him on the way out, so she walked around the side of the room to get closer to the stage, hoping to catch his eye.

'The talk in the press of a trade crisis between private caterers and British Restaurants is a needless distraction,' Mr Boyle carried on. 'The truth is that the public needs both. There is a need for meals outside the home and private caterers are already supplying more than fifty thousand meals a week to workers, but in some areas this is not enough. We must finish now, so I want to say thank you to our guests: Mrs Wight from the Association of Purveyors of Light Refreshments, Mr Hale from the National Caterers

Association, Miss...'

As he continued to thank the panel Rose couldn't help but think how sincere his presentation had been and how she believed what he said; she wasn't sure that Maggie and Eliza's idea that he had disrupted their supplies to save face with the private caterers could really be true.

Then the speakers were leaving the stage and the rowdy gathering began to disperse. Rose squeezed past, trying to keep Mr Boyle in sight but she was like a swimmer swept away by an outflowing tide, unable to reach the shore. Then she spotted him, shaking hands with the other panel members, a brief exchange before striding away.

She pushed harder, elbows meeting flesh, until she reached the edge of the crowd and hurried after him.

'Mr Boyle? Mr Boyle!'

He carried on walking and she fell into step beside him.

'Mr Boyle, I didn't mean to be rude or imply anything when we last met, I was just sticking up for Maggie.'

'Just as you should, Miss Barnard, just as you should.'

He seemed quite calm as he walked, unflustered by the rabble or by seeing her again.

'I've come to apologise, Mr Boyle,' Rose continued, struggling to match his pace. 'I should never have said those things and they certainly shouldn't reflect on Maggie. I hope you will consider that when you make your decision.'

He didn't respond.

'Please, Mr Boyle,' Rose begged. 'Will you accept my apology?'

At last he stopped and turned to face her.

'Emily was a very talented cook too. She also trained at Westminster Training College. She would have done exactly what Maggie has. Don't worry, Rose, Maggie will be fine.'

'I don't understand...' Puzzled, she searched his face for a clue.

'The family that isn't going to be there for me at the end of the war, the one that I can't make plans for...'

Her blundering interference gradually dawned on her and she gasped. 'Oh, Mr Boyle, I am so sorry.'

'Not another casualty of war – Emily died during childbirth. Our child died too. That is why we aren't all waiting and hoping for the end of the war, Rose; some of us would prefer to hold on to the past.'

'I'm so sorry, Mr Boyle. I really am. Please, can you forgive me for everything I said?'

Nothing, and then the glimmer of a smile; a sunrise on a grey horizon.

'Remember, Rose,' he said. 'Sometimes the past is what's most important, but it's the future that you have control over.'

He was looking straight at her and it suddenly struck her that she understood exactly what he meant. She appreciated her past too, so perhaps she should go back to what she had enjoyed. She had so wanted to help Maggie with the restaurant, but it wasn't working, and Rose knew that she had been a good sales assistant. Janek would never be interested in her, so that was it; Rose had made up her mind – it would be best for everyone if she just left.

Chapter Thirty-three

BRAISING:
Braising can be used for large or small joints, as well as for chops or pieces of steak. Meat cooked in this way is always tender and has a lovely flavour from the vegetables which are cooked with it.
Ministry of Food, War Cookery Leaflet No. 16

Eliza emerged from the storeroom red-faced and empty-handed. She had been up and down on the ladder trying to find ingredients but there was hardly anything left.

'It's all gone, even the powdered egg.'

'But there were two tins of Made In A Tick sitting right next to the Miller's yesterday!' Maggie shook her head. She was sure she'd seen them; she remembered thinking how they would have to make do with an egg custard if there weren't enough ingredients for the thrifty Christmas pudding.

'Well, they're not there now. One of the other cooks must have used them.'

Eliza had a point; since compulsory conscription had been introduced at the end of November, most of the trained cooks had left and they hadn't had time to show the new ones where everything was and they were making all sorts of silly mistakes.

'Surely not...'

'It's going to be alright, Mags – you do know that, don't you?'

'No, I don't,' Maggie said, 'but thank you.'

She wasn't at all sure that anything was going to be alright, ever again. She hadn't seen Janek since the night she'd asked him to leave, and Mr Boyle and the other divisional food officers were due the next day; it was the end of her notice period and they would be making their decision. She had finally told the rest of the staff and she wished she hadn't; Tom and Maeve had been treating her as if she had some kind of illness and it felt as though they were all walking on eggshells – if only they had been lucky enough to get any! In response, she was trying even harder to make it look as if she wasn't worried, and the strain was beginning to show. Thank goodness for Eliza, who was so distracted with booking the registry office and choosing her outfit that she didn't seem to be paying much attention to everything else.

Maggie decided to have a look for herself, but once inside the storeroom she could see that it was hopeless, and the grey stone floor was so cold that she stood shivering, feeling as desolate as the empty shelves in front of her. It took the equivalent of two dozen eggs to make the quantity of mixture required for the puddings tomorrow. It wasn't just the eggs, either; there was only one sack of sugar, a few tins of National Household skimmed milk and a single remaining packet of Bournville cocoa. With Christmas only weeks away, there was an unspoken agreement that they skimp on ingredients now in order to conserve a few pounds of sugar here and a few ounces of butter there to add to the festive table, but now they would have to forgo even that.

Not that Maggie was feeling particularly festive this year anyway. The only family she had left to celebrate Christmas with were Aunt Mary and Rose, and relations between them were somewhat strained at the moment. They'd had their usual Sunday afternoon tea on the weekend, and Maggie had finally tired of seeing her aunt putting Rose down; it was just too hypocritical after her visit to the restaurant, after what she had asked of Maggie.

'See, Rose,' Aunt Mary had said, talking through a mouthful of semolina pudding. 'It warms the cockles of your heart this food does. You really should spend more time learning to cook.'

'Why do you always do that?' Maggie had said.

'Do what?'

'Criticise Rose by way of paying me a compliment.'

'I don't know what you mean,' her aunt protested.

'Yes you do. What happened? I don't remember you being like this when we were growing up.'

Mary abruptly let go of the spoon and it clattered into the empty bowl. She sat back.

'Something happened when your mother left, Maggie – not just to you kids and your poor old dad, but to all of us...' She wasn't looking at Maggie; she was staring into space as if she had conjured the image of her sister there.

'We blamed ourselves, of course. If we'd been more help, more support to her after Ernest died, then she might never have gone. Me with only Rose and Joe to look after, I could have done more.'

'So is that what this is all about – your guilty conscience?'

'No, Maggie. Of course not...'

'What then?'

'Rose is so like your mother when she was young – I suppose I just don't want her making the same mistakes.'

'What mistakes? What are you talking about?'

'Some things aren't in our control, Maggie. There are things that happen to us by other people's hand, not by our own doing.'

'I've never heard you talk like this before,' Maggie said, shaking her head in exasperation. 'What's it got to do with Rose?'

Rose stood up. 'Don't, Maggie, please...'

But Maggie went on. 'Surely Mum leaving should have made you appreciate each other – not punish Rose because you didn't do enough to help your sister when you had the chance.'

When Mary turned towards her, the colour had drained from her face. 'In God's name, Maggie, I haven't meant to – I'm not that cruel. Please don't say that...'

Maggie had been angry; she wanted to leave her aunt sitting there alone in the chair feeling every bit as hopeless as she made Rose feel, but in the end she couldn't. Mary was family, and all that she had. In the end she had apologised and told her that she didn't believe her to be cruel, just thoughtless and a little unkind.

Maggie had only been standing in the storeroom for a few minutes recollecting, but the damp from the floor had made its way into her shoes and her toes were beginning to feel numb. Eliza was right, the powdered egg and flour had gone and so she retreated, also empty-handed. She sighed heavily as she slammed the storeroom door shut; it seemed that as soon as she dealt with a problem in one area, another sprang up somewhere else. It wasn't just the notice period and tomorrow's lunch she had to worry about; now she had to work out how she was going to get her regulars the Christmas meal they deserved.

Robbie was relieved his guts felt back to normal after all the pain and embarrassing stuff that had been going on. And he couldn't believe his ma had agreed to come back to the city; now they would all be there when his dad came back and he would be really proud when he found out how hard Robbie had worked and all he had done for Maggie. He was going to surprise her now, skipping school to follow the instructions Janek had left him for keeping pests out of the sacks of potato and seed.

He thought Maggie would be pleased to see him, but she didn't even say hello when he entered the kitchen. It seemed to be taking longer than he had hoped for her to forgive him for keeping the secret about his ma and sisters.

'So you get free time on Wednesdays and Fridays now?' she said without looking up from the cookbook she was reading.

'Yes,' he lied. 'They call it community service. We're supposed to ... to do an old lady's shopping or something, so I come and help you.'

'Cheeky monkey! Although since you put it like that, I can see the benefit to the community.'

'Good, that's what Ma said too.'

'How are your mother and sisters?'

'They're fine. Ma keeps asking after you though. I think she's waiting for an invitation.'

Maggie looked surprised. 'She doesn't need an invitation. She can come in any time.'

'Thanks, I'll tell her. What you doing anyway?'

Something smelled good and although he hadn't felt much like it after the food poisoning, it was his duty to try out all her recipes again now, especially the new ones.

'We've got a special lunch tomorrow so I'm braising some brisket.'

'If you're such a good cook, why does it take you so long to cook the meat?'

'God bless him,' Eliza said, running her hand over his shorn head. 'Have you not picked up anything since you've been here?'

'The reason is that some cuts need to be cooked long and low so they don't toughen up,' Maggie explained. 'Braising releases the fat and the flavour, keeping the meat moist.'

'So what's the difference between slow-roasting and braising?' he asked, moving to where Eliza stood, her thick tongs turning meat that sizzled in the bottom of a deep pan.

She pointed at the wire rack where a batch of freshly baked rolls cooled, indicating that he should take one. Who was he to turn her down?

Eliza said, 'Slow-roasting doesn't need liquid while you're cooking but braising does. And you have to brown the meat first, to seal in the juices.'

'Fatty meat makes a greasy dish, so we trim the fat off beforehand and render it to make dripping,' Maggie added.

'I've seen Ma do that. It's bloomin' lovely on toast.'

He remembered how his dad liked to eat it for Sunday tea with loads of pepper sprinkled on top.

Maggie picked up a soup ladle and skimmed a thin layer of fat from the oversized copper saucepan. 'When it's cooled down, I'll strain it and you'll be able to lift off the whole layer of dripping.'

'When will that be?'

'Couple of hours ... you should have a go, see if you can lift it in one piece. It's just like the ice on top of a frozen pond.'

'If I can do it, will you let me have some?'

'Yes.'

'With hot toast?'

'I don't see why not.' Maggie smiled.

It was about as interesting as watching paint dry but he could hardly wait for the two hours to be up and eventually lifted the top off without a single crack.

Maggie kept her promise and made him two rounds of thick toast, whopping great big doorsteps of crusty white bread, and he settled onto the end of a bench in the dining hall watching as leaves blew in and danced around him every time the door opened. He didn't want to stop eating in

361

order to move so he just stayed there, freezing, the cold reminding him of his long walk back to their new home on the other side of the Holloway Road.

Afterwards, he went to find Maggie to thank her, finally tracking her down to a quiet corner of the kitchen. Hoisting himself up onto the workbench next to her, he watched as her knife worked rapidly and he asked all sorts of questions about the locals and told her about the revolting mock fishcakes his ma had made, until he couldn't hold his tongue any longer.

'How come Janek doesn't come here anymore?'

'He doesn't need to. There's nothing for him to do now.'

'I don't mean outside; I thought he helped in here?'

'He used to, but I've got Eliza and Maeve, so we don't really need him.'

'Is everything alright?'

He could tell it wasn't; she wouldn't even look at him. 'Why ever would you ask that? Of course it is!'

'I might be a kid, but I'm not stupid.'

She exhaled and then looked up at the ceiling before she turned to him.

'I know you're not, Robbie, but I don't know what to say. Things just get a bit more complicated when you're older.'

'So you would like to see him?'

She looked as if she wanted to say something but was thinking about it really carefully.

'Yes, I would like to – very much, in fact. But I can't.'

'Why not?'

'I just can't.'

He didn't understand; he wanted to see his dad but he couldn't because he didn't know where he was. Maggie knew exactly where to find Janek.

'I know he's not coming back, you know.'

Maggie looked confused at first, but then her expression changed. 'Your dad?'

'I'm pretending for Ma's sake. I still go down to the docks, see his old friends, but I know.'

'I'm sorry, Robbie; the war's been hard on all of us.'

'Doesn't have to be though – you still have a choice.'

'No, Robbie, I don't. Just like you know about your dad, I know I can't see Janek.'

He shifted along the bench so he was close and she couldn't avoid looking at him anymore.

'Why, though? I don't understand. If you want to see Janek, you can just go over to the railyard.'

'I know, Robbie.'

'You say you can't see him, but how would you really feel if you could never, ever, ever see him again? If he went away and never came back?'

He worried that he'd gone too far because she was just staring at him, not blinking, like her mind was a million miles away. And then she leaned forward and kissed him. 'Thank you, Robbie. You might be only a kid, but you really are much smarter than me.'

'Am I forgiven then – for lying to you about Ma?'

'Yes, Robbie, you're forgiven.'

'In that case, can I get some more bread and

dripping ... please?'

'Yes.'

He looked towards the window where the howling winds swirled snow like confetti and he shivered.

'And can I stay here tonight – one last time?'

'Don't push your luck...'

At first he thought the answer would be no, until she took the pocket watch out of her apron pocket and handed it to him.

'Just make sure you're not late for school. And don't touch anything!'

He smiled, pleased with himself.

'And Robbie?'

'Yes?'

'This really is the last time...'

Chapter Thirty-four

IF AN AIR RAID SIGNAL TAKES
YOU FROM THE KITCHEN:
First thing to do is to stop the heat, turn off the gas
or electric and close the dampers of the kitchen
range. If you do this, the food cannot get burnt.
Ministry of Food, Food Facts

Mrs Bevan said they predicted snow so Maggie wasn't surprised by the small flurry of snowflakes. It was still light, melting as soon as it hit the ground, but it could change in a short space of time and Robbie could be caught in the thick

364

of it, a long cold walk alone in the dark. One last time sleeping here wouldn't hurt; Maggie had managed to get word to his mother, and Mr Boyle and the others wouldn't be arriving until midday, by which time he would be long gone.

The assistants had left already and the dining hall was empty except for piles of gleaming white plates and cups that looked like giant meringues. In her mind's eye, though, Maggie could still see Maeve and Gillian spooning out the day's specials and chatting with the customers, Tom at the register taking money, and Rose doing her level best to clear the tables in time for the next influx. She could also picture Mary Bevan in her usual spot with her morning cuppa and the market workers piling through the door and hurrying to finish their meals so they could get back before their short break was over. Even the girls from the depots and factories nearby had a favourite place they liked to sit – and God help anyone who tried to sit there in their stead. Her staff had become like family over these past months but so too had the customers she had got to know.

As she turned to leave, the Tower of London mural caught her eye and the tiny detail of the stone turrets; it too had once been someone's grand vision and had stood for centuries despite the fires and wars. Maggie's Kitchen may not be an imposing monument, but it was just as important to its customers now and she wasn't going to let anyone take it away. Why had it taken so long for her to realise? Mr Boyle was threatened by her. She thought back over all the conversations they'd had and the way he was always trying to make himself look smarter than her, smarter than everyone else. Well, she wasn't going to let him stand in her way. If he wouldn't let her carry on, she would appeal. If she lost the appeal, then she would go directly to the ministry. And Robbie was right: she did have a choice; he couldn't see his father but she could see Janek.

She pulled out the picture of the Black Madonna and turned it over; she had read the Mazovian poem dozens of times and knew it by heart: *True love requires courage and triumphs in the friendship it brings.*

She wondered where he was on this cold and friendless night; probably sitting alone in his tiny wooden hut. Nothing was ever going to happen between him and Rose, so why should she be responsible for Rose's happiness? Wasn't she entitled to some of her own? She and Janek had a chance, unlike Gillian and so many others – but she would need to hurry, and hope to God that she wasn't already too late.

He stacked his belongings against the wall of the hut: two bags of clothes and bedding that he would send for when the time was right. For now, he was leaving with all that he'd had when he arrived – barely enough to fill a small knapsack. Stefan hadn't made it clear what they had planned for him next, but he preferred it this way; he wouldn't be able to share anything if he was caught. He had fulfilled his task without a hitch, but they hadn't been pleased when they had to change the delivery location at the last minute, nor with the fact that he hadn't followed their instructions. At least once he was gone there would be no distractions, no Malgorzata to consider; his only concern would be getting the job done.

Janek took a final glance around; the seedling trays lay empty on the workbench, the metal equipment and tools lined up alongside. He was tired and his bones ached from cold since he had been up most of the night mending broken equipment and ensuring that the seeds were labelled and correctly stored. There would be someone coming to take over as soon as a replacement could be found, he had made sure of that, and that the railway company knew what in the gardens and allotments needed looking after. He had laid the old transmitter and headphones out with a note for Robbie in case the boy came looking for him. Robbie had always been so intrigued by the machine, and not just for the spare parts; he really seemed to want to understand how it worked. Janek was convinced Robbie would be an engineer one day and would follow in his father's footsteps. He walked over to the small metal wall cabinet and picked up a miniature motorcycle fashioned from scrap metal. Robbie had sat cross-legged on the floor listening to Janek's stories of motorcycle adventures with his brothers, his fingers nimbly working the small pliers to manipulate the springs and wires into shape. Janek was about to put it back when he hesitated. Taking his handkerchief from his pocket, he wrapped it around the model then slid it back into his pocket.

When he'd arrived here he had felt lost and broken, but now he was restored and felt as strong a pull to stay as a reason to go. He wasn't ready to leave, but he must prepare himself for whatever lay ahead.

He picked up his knapsack and crossed to the open doorway, the snow thickening into flurries that hopefully would not prevent his train from leaving. Poland could not be his home for the time being but he had to hold onto the thought that one day it would, and there was one last stop to make before he left. Even though Maggie had told him she didn't want to see him, he had to tell her how he felt; he needed do that before he left.

The worst thing about staying at Maggie's was listening to the rats scratching around under the floorboards and scrapping inside the walls' cavities. Robbie imagined them finding a hole nearby and squeezing through, and him waking in the morning to find his fingers missing. He pulled the blankets further up around him and tried to distract himself by thinking about food. The best thing about staying here was the possibility of a midnight feast, but he had been banished from the kitchen. Extra prep was laid out for the special lunch the next day and he had been ordered not to tamper with any of it. Maggie had looked so tired that he hadn't even bothered to cross his fingers behind his back as he promised not to; this time he really wouldn't leave the office. The pocket watch she had given him was uncomfortable in his pocket so he pulled it out and propped it against the pillow. There was no way he could miss it there and he would be up and out as promised and no one would even know he had been here.

The Morrison shelter had been furnished with a second-hand mattress, an eiderdown and assorted knitted blankets that Rose had brought from home and which at that exact moment he was extremely grateful for. He put the last of his sweets in his mouth, licked his fingers and tucked them back beneath the covers where the rats couldn't get them.

Still, sleep didn't come quickly. The usual night-time noises seemed louder than usual; the strong wind dragging debris along the street, branches scratching against the window, clawing to get in, and there was a low hissing noise coming from somewhere inside the kitchen. His neck bent crooked as he strained to hear the source but it kept coming and going, intermittently drowned out by other sounds.

His lids were too heavy, his yawns more frequent. He had promised not to enter the kitchen, so whatever it was it could wait until the morning now; he would ask Maggie about it then.

Her fingers skimmed across the brickwork, nails catching on the rough edges, slowing down as the solid wall disappeared with the pathway to a house.

The walk from the restaurant to the railyard only took ten minutes by daylight, but tonight it was taking much longer, guided as she was only by her memory and the touch of the walls. She had run as much of the way as she could but now she walked, eager as she was to get there without being careless on the fresh, squeaky snow.

When she reached the junction to the main

369

road she knew it was only a few hundred feet south to the bridge and the stairway down. No cars had passed her the whole way but now she waited, shivering, as a small fleet of late commuters travelled past on the New North Road, their dimmed headlights creating freckles of light in the snow.

Her footsteps were unnaturally loud on the stone steps, her heart beating faster as she imagined Janek's reaction when she told him how she felt, his expression changing from surprise to relief when he realised her feelings mirrored his own.

But as she reached the bottom of the stairs, she saw that the place looked deserted. There were no plants climbing trellises or flowering beds; the gardens were bare and Janek was nowhere to be seen.

There was a rustling ahead and she rushed forward, hopeful, but it was only a cat chasing another animal through the dirt.

She walked the rest of the way to the signal hut and stood with her ear against the flimsy wooden door, listening for the sound of him moving about inside. It was pitch black and all she could hear was the creak and groan of the old building shifting in the wind.

There was no point in knocking; she knew that he had gone.

Janek felt the tremor as he walked towards Essex Road and minutes later heard sirens before the two fire engines roared past. It wasn't until he was closer that he noticed the strange orange glow up ahead, as though the sun had chosen to set again.

He was breathless from running by the time he reached the restaurant, despite the slight limp that usually slowed him down. The emergency crews had just arrived and the onlookers were penned behind cordons, spooky silhouettes against the amber sky. Beyond them, the front of Maggie's Kitchen appeared to be still standing, but at the back only part of the kitchen still stood, the rest of the building tilting down into a shallow crater. As he drew closer, Janek saw the dining hall begin to collapse, a piece of the wall mural teetering precariously, Big Ben about to be engulfed in flame.

Smoke stung his eyes and the rage of the fire was deafening, but all he could think was that Maggie could be somewhere inside.

Weaving through the crowd, he ducked beneath the cordon, raised his arms up in front of him and walked towards the building's collapsing shell.

Flames stung his skin and smoke scorched his lungs as the long feathers of fire flickered out from its centre. The firemen shouted for him to stay back, but what if she was still in there?

He had deserted those he cared about once before. He would never do that again.

Chapter Thirty-five

During the past few years we have discovered how good a daily green salad can be. People who tell you that they feel much better now that they eat salads are not just food faddists. They are stating a fact that has been proved over and over again.
Ministry of Food, War Cookery Leaflet No. 12

Maggie often thought about Ernest but never as strongly as her memory of him now; he was in crumpled clothes, his light brown hair ruffled as if he had just got out of bed. He was towing his billycart in one hand and holding a slab of bread in the other, chewing as he walked away, ignoring her pleas for him to wait for her. Just another minute and she would be able to go with him – look after him as she had promised her mother she would. She could see him clearly now as she wandered through the emergency workers at the depot at Islington Green, and he felt like part of the dream that she was having. It was as if she was watching herself searching among the tents at the depot and pulling back the tarpaulins to see if Robbie was inside.

She had sensed that something was wrong as she left Janek's, feeling a growing unease, and then the smoke had come into view: thick choking clouds of it, the stench reaching her before she even crossed the road. Essex Road was cordoned off and it was difficult to see through to the fire trucks parked outside, so she pushed past the barriers, following the trail of the hose to where the firemen stood struggling under its weight as they directed it into the flames.

The fire had roared uncontrollably, flames dancing across the rooftop, in and out the windows, leaping up and down the restaurant walls.

'Miss, you can't go in there!'

'But what about Robbie?'

She felt someone holding her back and she struggled to break free.

'There's no one in there,' the fireman said. 'No one at all.'

She wanted to believe him. There had been no air raids tonight, no incendiaries or explosions; no clue as to what could have caused this.

Slowly more people had arrived, locals with their kind faces and soothing voices. Her landlady, Mrs Foster, had appeared, then Mr and Mrs Fox appeared, and Mrs Armstrong. Next came Henry and Julia, arm in arm, and they stood with her in silence and watched the timbers burn. After a while she felt Rose beside her and heard her cousin's quiet sobbing as she reassured Maggie that she would always be there for her, no matter what.

With the embers still smouldering she moved closer until she could see across to where the dining hall once stood; only a few chairs remained, the rest of them reduced to charred fragments on the floor with flattened tables or submerged beneath the collapsed ceiling beams.

One of the firemen shouted at her, warning her

to move back.

'It's my restaurant,' she said urgently. 'I need to see if there's anyone there.'

'It doesn't matter if you're King George, you're not allowed in!'

'Have you seen the warden? Have you seen Bill Drummond?'

'He went with the boy.'

'A boy? You found a boy?'

'One lucky lad,' the fireman confirmed.

'Is he alright?'

'Got to him just in time,' added the second fireman.

'Where did he go?'

'They took him to the depot.'

Now, she glanced down to the end of the row where the last tent stood; he had to be there. It was then that she saw her – the woman from the restaurant, the one who always left before Maggie had the chance to talk to her or to get a proper look.

The woman made no attempt to move this time, and as she drew closer, Maggie, who'd had her suspicions before, knew without a doubt; the resemblance was uncanny. The face was so familiar but the eyes were paler than she remembered, her lips thinner and the once-taut skin now sagging in soft folds.

'Maggie, you're safe!'

'Yes,' Maggie said simply.

'Thank God.'

'It is you then?' Was she hallucinating or was it really her mother?

'Yes. I'm so sorry about your restaurant. It was

such a wonderful place.'

So she had been right all along; her mother had been into the restaurant.

'How long have you been here?' Maggie asked.

'Not long, but I've always known how you are.'

'How?'

'Mary. I got in touch with her a few years ago. I always knew you would be alright, Maggie – but I want to give you something. I think you might need it now.'

Maggie couldn't focus on what her mother was saying; she was still trying to absorb the fact that her aunt had known her mother's whereabouts all along. Was that what she meant when she'd spoken of things that were beyond her control? And what about her cousin? Had she betrayed her too?

'Did Rose know?' Maggie demanded.

'No, only Mary. I don't expect you to understand, Maggie; I just want you to read this.' She held out an envelope.

Maggie reached for it, not sure if the moment was real or imagined, if it was her shocked mind conjuring the mother she had always missed to take care of her now or if she was really there. But when her fingers brushed across her mother's hand, she knew the woman before her now was flesh and blood.

Her mother's hand closed around Maggie's, pressing the letter inside.

Then the firemen and volunteers started arriving, bringing salvaged bricks and timber from the fire to transport to the council depot on Calvin Road, reminding her why she was there.

'I have to find Robbie,' she said.

For years after her mother left, Maggie imagined seeing her again, of a time when they would be reunited, discovering it had all been some terrible mistake, that her mother had had a good reason for leaving. After a while, though, she had stopped torturing herself with the belief she would come back, realising that it was pointless; she would be happier if she could put her mother out of her mind. After a while the memories faded and she daydreamed less and less.

Standing here now it didn't feel remotely like any of the scenes she had envisaged; she had no overwhelming desire to fling her arms around her mother or to tell her how much she had missed her.

Yes, they were her mother's eyes, as grey as stone, and as sad as she remembered them, but expectant too.

'What did we do?' Maggie asked.

'Nothing, love. You didn't do anything...'

Those few simple words and the years of imagining, a whole lifetime of blame and questions, and the emotion of the night; Maggie wanted to sink down, dissolve into the earth.

'Why now, why after all this time?'

'I thought you might need me.'

She didn't know what to say; there were dozens of times when she had needed her mother – when she was growing up, when Peter had gone – but now she had learned to cope on her own.

As if her mother somehow sensed Maggie's doubt, she moved closer, hands outstretched, seeking her daughter's touch.

'I know that I must seem cruel, but I thought that after all you have been through, I may be able to offer you the support and help that I've not been able to in the past...'

Maggie opened her mouth to say something but only a small whimpering sound came out.

'I shall never ask for your forgiveness or try to be your mother again, but I hope we can be friends.'

The snow had stopped falling and she could see her mother clearly now.

'But where have you been?'

'That doesn't matter now, I can tell you that later. Just read the letter...'

'What is it?'

'It's the deeds for the shop,' she said, glancing across the green to where the three-storey Victorian building stood. 'When your father died it came to me, since we were still legally married. He always meant for you three to have it, but with your brothers away I thought it would be of more use to you. Especially now.'

Maggie looked at the envelope.

'Mary told me that you had considered it for the restaurant... I knew you would be successful; you always were a marvellous cook.'

'What about Edward and John, do they know?'

'No. I'd like you to make sure they're taken care of with jobs and somewhere to live when this ghastly war is over. I know that you have always put them first, better than I ever could, and for that I am so grateful to you, Maggie.'

Her mother was fading, tears filling Maggie's eyes, obscuring her vision.

'You have grown into a wonderful woman and

Edward and John into fine young men, and it is my great sadness that I cannot take any of the credit for it.'

'Are you going?'

'That's up to you. I'd like to stay, but I know you've had your share of pain. I don't want to make things worse.' She took a step closer. 'Still, it has been unbearable for me, knowing that I've had to stay away all these years because I couldn't be the mother that you all needed me to be.'

Finally, the tears fell, silently streaking down Maggie's lace. 'My address is in there when you are ready...'

When Maggie finally wiped away the tears and looked up, her mother had gone and a fireman and warden were carrying a ladder across the place where she had just stood.

It hadn't been a dream though, the letter was clasped tightly in her hand and she could still hear her mother's voice: *I've had to stay away all these years because I couldn't be the mother that you all needed me to be.* She knew things had changed after Ernest died and suspected it had something to do with her mother's dark moods and the bitter arguments that accompanied them, but now she knew for sure.

As she remembered to breathe again, her disbelief gave way to an unconscious surge of relief. She didn't feel helpless anymore; she had a future after all. What Mr Boyle decided or even what the newspapers said didn't matter; with these deeds she could open Maggie's Kitchen again, give the locals what they wanted and cook whatever she pleased.

And her mother had come back.

It was then that she felt a gentle nudge against her leg and looked down to see Spoke.

As soon as she reached the tent she tore through the canvas entrance, walking straight past nurses and medical trolleys, searching the line of occupied beds until she came to the last one.

He sat up on the stretcher when he saw her, sending blankets cascading to the floor as he reached out. 'Dear God, Robbie!' She held back, afraid to touch him. 'Are you hurt?'

'Just a few cuts...'

His clothes were torn and bloodied but he was in one piece, and he wore a smile she thought she would never see again.

'You've got more lives than Rafferty,' she said, hugging him at last.

'I don't know what happened. One minute I was taking Spoke outside for a pee, then there was this huge explosion... I couldn't see through the flames but I didn't touch anything, Maggie, honestly. I didn't even go in there – I never went into the kitchen. You do believe me, don't you?'

'It's fine, Robbie, I believe you. No one is blaming you.'

'I was scared, Maggie. All those times I said I was okay on my own but I wasn't really. I'm chicken ... I'm sorry.'

'I'm sorry too, but you're not chicken, Robbie, never say that. You are one of the bravest people I have ever met.'

'I suppose I'm gonna have to sleep at home from now on?'

'I think that's probably a good idea.'

He handed her the pocket watch.

'It still works; I checked.'

She looked at it for a moment and then slid it into her coat pocket.

'It's such a relief that no one else was hurt.'

'Except for Janek...'

'Janek?'

'Yes – he rescued me.'

She hadn't noticed anyone else until now but then she followed Robbie's gaze to the corner of the tent, where the sides strained against the strong winds and a figure leaned forward out of the shadows.

'It was lucky I came to say goodbye.'

'You're leaving?'

'Yes.'

'When?'

'Soon.'

'But where are you going?'

'To France first...'

He moved unsteadily towards her, his singed clothing now visible, forearms thickly bandaged.

'Janek rescued me from the fire.'

Robbie sounded proud but her attention was still on Janek. She had thought she would never see him again but here he was, and every bit the hero he had never thought himself to be.

'Are your injuries bad?'

'They are not too serious.'

'But you won't be able to go now, surely. How would you even get there?'

'The same way I came.'

'Then what?'

'Across to Kresy.'

'You'll be killed!'

It was a conversation they had had before, but how could she let him go now, when he was injured – and before she had told him how she felt?

'I thought you understood; I must try to find my brother. There's nothing I can do here.'

'There's nothing you can do there either. You'll be just one more casualty, and what for? Wouldn't he prefer it if you stayed alive?'

Surely he couldn't really think he should still go, but his expression hardened; it was like talking to the stranger she'd first met.

'When people are desperate they don't always think about what is right.'

There was a flicker of the old Janek again as he came closer.

'Would you rather chase chances or certainties?' she asked.

She waited for him to answer, able to see him clearly now, those glacial eyes that made him look as if he were bound to nature and everything in it.

'We all prefer certainties, but there aren't any.'

'There is one,' she said.

'What is that?'

'That I love you.'

He said nothing in reply but she didn't regret saying it; it had freed her and she wanted to tell him again, only louder.

'I love you.'

A smile, and then confusion clouded his face. 'But you told me to go...'

'Of course I did; Rose has feelings for you. I didn't want her to get hurt.'

381

'Does that change things? Would you still rather I left?'

'No. Unless you need to go...'

'She is your family, you want to do what is best for her too.'

Perhaps she had misjudged him or was being selfish thinking that his loyalty to his family was less important than his feelings for her. She wanted to protect him, nourish him in the same way he had helped her. She remembered the Black Madonna and the prayer card: *True love requires courage and triumphs in the friendship it brings.* He had helped her emotionally with his support and friendship, and now she was ready to love again, unconditionally – and if that meant waiting for him to come back, she would.

'I'm sorry, of course you must do what's right for your family,' she told him.

There was a distant grumble of anti-aircraft fire from the far side of the city and they both looked up. It might not be long before they were ushered into the underground, the wail of the siren banishing any chance they might have to say goodbye.

'Maggie...'

'You must also think of yourself, Janek.'

'I know, I–'

The gunfire was fainter now, but she still had to move closer to hear him.

'What did you say?'

'I said I love you, Maggie.'

His body was only inches away, the smell of smoke on his clothing and the warmth of his breath on her face. And as the gunfire faded and the night clamped down, all thoughts of him leaving vanished like the dusk.

Whatever the future held, she could face it, because for now, they were together.

Afterword

On Tuesday, 13 January 1942, *The Times* reported:

Lord Woolton assured caterers yesterday that before any more British Restaurants opened the Ministry of Food will consult the trade. A deputation representing seven associations of the industry discussed with him for three hours the effect of British Restaurants on the livelihood of caterers. The Minister replied that British Restaurants had been brought into existence solely to meet a wartime need, and he saw no reason to antici-pate their continued existence after the emergency.

On Saturday, 22 August 1942, *The Times* edi-torialised:

The British Restaurant is one of the most interesting social developments of the war. Community feeding has obvious advantages in wartime. It is economical of fuel, food, equipment, labour, and transport. It provides an auxiliary emergency service, which can put lull periods to use in training people for disciplined action under attack. And – perhaps its greatest long-range value – it lessens the part played by income in deter-mining nutritional levels in the community... In their early days the establishment aroused suspicion among private caterers, who were apt to view these non-profit-

making and often volunteer-staffed undertakings as unfair competitors. Yet the catering trade has been helped rather than injured by their development. It is the people who formerly ate at home, not those who sought other caterers, that communal feeding has won over by its service. By inducing more people to eat out and by encouraging them to sample unfamiliar dishes, much has been done to tap a new source of customer for the trade.

Maggie's recipes

Hopefully you are suitably hungry now and eager to attempt one of Maggie's dishes; the following are all original recipes from the Second World War contemporised for modern tastes. The wonderful thing about these recipes is that although they were once suitable for feeding a fighting nation, many of them are still popular and combine fresh unprocessed ingredients. They include seasonal fruits and vegetables that you can grow at home or source from your local farmers' market or supermarket. This back-to-basics approach to cooking is also surprisingly practical; the recipes are both quick and economical as you only need a limited number of ingredients. By the end of the war there were only two hundred and fifty food products on supermarket shelves – now there are two hundred and fifty thousand! It makes you wonder how many of them we really need and what they all contain.

So, whether you are part of a book club taking it in turns to make a dish, cooking for friends or family, or just having a go at how your grandmother used to cook, put your food processors away, roll up your sleeves and enjoy the simple art of cooking.

CHURCHILL'S RAREBIT

While toasted oatmeal or mashed potato were sometimes added to bulk out this traditional dish, the addition of mustard gives it an extra kick. The ultimate comfort food; a great lunch served with Maggie's turnip top salad (see recipe from chapter eleven, below), a perfect afternoon tea on its own, or slice tomatoes or crispy bacon and arrange on top for a tasty brunch. It's best with a good soft white bread or sourdough for the great plump texture.

4 slices bread
2 tsp butter, softened
2 dstsp milk
4 tbsp grated cheese
½ tsp Colman's mustard powder

Mix the butter, milk, cheese and mustard powder and coat the top of the bread, then place under the grill until bubbling hot and golden brown. *Serves 2–4.*

NETTLE SOUP

If there isn't any decent woodland nearby to go foraging in, or it just hasn't been a great nettle season, then pop down to the supermarket and substitute the nettles with spinach.

2 tbsp olive oil
200g/7oz young nettles/spinach

A few sprigs chives or a small onion,
  finely chopped
6 tbsp barley or oat flour
2 litres/3½ pints vegetable stock
Salt and pepper

Wash the nettles and plunge them into a pot of
boiling water. Reduce water to a simmer and
cook gently until nettles/spinach are tender, 6–8
minutes, then drain and refresh in cold water.
Once you have drained off all excess water, chop
leaves finely, combine with chives and/or onion,
add flour and sauté in a pan with a little olive oil.
Add stock and simmer for 45 minutes in a
covered pan. Skim and season to taste. *Serves 4.*

BORSCHT

This is the vegetarian version of the dish, so if
you like your dishes salty or with extra punch,
then add ham hock during the onion-softening
stage. It's a meal on its own, especially if served
with some rustic bread or sourdough.

2 tbsp olive oil
2 onions, finely chopped
1 clove garlic, crushed
350g/12oz raw beetroot, grated or finely diced
225g/8oz carrots, finely diced
225g/8oz potatoes, peeled and finely diced
1 stick celery, finely chopped
Fresh bay leaf
2 litres/3½ pints vegetable stock

2 large tomatoes, skinned, deseeded and
   chopped
50g/2oz cabbage, finely shredded
2 tbsp apple cider vinegar
2 tbsp lemon juice
Sour cream (to serve)
Chives (to serve)

Heat the olive oil in a large pan and soften the
onions and garlic over a medium heat. Add
beetroot, carrots, potato, celery and bay leaf, and
sauté until tender before adding the stock and
simmering for 30 minutes. Remove the bay leaf
and add tomato and shredded cabbage and cook
for a further 10 minutes before removing from
heat. Stir through the vinegar and lemon juice
and serve topped with sour cream and sprinkled
with finely chopped chives. *Serves 6*

BEEF BROTH AND BARLEY SOUP

This recipe evolved because of its use of meat
stock, but it is often now made with the beef as
part of the dish. If you want to do this, then brown
450g/16oz of diced stewing steak first and then
add the vegetables and follow the recipe from
there, but leave food chunky rather than passing
through a sieve.

55g/2oz pearl barley
30g/1oz butter or oil
2 onions, chopped
450g/16oz diced carrots and turnips

Small stick celery, chopped
Sprig parsley and/or rosemary
2¼ litres/4 pints beef stock
Salt and pepper
285ml/½pint milk

Cover the barley with water and soak overnight, then drain. Heat oil in a pan, then soften onions and vegetables. Add the barley, herbs and beef stock. Season to taste. Bring to the boil and simmer gently for 1 hour until the barley is tender. Remove herbs and pass liquid through a wire sieve. Add the milk and bring to the boil again. Serve with fresh crusty bread. *Serves 4–6.*

WOOLTON PIE

The combination of oatmeal and vegetables is what makes this dish one of the most significant from the Second World War; both foods were home-grown and both full of nutrition. Oatmeal was added to many dishes because it increased the food's nutritional value and made it go further. The basic Woolton pie would only have contained potatoes, swedes, carrots, leeks, cauliflower or whatever was in season, but here sweet potato and broccoli are used for extra flavour, although you can use any combination of your most-loved vegetables.

450g/16oz each diced potatoes, swedes, carrots
    and cauliflower (or sweet potato and broccoli)
4 spring onions, sliced

1 tsp vegetable extract (or Bovril or Oxo)
1 tbsp oatmeal
Chopped parsley
225g/8oz sliced potatoes or pastry for topping
½ cup grated cheese
Gravy (to serve)

Preheat oven to 180°C/350°F. Place vegetables, vegetable extract and oatmeal in a saucepan and cover with water. Simmer gently for 10 minutes, stirring occasionally. Season to taste. Allow to cool and then place in a pie dish, sprinkle with parsley then cover with potatoes or pastry crust and cheese. Bake until topping is browned and serve with steaming hot gravy. *Serves 4–6.*

COD CASSEROLE

Although fish was not readily available, cheaper stock fished in the North Sea – such as cod – was obtainable more frequently than other varieties.

675g/18oz fresh salted cod (skinned)
450g/16oz parsnips, parboiled and thinly sliced
Small cabbage, shredded
1 leek, sliced
1 dstsp parsley, finely chopped
30g/1oz butter
1 dstsp cornflour
570ml/1 pint water

Preheat oven to 180°C/350°F. In a pan, bring cod to boil and simmer for 15 minutes, then flake, removing bones. Arrange parsnip, cabbage, leek and parsley in layers with fish in a casserole dish, dotting each layer with butter. Blend cornflour with water until smooth and then pour over dish. Cover and bake for 40 minutes. *Serves 4.*

LEMON SOLE

Sole is another fish that was both available and popular on the menus of restaurants and hotels at the time.

2 shallots, finely chopped
1 tbsp white wine vinegar
4 tbsp white wine
55g/2oz butter
Juice 1 lemon
2 tbsp chives, chopped
2 lemon sole, skinned and filleted
Wilted spinach, to serve
1 tomato, finely chopped
Salt and pepper

In a pan, gently simmer shallots, white wine vinegar and white wine until reduced. Add 2 tbsp water and simmer until reduced again. Slowly add butter, a small amount at a time, stirring constantly. Remove from heat and strain until the liquid is clear. Season and add the lemon juice and chives. Set aside and fry the sole in extra butter for 2 minutes on each side. Serve sole on a bed of wilted spinach with the sauce poured over and tomatoes dotted around the plate. *Serves 2.*

RABBIT STEW WITH
HERB DUMPLINGS

Rabbit was a notable source of meat protein during the war and more available than traditional livestock, which had been sacrificed to make way for crops. Close in flavour and texture to chicken, it can be substituted now by its feathered friend.

1 rabbit, jointed (or chicken)
30g/1oz plain flour
Salt and pepper
60g/2oz dripping or butter
3 rashers bacon, chopped
2 onions, chopped
2 garlic cloves, crushed
3 sticks celery, chopped
3 carrots, chopped
570ml/1 pint chicken stock
285ml/½ pint cider
½ tbsp tarragon or thyme, chopped

Dumplings
400g/14oz self-raising flour
200g/7oz butter
Parsley or sprig thyme, chopped
Salt and pepper
2 tbsp milk

Mix the flour and seasoning and coat the rabbit pieces. Heat dripping or butter and add bacon and rabbit. Cook until browned then remove from the pan. Add onions, garlic, celery and carrots and cook until soft, then return the rabbit and add stock, cider and tarragon. Cover the pan and simmer for 1 hour, checking and adding more liquid as needed. Meanwhile, rub flour and butter with herbs, salt and pepper until they form a breadcrumb mixture, then add enough milk to bind it together. Knead until smooth and then divide into half, quarters and so on until you have 16 dumplings. Add dumplings to the stew after 1 hour and cook for another 30–40 minutes. Sprinkle with parsley and serve. *Serves 4–6*

RABBIT CURRY

The slightly gamey flavour and ready availability of rabbit made it the ideal candidate for curry.

1 rabbit, skinned, deboned and cut into pieces
2 tbsp olive oil
1 onion, diced
1 cooking apple, peeled and diced
1 stick celery, diced
1 dstsp curry powder
1 tsp flour
1 glass water

Brown rabbit in oil and remove from the pan. Gently fry chopped vegetables and apple in same oil until softened and then add flour and curry powder, mixing and then stirring in water. Return rabbit to pan and cook gently for 2 hours before serving with rice. *Serves 4–6.*

LANCASHIRE HOTPOT

A classic that can make the most disciplined vegetarian's mouth water; it is flavoursome, has great texture and is real comfort food – and there's no need to use mutton now if you prefer to use lamb.

2 tbsp olive oil
450g/16oz scrag mutton, diced (or replace with diced lamb)
1 onion, thinly sliced
30g/1oz flour
570ml/1pint hot water
Salt and pepper
4 mushrooms, sliced
2 sheep's kidneys, sliced
450g/16oz potatoes, thinly sliced
Parsley, chopped

Preheat oven to 170°C/340°F. Heat oil and brown lamb or mutton in small batches, then fry the onions, separately. Remove from pan. Add flour to the oil, cooking until brown, and gradually add hot water. Mix well and season to taste. Grease a casserole dish and add the mutton or lamb in layers with mushrooms, onion and kidneys. Cover with thinly sliced potatoes, pour over browned gravy and bake for 2 hours. Sprinkle over parsley and serve. *Serves 4–6.*

OFFAL PIE

If you don't fancy going the whole hog with the offal, you could substitute with mushrooms or your choice of meat. While you might not want to eat the original offal version, wait until a grandparent or great-aunt or -uncle is coming over to visit; they will be suitably impressed!

2 tbsp dripping or olive oil
225g/8oz steak, diced
1 tbsp plain flour
2 sheep's kidneys or 225g/8oz ox kidneys, sliced
225g/8oz calf's liver, sliced
1 onion, chopped
1 rasher bacon
55g/2oz mushrooms, sliced
285ml/½ pint beef stock
Puff pastry

Preheat oven to 180°C/350°F. Heat half the dripping or oil in a pan. Toss steak in flour then brown in the oil. Place in the bottom of a pie dish and spread half the kidneys and liver on top. Sauté the onion, bacon and mushroom in the remaining oil in the pan, then place onion mixture on top of the layered meats and add the rest of the liver and kidneys as a second layer. Pour stock over and cover with a lid. Bake for 30 minutes. Remove from oven and cover with pastry, return to oven and cook for a further 30–40 minutes. *Serves 4.*

MUTTON STEW

Now that tastier cuts are available, mutton is rarely used except in stews or curries, so for an authentic dish, use mutton and cook long and slow – but if you prefer a more succulent piece of meat, then substitute with lamb.

900g/32oz breast and scrag mutton, diced (or
    use lamb)
15g/½oz dripping
450g/16oz mixed vegetables such as carrots,
    turnips, swedes, parsnips, chopped
450g/16oz potatoes, thickly sliced
Salt and pepper
2 tbsp fresh parsley, chopped (or 2 tsp dried)
850ml/1½ pints chicken stock

Heat dripping in a deep pan, then brown meat in batches. Add vegetables and potatoes and season well. Cover with stock, replace lid and cook for 1½ hours for lamb or 2 hours for mutton. *Serves 6–8.*

LIVER AND SAUSAGE HOTPOT

It sounds old-fashioned, but this meal delivered all the necessary protein and vegetables in one meal, and it's so easy to make.

450g/16oz liver, chopped
450g/16oz sausages, chopped
450g/16oz mixed vegetables, sliced

450g/16oz potatoes, sliced
850ml/1½ pints chicken stock
Salt and pepper

Preheat oven to 180°C/350°F. In a deep baking dish, layer meat and vegetables, seasoning well. Cover with stock and then layer potatoes. Cook for 1½ hours.

TOAD-IN-THE-HOLE

It's hard to believe this classic was born out of wartime necessity, but it was a good meal for home and a good one to serve in the canteen too.

30g/1oz dripping
450g/16oz sausages, left whole

Batter
140g/5oz plain flour
1 egg
140ml/½pint milk

Preheat the oven to 200°C/390°F. Melt dripping in a medium roasting tin and then add sausages and cook in the oven for 5 minutes. Remove and raise oven to 220°C/430°F. Blend ingredients for the batter, then pour over the sausages. Bake for 25–30 minutes or until golden brown. Serve with a crisp salad or green vegetables and a tasty onion gravy. *Serves 4.*

CRISP-COATED SCOTCH EGGS

There was a requirement for fast food that could be eaten in a hurry, hot or cold, and the humble Scotch egg fitted the bill.

4 eggs
450g/16oz sausage meat
Flour
Breadcrumbs

Preheat oven to 200°C/390°F. Hard-boil eggs and coat with sausage meat, moulding them into neat shapes. Dust with flour and roll in bread-crumbs. Line a baking tray with baking paper and bake eggs until crispy. *Serves 4.*

LEEK AND MUSHROOM GRATIN

This works really well as a side dish or can be the star of the show, as many of the vegetable dishes had to be during wartime. Otherwise, bake some fish or chicken in the oven at the same time so that you have a complete meal at the end.

4 tbsp grated cheese
4 tbsp breadcrumbs
40g/1½oz butter
2 leeks, sliced
4 large mushrooms, sliced
30g/1oz plain flour
235ml/½ pint milk
Pinch fresh thyme leaves

Preheat the oven to 180°C/350°F. Mix 2 tbsp grated cheese with breadcrumbs and set aside. Soften leeks in 20g/½oz butter in frypan, then add mushrooms for a couple of minutes. Once softened, place leeks and mushrooms in a small ovenproof dish and add remaining butter to frypan. When melted, add the flour and stir to form a roux. Cook, stirring continuously, for a minute or two, then gradually add the milk until the mixture thickens. Stir through the remaining cheese. Pour sauce over leeks and mushrooms, sprinkle with the cheese and breadcrumb mix, then bake in oven for 25–30 minutes or until golden brown. *Serves 4.*

TURNIP TOP SALAD

The delicious honey mustard dressing is the perfect accompaniment to the slight bitterness of the vegetables. Although you can substitute any vegetables for this recipe – courgettes, fennel, etc.

Salad
115g/4oz turnip tops or radishes, thinly sliced
115g/4oz white cabbage, finely shredded
115g/4oz red cabbage, finely shredded
55g/2oz raw beetroot, grated
55g/2oz carrots, grated

Dressing
1 tsp English mustard (or grain, if you prefer)
1 tbsp apple cider vinegar

2 tbsp rapeseed or olive oil
1 tbsp honey
1 tbsp chopped herbs – chives, parsley or
    whatever you like
Salt and pepper
Small handful of flower petals for garnish (or
    micro herbs if they are easier to find)

Prepare the vegetables by grating or slicing with a mandolin or a peeler – the different techniques give a combination of shapes. Make sure the serving dish is white so that the vibrant colours of the vegetables stand out. Drizzle with dressing, decorate with petals and enjoy! *Serves 4–6.*

APPLE CHARLOTTE

In the 1940s, substitutions would have been made by adding marmalade instead of sugar to the mixture and using available fruits instead of apple, but now, with the addition of almonds or walnuts, you can transform this tasty dessert into something a little more special.

450g/16oz apples
85g/3oz sugar
½tsp each nutmeg and cinnamon or mixed spice
55g/2oz butter, melted
170g/6oz day-old bread made into breadcrumbs
½ cup slivered almonds or chopped walnuts

Preheat oven to 180°C/350°F. Stew apples in a little water with half the sugar, then mix through half the spices. Grease pie dish and dust with a little sugar. Mix the breadcrumbs with melted butter and the remaining sugar and spices, then line the dish with alternate layers of breadcrumbs, apples and a handful of nuts. Sprinkle the top with some extra sugar, nutmeg and cinnamon and bake for 35 minutes or until golden. *Serves 4.*

MOCK CREAM

This is only for those truly dedicated to authenticity or if you get caught out when the shops are shut; otherwise, please buy a tub of fresh cream or fromage frais!

30g/1oz butter
30g/1oz sugar
1 tbsp dried milk powder
1 tbsp milk

Cream the butter and sugar together, then beat in the milk powder and the milk until the cream is the desired consistency.

HONEY AND WALNUT PUDDING

This is quite a labour intensive dish to make by hand, so maybe it's the one to whizz up in the food processor to save time and muscle-ache.

55g/2oz butter, melted
1 cup milk

4 tbsp honey
1 egg, lightly beaten
115g/4oz self-raising flour
55g/2oz stale breadcrumbs
55g/2oz chopped walnuts
2 tsp vanilla extract

Preheat oven to 180°C/350°F. Brush pie dish with a little of the melted butter, then mix the rest of the butter with the milk, honey and egg and warm gently in a pan. Mix the flour, breadcrumbs and walnuts in a basin. Add the vanilla to the milk mixture and pour it into the flour mixture. Mix and pour into the pie dish and bake for 1 hour. Serve with a generous drizzle of extra honey. *Serves 6.*

STEAMED RICE AND APPLE PUDDING

This is a flourless steamed pudding, so it's a good one for the gluten-free around the table.

170g/6oz short-grain or Arborio rice
5 medium apples, peeled
4 dstsp sugar
1 dstsp cinnamon
Pinch ground ginger
750ml water or milk
Golden syrup to serve

Cook rice with 1 dstsp of sugar in water or milk until tender. Core and dice apples and add to the rice, together with the rest of the sugar and spices. Mix well and place in a baking basin.

Cover with baking paper and leave rice to swell. Steam for 2 hours and then turn out and serve topped with warmed golden syrup. *Serves 6.*

STEAMED JAM PUDDING

Robbie knows the secret of this dish: plenty of rhubarb jam!

85g/3oz butter, melted
85g/3oz rhubarb jam
170g/6oz self-raising flour
2 tsp baking powder
55g/2oz sugar
Pinch salt
½ tsp cinnamon
½ tsp nutmeg
140m/¼ pint milk
1 tsp vanilla extract

Brush a pudding basin with a little melted butter and place jam in the bottom. Sift flour and baking powder into a separate bowl and add the sugar, salt and spices. Combine the butter, milk and vanilla extract and add to the dry ingredients. Mix well. Pour mixture into the pudding basin, cover with baking paper and steam for 2 hours. You can steam by placing the pudding directly into a steamer over a saucepan of simmering water, or use a large saucepan with an upturned saucer in the bottom and simmering water. Remember to check water levels regularly. Serve with custard. *Serves 6.*

THRIFTY CHRISTMAS PUDDING

Those who lived through the Second World War endured six wartime Christmases, and they were as much of a celebration then as Christmas is now – perhaps more so, as an occasion to look forward to and provide hope. Even though certain foods were limited, they were hoarded all year in order to prepare special dishes for Christmas – most importantly of all, the pudding.

85g/3oz bread
140m/¼ pint cold water
85g/3oz flour
1½ tsp baking powder
½ tsp mixed spice
½ tsp cinnamon
85g/3oz sugar
225g/8oz mixed dried fruit
85g/3oz rolled oats
85g/3oz carrots, grated
85g/3oz butter
2 eggs

Break the bread into small pieces and leave to stand in the cold water for about 20 minutes, then beat with a fork until smooth. Sift flour, baking powder and spices into a bowl. Add the remaining ingredients, including the bread, and mix thoroughly. Spoon into a greased 2½-pint basin, cover with baking paper and a cloth and steam over boiling water for 2½ hours. Leave to cool and then store in a dry place for 2–3 days. On Christmas Day, steam for 1 hour and then serve with brandy custard. *Serves 6–8.*

POLISH PANCAKES
(PLACKI Z KARTOFLI)

Some things are worth taking time over, and this is one of them.

510g/18oz potatoes
2 eggs, separated
285m/½pint milk
1 dstsp sugar
1 tsp cinnamon
30g/1oz butter

Boil the potatoes and mash until smooth. Gradually beat in the egg yolks, milk, sugar and cinnamon. In a separate bowl, whisk the egg whites until stiff and then fold them into the mixture. Heat butter in a frypan and ladle batter into pan, just covering the bottom for a thinner pancake and adding more for a thicker texture. Fry pancakes in batches for approximately 5 minutes, turning once. Serve straight away with fruits or jam. *Serves 4–6.*

CARROT COOKIES

Together with Potato Pete, Doctor Carrot was introduced in 1941 to promote eating more vegetables since they were high in vitamins and were not rationed foods. The Ministry of Food's War Cookery Leaflet No.4 contained many recipes using carrots and these cookies are still a tasty treat with your cup of tea and great for kids since they combine the delicate crispness of biscuit and the soft crunch of carrot, with no artificial ingredients – and you can even keep the key ingredient secret! They will be at their best within the first three days; keep them in an air-tight container.

40g/1½oz butter
80g/3oz sugar
A few drops of vanilla, almond or orange
   flavouring
180g/6oz carrot, grated
180g/6oz self-raising flour
½ cup slivered almonds (optional for extra
   crunch)

Preheat oven to 180°C/350°F. Cream the butter and sugar until fluffy then beat in the flavouring. Stir in the carrot and almonds, then fold in the flour. Spoon dessertspoons of the mixture onto a greased baking tray and sprinkle with a little extra sugar. Bake for 20 minutes. *Makes 20 cookies.*

CHOCOLATE BIRTHDAY CAKE

Birthdays would not be the same without cake and cakes would not be the same without chocolate. Children celebrating during the Second World War had to make do with all sorts of mock meals and eggless puddings, but when it came to cake, there was still Bournville cocoa.

55g/2oz butter
55g/2oz sugar
Few drops vanilla extract
1 tbsp golden syrup
140g/5oz self-raising flour
½ tsp bicarbonate of soda
30g/1oz Bournville cocoa
2 eggs
Milk or water to moisten
1 cup grated beetroot *
Jam, for filling

Icing
2 tbsp icing sugar
2 tsp butter, melted
1 tbsp Bournville cocoa
1 tbsp golden syrup
Few drops vanilla extract

Preheat oven to 180°C/350°F. Cream butter, sugar, vanilla extract and warmed golden syrup. In a separate bowl, sift flour, bicarbonate of soda and cocoa. Gradually add eggs to the creamed mixture, beating well between each addition. Then slowly add the flour mixture, stirring in enough milk to bind the ingredients. Gently fold in the beetroot and divide cake batter between two 18cm/7-inch greased and floured cake tins and bake for 25 minutes. Test with a metal skewer to check they are cooked. Combine ingredients for icing and set aside. Once cooled, sandwich cakes together with jam, then spread icing across the top of the cake.

*The combination of chocolate and beetroot is delicious, and since it was one of the staple vegetables of the wartime garden it seems appropriate to use it still.

GINGERBREAD

This favourite can make a great comeback with the addition of chopped stem ginger added to the batter, giving the gingerbread unexpected bursts of flavour. And with another added extra – lemon icing...

55g/2oz butter
55g/2oz black treacle or golden syrup
170g/6oz self-raising flour
1 tsp bicarbonate of soda
1 pinch salt
1 tsp ground ginger
1 tsp ground cinnamon or mixed spice
55g/2oz sugar
1 egg
2 tbsp milk
6 tbsp water
2oz stem ginger, roughly chopped

Icing
1 tsp lemon juice

½ cup icing sugar

Preheat oven to 180°C/350°F. Line an 18 x 10cm/11 x 7 inch cake tin with baking paper. Melt the butter and treacle or syrup in a saucepan. Sift dry ingredients into a bowl, then pour butter mixture over. Whisk egg and milk together, then add to bowl and mix well. Place water into empty saucepan and bring to the boil, stirring to make sure no ingredients are wasted, and then add to mixture.* Stir well to combine then pour into tin and cook for 50 minutes. Mix lemon juice and icing sugar to desired consistency and drizzle over the gingerbread once it has cooled.

* This stage of the recipe can be omitted and the water added with the butter and syrup; it was important during wartime to make sure nothing went to waste.

DRIED FRUIT

A great way of using windfalls or blemished fruit such as fallen apples or bruised pears.

Preheat oven to 65°C/150°F. Wipe the fruit and remove the cores. Peel apples, cutting out any blemishes, and slice into rings about 1cm/½ inch thick. Peel and cut pears into halves or quarters and steep all fruit in water containing 30g/1oz of salt to every 2 litres/3½pints of water for 10 minutes. Thread the rings on wooden skewers or spread on trays and dry in the oven for an hour, turning once or twice during cooking.

ROSE PETAL JAM

The traditional Polish recipe would have only combined rose petals and sugar and used a pestle and mortar to bruise the petals and release the oil. English recipes use liquid and lemon juice to make jam with a set consistency more like a jelly.

500g/18oz rose petals
500g/18oz sugar
Juice 2 lemons
1 litre/1¾ pints water

Place petals in a large bowl and sprinkle over half of the sugar, bruising the petals lightly as you turn them. Cover and store in a cool place or refrigerate overnight. The following day add the rest of the sugar and the lemon juice to the water and bring to the boil, then add the steeped rose petals and simmer for 20 minutes. If you like a thicker jam then boil for a further 5 minutes on a higher temperature. Test it is at setting point* and then spoon into sterilised glass jars, wait to cool and label clearly.

*You can test your jam is at setting point by following some simple steps: place an empty saucer in the freezer for 5 minutes and then place a spoonful of jam on it and return it to the freezer for a further 2 minutes. If it wrinkles and feels like gel then it is set.

RHUBARB JAM

This jam is a real star to have in the pantry as a delicious compote for porridge in the winter, as a rich fruity jam on scones or toast, and as a tantalising spread on the sponge for Maggie's trifle. Certain people (who shall remain nameless) have even been known to dip a spoon into it for an instant sugar hit!

900g/32oz rhubarb, washed and roughly
   chopped
450g/16oz sugar
Zest 1 lemon and/or 1 dstsp root ginger, grated

Stand ingredients together for 24 hours then boil for 15 minutes in a few tablespoons of water. Once cool enough, spoon into sterilised glass jars and label with date. Store in a cool place and then move to the fridge once opened.

Acknowledgements

This is a work of fiction and combines historical facts with both real and fictional events. I have used several references during my research, and where the original sources have been used directly or quoted from, the sources have been attributed. Specifically, these include material from the Ministry of Food held by the National Archives in the United Kingdom, which contains public sector information licensed under the Open Government Licence v3.0, and *The Times* digital archive.

One of the reasons that I wanted to write this book was because of an interest in how and why British Restaurants evolved during the Second World War and how they are still relevant today. They were created to solve problems surrounding food supply, food safety and the health of the nation; issues that societies are still concerned with now. I also noticed that there was renewed interest in 'paddock to plate' or 'nose to tail' eating, perhaps because of concern for our health, our environment and our animals, but it is how they ate during the war out of necessity. As we continue talking about the health and economic issues surrounding food, it seems worth exploring our past and seeing what we can learn from it; if we look closely at how they evolved a whole new way of eating, what they ate and how much they ate, then maybe we can find ways to help us in the future.

The recipes are an amalgam of many recipes from the archives and the popular dishes of the time, with a new twist from Maggie, some tested in my kitchen; thank you to my family for being willing guinea pigs.

In addition, the following books were used for background reading and research:

Isabella Beeton, *The Book of Household Management* [London]: Ward, Lock and Tyler, 1869

Richard Broad and Suzie Fleming (eds), *Nella Last's War: The Second World War diaries of housewife, 49* [Great Britain]: Profile Books, 2006

Gill Corbishley, *Ration Book Cookery: Recipes and history* [England]: English Heritage, 1985

R.J. Hammond, *Food, Volume II: Studies in administration and control* (History of the Second World War, United Kingdom Civil Series), [London]: H. M. Stationery Office and Longmans, Green and Co., 1956

Brian Lavery, *The British Home Front Pocket-Book* 1940–1942 [London]: Conway, 2010

Eating For Victory: Healthy home front cooking on war rations. Reproductions of official Second World War instruction leaflets, foreword by Jill Norman [Great Britain]: Michael O'Mara Books, 2007

David Notley (ed.), *Wartime Recipes: A collection of recipes from the war years* [Great Britain]:

Jarrold Publishing, 1998

Marguerite Patten OBE, in association with
    Imperial War Museum, *Victory Cookbook:*
    Nostalgic food and Facts from 1940–1954:
    [London], Chancellor Press, 2002

Nicholas Webley (ed.), *A Taste of Wartime Britain*
    [London]: Thorogood Publishing Ltd, 2003

Good Fare: A Book of Wartime Recipes Produced by
    the Daily Telegraph [United Kingdom]:
    Macmillan, 2008

And some cooking tips from:

Reader's Digest, *What Our Grandmothers*
    Knew: Hints, recipes and remedies of a bygone age
    [London]: Reader's Digest Association
    Limited, 1979

Writing this book was a communal affair, a lot
like Maggie's Kitchen, so I would like to thank all
those who contributed information and support.
In particular, the archivists for the fascinating
research that gave kindling to the idea, Peter
Thompson for advice, John and Anne Whaite for
help with recipes, and Daniel Puskas for sharing
his chef's secrets. My grandmother, Mary Ellen
Taylor, who was in the Land Army during the
Second World War and provided great detail on
life at the time. And to my parents, Jackie and
Alan, for always being there and for cooking the
offal dishes that I couldn't!

Thank you to Kathryn Heyman who helped
start me on the novel-writing journey, and also to
James Bradley and Sophie Hamley. Sincere

personal thanks to Annette Barlow for believing in Maggie, and I am deeply grateful to the team at Allen & Unwin, especially Christa Munns and Ali Lavau, for their work on the book.

Finally, for the men and women who, like my grandmother, have shown bravery in the most unlikely of places...

This Large Print Book for the partially sighted, who cannot read normal print, is published under the auspices of

THE ULVERSCROFT FOUNDATION